THE GALLOWSMAN AND HENRY KIDD, OUTLAW

TWO FULL LENGTH WESTERN NOVELS

CAMERON JUDD

WOLFPACK PUBLISHING
— EST 2013 —

The Gallowsman and Henry Kidd, Outlaw: Two Full Length Western Novels
Paperback Edition
Copyright © 2022 (As Revised) Cameron Judd

Wolfpack Publishing
5130 S. Fort Apache Rd. 215-380
Las Vegas, NV 89148

wolfpackpublishing.com

Paperback ISBN 978-1-63977-699-3
eBook ISBN 978-1-63977-312-1

THE GALLOWSMAN
AND HENRY KIDD,
OUTLAW

THE GALLOWSMAN

To Don D'Auria, with appreciation

CHAPTER 1

With stage fare at two bits a mile, he couldn't afford to ride, and so he walked, with the single feed sack containing his entire worldly fortune slung over his shoulder. He was not happy to be afoot. Usually he enjoyed walking, but that was in the lowlands, where a man could breathe and enjoy some benefit from it. Here in the high Colorado mountains, every breath seemed thin, empty of sustenance and unable to satisfy.

Pausing for what seemed the hundredth time to let his gasping subside, he felt much older than his forty years. As he stood panting, he examined an odd heap beside the roadway, which was still partly covered with snow despite the spring season. A dead mule. Another beast worked to death hauling heavy mining and smelting equipment up these mountain roads in this cussedly thin atmosphere. How many dead mules was that? Twelve, he believed, since he'd started keeping count in this endless hike up toward Ferguson.

When he had his wind back, he shifted the canvas sack to his other shoulder and set out again. The road still climbed, but leveled somewhat ahead. Nearing the crest at last! Once beyond that, he would see the town of Ferguson, newest of

Colorado's silver boomtowns, and a destination Ben Woolard looked forward to with a combination of unfamiliar hope and all-too-familiar dread.

A sound behind him made him turn. A wagon came up past the dead mule and toward him. A tall, broadly built black man drove it, and flashed a big grin at Ben as he neared.

Ben grinned back, being friendly, but also because he was amused: The wagon driver's teeth flashed like the palace of Midas. Every tooth in his head, or at least every tooth that showed, had been capped over in bright gold.

"Howdy," Ben said.

"Hello, sir," the cheerful driver said, pulling his mules to a halt, studying Ben for a moment. Apparently Ben passed his test. "Can I offer you a ride?"

"You can, and I accept."

The driver reached down, took Ben's sack, and Ben climbed into the seat beside him. "Hard thing, keeping your wind here in the mountains, until you get used to it," the driver said.

"It shows on me that much, huh?"

"Shows in every newcomer, sir. This is a different world up here among these peaks than what's lived in down below."

"My name's Woolard," Ben said, putting out his hand for a shake. "Ben Woolard. Mighty obliged for the ride."

"Woolard! Well, that's a name well-knowed in Ferguson. There's a Jake Woolard there who owns him a big store and a sleeping house and some other stuff. Mine stock, too. Doing mighty well for himself."

"Jake Woolard is my brother," Ben said.

"No! I be! Well, sir, that's really something! You and Mr. Jake are brothers!"

"What's your name?"

"Roanie, sir. Roanie Piatt."

"You a miner, Roanie?"

"Me? No, sir. Mostly I work for myself, sir, me and my brother together. We haul stuff about in wagons, anything that needs hauling. And we drive ore wagons, too, for one of the smelters there in town, every now and then." He pointed ahead. "Look yonder. You can see the town now."

Ben could smell it, too. A smoky, heavy smell in the thin air, the stench of smelters mixing their noxious fumes with the cooksmoke of hundreds of rough chimneys. Ben studied the town as it gleamed in the sunlight beneath the bench of low-lying smoke.

A yellowish pallor marked the irregular jumble of buildings that comprised Ferguson. Ben couldn't account for the distinctive coloration at first. As the wagon rumbled nearer, he figured it out: The yellow was that unique hue of unpainted pine lumber, the predominant building material of Ferguson. So new was most of the town that the yellow of the boards had yet to be weathered away.

Ben squinted as the wagon circled around a bend in the road. "Where's the streets?" he asked Roanie.

"There ain't nothing of what you could rightly call a proper street, sir," he replied. "Except for Center Street. Right there it runs through the heart of town, and you can see that somebody's throwed up a hut right in the middle of it, but it won't last. The town commission'll have that pulled down right swift. All the rest of the town is kind of just built wherever, you see—no real pattern to it, nothing but alleys and trails and such instead of streets. You know much about the town, sir?"

"Not much. Used to be a placer-mining town, I believe."

"That's right, yes, sir. Them was the gold days, back before the town even had a real name. You can still find old cabins and huts all through the hills where the gold miners lived. And the pressure cannons south of town—see them there?—still uncover some of the old places that got buried under slides and such since the old days."

Ben gazed with interest at the pressure cannon, which to his disappointment were not operating at the moment. He'd read about the devices: big pipelines that brought water down from the peaks, narrowing all the way, so that when the heavy water reached the narrow nozzle openings, it was under enough pressure to blast away stone and soil like so much dust. The pressure cannon were the last vestige of the gold-mining days of this community. Day by day the cannon blasted through dirt and rock that had been panned by placer miners years before, and day by day the pressure miners were rewarded by the discovery of gold that had escaped the earlier, less technologically advanced miners. But even so, it was all a mere shadow of the old and lost glory days of gold; the color of primary wealth found in these mountains these days had a silvery sheen.

Ben turned his eyes back to the town. It sat on a slight slope, surrounded on all sides by hills and high mountains. He'd never seen such a shapeless farrago of structures. Among the predominant pine buildings he now made out as many tents and frame-and-canvas structures, as well as countless log huts and cabins. An improvised town, this one, a grown-up version of a child's tiny city of upturned crates and boxes, but with less order.

"Yes, sir," Roanie went on. "This place wouldn't be what it is now if there'd only been the gold. Most of that was gone long ago. It was the carbonate, with the silver in it, that caused this town to be. One of the first of the gold miners is who figured out that there was more fortune to be made from the silver than the gold. It was his boy, in fact, who the town's named after. Poor boy. Poor little Ferguson Jones!"

"Why 'poor little Ferguson'?"

"Well, the little fellow died, that's why. Partly because of his father getting so worked up when he found out there was silver to be had. The little boy, maybe eight or nine years old, was sickly, they say, and his father stayed too long up here instead of going down to the lower lands when the winter begun coming in. He tried to leave too late, and a snow bank fell and caught his boy. Smothered the life out of him before they could dig him out. The father, Chance Jones, named the town Ferguson in memory of his child. I think it'd have been better if he'd named the town after hisself. Chance. It'd be a good name for a mining town. 'Come take your chances at Chance.'"

"Sad story. About the little boy dying, I mean."

"Yes, sir, it is. And there's plenty of other sad stories in this town. Folks come in thinking they'll make it big and rich real fast, but a lot wind up going broke, or getting hurt or killed some way or another. There's a graveyard east of the town, and I know the fellows who dig the holes. They keep three or four holes dug ahead, knowing there'll be need for them before long, and sure enough, they'll have them holes filled before they've been there two days. Every time."

"Dangerous place, this town?"

"Dangerous enough. And no good law. None that's lasted, anyhow. There's a town marshal, but he don't do squat. Spends most his time prospecting. And who can blame him? Why would anybody come to a town and risk his skin fighting drunks and thieves and shooters and such for what little bit a peace officer gets paid, when instead he can go out and dig him a hole or two, and maybe strike it rich?"

They rolled into the town itself. Ben examined the mob of humanity there, mostly young, male, and unkempt. A dirtier rabble he'd not seen since the war.

"All these folks miners?" he asked as Roanie weaved a course down the milling, crowded street.

"Most. But not all. See that building there? Two lawyers operating in there. Yonder tent has a doctor, though as best I know there ain't but two doctors in town who went to no doctoring school. And there's plenty of merchants, all kinds, and dentists, and teamsters like me, and assayers...every kind of business you can think of, there's somebody here already trying to do it. And if there ain't already, there'll be two of them show up tomorrow to do it. What brings you to Ferguson, sir? You going to mine?"

Ben paused. "I've just come to work with my brother. I don't know just what I'll be doing, exactly."

They rolled on, deeper into town. Or was it a town at all? No railroad yet reached this place, and there was no sense of pattern and settlement that normally went with the concept of township. No, Ben decided, this was little more than an overgrown mining camp, a place where function overruled form, and beauty didn't matter a whit. The buildings were irregular, the boardwalks even more so. Signs were everywhere, offering two drinks for two bits, rooms for rent, laundry service, shoe shines, groceries. The street was a pitted expanse of trampled dirt, filled with horse droppings that were trod underfoot along with the mud.

"Hey!" Roanie declared abruptly. "Dang if it ain't my brother yonder! Hey, Billy!"

Ben saw the indicated man, a slightly smaller version of Roanie himself, seated on a keg on a street corner, head tilted back, mouth open, and another man working hard on his teeth. Only his eyes turned in response to Roanie's shout. He waved as best he could without moving.

Ben asked, "He's getting a tooth pulled?"

"No, sir, no sir, getting another tooth golded over...like mine." He grinned his bright gold grin at Ben. "Billy's been jealous of my gold teeth since I got 'em done, and he's been having his own golded over, one at a time, as he can afford it."

"I never seen a dentist on a street corner before," Ben said.

"There's a lot in Ferguson you've likely never seen before," Roanie replied. "Like the buildings. This town lives in tents and cabins. Your brother's got one of the few real houses in the whole dang community. Big old porch on it, carpet on the floors, calico on the walls, muslin on the ceiling. Good furniture, too. Me and my brother hauled it in for him. He'd bought it in Denver. Your brother's done good for himself here, and it ain't took him long to do it."

"Jake's always got a way of making things work out."

"Yonder's a casino," Roanie said, pointing as the wagon made another turn and scattered a flock of chickens freely roaming the streets. "Casinos and smelters in this town got one thing in common: They both go 'round the clock, seven days a week."

"What's that place?" Ben asked, indicating a big, warehouse like building to his left with a sign reading CATHEDRAL OF REST on its front. "Some kind of big funeral place?"

"Lord, sir, no! That your own brother's sleeping house. Smartest business in this town, if you ask me, which you ain't."

"What's so smart about it?"

"One of the things that's hardest for a newcomer to find in this town, sir, is a place to sleep. Men sleep wherever they can—saloon floors, under boardwalks, in alleys, on rooftops. I seen a whole family in a big crate behind a grocery store just two days ago. But the best place for a new man to go for his snores is the sleeping house."

"Looks like a storehouse to me."

"It's just a big old building, sir, with row and row of bunks in it, two deep. You go in, pay your fifty cents for the night, and you can sleep on a good mattress and with a warm blanket. A lot better than a saloon floor, I can tell you."

"You slept there?"

"No, sir, not me. I'm colored. I ain't allowed." He said it matter-of-factly, a man accustomed to discrimination. "Sir, is your brother expecting you at a spific time or place?"

"No. He knows I'm coming, but not when. Where's his house?"

"Not far. I can take you there, if you want."

"I'd appreciate it. But, Roanie...I'm a little short on money. I feel I ought to pay you."

"No pay needed, sir. I'm glad to lend a hand. I ain't one to let a man walk when I got room on my wagon."

"You're a kind man."

"Your brother will be pleased to see you come, I'll bet," Roanie said. "Me and my brother are close as we can be. A brother's a fine thing to have. Yes, sir, he'll be happy to see you show up."

Ben looked away. "I hope you're right."

———

Jake's house, like most things in Ferguson, wasn't much to look at.

Ben stood for a long time in the shade of a little grove of trees that had somehow escaped destruction as firewood, and studied his brother's home. Shaped like an L and only one story tall, it was distinctive only for being somewhat larger than the typical Ferguson hovel, and for its long porch.

Now that he was here, Ben was reluctant to make his presence known. He'd already swallowed much pride merely to accept his brother's invitation, and many times he'd come within a hairsbreadth of turning back during the long journey from St. Louis to here...but there had been nothing to turn back to.

He turned away, sighed, and meandered back into the town, onto Center Street, putting off for a while the actual moment of reunion. Wandering along, he eyed the many saloons, none of them fancy by any standard, but all of them offering the kind of liquid refreshment he'd certainly enjoy just now. But he couldn't. He'd struggled hard to break liquor's hold on his soul, and he wouldn't throw that away. Liquor belonged to a past that he was determined to let go... if only it would let go of him.

He stopped on the boardwalk, looking around. Ferguson, Colorado. A place of hope for those already here and the scores who arrived every day. Most came seeking their mortal salvation in the black carbonate ore that lay beneath the surface of this rugged land, others through the network of commerce that inevitably grew in a mining boomtown.

Ben Woolard, on the other hand, sought his salvation and reformation through his brother, the brother who had always seemed to succeed even as Ben inevitably failed.

He hadn't seen Jake in years. Funny thing. His own brother, to be met again this very day, and it felt like he was going to meet a stranger.

He roamed the street the rest of the day, watching the bustling activity all around, and did not turn his steps back toward the house of Jake Woolard until the sun dipped its lower edge below the highest of the peaks looming in the west above the town.

He was halfway to his destination when he realized he was being followed.

CHAPTER 2

A street robber, maybe. What he would later learn the folks of the Colorado mining towns called a "foot-pad." Ben increased his pace slightly and ducked around a trio of half-drunken miners coming his way on the board-walk, and during the brief moments their big forms hid him from the man trailing him, ducked into the nearest alley and backed up against the wall.

The man passed the mouth of the alley a moment later and paused there, looking uncertainly up and down the street.

"Behind you," Ben said.

The young man, in his mid-twenties at most, jumped in his boots and cursed. Wheeling, he faced Ben.

"I do believe I know you," Ben said, stepping forward. "Andrew? Andy Woolard? Is it you?"

The young fellow shook off his look of startlement and replaced it with a smug and contemptuous expression. "Well! I *thought* that was you I saw roaming about, Ben."

"So I'm just plain Ben now, eh? No more 'Uncle Ben'?"

"I ain't a child no more, and I don't talk like one. I'm as much a grown man as you now." He smiled rather bitterly.

"The folks tell me, matter of fact, that I look quite a lot like you." He eyed Ben up and down. "God, I hope not. You look like you've been through it and back again."

"I have. You know that story, I reckon."

"Oh, yes. I know. I've heard it all. And from what I've heard, it appears you and me are alike in more than looks." With that he reached beneath his coat and pulled out a flat metal flask, which he uncorked and swigged without breaking his gaze from Ben's.

Ben watched the young man drink and hoped to heaven that the fierce liquor-hunger the sight roused in him didn't show. He longed to reach out and grab that flask, put it to his own thirsty lips...

Andrew Woolard recorked the flask and put it back into his pocket. "I do love my whiskey, Ben. Fine stuff. I hear you hold a similar point of view."

"I did. I've put it behind me now. It would have killed me."

"Could be worse ways to die."

"What's wrong, Andy? What's this crazy talk? Something bothering you?"

"Why did you come here?"

"Because your father invited me to."

"You've come to be his servant? Going to let brother take care of you?"

"I've come to do honest work for Jake, and I'll do a good job of it."

"Doing what? You going to wipe his butt for pay or something?"

"You got quite a smart mouth on you, don't you, son? If I didn't know better, I'd think maybe you weren't glad to see your old uncle."

Andy put on a fulsome look of shock. "Why, did I give you that notion? Forgive me! Why, I surely do hate you thought that!" He pulled out the flask again and took another slow, deliberate swig. Then he shoved the flask toward Ben. An invitation.

"No," Ben said. "I told you. I put that behind me."

Andy laughed. Ben wondered why. Andy put the flask away again—for good this time, Ben hoped.

"You'll be heading for the house now, I reckon," Andy said.

"Reckon I should."

"Pa won't be there. Ma will, and Judy. Judy's twelve years old now. Eats like a pig. Spends most her time stuffing her mouth."

"What about you, Andy? What do you spend your time doing these days?"

"Trying to drink myself to death. Want to join me?"

Ben didn't know what to say to that, so he didn't say anything. He turned and began striding down the boardwalk, toward Jake's house, having had quite enough of Andy.

Andy watched him go, then pulled the flask out for another drink. When Ben was out of sight, he sighed and turned the other way, heading for the nearest saloon.

———

Sally Woolard had been pretty as long as Ben had known her, but the years were finally beginning to leave their traces. Not as much, though, as on Ben himself; this he had detected by the quick look of shock when she'd first seen his craggy face in the light.

Now she and he were engaged in a rather forced conversation. When his eyes caught hers she smiled broadly and a bit too nonchalantly. Ben was making her nervous, obviously. He wished he'd lingered outside a little longer and not approached the house until after Jake came home.

Judy Woolard, meanwhile, seemed not at all discomfited by the presence of this long-absent uncle. She stared with the honest interest of the typical adolescent, eyeing him from the corner while nibbling on a plate of potatoes and bacon. A pretty girl, but tending toward heft. Ben recalled that Sally's family, whom he had met many years before at Jake's wedding, had several sizable members. Young Judith, namesake of her two-hundred-pound maternal grandmother, seemed destined to carry on the family tradition.

"So Jake's got some mining interest, does he?" Ben said, trying to advance a struggling conversation.

"Yes. Some. He's taken a lot of mine stock in trade for this or that, and he does some grubstaking. He owns little pieces of at least a score of mines. A few have struck, and a lot of the others look promising, he says."

"We're going to be rich," Judith said around a mouthful of potato. "We're going to move back to Denver someday and build a mansion."

"Hush, Judy!" her mother remonstrated. "We don't know that we're going to be rich. And we don't need a mansion in Denver—we're doing quite well here."

"Very nice house you got," Ben exaggerated. "Very nice. One of the best in town, from what I saw."

"Thank you. It's not that much, really. Anywhere else but Ferguson, and it wouldn't look at all special. Among a bunch of cabins and glorified tents, it seems much more than it is."

"Better than what I've lived in the past couple of years," Ben said.

"Tell me, Ben...are you well now?"

"If you mean have I gotten over being a drunkard, yes, I have. Oh, I still want the whiskey as much as ever. The difference now is, I don't drink it."

"Never?"

"Never."

She smiled at him. "I'm so glad. It must mean you've been able to finally get over your losses and sorrows."

"I haven't gotten over anything. I never will. All I've gotten over is trying to drown it all away in whiskey. Doesn't work, you know."

He was seated at the kitchen table, leaning on his elbows with his hands clasped before him as she busied herself around in tasks he knew were undertaken merely to keep a comfortable space between them. Now, however, she stopped and came to the table herself, and took a seat across from him.

"I'm sorry I never got to meet her," she said. "She was pretty?"

"Beautiful."

"And the children too, I'm sure."

He blinked. It hurt terribly to think about Molly, even worse to think about the children. Three grand, lovely children, a dear and affectionate wife, prettiest woman he had ever known...and all of them gone. Buried in Kentucky. And buried with them, the best part of Ben Woolard's life.

"They were all wonderful children. Very dear to me."

"Measles, was it?"

"Yes."

"It's awful."

Ben looked at her with eyes encircled by lines and shadows that hadn't been there the last time she had seen him so many years before. "It is awful. And the worst of it, the pure hell of it for me, is that it was me who brought the disease to them. Me. I caught it, suffered out the fever and the spots, and lived. They caught it, one by one...and died. One by one."

Sally's eyes filled with tears. A sympathetic woman, even if almost a stranger to him. She said nothing because there was nothing to say. Over in the corner, Judith had stopped eating and stared in silence.

"I lived and they died. Why? It's that that drove me to the bottle. Asking why. Asking again and again, and never getting an answer."

"Ben, I...I just want you to know that...Oh, Ben, I don't know what to say. I wish it had never happened."

"Me, too."

She brightened by an effort of will, and beamed a smile at him with tears still in her eyes. "But things will be better now that you're here!" she said chipperly. "Jake will get you work, grubstake you if you want to mine, lend you a hand until you can find the kind of situation that suits you, and you can start building a new life for yourself. Here with us. You'll see how good it can be after Jake shows you around the town. There's such opportunity here, Ben! Why, there's people who come to this town as paupers, get themselves a grub-stake from people like Jake, and before you know it, they're running a successful mine. Happens all the time! And the beauty of it is, a novice has as much chance at a silver strike as a veteran prospector. There's a layer of ore underlying this whole region, Jake says, and it's just a matter of sinking a shaft at the right place and to the right depth. Sometimes the ore is right at the surface! Why, there've been a few who have turned over a shovel three or four times and struck wealth!"

"Is being a miner what Jake has in mind for me?"

She opened her mouth to answer but never got the chance. The front door burst open so suddenly that Ben came to his feet and barely stifled a shout of alarm, as through his mind flashed vivid and well-remembered scenes of fire and lead and uniformed men in blue and gray and butternut screaming as death claimed them...

It was Andy who had come in. "Mother! My dear old ma!" he bellowed, voice slurred. He was raging drunk. "Dear old mother who bore me in her own body! And, why, looky here—it's *Uncle Ben!*" The emphasis on the last two words dripped with sarcasm. "Old Uncle Ben, the Woolard who tried to drink himself to death and failed!" He reached under his coat and pulled out that familiar flask once again. "Here's to you, Uncle Ben, from the Woolard who's trying to drink himself to death and—unlike you—will succeed!"

"Andy!" Sally yelled, rising. "Andy, for God's sake— how dare you..."

He had turned up the flask, but there was nothing in it. He made a wry face and put on a show of peering into the flask's mouth, shaking his head.

Judith, hugging her plate over in the corner, quietly began to cry.

"Andy, I won't have you in here like this. I won't have you in this house drunk!"

"Why, are you throwing me out, Ma? What, there room for only one drunk at a time in this fine dwelling? Has dear pitiful old Uncle Ben taken my place as the family charity project?"

"Andy, get out of this house! Get out before your father comes home!"

"Why? You think he might get mad at his little Andy? His bad little boy?"

"Andy, your uncle has come and he is a guest in our house, and I expect you to show the sort of respect that—"

"Oh, Uncle Ben and I met earlier today, on the street," Ben said. "Didn't he tell you? Why, we had the best talk, and sat down together for some of the finest whiskey to be found in all Colorado!"

"Sally, it's not true," Ben said. "I did meet Andy earlier, but there was no drinking. Not on my part, at least. I didn't tell you I met him because of...well, he was half drunk and rude as could be at the time."

Judith dropped her plate from her lap and turned her face away toward the wall. Andy, meanwhile, put his hand to his head as if it hurt suddenly, and winced. He turned and left the house without another word, the sarcasm and fire all at once gone from him.

Ben Woolard wondered just what kind of household he had come to. A troubled one, to be sure. Obviously he wasn't the only Woolard with a full share of problems.

When Andy was gone, several uncomfortable moments of silence followed. Sally turned a pallid face to Ben, opening her mouth to say something, but somehow failing to find words.

"It's all right," Ben said. "I reckon my nephew ain't glad to see me."

"It's...it's more than that," she said. "There's things that have happened. Troubles that Andy has had. Bad things that have come his way, and made him all angry and bitter."

The door opened again, not so loudly or suddenly this time. Ben turned and, for the first time in many a year, looked into the face of his elder brother.

CHAPTER 3

B en would later ponder why his first sight of Jake after so long a separation took him back not to the last time he and his brother were together, but all the way to a time of an ending war in the Federally occupied city of Nashville, Tennessee, and a view of his brother that had ingrained itself as a recurring memory: Jake, then a uniformed new veteran of the 12th Kentucky Cavalry, standing on a corner of High Street, nervous but trying not to show it, and looking handsome as the devil. He was waiting to enter the courthouse and give testimony in a military trial that for a time made him famous in the region. Ben had been involved in that trial, too, far more deeply than his brother. He, too, had become briefly famous.

Ben, more than any other man who testified in that trial, was responsible for the aftermath of it, in which an infamous and shadowy figure of war went to a prison-yard gallows and died with the jerk of a noosed rope, a macabre smile on his face even as the trap dropped. When it was done, Jake had turned and said to no one in particular, "Well, it's finished, then."

The memory passed, and Ben saw Jake as he was: much

older, thicker around the middle and thinner in the hair, and with a look of surprise on his face that erupted into a smile.

"Ben? *Ben!*" He came forward, arms spreading, and Ben went to him, grinning like a fool. The brotherly embrace that followed was long and crushing.

"Ben, by gum, you've made it at last! I've wondered every day when you'd arrive!"

"Took me a while, but I finally did."

"So you did. So you did. Sally, why didn't you send word out to me that Ben had come in? I'd have come home early if I'd...Sally? What's wrong?" He'd just noticed his wife's distraught expression, and his eyes shifted as well over to Judith, who huddled in the corner, looking scared.

"It's Andy again," she said. "He came in, in a very bad way. He was rude, disrespectful to me and to Ben...awful. He was awful."

Jake grew sober, glanced at Ben, obviously embarrassed that his brother's initial reunion with his only living close kin had been far from flawless. "In a bad way, you say...drunk?"

"Yes. Very."

Jake spoke apologetically to his brother. "Ben...I'm sorry for whatever bad things you've seen here. We're having some trouble out of Andy."

"I surmised that."

"I'm embarrassed. I'd hoped for your arrival to be a happy time."

"Well, I am happy. Surely happy to see you, Jake. And Sally and Judy have been nice as can be while we've waited on you to get back."

Jake grinned. "Good. Good. Well, I'll have to deal with Andy for how he's behaved, but in the meantime let's forget about it. My brother's here! And to stay, I hope."

"To stay...if you want me to. If there's proper work for me. I'll not stand for being a burden to you."

"No, you won't be. For one thing sure is true about this

town: There's work for any man who wants it. Any man who wants to can make his own work with a pick and a mule."

"Sally's told me some about you and your success. I'm impressed." Ben smiled. "I'm glad one of the Woolard brothers has made something good and worthy of himself."

"There's *two* good and worthy Woolard brothers, by gum, and I'll hear nothing to the contrary. But one of those brothers has suffered some hard blows in his life, worse than any man should, and he's had a rough go of it because of it." He spoke the next words very deliberately and with force: "A rough go that has now come to an end."

"I hope that's true. I've made some bad decisions in my time, and I don't deny that now. I want to make good ones from here on out." Abruptly, tears rose in Ben's eyes, and it was his turn to feel embarrassed. "Jake, I want you to know, I appreciate the fine thing you're doing for me. Offering me work, a home—a man like me don't deserve it."

"Nonsense. Every man deserves a chance to make the best of himself. That's what this growing nation of ours is all about. And if what you say is true, about wanting to make good choices and a better way for yourself, then, by gum, you've come to the best town in the nation for it. There's opportunity here, Ben. True opportunity. A man can get rich here by digging a hole! How many places can that be said about, huh?"

"Reckon not many."

"So how was your travel? Enjoyable?"

"Mostly. Less so the farther up into these mountains that I came. There's some mighty thin air up here for a low-lander. If I hadn't caught me a wagon ride I'd probably still be out there huffing toward town, stopping to rest every five steps."

"Who'd you ride in with?"

"Colored man with a mouth full of gold teeth. Name of Roanie something-or-other."

"Oh, yes! I've seen that fellow. Roanie Piatt. I believe he's got a gold-toothed brother, too."

"He knew who you were right off," Ben said. "Declared you a prominent and powerful man."

"I've done well enough, I suppose. You'll do well here, too. You and me have a lot of talking to do this evening, Ben."

Sally cut in. "What about Andy? Aren't you going to do something about him? He was...*awful!*"

Jake turned stern. "Andy is a grown man now. Even if he doesn't act like one. I'll not spend this night poking through every saloon and dive in town, trying to find him when he doesn't even want to be found. Especially not now that Ben is here."

She looked sad. Ben felt sorry for her, a mother grieving for a son obsessed, for whatever reason, with ruining himself, even destroying himself.

"You'll be wanting your supper now," Sally said to her husband.

"I'm starved. Ben, you eaten yet?"

"Sally fed me well."

"Come sit with me while I have my supper, then, and after that we'll have some cigars and good talk. You still like cigars, don't you?"

"Love 'em."

"Good. Good." Jake went over to where Judith still sat, and rumpled her hair with his hand. "How you, Punkin?"

"Andy acted real bad," she said.

"I know. I know. I'll be dealing with him soon. Don't you worry."

He sat down at the table as Sally loaded a plate for him. Grinning at Ben, shaking his head as if in pleasant disbelief that he was really there, he was a man Ben might envy. If not for the shadow cast onto this household by the troubled Andy Woolard, Ben could have perceived his brother as the world's most fortunate man.

———

The hour was late; Sally and Judith were asleep in their beds. Andy had not come home, but Jake wasn't particularly disturbed by this, telling Ben that Andy was seldom home anymore, spending nights with drinking companions, in cheap rooms, on saloon floors, and likely as not, in the cribs and chambers of the kind of fallen women that Ferguson, like any mining town, possessed in abundance.

"He said some troubling things to me today," Ben confided. "He talked like someone trying to kill himself slowly—and I know that kind of man well, having been one myself not all that long ago."

"Andy has suffered a hard blow, and it's left him very changed. Very hurt."

"May I ask what kind of blow it was?"

"One rather similar to yours, now that I think about it," Jake replied. "He was engaged to be married last year, and lost her."

"She left him?"

"She died. Killed. And the worst of it was, Andy was the one who killed her."

"What?"

"It was accidental. A shooting. A rifle he'd just bought. Somehow, when he laid it on a tabletop, it fell, and fired when it hit the floor. He hadn't even known the blasted thing was loaded. The bullet struck her in the side. She lingered for two weeks, suffering very terribly, before she died. Andy blames himself."

"He shouldn't. It wasn't his fault."

"No. No more than it was your fault you happened to be the first in your family to catch the measles."

"I know. It wasn't my fault...but it *feels* like it was. Same way Andy feels, I guess."

"Andy's following the same course you did. Liquor, self-destruction. I worry for him. His mother worries all the more. It's destroying her, right along with Andy."

"I gather that Andy resents me," Ben said. "Just some things he said when I first saw him today."

"I'm sure he does. You remind him of what he's doing to himself. Because despite all his talk about wanting to drink himself to death, I don't believe he really wants to. He wants to be pulled out of it, somehow, but now he's in so deep he doesn't know how to get back out again. And then you show up, a man who by all rights should have died long ago, the way you drank and such, yet you've made it through alive. He ought to see you as inspiration, but I suspect that right now, you're just someone to be envied."

Ben chuckled ironically. "I'd have never thought anybody could find anything in me to envy."

They talked another hour, the topic shifting to Ben and his own difficult experiences—the good times that turned bad with the death of his family, the liquor that almost consumed him, and Jake's last-ditch bid to save his brother's life by offering him work and a new chance if only he'd shake off the whiskey and come join him in Ferguson. In Ferguson, Jake had promised, opportunity would be handed to Ben. He'd have a place, work, a hope and promise. But only if he'd cast off the liquor. Only if he'd come to Ferguson on his own, when he was ready, as a show of evidence that he was serious about wanting to reform.

The conversation dipped farther into the past, back into their Kentucky boyhood, the days of hunting, working the farm, racing their horses across the bluegrass countryside.

The companions, the girlfriends, the youthful carousing. Good days. Good memories.

Then darker times, a few years past the boyhood joys. Hard and grim days of war. Two brothers joining the Union cavalry, making excellent showings for themselves as soldiers. Then the special service they had been called into, covert work that had taken Ben down into Tennessee and into the heart of a bushwhacker-infested region, his commission being to infiltrate a particular bushwhacker's band, to gather damning facts, evidence worthy of a military courtroom...

Hard times, those. Dangerous times. But Ben Woolard, obedient soldier, had fulfilled his assignment. Working with his own brother Jake as his secret contact, he had filtered intelligence out to the Union military. When at last the bloody bushwhacker named Henry Champion was brought to trial in a Nashville courtroom, Ben had faithfully testified, unveiling the evidence he had gathered, the things he had witnessed and heard, while glint-eyed Henry Champion sat glaring at the young man he had thought was a fellow reb bushwhacker, an underling and follower, but who in fact was a Judas, betraying him to those who would see him killed.

Ben talked quietly about that episode of his life, so distant now in his experience, and seldom thought about any longer.

"You know, Jake," he said as he took the last puff from his third cigar of the night, "I recollect how I felt when Champion was finally hanged. It was odd, really. I felt kind of sorry for him, for I'd ridden with him and got to know him. Even to like him, sometimes...what rare part of him there was to like. But I was also relieved to know he was dead. The way he looked at me while I testified...I knew that he'd kill me, if he could, for what I was doing to him. He'd have killed me like I'd seen him kill so many others."

Jake, rolling his own cigar around in his mouth, stared at the wall and said nothing.

"Looking back now, I have trouble believing I actually did what I did," Ben went on. "To think I actually became part of a reb bushwhacker gang! Rode with them. Helped them rob folks, burn houses. But never did I kill anyone for them. That I wouldn't have done, though I tell you my heart was in my throat every day for fear Champion would call on me to prove my worth and loyalty by killing somebody at his behest. But it never happened. Thank God. It was always Champion or one of his higher followers who pulled the trigger or tied the noose. But even then, it haunted me. Standing by, watching men and even boys killed by that murdering scoundrel...and me doing nothing. Not that I was supposed to do anything—my charge was to observe and gather evidence, not to interfere. But I remember how many died, and how bad they died. You know what I'm talking about, Jake. You know how many I told you about personally, and you heard me give testimony. You even gave testimony yourself."

"I did, yes."

"He hated you, too, you know. He hated everyone who testified against him. It's a good thing for me and you both that he was hanged."

"Yes. It is." Jake lifted his head sharply. "Listen! Did you hear that?"

Jake's sudden motion had startled Ben, lulled as he was by rich cigar smoke and reverie. "I didn't hear anything."

"Outside...something..."

Jake rose and went to the door. Ben felt a pins-and-needles edginess that he hoped didn't show. He'd been so lost in thought about long-ago days of espionage among Civil War bushwhackers that he caught himself halfway fearing that Jake would open that door and reveal the living phantom of Henry Champion himself, back from the dead to punish the two brothers whose work had helped spur him to the gallows.

Ben felt foolish, of course, when the open door revealed nothing but the passed-out form of Andy Woolard, curled up like an oversize fetus on the front porch.

"Look at him," Jake said, shaking his head.

Ben came to his brother's side. "Help you carry him in?"

"If you would. Thanks. Look at him, Ben. My own son."

"Not long ago, it was also your own brother who was curled-up drunk like that. But I'm still alive, and sober now. If that can happen to me, it can happen to him, too. Just be glad he came home, Jake. He could have spent the night on some saloon floor, lying in spit and sawdust."

CHAPTER 4

Ben walked at his brother's side down Center Street, listening to Jake expound upon life and growth in Ferguson, Colorado, and noticing, too, the number of glances and reactions Jake received from those they passed Impressive. The surest test of a man's importance, Ben knew, lay in how people reacted to him, and judging from what he saw here, Jake Woolard enjoyed a wealth of influence in this town.

"There are two routes to success here," Jake was saying. "The first and most fundamental is mining. It's the heart and soul of this town. Without it there would be no Ferguson. Nor would there be commerce, and that, by the way, is the second of the two routes."

"Commerce."

"Yes. Supply and demand and all that. Fulfillment, for your own profit, of another man's requisites for making a profit of his own."

"In other words, if a miner needs a shovel and a miner's candle, sell it to him."

"Right. Or, more applicable to what I have in mind for

you on the immediate level: If a man needs a place to sleep in a new town, sell *that* to him."

Ben looked at a building looming up ahead of them. "I have a suspicion that I'm about to become the headmaster of the Ferguson sleeping academy."

Jake laughed. "And so you are...if you'll have it. And only temporarily."

They reached the big Cathedral of Rest warehouse, with walls two stories high but only one vast room inside, with its rows of curtained windows just above head level. A man inside could look out, but one on the street couldn't look in. "Clever idea, Jake," Ben said. "Not quite a hotel, but better than putting up in an alley or on a billiard parlor floor."

"Indeed it is. And there's never a shortage of business, and won't be, not as long as this town attracts newcomers. And that's going to be going on for a long time to come."

Jake pulled a key from his pocket and thrust it into the door. The door swung inward into a great, hollow, shadowed emptiness. The two men stepped inside, and as Ben's eyes quickly adjusted, he saw that the place wasn't really empty at all, but filled with row upon row of double-level bunks. Not a living soul was in the place.

"I figured there'd be somebody in here taking an afternoon snooze," Ben said.

"Nope. One of my rules is that the place is empty by eight in the morning, and stays that way until eight at night. No stragglers and loiterers that way. You want to sleep here, you show up when it opens for an evening, and get in line. First come, first served."

"No weeklong reservations, eh?"

"No. One night at a time, fifty cents a night. No credit or paying in advance."

"But what if a man has luggage and such? Does he have to take it out come morning and haul it around with him all day?"

"He does...unless he wants to rent a lockbox." Jake pointed toward a row of padlocked, heavy wooden lockers lining one portion of a wall. Ben smiled and shook his head in admiration.

"Jake, you are indeed a caution. I never knew you had such a nose for making a dollar."

"I've caught the itch, I reckon. Seen the elephant, as they used to say back in the California gold rush days. Maybe it's because I've struggled so for money for so many years that I've took such a passion for making it here, where the opportunity is so good. And I'm doing well, no denying. I make good money with my sleeping house and my stores, too. And there's mining. I don't do any mining myself, but I have stock in several mines."

"I heard. Sally said you grubstake new miners."

"Some, yes. Those I have a good instinct about. I supply the tools and such in advance in return for a bit of stock in whatever productive mine the prospector might find. Some never amount to much, but others have done quite well for me. And I'm ready to grubstake you, Ben...if you want me to."

Ben shrugged. "I don't know a thing about mining."

"It's not hard to learn. There's every kind of man in the world digging in these hills—veteran miners, college professors, bookkeepers, preachers...every kind of man in the world short of a Chinaman. No Chinamen in Ferguson. No Celestials allowed. It's a town rule, written right in the ordinances."

"Speaking of rules, what would I have to know to run this sleeping parlor of yours?"

"Not much. Payment in advance, no exceptions. No drunks, no exceptions. No food, no gaming, no smoking while in bed, and no talking."

"Strict house."

"It's a sleeping house. That's all. You don't want to sleep, don't come in. Oh, and no women. Not even alone, and certainly not with a man."

"Not even a man's wife?"

"That's right. This is a one-night-at-a-time sleeping facility for single, sober-minded men. And that's all."

"Who's been overseeing it for you before I came?"

"Lately just a string of short-termers. Before that, Andy did the job. But he ended up ignoring the rules, letting people carouse and drink. Joined in with them, in fact. I had to relieve him of the job. Fired my own son, I did."

"Oh."

"It's hard, anymore, dealing with Andy." Jake looked thoughtfully into a corner of the shadowed room, frowning, his mind on the wayward son who even now was sleeping off last night's drunk back at the Woolard house.

"So what do I do if some two-ton Thomas violates a rule and declares he won't be evicted?"

"You work it out any way you can. Level a shotgun at him if you have to. Generally the others in the place will help get rid of any rule-breakers. It's their sleep that gets disturbed, after all."

"Where do I sleep?"

"There." Jake pointed to a curtained-off little section with a single narrow bunk inside. It was the only segregated chamber in the vast warehouse.

"All right. Will this place be full tonight?"

"It's full every night. Or almost so. Four hundred men. Well, Ben, do you want the job? At least until I can get you grubstaked and make a miner out of you?"

Ben looked around. The truth was, he didn't relish the task of supervising four hundred sleeping men a night, playing landlord, nursemaid, and bouncer all at the same time—but he'd come here to turn his life around, to work. He wasn't likely to be offered anything better anytime soon, and he wasn't willing to freeload off his brother like some tramp.

"I'll take the job," he said. "At least until you can find you somebody reliable to take it over for good. I'm beginning to like the notion of mining. It's my best chance to make something good out of myself. But for now, I'm glad to help you out here."

Jake grinned and slapped Ben's shoulder. "Good. You can start now."

"Doing what?"

"Stripping dirty linens and carrying them to the Smithers Laundry on up the street. Don't let the abundance of laundry signs in this town fool you: Smithers is the only one worth its soap. I've got an account there. Pay it once a month. Laundry and stolen blankets are my biggest expense."

"How do I decide which sheets are dirty?"

"If they look stiff enough to stand up by themselves, they're dirty. Otherwise, leave them be."

Ben leaned over and examined the nearest exposed sheet with a wince of distaste. "Stains don't count, eh?"

"Stains don't count."

Ben grinned. "I appreciate what you're doing for me, Jake."

"Think nothing of it. Glad to do it." He paused. "It seems I'm unable to save my own son from destruction. At the very least I can help my brother."

"Andy will come around," Ben said.

"Maybe. If he lives long enough."

———

Three nights later, Ben sat quietly in the darkness on his bunk, staring at the thin fabric wall separating him from the main chamber, listening to the cacophony of snores rumbling and echoing through the big warehouse. He smiled, thinking that it was a good thing that Jake's strict house rules didn't forbid snoring as well as talking and card-playing. Otherwise he'd have to evict half his customers.

He rolled over on his side. Who'd have thought he'd wind up here, high in the mountains where air was thin and veins of ore were thick, where wealth was abundant in the land all around but most men were still poor? When he'd left the service of the Union Army at the close of the great conflict, he'd envisioned quite a different future for himself —a wife, good home, houseful of children, maybe a career in law or business. That future had seemed to be shaping itself for a long time, until death intruded and his family left him for the great world beyond earthly life...and he was alone, and miserable.

How many times had he struggled with the desire to see it all end? How many times had the thought of death seemed as sweet and enticing to him as those soft bunks out there surely seemed to the weary men now occupying them? He couldn't count on two hands the times he had forced himself to cling to life and hope by sheer force of will, by a pure leap of faith that somehow there was something worthwhile remaining in life, even for a man alone.

There were, after all, things worse than the kind of loss he had suffered. Worse ways to have one's life and loved ones taken from him. He'd seen plenty of that in the days he had ridden with Henry Champion, gathering the eyewitness evidence that finally made a gallowsman out of the murdering devil. Horrible times, those. Men murdered before their families, mere boys shot to death for the sins of their fathers, or because Henry Champion was in the mood to see some poor Union-sympathizing lad jerk and fall at the kiss of a pistol ball.

Ben fell into a deep and undreaming slumber that lasted until the first light of morning began spilling through the big warehouse windows. He sat up and glanced at his watch. Ten minutes later, dressed and with his face washed clean in the basin beside the bed, he stepped out from behind the curtain and clanged the wake-up bell. He was greeted with a chorus of groans and muttered curses as a sleeping army stirred awake.

They filed out past him, most of them grumbling and grumpy, others still half asleep on their feet, and the inevitable few bright and eager early-morning types smiling and looking as if being rousted too early from a comfortable bunk was the finest thing that could happen to a man.

The last man in line was a bald fellow in his mid-forties. "Pardon me, sir, but might I have a word with you?" he asked.

A complaint, Ben figured. "What can I do for you?"

"Is your name, by any chance, Woolard?"

"It is."

"Benjamin Woolard, perhaps?"

"Yes. Do I know you?"

"No. But I do know you. Or who you are. I once watched you sit on a witness stand and talk a wicked man onto the gallows. Back in Nashville. I was a guard in that courtroom, sir, and I stood there listening to you, and I want you to know, sir, I admired what you were doing."

"Well, I...I don't know what to say. Thank you."

"No, sir. Thank *you*. You were a brave man to do what you did. Infiltrating that bunch of bushwhacking murderers, riding with them, gathering the facts to put Henry Champion where he belonged...God bless you, sir. If you never do another fine thing in your life, you've already done the work of the saints by ridding this world of Henry Champion."

"Thank you. Thank you very much. That means a lot to me to hear you say that, Mister..."

"Wilkins. Peter R. Wilkins, from Albany, New York." He

stuck out his hand for a shaking. "Pleased to know you in person, Mr. Woolard."

"Pleased to know you, too. You're going to mine, I take it?"

"If I can. A man has to take his opportunities when they come."

"Indeed. Indeed. Good fortune to you, Mr. Wilkins."

"And to you too, Mr. Woolard, sir." He chuckled. "Quite an odd thing, you know, meeting two men who were involved in bringing the demon Champion to his end!"

Two men? Ben was momentarily confused, then realized that Wilkins must have met or seen Jake. "My brother, I suppose you mean."

"Brother?" Wilkins laughed heartily. "I'd say not! This fellow is black as the night sky, and has himself a mouthful of gold teeth."

"Is his name Roanie? Roanie Piatt?"

"I do believe so."

"I know him. But what did he have to do with the Champion business?"

"He was at the hanging. Saw it happen. You remember the company of Negro soldiers they brought in..."

"Yes, yes—because of what Champion did at Saltville. I do remember. But I didn't know that Roanie was among them."

"He was. He and I had quite a good talk about it only last evening. We'd met one another the day of the Champion hanging, and he recalled me before I recalled him. Quite a nice man. Those teeth are a sight, eh?"

"They are. Well, sir! Thank you for telling me about Roanie. I'll have to talk it over with him if I run across him again."

Wilkins put out his hand again. "Good day to you, sir."

"Good day to you."

When Wilkins was gone, Ben marveled over the remarkable encounter, and the even more remarkable news about Roanie. The past, it appeared, wasn't always as dead as it seemed. It had a way of intruding itself unexpectedly into the present.

He'd almost forgotten that band of black soldiers who had been brought in to see Champion hanged. A deliberately ironic presence theirs had been. Champion, who had murdered wounded black soldiers at Saltville, Virginia, shooting them in their faces without a trace of remorse, had been forced to see black faces staring back at him when his own death came to claim him. A nicely fitting touch, it seemed to Ben.

He locked the door, then made the rounds through the warehouse and checked the sheets. None so dirty as to require laundering, at least not by the standards Jake had laid down. And all the blankets still in place.

He let himself out and locked the door behind him again. The morning was bright and clear, and over at Jake's house, Sally would be cooking one of her excellent breakfasts. He strode into the street and made his way in that direction as fast as he could walk.

CHAPTER 5

Ben lay awake, hands behind his head, staring at the high sloped ceiling of the Cathedral of Rest and listening to the snores rising from, it seemed, at least half of the bunk occupants on the other side of the curtain.

The noise wasn't what kept Ben awake. He'd been at this job for almost a week now and was accustomed to the nightly serenade of snores. Something else was bothering him, and he couldn't quite pin down what it was. A sense of brewing trouble, as yet undefined.

He was finally about to drift away into slumber when he heard a man's voice, talking in a rough and far too loud whisper, somewhere out in the Cathedral of Rest.

"Come on, you! Show yourself! You ain't fooling me!"

Drunk, obviously. Ben could tell from the slurred words. So this was it: His first round of trouble in his new job. He'd have to evict this man.

Sighing and rising, he pulled his trousers up over his long-john-clad legs and hitched them. Finger-combing his hair, he pushed aside the curtain and exited into the big, dark chamber.

"Come on! Ain't no use in fighting me—I done seen through your game, yes indeedy!"

He tracked the voice and found it belonged to the very man he'd hoped it wouldn't—a burly, ugly, bearded fellow who surely was a prizefighter or strong-arm man. He'd seemed a touch intoxicated when he passed into the Cathedral of Rest earlier, but not enough to make Ben call him down. Clearly, though, he'd slipped a bottle in and had been continuing to drink after climbing into his bunk. The smell of liquor hung like a cloud around his area.

He was in the top bunk, leaning down over the edge, eyeing from an upside-down position a very small and timid-looking fellow in the bunk below him who, curiously, was sleeping with his hat on. His big paw of an arm extended almost to the little fellow's bedclothing, and it appeared he was trying to grab them and pull them away. Or was it the hat he was going after? Ben couldn't tell.

"What's going on here?" Ben demanded, trying to sound as tough as possible.

The bearded head turned up and gazed at him in the darkness. Ben had brought a lamp with him, and now struck a match to it. Light spilled out in a golden circle, and men sat up in their bunks all around, blinking and squinting. Most had been awake already, disturbed by the voice of the drunk.

"Ain't nothing to do with you," the drunk said. "Just get on back to your place."

"Sorry, friend," Ben replied. "There's rules here, and you just broke one of them. No talking. Now, you going to quiet up, or get out?"

"Get the hell away from me, little man," the drunk said again, and reached down again toward the cringing occupant of the bunk below him.

Ben set the lamp on the floor, grabbed the extended arm, yanked back and down, and tumbled the drunk out of the bunk and onto the floor. Twisting the arm around behind the man, he dropped a knee into the small of his back and pinned him.

Ben glanced around. "A little help here would be appreciated," he said.

No one responded—and the pinned man didn't stay pinned long. With a roar and great heave, he dumped Ben off him onto the floor.

Coming to his feet, the drunk swore and said, "You're going to wish you'd minded your own 'fairs, little man!"

Though the drunk had the advantage of size, Ben had that of speed and sobriety. He managed to avoid the man's stomping foot. A bare foot, but a heavy one that would have hurt terribly had it connected.

"Somebody!" Ben yelled. "Give me some help here!" He came to his feet and gave a quick punch; the drunk took it on the nose and grunted, falling back against one of the bunks.

Cursing and furious, the drunk came at Ben, but this time someone did intervene. A nervous but strong-looking man appeared from a nearby lower bunk and stepped in front of the drunk. "You leave that man be!" he shouted with surprising force.

For some reason, the drunk faltered. He paused, staring with confusion at the interloper. Ben took advantage of the moment to come forward and strike the drunk in the jaw as hard as he could. The man collapsed onto his rump, hard. Stunned, he sat there as others now surrounded him. Too many to be defied.

Ben looked around, grinning feebly. "Thanks."

They got the drunk to his feet and hustled him toward the door. Someone found and gathered the man's belongings, most of them still in the cloth sack he used for luggage, and dumped it out the door after him.

The drunk turned on the dark street—still not an empty street, even at this hour—and pointed waveringly at Ben. "I ain't going to forget you!" he yelled. "And you ain't seen the last of me!"

"Don't you try to come back here again," Ben replied. "You're barred from this place."

The man muttered curses, gathered up his possessions, and vanished down the street, which was mostly dark but lighted here and there by saloons and gambling halls that remained open all night.

As Ben started to turn to go back into the Cathedral of Rest, he happened to glance toward the doorway of one of the nearer saloons. There were men there, attracted by the ruckus generated by the ouster of the drunk.

Ben's eyes locked onto the face of one of the men, dimly visible, but clearly enough seen to bring an expression of shock onto Ben's own face.

He stepped forward, staring...and the crowd at the saloon door dispersed and was gone.

"What is it?" someone asked.

"Nothing," Ben replied. "Nothing. Well, I reckon we can go back and get some sleep now."

They all reentered the Cathedral of Rest, closing the door and shutting out the night.

———

As the men filed out of the building come morning, the altercation of the night before was a subject of lighthearted commentary. The light of day had stripped it of its ominous quality, and Ben found himself a warmly regarded hero.

As the small-framed fellow who had occupied the bunk below the belligerent drunk passed by, Ben reached out and touched a shoulder. "Hold up a minute, if you would. I'd like a word."

The dirty face, thin and gaunt, was suddenly full of fear.

A quick nod, and the small fellow stood aside until the others were out.

Ben closed the door and looked closely at the fellow. He slowly reached out and removed the hat. Long auburn hair spilled out around the delicate face.

"How did you know?" she asked.

"Same way that drunk last night did, I reckon. Just something different in the look of a woman, even when she's trying to make herself look like a man."

"Nobody else seemed to notice."

"Maybe they didn't. Maybe they did and didn't want to get you in trouble by saying something about it."

She looked dejected. "I'm sorry. I shouldn't have tried to fool you. But I had to have a place to sleep."

"I know. That's why I didn't say anything last night when I first noticed."

"Thank you."

"But it is against the rules. I can't let you do it again."

"I know."

"You have a place you can go?"

She looked solemn, and drifted her gaze away from him. "Yes." And he knew from the way she said it that in fact she didn't. But it wasn't really his affair.

"Well...I wish the best for you. Where'd you come from?"

"Oh...it doesn't matter."

"Sorry you had that trouble last night."

She smiled sadly. Sort of pretty, he noticed, though it was hard to tell through the grime on her face. Put there, he figured, to help disguise her femininity.

"What's your name?" he asked.

"That doesn't matter, either. Good-bye," she said.

"Good-bye."

———

When she was gone, Ben made the rounds of the sleeping chamber, checking the linens, removing those that demanded a washing. When he reached the place where she had slept, he paused an extra moment.

Intriguing woman. He wondered who she was, and what her circumstances were.

He started to move on, but noted something peeking out from beneath the blanket. He picked it up. A small leather packet, unmarked, held closed by a leather tie. He paused, wondering if he should look inside for identification.

Probably not. She'd surely note she'd left it, and come back for it. Resisting temptation, he tucked the packet under his arm and continued his rounds. When he was through, he placed the packet in one of the lockers, secured it there, and headed out to meet the day.

Outside, he stopped a moment and stared at the place where, the night before, he had seen the shadowy figure that so startled him. He shook his head slowly. Surely not.

Surely it had been his imagination, or some odd coincidence of similarity.

He stepped into the street and strode away.

———

"Pardon me, sir."

Ben turned. He faced east, toward the rising sun, and had to squint to make out the man who had hailed him. "Howdy."

"Yes. Hello." The man moved to the side, into a more comfortable light. Ben recognized him as one of the men who had helped him evict the drunk. "Sorry to bother you."

"No bother. Thank you, by the way, for the help last night."

"Glad to. Glad to. My name is Hammel. Roscoe Hammel. I've come to Ferguson to mine, like most everybody else, and I've been hoping to find a partner. Well, I figure a man like you, who sees so many folks, might be in a position to know of who else might be looking for somebody to mine with."

"Well, the truth is, I do see a lot of people, but not to get to know them. It's pretty much like you saw it last night: You come in, pay your money, take your bunk, and sleep. No real socializing."

"Right. I see. Well...it was just a thought, Mister..."

"Woolard. Ben Woolard. Listen, you shouldn't have trouble finding somebody to mine with you in this town, I wouldn't think. The place is crawling with men wanting to mine, and a good number probably need a partner as much as you do. I'll be looking for one myself before long, most likely."

The man brightened with interest. "So you plan to mine?"

"Probably. I'm working the Cathedral right now to help out my brother. He owns the place."

Hammel paused, then said, "Perhaps when the time comes, you might consider me as a possible partner."

Ben was honestly surprised. "I don't really know...what I mean is, you don't really know me. Wouldn't you want to work with someone you knew?"

"Unfortunately, Mr. Woolard, I don't know a soul here. You strike me as the kind of man who can be trusted, and I tend to trust my instincts."

Ben studied Hammel. He had an open and honest face and manner. If instinct was the issue, then Ben's instinct was positive toward Hammel, as Hammel's was toward him. "I'll give it some thought."

"Will I be able to reach you at the Cathedral?"

"There, or through my brother's store. He has the mercantile and mining supply store that stands yonder." He pointed.

Hammel smiled. "Very good. Hope you have a fine day, Mr. Woolard."

"You, too, sir."

————

Late that day, Ben was striding out of the door of a cafe when he saw Roanie standing at the corner open-air dentist parlor, the smiling dentist at his side, holding a mirror in which Roanie was admiring his brilliantly gleaming mouth. Nodding his satisfaction, he said something to the dentist, placed money in his hand, and turned away, catching sight of Ben as he did. He came over, smiling.

"Covered you over another tooth, eh?" Ben asked.

"Yes, sir," Roanie replied. "That's all of them. Every tooth in my head is gold now."

"What do you reckon your brother will think about that?"

"He'll be jealous, Mr. Woolard. We been racing to see who can get all his teeth golded over first."

"Congratulations on your victory. By the way, Roanie, I met somebody who told me something interesting about you. I hear you were there when the army hung Henry Champion."

Roanie's brows flickered and his bright manner lessened just a little. "Yes. I surely was."

"I was involved in that situation myself."

"Oh?"

"That's right. I testified against him in the trial. I knew some things about his crimes. It was me, I suppose, who was most responsible for putting him on those gallows."

Roanie lifted his head and looked at Ben in a whole new way. "Then, sir, I salute you. Because Henry Champion took something from me. He killed my oldest brother. Murdered him while he lay wounded on a battlefield."

"I'm sorry."

"But I got to see him die for what he done. I watched him hang."

"So did I. You were one of the colored soldiers there, I guess."

"That's right, sir."

"Those were hard days. That bloody war."

"Yes, sir." Roanie paused, running his tongue across his teeth, feeling the smooth gold covering them. "Mr. Woolard, it's funny you should talk about Henry Champion. I was just thinking on him yesterday. Wondering something. Did he have a brother?"

"Champion? No. No. I'm sure he didn't."

"Not disputing you, sir, but I'm feeling sure he did. A twin, matter of fact."

"Henry Champion had no twin brother. No brother at all. I know a lot about the man, and if he'd had a twin, I'd know it."

"But there's got to be a twin, sir. Because I seen him with my own eyes."

"What are you talking about?"

"I seen Henry Champion's twin. Just a few days ago."

"Here? In Ferguson?"

"That's right, sir. Standing inside a saloon, at the bar. I passed it, nighttime, and looked in. And when I saw him, sir, I right nearly died on the spot. Felt a jolting in my heart, and that's the truth. It was like seeing Henry Champion himself again, in the flesh. But older. Like he'd be now, if he hadn't been hung."

"But he *was* hung. He's dead."

"I know."

"I mean...I *saw* him hanged."

"Yes, sir. Me, too."

Ben, more unnerved by this odd tale than he wanted to admit, thought it over. "It has to be a mistake. There is no twin. And Champion himself is dead. So it must be someone who looks like him."

"Just like him, sir. So much like him that it's nigh a miracle if it ain't him. Mr. Woolard? Are you feeling all right, sir?"

Ben was shaken, and apparently it showed. "I'm fine." He forced a smile. Suddenly he didn't want to talk about this matter anymore. "Congratulations on getting your teeth finished up like you wanted."

"Thank you, Mr. Woolard. Did you find your brother?"

"I did. I'm tending his sleeping house for him for now. I'll probably take to mining a little later on."

"All the best to you, sir."

"Thank you."

They went opposite directions. Abruptly, Ben turned. "Hey, Roanie..."

Roanie pivoted. "Yes, sir?"

Ben opened his mouth but paused, then did not ask what he had been about to ask, the question that stemmed from the unexpected vision he had seen in that saloon doorway the night before across from the Cathedral of Rest, and which fit all too well, if all too uncomfortably, with what Roanie had just told him.

"Nothing, Roanie. Never mind."

"Good day to you, sir."

"Good day to you."

CHAPTER 6

Ben knew who had jumped him even before he hit the ground, and chided himself for not having considered the possibility of retribution aimed his way by a man humiliated before an entire warehouseful of others.

He grunted at the impact of the well-trodden alleyway ground against his chest, then yelled when a hard-toed boot caught him in the left ribs.

"Think you can throw *me* out, do you? Think you can make *me* look a fool before four hundred men?" And then the evictee of the prior night kicked him again.

Ben took that blow painfully, but when the laughing attacker drew back and launched a third kick, Ben was ready. His hand shot out, grabbed the man's ankle, and pulled at just the right moment to bring the fellow crashing to his rump.

Ben came up, planning to light into the man while he was down. He hadn't factored in the pain that movement brought to his ribs, however, and that slowed him just enough to allow the big man—who was drunk again, though not quite as drunk as the night before—to rise again and drive a fist into his jaw.

Ben saw stars explode inside his head and staggered back, bumping hard against the side wall of the Cathedral of Rest. He'd been on his way here to open up for this evening's round of sleepers when the drunk had come upon him as if from nowhere.

Stunned and suddenly unable to focus his eyes, Ben groped out blindly and tried to hit his enemy. No connection. The force of his own blow made him stumble out and toward the attacker, leaving him in excellent position to receive the next blow, which caught him on the chin. Consciousness threatening to flee, he went weak in the legs and fell like a puppet with severed strings.

He landed on his knees and somehow managed to stay upright. Putting out his hands blindly to ward off the next blow, he was surprised by a sudden explosion of motion and violence in his swimming field of vision. The drunk cursed and fell; there was thudding and yelling and more cursing...

Ben managed to clear his vision enough to see that his attacker had been attacked in turn, and to Ben's surprise, the man who had done it was his own nephew, Andy.

Ben rose weakly and tried to step forward to join the fray. Instead he merely staggered backward, up against the wall again.

"Hey now, wait a minute there...that's my nephew you're...pounding on..." Ben's voice was breathless and slurred; he sounded intoxicated.

He was also inaccurate about who was pounding on whom. The drunk was doing very little pounding on young Andy, who despite a great disadvantage of size and weight was thoroughly pummeling the man. He fought with a vigor and fury that spoke of pent-up rage and frustration.

Ben opened his mouth to speak again, then swooned and fell to the ground. When he opened his eyes, Andy was looking down at him in the shadowy twilight, an abrasion on his forehead and blood at the corner of his mouth...but also a big smile lighting his face. The drunk was gone.

"Ben? You going to be all right?"

"I'm...yes...I think..."

"What the devil did you do to get that man to jump you? He might have killed you if I hadn't been here."

"I was...last night...threw him...out of..."

"Come on, Ben. Get up from there and let's get you inside. Wash you up a little and pour a little whiskey down you. Whoops! No whiskey for you, I guess. Coffee'll have to do. Come on. I'll help you up."

"Pleased that...mighty obliged you..."

"Hush. Don't try to talk while you're still addled. Whoooeee! That was a fine time there! I ain't had such fun in Lord only knows!"

"Didn't much think it...was fun myself..."

"Hush. Come on." He got Ben to his feet and draped Ben's arm across his own shoulder. Supporting his uncle, he began carefully walking out of the alley, around to the front of the Cathedral of Rest. Ben more or less hung on, shuffling his feet and managing to walk, and wishing his head would quit ringing so loudly.

———

"I was waiting for you to show up," Andy said, dabbing at Ben's abraded and bloodied chin with a damp cloth. They were inside Ben's little curtained-off chamber, the exterior door closed and locked behind them to keep out customers just yet. "Wanted to talk to you about something. Good thing, huh? I knew there was some kind of trouble soon as I heard that ruckus commence in the alley. Word of caution to you: Don't walk in the alleys in Ferguson at night without looking for somebody to jump you. Half the time somebody will."

Ben's head still hurt but wasn't ringing anymore. He was able to think again, too. "I do thank you, Andy. But what was it you wanted to talk to me about?"

Andy's cheerfulness diminished noticeably, but he retained an open and friendly manner that Ben was only just now beginning to comprehend as quite a significant change from his usual past demeanor. "I wanted to tell you, first off, that I'm...sorry. It ain't easy for me to say, but I do mean it. I've been mighty rude to you since you came to Ferguson. I shouldn't have been."

Ben was so stunned, he almost felt he'd been hit again. "Well, I forgive you, then. And I know, by the way, that you've had good reason to feel bitter and sad."

Andy glanced at Ben, then drifted his gaze floorward. "They told you what happened?"

"Yes. And it was an accident, Andy, nothing you need to feel responsible for. It wasn't any more your fault that she died than it was mine that my own family died. It took me a while to see that, though. Sometimes I still feel guilty for it."

Andy looked at him. "It was awful, knowing it was my gun that killed her. I didn't even know it was loaded."

"Forget about it. Forgive yourself and go on. All you can do."

Andy remained quiet for several moments.

"Andy, let me ask you. What made you decide to come apologizing all at once?"

"I don't know, really. Just came around to it, I reckon. I got to thinking about myself, what I was doing, and about you, and how you'd done the same kind of thing after your own tragedies...and all at once I knew I was jealous of you. You'd survived. Made it through alive. I was talking every day about destroying myself, but down inside, I didn't want to. I wanted to live again. Like you are."

"I'm not quite living yet," Ben said. "I mean, I'm forty

years old, well on through my life, and I've got nothing but a job handed to me by my brother."

"Maybe you can have more."

"What do you mean?"

"It's the other thing I wanted to talk to you about. You interested, maybe, in doing some prospecting?"

"Matter of fact, I am. You?"

"Been thinking about it last day or two. Thinking maybe you and me might do it together."

"Partners?"

"Yep. If you want to."

"Sounds right good to me."

Andy grinned; he was more like the boy Ben had known years back than he'd been since Ben had arrived at Ferguson. "Good. You know, the best way would be to have a third man, too. It's easier with three."

"Well, there was a man who stayed here last night who expressed an interest in finding a partner. I don't know him beyond one conversation, but he seemed a likely enough fellow."

"What's his name?"

Ben searched his mind. "Roscoe Hammel."

"Strong-looking man?"

"Yes."

"Well, heck...fine with me, I guess."

"If I see him, I'll talk to him."

"So you really want to do it?"

"Your father's been talking to me about grubstaking me since I came. He just hasn't been wanting to push too hard about it, as best I can tell. But yes, I really want to do it. On one condition."

"What?"

"You do what I've done and give up the drinking."

Andy thought about it and nodded. "I will. I will before I get so lost in the stuff that I can't."

"Wise young man, you are. Proud to claim you for a nephew."

"I am sorry about how I've been."

"You know who you really need to say that to, don't you?"

"Yes. My mother."

"Right. She worries half to death over you."

Andy nodded, then thought seriously, in silence, for several moments. "Ben, does me wanting to change my ways mean that I've given up caring for my lady like I did? Am I forgetting her?"

"You're forgetting the tragedy a little, maybe. Not forgetting her. You'll never forget her. But you have to understand that punishing yourself for an accident does nothing, *nothing,* for the one you've lost. All it does is hurt you and all those who care about you."

"I'll never get over what happened. Not all the way."

"That's true."

Andy chuckled all at once, happiness bursting in from somewhere, making him thrust out his hand for Ben to shake. Ben did shake it, firmly, and knew from the light in his nephew's eyes and the joy behind the wide grin that the lad had turned a corner and was on his way to better things.

"Ben, I'm glad to be your partner. When can we get started?"

"Tell you what. Let's talk to your daddy tonight and see when he can get us grubstaked. But let me warn you about something: You've taken on a partner who don't know a blessed thing about mining nor mining law. I can dig a hole and shove a cart, but when it comes to the rules..."

"Don't worry. I know most of that already, and Pa can guide us through the rest."

Someone rattled the door; customers for the night were already beginning to gather.

"Well, best open up," Ben said.

"Want me to stay with you tonight, you having took such a pounding?"

"No need. I believe I'll make it. Do I look a sight?"

"Like you've wrestled a pit saw and lost."

"That bad, huh?"

"That bad...Come on. Let me stay. I can take care of everything for you tonight, and sleep out in one of the bunks. You can stay back here behind the curtain and not have everybody wondering what bear you went three rounds with."

"Fair enough. I'll owe you one."

Andy grinned and nodded. "I'll go open the door."

———

The next two days were filled with activity. At the Jake Woolard household, all was joy. The prodigal had returned! Andy was himself again! Furthermore, he and Ben were going to be partners, mining together, and with Jake naturally sharing some ownership as the provider of the grubstake, it would be a true family venture. Roscoe Hammel, whom Ben found on the street the very day after the initial conversation with Andy, and who had gladly accepted Ben's offer, would be the only involved party not a part of the Woolard clan.

In the meantime, an event happened that generated much interest in Ferguson. The town's first newspaper opened. No warning or prior ceremony, just a cleanly printed first edition hitting the streets, being hawked by paper-waving, loudly shouting boys in classic style.

Owned and published by a trio of local businessmen who had been victimized in one way or another by crime in Ferguson, the *Ferguson Law & Justice* declared its central theme and purpose in its very title, then spelled it out in full in a lengthy and scathing editorial published just beneath the nameplate.

Ferguson, the newspaper declared quite accurately, was even yet, and to its shame, an oversize mining camp as opposed to a true town of civilized men. The problem: a lack of proper and dedicated law enforcement. The town sheriff, professed the newspaper, was little more than a figurehead, an idle and incompetent symbol who held no true authority, and even worse, no true interest in maintaining law. No wonder men and women were robbed in alleyways by footpads! No wonder prostitution and lewdness thrived in the gambling dens, the upper rooms of the saloons, and on the stages of the theaters! It was time for a new and vigorous assertion of civilization in the high mountains, asserted the *Law & Justice*. Time for Ferguson to rid itself in orderly fashion of the present joke of a town marshal and appoint an authentic and effective replacement, creating a law-enforcement agency well-staffed with tough and fearless deputies who could keep the roughs and rowdies in their places.

Ben, like most everyone else, read the newspaper with great interest. He discussed the matter of the town marshal with Jake, who agreed heartily with the newspaper's sentiments. "The problem with a place like Ferguson is that you get all types, from all over," he expounded to Ben, Roscoe Hammel, and Andy over cigars after a satisfying supper. Sally, filled with a new joy of life, was cooking fine, fine meals now that Andy had declared himself reformed. "There's no sense of permanence and 'home' about a new town. Men come here planning to make a quick fortune, and they think of little else. As long as the rowdies bother the other man and not them, all is fine.

"And rowdies we have, with more coming every day. The lack of good law is like a lure to bad men. They'll swarm to a lawless place like flies to bad meat. I daresay that one out of every ten faces you see on Center Street on a busy day belongs to some man who has reason, beyond the desire for wealth, for forsaking the civilized lowlands for the uncivilized mountains."

"I can vouch for that," Andy threw in. "In the circles I've run in lately, there's plenty of old dark secrets crawling around in the shadows of a lot of men's lives."

"So what will happen?" Ben asked. "Will there be a new town marshal named?"

"Eventually," Jake said. "Having a newspaper to push for it will help a lot. Make people think, you see. Give them a corporate point of reference in addition to their own individualized ones. A newspaper is just the thing to make a town feel like a town, not just a hodgepodge."

"I hope you're right," Ben said, thinking about the attack he had suffered in the alley, and how badly it might have gone for him had Andy not shown up. "I just wonder how bad things will have to get before folks really decide to do something about it."

"Some people getting murdered, most likely," Roscoe said. "I've noticed it always takes people getting killed before folks will get stirred up to fix things."

"You, sir, are a prophet and a philosopher," Jake said, drawing placidly on his long cigar. "Yes, sir, a prophet and a philosopher."

Roscoe looked very pleased. "Really? Thank you, sir. I don't hear that kind of thing much. Most people I know tell me I'm stupid."

CHAPTER 7

Andy Woolard held a tack between his teeth and another between thumb and forefinger, the latter being gently but firmly embedded in the trunk of a tree. That one in place, he nailed in the second one as well, then stepped back to examine the document he'd posted on the trunk. A quick nod revealed his satisfaction, and he turned to Ben and Roscoe with a manner much like that of a lecturing professor. The high and beautiful Colorado mountains spread out behind him; before him in the distance lay the smoke-belching, brown and yellow town of Ferguson.

"There, now," he explained. "We've officially posted our notice of claim upon this spot. Later I'll also peel off some bark and etch the same claim right into the wood of the tree, then let the sap run over it and glaze it in to stay. Nobody can swipe off a claim notice that way, you see."

"Now, how big a plot we claiming?"

"Three hundred feet wide, fifteen hundred feet long," Andy said. "That's the law. We'll mark off the rough boundaries in just a few minutes. Now, after we do some digging, and if things then look promising here, we'll bring in a surveyor and get our boundaries clearly defined and registered."

Roscoe shook his head. "I don't need a surveyor to know that we're already overlapping another claim. There was due notice posted on a tree, just like you've done, and yonder is one of the boundary markers already in place. And look there—he's done some digging right yonder, already. How can we just run over another man's claim like that, with him having worked it and duly marked it as his?"

Andy whistled between his teeth. Roscoe Hammel was set on obtaining wealth as a miner, but he surely already possessed a wealth of ignorance about how Colorado silver prospecting functioned.

Ben answered before Andy could speak. "Have you heard of 'surveying in,' Roscoe?"

"No."

"Well, I'm far from an expert, and Andy can correct me if I'm wrong, but what it amounts to is that it don't matter if our claim overlaps some other fellow's, or his overlaps us. The issue is who makes the first strike."

"That's right," Andy said. "What'll happen is this: We'll dig around in this land here, just like our neighbor's already done. Then, if we strike silver first, we gain the right to our whole claim, including even the parts of it that overlap his claim—unless, of course, he strikes on his claim first, and then he has the right to any part of his that includes part of ours."

"I don't understand," Roscoe said.

"It's just this simple," Ben contributed. "What counts is who strikes first. You have a successful claim, you get all the claim, and nobody can come along and take part of it from you just because their *unsuccessful* claim happens to overlap your *successful* one. See? That means that even if we encroach on our neighbor there, we aren't really taking anything of value from him. If he gets lucky and finds silver, then that claim is his, and there's nothing we can do to take it from him. Our boundary cuts off where his begins, if he strikes before we do. Same for us if *we* strike first."

Roscoe shook his head and looked sad. Nice fellow, Ben thought, but surely dumb as a rock.

"Never mind," Andy said. "Don't worry about it. Me and Ben understand it, so you don't have to. All you have to do is dig."

"Well, explain that to me, too," Roscoe said. "Just how does a man go about actually running a mine?"

Andy drew in a deep breath and searched for the simplest way to explain. "All right. First thing is you bring in your tools. Picks and shovels and such. Most haul them in on the back of a mule or two or three donkeys. You pick a spot and you commence to sink a shaft. Down you go, deeper and deeper, putting in timber to keep it braced as you go on down, hauling up dirt and rock with a windlass. You might go deep as a hundred feet or more and find nothing. Sometimes you strike right below the top of the ground. Anyhow, say you've gone down a hundred feet or so, and you've been lucky not to get flooded with water, and you finally hit your contact."

"What's 'contact'?" Roscoe asked.

"It marks off where the barren rock ends and the mineral-bearing rock begins. Well, if you can tell you've hit ore, or are about to, you put up a gallows atop the shaft."

Anticipating the inevitable query, Ben said, "A gallows is what the miners call the timber framework they build over the shafts to put their pullies and buckets and such."

"Right," Andy continued. "Once you get your gallows in, that's where the mule does his work. You tie your rope to him, run it through the pulley on the gallows, and tie the other to your bucket that drops down into the hole. Digging below, you fill the bucket and the mule takes a little walk, pulling up the bucket as he moves away from the shaft. You understand? We saw a mule doing just that while we were coming here."

Roscoe remembered, and smiled, nodding.

"All right. Now say you're doing good and you're going to keep on digging, expanding your mine. You'll probably want to put in a whim at some point. That's kind of a drum that your bucket rope can wind around. The mule turns the drum and winds the rope. Better than the other way, you see. More stable and powerful, and works without the mule having to walk to all creation, back and forth. And once you hit ore that assays out at a hundred or so ounces a ton, you build a shelter house over the shaft."

"Does the shaft just keep going straight down forever?"

"Of course not. When you hit your mineral, which generally is a hundred or more feet down, you begin running drifts."

"That's tunnels that run to the side instead of straight down," Ben presented. He'd been doing his research for the last little while and was proud to show up smarter than Roscoe...not that being smarter than Roscoe was a hard hurdle to leap, he was beginning to notice.

"Right again, Ben. The drifts run out from the bottom of the shaft, and you keep them shored up all along with lagging. That just means posts and lintels, put there to hold back cave-ins. You work on out the drift, and the end of it, where the digging goes on, that's called the breast of the drift. You use tallow candles for lighting, and put in timbers every four feet."

Roscoe nodded. "That's all I need to know for now."

Ben and Andy shared a private glance of amusement. *All* he could comprehend for now was probably more the truth.

"Well, gentlemen," Andy said, looking from one to the other. "We've posted our claim, we've got our grubstake, and it's a pretty day. What do you say we begin scouting about to figure where to begin digging our hole?"

———

The Ben Woolard who headed back late in the day toward Ferguson and the Cathedral of Rest was a weary, filthy, and aching version of his former self. He was beginning to have doubts about his fitness as a miner.

He hadn't worked so hard in years, and when it was done there hardly seemed to be more than a dent in the landscape. Thoughts of shafts sinking a hundred feet, even two hundred or three hundred feet... It was more than he could bear to think about just now.

Roscoe had done much better. With the explanations and thinking portions of the business behind, he had fallen to the labor with enthusiasm, working so hard and so enthusiastically, and with such remarkable strength, that Andy had privately joked to Ben that maybe they had wasted part of their grubstake in buying the mule. Roscoe could probably do the work of a mule all by himself.

When the work had begun, Ben was unhappy with the fact that he would have to cease labor earlier than the other two in order to return to the Cathedral of Rest. Jake, unable to find a reliable replacement for Ben at the sleeping warehouse, had begged him to continue his nighttime duties there for a while longer. Ben agreed, on condition that Jake try as hard as possible to find a permanent replacement so that Ben couldn't be accused of leaving his partners to bear more than their share of the mining load.

He didn't feel quite the same now, with muscles throbbing and weariness draining him. He was grateful for the excuse to leave, and the thought of his comfortable bunk enticed deliciously. Striding toward the town, he wondered if he would ever adjust to the physical demands of being a miner.

A stream trickled down from the high peaks. Ben paused, knelt to drink, then looked down at his filthy body.

He could hardly crawl into his bed in this state. Looking around, he assured himself he was alone, then stripped down and began to wash, letting the cool water bathe away his aches along with the grime.

Finishing, he let the breeze dry him, then put on his clothes again. Not very pleasant; they were as dirty as he had been. Clearly he'd have to buy himself some extra changes of clothing if he wanted to maintain a modicum of cleanliness.

Motion caught his eye. He looked across the stream and saw a rider descending toward the creek from the nearest ridge. Concentrating on the trail, the man hadn't looked up, hadn't noticed Ben—and when Ben caught a semi-profile glimpse of the face, he was glad of it.

Darting to a nearby grove of trees, he sank to the earth and watched the rider draw near. He obtained an even clearer view of the face now, and was chilled.

God in heaven, it was true. The man he was watching was none other than Arthur Rellon. Much older-looking than he had been those years before when he rode as the right-hand man and chief assassin for the bushwhacker Henry Champion, but the same man, sure as the world.

Arthur Rellon, a ghost from a dark past, alive and right here in Ferguson! It was enough to make Ben feel sick to his stomach.

He watched as Rellon dismounted at the stream and knelt to drink. Rellon looked about as he cupped water to his mouth, studying the landscape just as Ben had seen him do a thousand times before in the war-torn backcountry of Tennessee and Kentucky. The same small, animal eyes, keen and discerning; the same foxlike cunning in the expression of his narrow face.

Ben hated to admit it, but he had always been afraid of Art Rellon back in his days with Champion. More afraid of him than of Henry Champion himself. Champion killed without mercy, but usually not without at least a perceived reason. Art Rellon killed because he liked it.

It seemed to take an eternity for Rellon to finish his drink and mount up again. He rode on, heading west, vanishing over the next rise.

Ben stood, shaken. Arthur Rellon. It couldn't be...but it was.

He recalled the figure he had seen in the doorway of the saloon near the Cathedral of Rest. Jim Masker, or so it had appeared...another of Champion's band of wartime murderers. And then there was that wild claim of Roanie Piatt, that he'd seen a man who seemed the image of Henry Champion himself.

It was nightmarish. And impossible. Henry Champion was dead. Art Rellon and Jim Masker and all his other agents of death were surely now either dead themselves, or scattered to the corners of the nation. They couldn't be here. It was too much to believe. And Champion, being a dead man, couldn't be anywhere but hell itself, the hell he had richly earned in his foul and wicked life.

Ben headed back to Ferguson, feeling as if the dimming twilight descending upon him was fraught with unseen dangers, full of ghosts.

He reached the Cathedral of Rest and opened it hurriedly, eager to get inside and out of the night.

She showed up an hour later. Still wearing her man's garb, still with a face begrimed in a nearly successful effort to feign the darkening effect of a man's whiskers.

He smiled at her. "I knew I'd see you eventually," he said. "I found your packet after you left. It's locked safely away. I'll get it for you."

She smiled, seeming both relieved and uncomfortable.

He brought her the packet, which she took and pulled close to herself.

"Thank you," she whispered. Whispered, Ben figured, because if she could pass herself off as a man in appearance, at least to those who didn't bother to look closely, she certainly couldn't alter the femininity of her voice. She turned to the door and began to walk slowly toward it, clearly not eager to go back onto the street.

"Wait," Ben said.

She turned, looking puzzled, almost scared.

"Step in here a moment."

She looked shocked now.

"No, no. It's not what you're thinking. I want to have a private word with you, that's all."

Reluctant, clearly nervous, she came into the chamber. He drew the curtain closed.

"May I ask you again what your name is?"

She hesitated, then whispered, "Deborah Bray."

"Hello, Miz Bray. My name is Benjamin Woolard. Don't worry, I'm not going to give it away to anyone that you're a woman. But I do have some concern about you. Do you have a place to stay?"

Her eyes, he thought, moistened slightly in the pause that followed. "No."

"I thought not. You been on the street at night?"

"Yes." She nodded, her eyes very wet now, and her voice growing bitter. "Day and night."

"It's not good, you know, a woman being on her own that way. What I mean is, it's dangerous for you. There's bad men in a town like this."

"I know." She paused. "There are bad men other places too."

"Men—or maybe just one man—that you're running from?"

"Maybe."

"Listen, I don't mean to pry into your private business, but do you mind telling me how old you are?"

"Twenty-five."

She was beginning to speak more readily, beginning to trust him. "Twenty-five. A twenty-five-year-old woman, roaming about unprotected in a dangerous town, hiding, trying to pass herself off as a man. It won't do."

"I have no choice."

He rubbed his chin, thinking. "Do you have a place to sleep tonight?"

"No."

"You do now. You can stay here."

"Out there?" She waved a shaky hand toward the curtain, indicating the building beyond.

"No. In here."

Her eyes, and the way she backed off from him, told him how she took that. He spoke quickly. "No! No! Don't think I'm suggesting anything like what you might be thinking. I'm talking about you sleeping in here, and me sleeping out there."

She frowned. "Why are you being so kind to me?"

"Why shouldn't I be?"

"I just don't understand."

"Look, Miz Bray, I'm just trying to befriend someone who needs it. I can't in good conscience ask a woman to leave a place of safety for the streets, not when I can do something about it."

"But the rules..."

"I don't intend to advertise any of this. If you don't either, then there's no problem."

She staggered. Without warning. Her face paled. He reached out and steadied her.

"I'm sorry," she said, embarrassed.

"How long since you had anything to eat?"

"I don't remember. A day or two."

"Sit down," he said, waving toward his bunk. "I'm going to get you some food. You stay put until I get back."

"Thank you, Mr. Woolard."

"Glad to help. Now, sit down."

He didn't know what Jake would think about him deserting his assigned place, but Jake wasn't here, and he suspected that if he was, he'd do exactly the same thing. Ben left the building and headed for the nearest cafe. When he returned, bearing food, he found her asleep on the bunk. Awakening her gently, he gave her the victuals and left her alone in the chamber, going out into the big main chamber and claiming one of the unused bunks.

He lay awake only a few minutes, weary as he was from his day of digging. When he fell asleep, he was thinking of her, wondering just who she was, and who it was she was running from, and why.

CHAPTER 8

T hat night in the Cathedral of Rest, a man screamed out in the darkness, a terrible scream as if hell had risen to claim him. Every soul in the building awakened and sat up, and Ben came to his feet, lit a lamp, and went to the screamer's bedside.

He found the fellow, a mid-fortyish man with a bald head and stooped shoulders, weeping in his bunk, aware now that he had merely dreamed and feeling ashamed of his screaming...yet also still very shaken by whatever vision he had experienced.

"It's all right, friend," Ben said soothingly. "Just a night-mare. Nothing more."

"I know...I'm sorry."

Ben took a guess. "The war?"

The man looked at him through red and swollen eyes. "Yes. Shiloh."

"Ah, yes. You were there?"

"Yes. I was. And when I dream about it... God, it's like I still am."

"No talking!" someone across the warehouse shouted grumpily, reminding Ben of the house rule. Ben ignored it.

As overseer of the place, he could break the rules if there was reason—and calming this man down enough to let him sleep again seemed reason enough to him.

"I wasn't at Shiloh, friend, but I was in the war. I saw things I wish I could forget. When I start to remember them and dwell on them, I have to remind myself that them days are gone. Them situations are past. And all the horrors of it, they're dead and gone."

"I know," the man said. "But sometimes the horrors are like ghosts. Sometimes they rise again. Sometimes they come back."

Ben had no reply. Something in those words shook him. He backed away, frowning.

"Good night, friend," he said. "Try not to dream anymore."

"Good night," the man replied.

Ben took his lamp and headed back toward the bunk, glancing at the curtain that separated his usual sleeping place from the rest of the building. He saw the curtain move and knew she had peered out. He wondered again just who Deborah Bray was, and why she roamed the streets of a mining town dressed as a man and hiding from something, or someone.

He blew out his lamp and lay down. *Sometimes they rise again. Sometimes they come back.* He hoped not. God in heaven, he truly hoped not.

He awakened sometime later in the night, having heard a thudding or bumping sound. He sat up and looked around. Nothing out of place he could see.

Lying back down, he closed his eyes and dreamed about Arthur Rellon, kneeling at a mountain stream and drinking from his hand. The water that streamed through his cupped fingers was as red as blood.

She was gone when morning came. Ben stared at the empty bunk and realized that the bumping he had heard was the thud of the door as she let herself out.

He was surprisingly disappointed that she was gone. Of the mysteries this community was beginning to throw his way, she was the most enticing.

He wondered if she was pretty. Hard to tell, given the man's hat, the hidden hair, the smudged face. If he had to bet, though, he'd bet that she was indeed a beauty. A man could just kind of feel it, even when it was hidden.

He hoped he'd see her again.

———

Ben, along with Andy and Roscoe, took supper that evening at Jake's house, Ben hurrying through the meal a little to make sure he would make it to the Cathedral of Rest in time to get the doors open at the usual hour.

They talked about mining, of the progress of the shaft, of whether any clear sign had yet been found to indicate good diggings instead of bad. None had. But Andy declared he had a feeling...

Mostly, though, they talked about the big news item of the day in Ferguson. Jake was much more informed about it than the others, having been in town all day instead of out digging in a mine as they had been. Besides, the *Law & Justice* had come out with a special edition that afternoon, full of all the details, and virtually chortling with delight as it reported the abrupt resignation of the town marshal. Jake was the only one of the men at the table who had had time to read the edition.

"The newspaper, as you might guess, hints pretty strongly that it deserves all the credit for bringing the man down," Jake said over a cup of after-dinner coffee, while the smoke of his cigar rose around his fingers. "And no doubt they played a big part. From the way it's reported, it appears he didn't submit a formal resignation letter. It was more or less just: I quit. He declared that the criticism of him isn't justified, that he's done the best job he could, and that the main reason he's quitting is that he hasn't had the mining success he hoped for, and wants to move on somewhere else." Jake puffed his cigar. "But the talk among the merchantry is that there's more to the resignation than that."

"What do you mean?" Andy asked.

"The word is that the marshal is scared. Says there's some 'elements' around Ferguson that he doesn't want to deal with, and that are more dangerous than anyone can know."

"I wonder what that means," Ben said. He was thinking solemnly about Arthur Rellon at a stream side, Jim Masker in a saloon doorway, Roanie Piatt talking about a man somewhere around Ferguson who looked for all the world like Henry Champion, and about ghosts that sometimes rise again, sometimes come back.

"I don't know," Jake replied. "He could mean any number of things. A mining town always attracts some undesirables. Bold and brazen ones, too."

"Maybe the marshal just didn't have no backbone," Roscoe suggested.

"Maybe."

Andy asked, "So what happens now? Ferguson has no law at all?"

"Not right at the moment. There'll be a new marshal appointed by the town council very soon. The newspaper is editorializing for one who is tough and experienced and ready to hire deputies who are the same. And it's asking the town council to vote in a decent budget for law enforcement...and I believe the council is ready to go along with that."

"Any specific potential new marshals named?" Ben asked.

"I've heard a name or two, no one that I know. The one who seems to have the strongest lead, as I hear it, is a man named Jimmy Fraley. He seems to have been doing some self-promotion among the councilmen, and it must be working."

"Hope he'll be a good one."

"Me, too. This town needs to get a strong grip on law and order. Otherwise the wrong elements get too strong, until it's virtually impossible to cast them out. Now's the time for the right kind of citizens to make their claim on this town."

Ben stood. "Well, folks, got to go. Time to open the Cathedral. Sally, the food was delicious."

"I made the pie," Judith chimed in.

"And good pie it was, young lady," Ben said. "Best I've tasted. Well, good night, everybody."

In almost perfect unison they all said their good-nights in return. Ben headed out the door and headed toward the sleeping warehouse, glancing down the street as he neared it.

A town with no law. Not a permanent state, apparently, but certainly the state at the moment. It was frightening, considering what could happen in a town like that. If there was trouble here tonight, for instance, there was no one he could call upon for help.

He hoped the council got that new marshal in place promptly, and that he hired himself a strong force of deputies.

Soon. Before anything really bad happened.

———

Ben was almost asleep in his chamber when he heard whispers and laughter out in the main section. Shaking his head, he got up, hoping that there wouldn't be a problem this time as there was the last, and feeling a bit headmasterish for having to go hush up a group of grown men. Despite the comfort of his bunk and the security of sleeping in a big, strong, closed building, he was beginning to get tired of this job. He wondered if Jake was really trying hard to get a new overseer, or just sort of letting everything slide conveniently along.

He trudged down one of the rows to where three men, out of their bunks, leaned together, looking at something in the hand of one. They were whispering and laughing like little boys doing something naughty.

"Gentlemen, I'm sorry to intrude on you, but you know the rule," Ben said, and as he spoke the one with something in his hand closed that hand and jerked it behind him very quickly. "Once the lights go out, there's to be no one talking. It disturbs the others, you see." Ben did his best to sound like the cordial voice of reason. He didn't fancy a fight with anybody tonight.

"Why, yes indeed," the man with the hidden hand said. "Very sorry, friend. We'll get in bed right now, and keep quiet."

This *was* like being a headmaster. It made Ben feel old and dowdy. "Very well. Hope all of you sleep good."

"Why, thank you. Same to you."

Ben turned his back and trudged back toward his chamber. He could hear them snickering behind him and could envision the derisive glances they threw toward one another. Again, that headmaster sensation. Oh, well. Went with the job, he supposed. Maybe he and his partners would get lucky at the mine tomorrow and strike ore, and he could tell Jake he was through with this task whether Jake had a replacement yet or not.

———

When Ben and his partners returned from the mine the next evening, they found that again the day had brought big news in their absence.

There was again law in Ferguson. A new marshal had been appointed—as predicted, Jimmy Fraley—and he was busy building a staff of deputies sufficient to ride herd on so busy and growing a town.

There was a palpable sense of general relief among the law-respecting residents of Ferguson. How the law-disrespecting crowd felt didn't matter. Jake, who told the three miners the news, declared himself among the pleased. Though he hadn't yet met this Fraley fellow, those who had seemed impressed with him.

"A man of grit, that's what they say," he reported. "A man of grit. I've heard that identical phrase about Mr. Fraley from three different men this very day."

Ben asked a question that hadn't even occurred to him until now. "Is there a jail in this town?"

"There is, of sorts. Just planks laid flat and nailed together, one atop the other. Makes for a heavy wall that can't be knocked down. But still not a proper jail, and no proper office for the marshal, either. But one is to be built, a jail and marshal's office together. The council voted that in at the same time they voted in Fraley as marshal, and gave him a good budget besides."

"Well, may he succeed and thrive," Ben said. "I'm just glad to know there's someplace I can go to if there's any big problem at the sleeping house. By the way, Jake, I'm ready to be replaced, anytime."

"I know. I'm looking. But don't you like having a good place to sleep every night? And how many men get paid for sleeping?"

"I don't get paid for sleeping. I get paid for scolding grown men for talking to each other, and for getting the holy fire beaten out of me in an alley because I booted a fellow out, and for worrying all night long that something will happen to somebody while I'm sleeping, and I'll be held responsible."

"All right! All right! I get your message. I'll find you a replacement before the week is out."

"Promise?"

"No...but I'll try. I do promise I'll try."

"Good. By the way, if there is trouble that I had to call the law in on, where does the marshal make his office until a real one's built?"

"The Palace Hotel, two buildings down from my store. You've seen it—it's the only two-storied building in town. First room on the left on the lower floor."

"Glad to know it. But with any luck I won't have to ever pay call there. With any luck everything will be nice and peaceful until you find me a replacement, and I can be nothing but a full-time miner and work toward repaying you for that grubstake."

"I'll find you that replacement as quick as I can." He glanced at his son. "Andy, now that you've settled yourself down, maybe you'd like to consider going back to your old job and—"

"Nope. Not me. I'm with Ben on that one. Mining is enough of a job by itself. You can find you some desperate fellow to run your sleeping house. There's plenty roaming the street every day who'd love to have the job just to have a place to sleep safe at night. Speaking of that, where will you sleep once you leave the Cathedral, Ben?"

Ben hadn't thought about that. "I don't know. Maybe I'll go from overseeing the Cathedral to being a paying customer."

"How you going to pay without a job, and until you strike ore?" Jake asked tellingly.

Ben paused. "I hadn't thought about that, either. Jake...

maybe there isn't quite the hurry I thought there was to get out of the Cathedral."

Jake smiled. "Maybe not."

"Don't worry," Roscoe said. "We'll be striking ore any day now."

"How do you know?"

"I can feel it."

"Is that right? Well, we'll just see how accurate your feelings are," Jake said. "How deep are you now?"

"Fifty feet or so."

"You've got a lot of digging left to go before you're likely to hit ore, then."

"I don't know, Pa," Andy said. "It's been found just inches down at some places. I'm like Roscoe. I got a feeling myself."

"Feelings are fine things, but they assay out at zero to the ton. What I want to hear about is ore, real ore, not feelings."

"Then just keep listening. You'll be hearing about ore real soon."

"That's just a feeling, I suppose, Andy?"

"Just a feeling. But a strong one."

CHAPTER 9

The next morning, after another night's round of sleepers vacated the Cathedral of Rest, Ben made his usual rounds to gather dirty linens.

He was passing by the spot where he had scolded the trio of talkers the night before last, when a golden gleam beside one of the bunk legs caught his eye. He knelt, examined it, picked it up...and had there been anything in his stomach, he might have vomited it up right on the spot.

He stared for several moments, trying to convince himself that there were explanations for this other than what came to mind. But what if? What if?

Pocketing the item, he left the Cathedral in such haste that he didn't even bother to lock the door behind him.

———

The Palace Hotel did not live up to its grandiose name. Poorly built and ugly, it seemed bigger than it was because of its false front, which leaned out slightly toward the street even as the entire building seemed tilted to the left. Still, this was one of Ferguson's most substantial buildings, and its only two-story structure. Only the Cathedral of Rest was as tall, though it was only one floor tall, its height resulting from its high, barnlike roof.

Ben pushed past a fat man coming out of the double front doors and ignored the man's protest. The first door to the left stood slightly ajar. Ben walked in without knocking, and a man as fat as the first one, but wearing a homemade badge on his vest, turned a mustached face toward the intruder. The room around him was a disarrayed, makeshift, minimal office, with a roll top desk and a few chairs here and there. The room smelled of stale tobacco smoke and flatulence.

"What do you want?"

"Are you Fraley? The marshal?"

"No. I'm Wilbert Smith. A deputy."

"Is the marshal about?"

"Not just now, no."

"Then you'll have to help me in his place."

"Help you with what?" The deputy suddenly looked suspicious, as if maybe nobody had informed him that doing this job might actually entail having to *help* somebody.

"I think there's been a murder."

"Murder! Who?"

"Maybe of a man named Roanie Piatt. Maybe his brother. Billy, I think his name is."

"What, now? There's a murder, but you don't know who?"

"That's right. Listen, let me explain. My name's Woolard. Benjamin Woolard. I oversee the Cathedral of Rest on up Center Street. You know, the big sleeping place with the bunks."

"I know. Somebody been murdered there?"

"No. But I found this beside one of the bunks." He reached into his pocket and pulled out what he had found: a gilded human tooth, seemingly freshly pulled, still brown-stained from blood around the long and deep pronged root.

Smith squinted piggishly at the tooth. "It's gold."

"That's right. I believe it came from the mouth of either Roanie Piatt or his brother. Both of them have all their teeth gilded."

The man frowned. "Wait a minute—you talking about them two negro wagon drivers with the gold mouths?" He laughed. "You think somebody's been murdering our local negroes, do you?"

"I don't see anything to laugh at here. It seems to me that it's worth checking into. Some people in this town would be mean enough to kill a man for the gold on his teeth, especially if he was a Negro, and looked down on...by some."

"Listen here, feller, you can't go thinking somebody's murdered just 'cause you found a gold tooth. There's a lot of folks got gold teeth."

"But this one's been pulled out."

"And from that you figure there's been a murder?"

Suddenly Ben started to feel a little foolish. Maybe, as much as he hated to admit it, this porcine deputy had a point. "Well...I don't know that anyone's dead, I admit. It just seemed suspicious enough to me that I thought you'd want to look into it."

"Well, let me have that tooth, and hold it for evidence. I'll see if I can find out who it might have come from. But I tell you, I figure that you're going to find them two negroes still alive and kicking—and there's sure no way I'm going to head off assuming a murder when there's no corpse even been found, nor nobody missing."

"How do you know nobody's missing? Have you seen the Piatt brothers anytime the last day or so?"

"I ain't looked. But I will now. And you can do the same. And when you see them, come tell me about it and I'll give you this tooth back. Finders keepers, I reckon."

"I don't want the tooth. And I will look for the Platts. And if one or both of them turn up missing, I expect Marshal Fraley will want to find out what's happened."

"Let's just take 'er one step at a time and see. And keep in mind, this ain't as big a thing as it might be, even if there has been a killing. We're just talking about a couple of negroes, after all."

Ben drew in a deep breath, not sure what to say to a man like this. "I'll let you know if I find out anything," he said.

The deputy grinned, a vague edge of mockery hiding beneath the yellow-toothed smile. "You do that, feller."

Ben glanced back as he left. The deputy was looking into a cracked mirror on the wall, finger hooked under his upper lip, the other hand holding the gold tooth against one of his own, just so he could see what it would look like.

Ben knew there would be no inquiry from the marshal's office about the Platts. And if this man was typical of the kind of deputies the new local law was hiring, he didn't have too high a hope for the future of law enforcement in Ferguson.

If the Platts were to be found, he'd have to do it. But how could he go about it without shirking his duties at the mine? He'd sworn to himself that he would carry his share of the load. He was the oldest of his group, but determined to work as hard as Andy, the youngest.

He'd have to wait to find the Platts, that's all. Maybe the deputy was right. Maybe a gold tooth found by accident didn't really mean much. Maybe he was jumping too far to the conclusion that a gold tooth equaled evidence of murder.

Suddenly hungry for his breakfast, he headed for one of the nearby cafes, from whence the smell of eggs and grease wafted in a thick, almost visible effluvium. Miner's food. Fare for men who would work off whatever they ate and more before their long day finally ended.

Ben ordered ham, coffee, biscuits, potatoes. He ate it all

without tasting a bite, thinking about that golden tooth, and keeping an eye toward the window all the time, hoping he'd see either Roanie or Billy pass by outside. He saw neither. After wiping his mouth on the checkered napkin, he paid his bill and left, heading for the mine and trying to put aside thoughts of anything but the job at hand.

———

They worked hard all day, making their shaft deeper, shoring it with timbers, and beginning to wonder, secretly, if they were going to find any wealth in this place at all.

It was easy to dwell on the promise of mining in the days before the work began. Wealth, lying right in the ground, ready to be claimed, ready to transform a man's life...it seemed magical and marvelous.

Only when the actual grueling labor came about did the other side present itself. Sure, wealth might be there...and equally so, it might not. No, more than equally so: The odds against success were greater than those favoring it. For every man who came to the mountains and became a tycoon, how many were there who lost it all?

Ben had never worked so hard with nothing to show at day's end but a hole that was a little deeper. What if they went down into the depths and found nothing? All this digging, all this framing of timbers, hauling of load upon load of rock... In the end there might be nothing to show for it but a dark pit, and the prospect of starting another such pit somewhere else, with equally chancy odds of succeeding.

"Let me ask you boys a question," Roscoe said when they broke at midday to eat the food they'd packed for themselves. "Once a fellow hits him some ore, what happens after that?"

"Well," began Andy, the usual answerer of Roscoe's endless queries, "what happens first is that somebody looks the ore over as it comes up out of the hole. Most likely that'll be me, in that I've been here the longest and have learned a bit more about this business than the rest of you. After time, it may be one of you doing it, if you prove to have a good eye for it. The ordinary ore will go into a pile, or a dump, and that will go in the back of a wagon and get hauled down to one of the smelters in town. That gets sold by the ton.

"The good ore, on the other hand, that'll probably go entirely out of Ferguson. The good stuff is generally bought up by purchasers out of the smelters in Pueblo or Omaha, or maybe even St. Louis. That's sold in hundred-pound quantities, bagged up."

"How do you know the good ore from the bad?"

"Well, like I said, some have an eye for it, can tell from looking about what an ore is going to assay. But to really know, you've got to have the stuff assayed out in town. If you're really lucky, you can make fine money. I know of one mine that stumbled here recently into some ore assaying out at a thousand ounces of silver per ton. We'll do the same. I can feel it."

"Your mouth to God's ear," Ben said.

When the too-short luncheon was finished, it was back to labor again, until finally the hour began to grow late and Ben took his welcome leave to return to Ferguson and Jake's warehouse full of bunks.

He washed again in the stream, but felt very odd and endangered while doing so, thinking that any moment Art Rellon might show up like he had the time before, recognize the miner at the stream as the very man whose testimony sealed Henry Champion's fate on the gallows...and then it would be over for Ben Woolard. His blood would stain this stream red, and nobody would ever know who had killed him.

Rellon didn't appear, however, and Ben made it back into town without incident...and saw, to his joy, the distinctive form of Roanie Piatt striding down one of the board-walks, going away from him.

Thank God! Ben felt a joyous wave of relief.

"Roanie!" he called, jogging toward him. "Roanie, wait!"

Roanie turned, but no golden smile beamed this time. He looked at Ben with the strangest expression. "Howdy," he mumbled when Ben came near.

"Roanie, I'm glad to see you. I been worried about you today."

"Worried?"

"Yes. I'd thought...well, never mind what I thought. You, uh, ain't lost a tooth by some chance lately, have you?"

"A tooth? Why you asking me about teeth?"

Ben could tell something was weighing heavily on his black friend. There was no cordiality, no "sir" at the end of every phrase. "What's wrong, Roanie?"

"It's my brother Billy. He's gone. I ain't seen him for three days now, and I can't find nobody knows where he might be."

Ben felt his legs turn to water and his hands begin to tremble. "Roanie...there's something I need to tell you."

"Something to do with Billy?"

"Maybe. The reason, you see, that I was worried about you today, and the reason I asked about your teeth, is because of something I found in the Cathedral of Rest. It was a gold tooth. Like yours...like Billy's. Pulled out by the root. Somebody had dropped it on the floor."

Roanie drew in a long, trembling breath and stared at Ben a few moments. "Let me see it."

"I can't. I took it to the town marshal's office, asking for him to look into it, to make sure you and Billy were all right. He wasn't there, but a deputy was, and he took the tooth as evidence."

"He going to be trying to find out if it's Billy's?"

"He said he would, but he won't. He...didn't seem to think a colored man was worth worrying about."

Roanie was silent again. "Billy's dead," he said at last, very flatly. "Billy's dead, and somebody's pulled out his teeth for the gold on them."

"That's the fear I had. But my first thought was that maybe it was you who was dead. That's because it's you I know, not Billy."

"Murdered. I was afraid of that." Roanie was struggling not to cry.

"You don't know he's murdered, that he's even dead. We don't know that the tooth I found was his at all."

"He's dead, sir. I been feeling it in my heart and my bones all day. He's dead. And I believe I know who killed him, sir."

"Who?"

A pause, then: "Henry Champion, sir."

"Henry Champion is dead, Roanie."

"No, sir. He ain't dead. He's alive, and he's here, and he's killed Billy."

"You're not making much sense. How could a dead man be alive?"

"Because he just is, sir. I seen him again. With my own eyes. And he seen me, outside of town it was, and tried to get two of his men onto me, to catch me. He'd have killed me, sir, if they had caught me. For my teeth, I reckon. Or maybe he recollects my face from seeing me in the crowd of nigras who watched the day they hung him. But no. No. He wouldn't remember that. One dark face would look like any other to him." Roanie ducked his head suddenly, and tears came. "I reckon he wanted me just so he could get my teeth. He didn't get me, but he must have got Billy. And now Billy's dead. Dead."

"Roanie, listen. One, we don't know that Billy's dead at all. All we've seen is a gold tooth, and that could have come from anywhere. Two, we *do* know that Henry Champion is dead. We saw him hanged back in '65. Three, I believe I know who had this gold tooth to begin with, and it wasn't Henry Champion. There were some men in the Cathedral, talking after the lights were out. I called them down, made them shut up. One of them had something in his hand he was showing the others. I believe it was this tooth."

"Why would he be showing off a gold tooth unless there was a reason? Unless there was a story to go with it?"

"I don't know. All I'm saying is, don't jump to conclusions. Billy may turn up at any time, alive and well, with every tooth still in his mouth. Then you'll feel silly about all this Henry Champion nonsense."

Roanie was firm. He shook his head. "I respect you, sir, and 'predate what you're trying to do here. But there's two things I'm sure of, and I'll not be shook from them: My brother Billy is dead, and the man I saw was Henry Champion himself, just as alive as you and me, and right here in Ferguson."

And with that Roanie turned and walked away. Ben watched him go, then headed for the Cathedral, eager to get inside, into his chamber and his bed. and to pull the curtain across like a child pulling his blankets over his face to hide from the dark ghost in the corner of the nursery.

Chapter 10

B en found himself confused when he pulled out his key to unlock the Cathedral door and found it already unlocked. Had Jake come and let himself in for some reason, or had Ben simply neglected to lock the door when he left that morning?

Remembering the state he was in during that departure, he decided the fault was his. Chagrined and hoping that no one had taken advantage of the unlocked door, he poked his head in, looked around, and took a quick tour of the building. Nothing amiss that he could tell. Heading to his own sleeping area, he yanked back the curtain, then leaped backward with a yell of surprise.

The person on his bunk let out a yell, too, and bolted upright. Ben stared into the fear-paled face of a person freshly jolted out of deep slumber.

He let out a slow breath. "Miz Bray, I do believe my heart almost gave out on me just then."

"I'm sorry," she said. "Please, don't be angry at me."

"You shouldn't have come in here with the place not open."

"But the door was unlocked."

"I know. My mistake." He sighed loudly, his heart now slowing to its usual rhythm. "I left in a hurry this morning and failed to lock it behind me."

"It was a godsend for me," she said. "I needed a place to hide."

"Something wrong?"

"Yes. Mr. Woolard...I'm in trouble. In danger, I think. I need help. You're the only person in this town I know to turn to."

"What kind of danger?"

"There's someone in town now who might hurt me."

I think I know the feeling, Ben thought wryly. "Who?"

"A man."

There was a stool just outside the curtain. Ben pulled it in and sat down. Deborah Bray, meanwhile, had swung her pantalooned legs down to the floor, and sat facing him with her hands resting on the bed on either side of her. Ben asked, "Your husband?"

"No. I have no husband. It's my brother. My *half*-brother, actually."

"Why would your own half-brother want to hurt you?"

"Because he's afraid that I might hurt him. And I will, if I can."

"What have you got against him?"

"Nothing but the fact that he murdered my father."

"That's a serious charge. You can prove it?"

"Yes, I think I can." She reached beneath the covers and pulled out the same packet she had left in the Cathedral once before. "With these."

"Papers?"

"Documentation. Copies of letters between my half-brother and one of his business associates. Letters that were supposed to be destroyed, but which I managed to save from the fire. They contain communications concerning the planned murder of my father. He'd become wise to some of the thievery and crime my dear brother and his associates had involved themselves in. He was prepared to turn them over to the law. They had to get him out of the way."

"If that packet contains documents as important as all that, why did you let yourself forget it the other day?"

"Because I'm so tired, so hungry, so scared, that sometimes I almost forget who I am." Her voice began to crack with emotion. "I came to Ferguson because I thought I could find the help I needed here from an old friend...but he wasn't here. He was supposed to be, but he wasn't. I looked for him for days, disguising myself in case Daniel—that's my half-brother, Daniel Bray—came looking for me. Finally I found the man I was looking for. He's buried in the cemetery at the edge of town."

"I'm sorry. A beau?"

"In a way. Some years ago. It doesn't matter now."

"Deborah—may I call you Deborah?—would this brother of yours actually *hurt* you?"

"He'd not only hurt me, he'd kill me. He's a wicked man, Mr. Woolard."

"Ben. My name's Ben. Listen...I don't quite know what to do. I'm glad you felt good enough about me to come here, but obviously you can't just keep hiding here forever. We could go to the law..."

"I don't trust the law. I've seen the law put into the pocket of too many wicked men to trust it anymore."

"Well, from what I've seen so far of the law in this town, I ain't too impressed myself. There is a new marshal, but I haven't met him. Just one fat deputy."

"I don't want to go to the law. I want to hide until I can get away, and get these papers to...someone. I don't know who. Someone who would know what to do, and who would prosecute Daniel for what he did."

Ben rubbed his chin, thinking. "Tell you what. Why don't you stay here another night—I'll sleep out yonder with the rest of them again—and tomorrow I'll take you to my brother's place. His name is Jake Woolard, and he's a good man. He has influence here. He'll have good advice, and his house is big enough that they can keep you safe for a while."

She smiled. "Thank you. Thank you so much. I felt that I could trust you."

The smile answered the question: She *was* pretty. Ben smiled back. "I'll do all I can for you. Tell me. When was your father murdered?"

He wished he hadn't asked that, for any happiness she had shown instantly vanished. "I don't much like talking about it."

"I'm sorry. Well...it's time for me to let in the evening's customers. Are you settled back here?"

"I'm fine."

"Had anything to eat lately?"

"No."

"I'll fetch you something in a few minutes, then."

"I have no money..."

"You don't need it. I'll take care of it."

"You're too kind to me, Mr. Woolard...Ben."

"Nah. Just trying to be the gentleman my mother raised me to be."

"I'll repay you when I can."

"Forget about it. Now settle in, and let me go out to fetch the food. I'd best do it before I let any customers in, or else my brother would have my head for leaving the place untended with folks inside. He owns this place, you see. In fact, he'd probably have my head for forgetting to lock the door this morning."

"I'll not say a word."

"Thank you. Now stay put, and I'll be back quick as I can."

He strode down the crowded street, lost in thought, feeling a mix of excitement, intrigue, and doubt.

The excitement and intrigue were easily accounted for. What man wouldn't be pleased by having a young and attractive woman coming to him for refuge, seeing him as a source of strength and security in time of danger?

He wasn't sure where the doubt came from. Here was this strange woman, disguised as a man, roaming the streets of a town for days, carrying about a packet of supposedly important papers, and now turning to a virtual stranger for help and telling a wild story of a patricidal half-brother roaming about, ready to kill her... It was a lurid and strange tale, to be sure. One he wasn't sure he could believe.

There was a lot going on, come to think of it, that strained his credulity. All this talk of a hanged man actually being alive, these visions of old enemies popping up like flesh-and-blood ghosts all about...who would have thought it? Even now, Ben wasn't sure what to think about it all.

He reached a cafe, ordered up a box of bread, beans, and beef, and carried it out into the darkening street. Glancing at his pocket watch, he realized it was after his time to open up the Cathedral. He hoped Jake wouldn't chance to come by and wonder why his brother and employee was failing to do his job in timely fashion.

He quickened his pace, then came to a dead stop.

Directly before him on the boardwalk, staring into his face, was Arthur Rellon.

Ben stood like a statue, looking at Rellon in disbelief, and seeing in Rellon's eyes the rising light of recognition. No words were said, no expressions changed...just mutual stares, mutual recognitions, mutual remembrances of a time long past, when they had ridden together in a bushwhacker's band, and a time shortly afterward when Ben had betrayed that band's leader on the witness stand in a military courtroom.

Ben found himself wanting to speak, yet also wanting to do anything but speak. He wanted to walk on and pretend that he hadn't seen this man, that nothing important had happened here.

But all he could do was stare.

Art Rellon was the first to move. He broke off the gaze and walked on past Ben, his shoulder actually brushing against him. Ben turned and watched him go, and when Rellon was half a block away, he turned as well, and looked back at Ben another long moment.

Ben actually had to fight the impulse to run, and he wasn't by nature an easily frightened man.

When he reached the Cathedral, men were already lined up at the door. He apologized for his lateness, told them to be patient another moment or two and he'd have the door opened for them. He then admitted himself, closing and locking the door in their faces, with further apologies.

She was eager for the food. He didn't think he'd ever seen a human being eat with such vigor. After drawing the curtain and closing her in, he returned to the door, opened it, and began admitting another night's army of soon-to-be sleepers.

He studied the face of each man who entered, fearing that he would see again the face of Rellon, or Masker, or even Henry Champion himself. Henry Champion, the dead man.

Henry Champion, the man Roanie Piatt swore wasn't really dead at all.

He saw the curtain move, and glanced that way. She was peering out like a mouse from a hole, watching the men file in. She, too, he knew, was looking for a particular dreaded face.

The last man entered, and Ben closed the door. Another nearly full house.

Ben went to his bed and lay down, looking at the ceiling.

Imagining that he could see Arthur Rellon up there in the darkness, staring down at him like a hanging bat.

———

He had only just drifted off to sleep when he heard movement near the door. Sitting up, he caught a glimpse of the door opening, shutting, and someone slipping out.

Deborah Bray. Leaving again.

He'd fallen asleep fully dressed except for his boots, and so he rose quickly and darted after her, shoeless. What was this business of leaving on the sneak, after all this talk about danger and needing a place to hide?

She had gone less than a block when he saw her. He ran after her and put his hand on her shoulder...

She wheeled and gave a low, muffled screech, and waved a knife at him, almost nicking his face.

"Be careful!" he snapped. "What are you trying to do—kill me?"

"I'm sorry," she said, her voice very strained. She was taut with fear. "I'm sorry."

"Why are you leaving? I thought you needed a place to stay."

"He's in there, Ben. Daniel came through that door. The last man. I almost died to see him... I waited until everyone seemed to be asleep, and I fled."

"Look, if he's a murderer, then maybe we're just going to have to trust the law after all, and go have a talk with the marshal."

"No! No. I can't." She pulled away from him and turned.

"But what about my brother's house? Tomorrow I was going to take you there, and—"

She ran down the street and was gone.

Ben turned slowly and walked back to the Cathedral.

The devil with her. It was probably all lies or insanity anyway. What sensible woman behaved the way she did?

She'd best not come back, he told himself. She'll get nothing more from me.

———

Ben watched every man leave the next morning, trying to recall which had been the last to enter the night before. He couldn't recall. Didn't matter anyway. He had enough to deal with without taking on the fantastic concerns of an unstable woman.

Half an hour later, he was on his way to the laundry with another load of dirty linens when he heard a hubbub down the street. It was continuing, and a crowd gathering, when he came out of the laundry again.

He overheard the word *murder,* and something about how awful it was, this business with the teeth...

He joined the crowd, pushing his way through until he was near the front of it.

The fat deputy was there, with another deputy, and a slender, young man who he assumed was the new marshal.

On the ground before them, covered with a sheet but with the face momentarily exposed, was the body of Billy Piatt. His mouth was open. All his teeth were gone.

CHAPTER 11

B en stared. The dead, dark face, eyes partially open, formerly rich-colored flesh now taking on a graying hue...and most of all, the jaws wide open, dark holes where teeth had been, flies buzzing in the gaping mouth, crawling upon the wounded and ugly gums.

"What happened?" Ben asked a man beside him.

"They found him hidden in a gully an hour or so ago. Found him by the smell. Stinks, don't he!"

Another man joined the conversation, as strangers will at such times. "What I can't figure is the teeth. I know a lot of men with no teeth in their head, but them gums look like his was fresh-pulled."

The first stranger answered, "Torture, I'll betcha. Lot of old hardshell Confederates and such still roaming this nation, despising your coloreds. Pulled them out to torture him, then killed him. That's what happened."

"At least it didn't happen to a white man," the second stranger said, shuddering.

"It was for the gold," Ben said, feeling and sounding somewhat dazed.

"What?"

"His teeth were gold. They pulled them for the gold."

"You knew this coon?"

"Know his brother."

As if cued in by those words, Roanie Piatt appeared at the edge of the crowd and shoved his way through rather roughly. Such behavior from a black man would have been scarcely tolerated at most times, but the crowd quickly clued to the suspicion that the dead man and the newcomer were probably related, and allowed Roanie to shove in without protest.

Roanie stared at his brother's dead form. Just stared, said nothing.

Ben approached him and touched his shoulder. Roanie didn't seem to feel him. "Roanie. I'm sorry."

"It was Champion," Roanie mumbled. "Henry Champion murdered him."

The same old impossible story...or was it impossible? There was the matter of having encountered Art Rellon on the boardwalk. Ben scanned the crowd quickly, looking for Rellon's face. He wasn't there.

The young neophyte marshal rose from his position by the corpse and faced Roanie with a frown. "Who are you?"

"My name's Roanie Piatt, sir."

"You know this dead negro?"

"He's my brother...sir."

"Your brother, huh? Hey, open that mouth wider."

Roanie complied. The marshal gazed at the golden spectacle, then turned and grinned at his deputies. "You see that? Ain't that just like a negro, wanting his teeth gilded over!" The smile vanished and he addressed Roanie again. "Why your teeth like that?"

"Just because I want 'em so, sir."

"This dead boy, he have the same thing?"

"Yes, sir."

"Don't it strike you as a bit foolish, running around a

town with a mouth full of gold? There's a lot of folks struggling to make their living, struggling to keep food in their bellies until they can make a strike, who'd likely resent seeing a common buck negro running about with his mouth full of gold."

"I expect so...sir."

"You think it's the job of the law to protect foolish negroes who ain't got the sense to avoid provoking the public?"

"My brother was murdered, sir. I believe it's the job of the law to find who done it, and punish them."

Ben stepped forward. "Pardon me. My name's Ben Woolard. I run the Cathedral of Rest for my brother, Jake Woolard. I saw something the other night that might be relevant to this, and I already brought it to the attention of one of your deputies." He pointed at the fat man. "That one."

The big deputy gave Ben a hateful look, then turned it to an expression of innocent confusion and shrugged at his superior. "Marshal, I don't know what he's talking about."

"Yes, you do. The gold tooth I brought you. The one I found on the floor of the Cathedral. The one you kept as evidence."

"I ain't never seen this man before, Marshal," he said. "I swear."

Marshal Fraley frowned at Ben. "Mister, I'm trying to conduct a proper investigation of a negro murder here, and would appreciate it if you'd stay out of it."

"Your deputy's lying to you, Marshal."

"Step back, sir, and keep your mouth shut." Fraley turned back to Roanie. "What'd you say your name was, boy?"

"My name is Roanie Piatt. My brother there is...was named Billy."

Fraley glanced at the fat deputy. "Write that down." Back to Roanie. "When did you last see your brother?"

"Been some days ago, sir. Right now my mind's all foggy, Marshal, and I can't recall exactly."

"Can't recall, eh? Can't recall." He said it as if it were significant.

Somebody approached Fraley from the crowd and whispered in his ear, with their eyes cut toward Roanie all the while. They withdrew, and the marshal gave Roanie a piercing look. "Tell me, boy, is it true that you and your brother had a little contest going over these teeth, trying to see who could get the most teeth gilded over first?"

"We did, sir. Just a friendly thing."

"Friendly. Friendly. Looks to me like somebody wasn't feeling too friendly toward your brother."

"I know who killed him, sir."

"Do you, now?" At this point, it seemed to Ben, that the professional approach would be to take this rather absurdly progressing interrogation off the street and out of the public eye and ear, but Fraley, despite all the talk of his experience as a peace officer, didn't seem to be as professional as Ben would have expected. He went ahead and asked the question. "Who done it, then?"

Roanie glanced around, caught and held Ben's eye a moment. "Henry Champion, sir."

Fraley cocked his head. "Who?"

"Henry Champion, sir. He murdered Billy. And he tried once to murder me."

"Who the hell's Henry Champion?"

"He was a rebel, sir. A bushwhacker in the middle part of Tennessee and Kentucky during the big war."

"*That* Henry Champion?" Fraley grinned. "Boy, the Henry Champion that bushwhacked in them parts is long dead. He was hung by the neck in '65, best I've heard."

"Yes, sir. I know. I was there to see the hanging."

"But you think this hung man killed your brother?"

Fraley laughed. "What's wrong with you, darky? You lost what mind you ever had?"

"Henry Champion ain't dead, sir. I seen him myself, more than once, right here about Ferguson."

"Know what I think, boy?" Fraley said. "I think that what we might have here is a case of two negro brothers getting all caught up in competing with each other over these fool gold teeth, and when one got ahead of the other, the other got mad, maybe drunk at the time, and murdered the other one over it, and pulled out the teeth for spite."

"I didn't kill Billy, Marshal, sir."

"What I can't figure is why you'd make up such a fool tale to try to cover it. Least you could have done was blame it on somebody who's really alive!"

"I ain't lying, Marshal. I didn't kill Billy. Henry Champion did. And he *is* alive! He is!"

"Come with me, boy. You and me got a lot of talking to do." Fraley nodded to his deputies. "Get this body took care of. Get it off the street before it stinks the whole damn town up. And find us a picture-taker to get some pictures took before we bury him."

Ben stepped forward and took Roanie's arm. "I'll talk to you later."

"Get away from the prisoner, friend!" the fat deputy snapped.

"What'd you do with that gold tooth I brought you?" Ben asked sharply. "You sell it, or gamble it off?"

Fraley intervened. "You keep claiming you had a gold tooth in your possession, and we may be talking to you, too. Now, be on your way. All you folks! Clear out!"

Ben longed to speak, but knew it would be ill-advised. He bit his tongue, gave Roanie a final glance and nod, and turned away, heading on down the street for some fresh air.

———

Ben worked all day in distraction, hardly able to concentrate. He said nothing about the murder to the others. It had nothing to do with them or anyone they knew...and the whole angle involving Champion seemed ridiculous.

And surely it was ridiculous. As he worked with pick, shovel, bucket, and pulley, Ben forced himself to pull back from the situation and evaluate it objectively. Obviously Henry Champion was dead. The federal government had made sure of it long ago. Just as obviously, Roanie Piatt, who had more reason than most to be sure that Champion was in his grave, was convinced that he had seen none other than that very man. Had even been attacked by him.

The only possible answer was that Roanie had seen someone who looked like Champion. And was that so unreasonable a hypothesis? Champion had been a fairly ordinary-looking fellow. It had been years since Roanie had seen him, and even then he'd only had a view of him from a prison yard, with Champion briefly standing unmasked on a gallows before the trap was sprung. There was no reason to think that Roanie's knowledge of Champion was so intimate that he couldn't easily be mistaken, especially after all these years.

And hadn't Roanie said that Champion had murdered another of his brothers during the war? That was entirely believable—Champion had murdered several wounded black soldiers—and might account for Roanie's readiness to link the idea of another murdered brother with Champion. It was all a mental misfire on Roanie's part, brought on, no doubt, by the stress of worry and hard work.

And what of Ben's own sighting of Art Rellon? Well, it was in fact possible that it was Rellon he'd encountered. Rellon had survived the war; unlike Champion, he'd been neither tried nor hanged. He might well be in Ferguson. Or, again, it might be a coincidence of physical appearance. Someone who looked a bit like Rellon might look after so many years. That look of "recognition" he'd seen on Rellon's face might have instead been a look of concern or surprise at the intense way Ben himself was probably staring at him.

And as for that brief sighting of a man who looked like Jim Masker—hang it all, that had been a nighttime sighting in far from ideal circumstances. It probably wasn't Masker at all. And even if it was, there was nothing inherently inconceivable about the notion of Jim Masker being alive.

By the end of the workday, Ben had substantially convinced himself that the world was a far more reasonable and common kind of place than he had been letting himself think. Henry Champion was dead and gone, Art Rellon and Jim Masker were either absent or irrelevant, and Roanie Piatt was operating under illusions to which he, Ben Woo-lard, would not let himself fall victim.

If there was any dangerous person in and about Ferguson with whom Ben should concern himself, it wasn't Champion or any of his old cohorts. It was Daniel Bray, the threatening brother of the lovely Deborah Bray, a woman who, no matter how unusual, was yet the object of many an increasingly pleasant thought for him.

He worked until it was time to go back to town. Bidding his partners farewell and feeling more at peace with the world than he had for the last little while, Ben strode through the late of the day toward Ferguson, whistling and wondering how things had gone for Roanie.

———

At the edge of town, Ben paused at the graveyard and noted a freshly filled grave. Billy Piatt's probably. He shook his head. Sad, the poor fellow being murdered like that. He only hoped, for Billy's sake, that the tooth-pulling had occurred after death, not before.

He would later think it ironic that he was thinking about

that when he spotted the man who had been in the Cathedral, talking and showing something—the gold tooth, Ben presumed —to those other fellows. The man was walking along, much as Ben was, heading back toward town from another of the trails leading down from the higher climes. Ben glared at him, unseen, then on impulse decided to have a talk with the man.

"Hey, there! Friend! Can I have a word?"

The man stopped and watched as Ben trotted toward him. He seemed wary, so Ben put on a smile and a congenial manner.

"Howdy, there. Sorry to bother you. Do you remember me?"

The man frowned at him and shook his head.

"I met you the other night in the Cathedral. The sleeping house."

"Oh." The man looked closer, then remembered. "Yeah. It was you who came over like a schoolmarm and told me to shut it up."

"Sorry about that. House rules, and my brother owns the house. In fact, I'm only working there for him temporarily, until he can find a permanent replacement." He grinned warmly, doing his best to show that he was just a regular old fellow, no schoolmarm after all.

"Yeah. What can I do for you today, then?"

"Well, it happens that I found something over near your bunk sometime after you left, and wondered if it might be yours. A gold tooth."

"You found that, did you?"

"Yep. Thought maybe that was what you were showing off to those other men, and that maybe you'd been wondering where it was."

"It was mine, yes. But that wasn't what I was showing to the other men."

"No?"

"No. I was showing them something else. You like pictures? Special pictures, if you know what I mean?"

"I don't think I do know what you mean."

The man reached a dirty hand into a pocket and produced a tintype that he put under Ben's nose. Ben arched his head back so he could see, and saw a lewd image of a naked woman. Some backstreet prostitute, most likely.

"Oh. That kind of picture."

"That's right." The man put the picture away. "But that tooth was mine. I didn't even realize I'd lost it. Guess it fell out of my pocket when I pulled out the picture."

"Where'd you get it?"

"Bought it off a man in St. Louis who has some women who work for him, if you know what I mean."

"I didn't mean the picture. The tooth."

"Why you care so much about a gold tooth?"

"Well...just interested."

"I found it. Lying on a road on the other side of town from here."

"Just one tooth?"

"Listen, friend, I don't know why you're asking me so many questions. I don't much like it. Why you so curious about a good tooth?"

A new voice spoke from behind Ben. "Bet I know." Ben turned and saw another of the group who had been examining the picture in the Cathedral. He had approached Ben unseen while he was talking to the first man. "There was a man murdered in Ferguson. His body was hauled in this morning, and talk was he had gilded teeth. They'd all been pulled out."

"Who are you?" Ben asked.

"Never mind who I am. I'm just me. And that man you're talking to there is my mining partner. And from what I'm hearing, seems to me you might be trying to find out if my good partner had something to do with that negro's murder."

"Look, all I'm trying to do is find out where that gold tooth came from. I don't know anything about any murder."

"That's a lie. I saw you standing amongst the crowd around the corpse this morning. Seen you talking to the marshal."

The first man, his manner emboldened now that he had a cohort, stepped closer to Ben, glaring. "You talked to a marshal? You tell him about the gold tooth you found?"

"Gentlemen, I regret I even brought the matter up. I'll be going on now."

"No, you won't! Who are you, and why are you so interested in our affairs?"

"My name's Campbell. Harve Campbell. And I ain't interested at all anymore."

"Your name ain't Campbell. Not if you're the brother of the man who owns that sleeping house. His name is Woolard."

Ben said nothing, wondering what was going to happen.

"Give me back that tooth."

"I can't. Don't have it on me."

"Where is it, then?"

"I'll tell you," the second man said. "This morning he was claiming to the marshal that he'd give the tooth to a deputy earlier, for evidence."

"I be damned! You're trying to get me tied in with some negro murder! I don't much care for that, mister."

"Look. My mistake. I'll forget about it. Good evening to you both."

Ben turned and started to stride away. He wasn't surprised that it didn't work. One of the pair, he didn't see who, jumped him from behind, and next thing he knew he was down, struggling, being beaten and kicked and generally abused, and though he fought back hard, it was two against one, and hopeless. As the sky darkened and evening descended, the struggle went on, silent but for the thuds and grunts and curses of the attackers.

It seemed to Ben that it continued for an inordinately long time.

CHAPTER 12

J ake's face in the lamplight was a fuzzy, vague imitation of itself, and no matter how many times Ben blinked his swollen eyes, it didn't seem to look quite right.

He could, however, easily make out Jake's forced smile, there, he figured, in an effort to make Ben feel that all was well, nothing really important had happened, that almost getting beaten to death at the edge of town didn't really amount to much.

"You know how to make an entrance, I'll grant you that," Jake was saying. "When Sally pulled open that door and we saw you standing there with blood and bruises and dirt all over you, we all just about fell over. I'm surprised you were able to stand at all."

"I don't even remember it," Ben said, as best he could with a swollen mouth.

"You seem to have an affinity for getting beaten up, brother of mine. This is twice since you've been in Ferguson, and this time Andy wasn't there to stop them before they knocked you senseless."

"Just lucky this time, I reckon."

"These men who did this to you, do you know their names?"

"No. Only their faces." He described them briefly.

"Why'd they do it?"

"Thought I was trying to accuse them of something. Jake, I don't much want to talk right now. Hurts."

"Fine. Keep quiet, and still. Rest up. We've got a doctor coming to look you over. And I'm going right now to talk to the marshal."

"No... no marshal."

"What happened to you was a crime, Ben. It ought to be reported."

"Not to this marshal."

"Why?"

"Don't like him...don't trust him, nor his deputies."

"Explain yourself, Ben."

"Later...when I can talk better."

Jake had a dark look. "I don't like this. You got something to hide from the law?"

"No. Trust me, Jake."

"I can at least fetch a doctor, can't I?"

"You can."

"Good. Because he's already on his way."

————

For a man who looked and felt as bad as he did, Ben was hurt surprisingly little. Nothing that would create any lasting damage, anyway. The doctor predicted several days of soreness and pain, followed by quickly diminishing discomfort and lessening stiffness. He asked pointed questions about how the injuries were inflicted, suggested that the law might need to be involved, then left. He'd say no more about it, get no further involved. In a town such as Ferguson, a man of medicine learned to mind his own business.

Ben slept after the doctor departed. When he awakened, Jake was at the bedside, dozing in a chair. Ben stirred a little, seeking a better position, and felt a stab of full-body soreness that made him groan loudly. Jake awakened.

"Ben, you all right?"

"Hurting. Thirsty, too."

"I'll get you some water." He rose and disappeared, came back with cup in hand.

"So, you going to tell me about what happened?"

Ben relaxed and tried to quit hurting. He felt that maybe he could talk now, without too much difficulty. "You hear about the murder, the Negro fellow they found outside town?"

"I heard about it."

"It was Billy Piatt. The brother of the teamster who gave me a ride into town. The one with the gold teeth."

"Yes. I know."

"I thought that one of these fellows maybe had something to do with it." He told, briefly, the story of the gold tooth and his visit with the fat deputy, and the attack that now had him laid up.

"Why didn't you leave it to the law?" Jake asked.

"Because it was clear that the law has no plan to do anything about it. That deputy denied I'd even brought him the tooth. And the marshal had no interest in anything I had to say."

"Still, it wasn't your affair."

"Jake, do you know who Roanie Piatt believes killed his brother?"

"Who?"

"Henry Champion."

A pause, then a chuckle. "Champion? *The* Henry Champion?"

"The same."

"Why, for God's sake? It's absurd."

Ben took a deep breath and began to talk. He told the entire story, from Roanie's presence at the Champion hanging years ago, to Roanie's claim to have closely encountered Champion, alive and breathing, right here in Ferguson, to his own encounters with men who seemed to be Art Rellon and Jim Masker.

"So you believe this notion about Champion?" Jake asked.

Ben closed his eyes. "No. No. I know it isn't possible. We saw the man die, you and me both. But Roanie seems convinced of it."

"And he saw Champion die, too."

"I know."

"The man doesn't have much sense, if he believes Champion is alive after having seen him hang with his own eyes."

"I know."

"Ben, you going to leave this thing alone now? Mind your own business?"

"I am."

"Good."

"Do you know, Jake, if the marshal still has Roanie in his custody?"

"No. I suppose we can find out come morning. It'll be in the newspaper, I guess."

"I guess." Ben felt very sleepy again. "Think I'll sleep some more. No need for you to sit up with me. Go on to your bed."

"Well, maybe I will."

"Jake...what about the Cathedral? Who's there tonight?"

"Your partner Hammel."

"Roscoe's doing it?"

"Yes. Andy went with him to explain the rules and so on. He didn't come back, so I expect Roscoe talked him into staying over, too."

"Never thought of Roscoe doing that job."

"Me either. But maybe I will now. If you're still wanting out, that is. He might make a good replacement for you whenever you do give it up for good."

Conversation dwindled, and Ben slept. He awakened late in the morning, very stiff and aching. He talked Sally into letting him look at himself in a handheld mirror, then groaned at what he saw.

"They might have killed you, Ben," she said.

"Looks to me like they did," threw in Judy, who was nibbling a biscuit and staring at him with undisguised fascination.

Ben was visited soon after by Roscoe and Andy, who scolded him playfully for taking such an extreme approach to getting out of mining labor.

"I'll be of little use to you for a couple of days, I'm afraid," Ben said.

"Longer than that, if you ask me. Hey, did we tell you? A woman came by the Cathedral last night, asking for you. Odd thing about it, she was dressed in a man's clothing. I don't think she meant for us to see that she wasn't a man. She came up and whispered to me while my back was turned, calling your name, and seemed mighty surprised when I turned around and she saw I wasn't you."

"Yeah. I know who you're talking about." Ben said no more, not wanting to advertise that he had violated the Cathedral rules more than once in allowing her to stay. "Did she say what she wanted?"

"No. Seemed mighty frightened. Like a scared rabbit, wasn't she, Roscoe? She turned and all but ran the other way."

Ben frowned, but it hurt and so he quit. "Did she seem scared before she realized that you weren't me, or just after?"

"Before, or so it seemed to me," Roscoe said. "I noticed her manner even before she spoke to Andy. Who is she, Ben?"

"Just a woman. A little bit crazy, maybe. I don't really know her, just talked to her a time or two."

Andy gave Ben a final gaze and shook his head. "My, my, but ain't you a sight! Well, Roscoe and me will be going. Doing our work and yours too."

"If you strike today, will you still share the wealth with me?"

"Oh, I reckon we'll give you a few dollars. You rest now. See you this evening."

————

Jake entered the room as Ben completed a delicious supper.

"Howdy, brother. Feeling all right?"

"Sore as can be. Stiff. Good food, though. You married yourself quite a cook."

"I know. Believe me." He patted his stomach. "Listen, Ben. I've done some asking around today, general questions and such. Talked to one of the deputies, not that same one you talked to. Couple of pieces of news for you."

Ben bit off a bite of bread. "I'm all ears."

"First off, the marshal let Roanie Piatt go. He questioned him close, then decided there really was no good grounds for holding him, no reason to think he'd killed his own brother."

"I could have told them that."

"Yeah. Apparently a lot of people could, and did. Roanie Piatt has an excellent reputation around this town. A good, levelheaded fellow. His brother, apparently, was the same sort."

Ben wondered how levelheaded Roanie really could be considering his conviction that a man long hanged and buried was at large and committing murder. "So where's Roanie now?"

"I don't know. Out trying to find the killer, probably. I doubt he expects the marshal to put forth much effort, and he's probably right. You know as well as I do that the death of a colored man doesn't count for much in the eyes of a lot of people."

"I know." Ben sipped his coffee.

"Now, another thing. It seems a pair of men matching the description you gave of the two who jumped you were seen leaving town this morning, early. Taking a wagon out and down the mountain."

"The deputy told you this?"

"No. I found it out all on my lonesome. Talking to an ore wagon driver, to tell the truth. Sort of an accident that I learned it. Anyway, this pair seemingly are a couple of no-accounts who'd drifted into Ferguson some days back, made a meager try at digging a few prospecting holes, but mostly just lay around the saloons and gambled. I'd say we'll not see them again. That means you won't be able to have them prosecuted, of course."

"That don't matter much. I'd rather have them gone, to tell the truth."

"Yeah. I'd feel the same. Anyhow, that's my news."

"I wonder what'll happen if Roanie finds whoever killed his brother."

"He won't find him. Can't. Not if he keeps with this notion that it was Henry Champion. Unless there's really such a thing as a ghost after all."

———

Ben passed a relatively comfortable night and the next morning became mobile again, however slowly and cautiously. He took advantage of Jake's wide porch, settling himself into a rocker, pillows stuffed around him here and there to make him more comfortable and to shield his many bruises. It was there that Roscoe Hammel found him when he stopped in at twilight, on his way from the mine to the Cathedral of Rest.

"Well, how's it feel to be following my old routine while I lay up like some lazy old sot, Roscoe?"

"Well, Ben, I don't much mind it. It lets me leave the mine a mite earlier, anyhow. Hey, we're missing you there. It ain't as easy with just two."

"Didn't seem much easy when there was three, to me."

"When you be back, you think?"

"Not long. I'm moving around pretty good. Not nearly as sore as I was. It was just a beating, after all. Nothing I ain't had before, and not as bad as it could have been."

"Hey, you had a visitor at the Cathedral last night."

"The woman?"

"If you mean the woman who wears the man's clothes and carries around that leather pouch, yes. She wouldn't tell me her name. She was coming hoping to find you."

"Her name's Deborah Bray. She's an odd woman. Very scared. Claims to have some sort of wicked brother who's trying to find her. That packet she has contains papers that will get him in some kind of trouble, she says, and he's supposedly searching around Ferguson to find her. That's why she disguises herself."

Roscoe had an odd look. "Now...what did you say that pouch had in it?"

"Papers of some sort. Legal documents, I suppose. Some kind of records or some such that will supposedly get this brother of hers in trouble with the law."

"I don't see how," Roscoe mumbled, as if to himself.

Ben frowned. "Roscoe, what do you know that you ain't saying?"

The big, gentle man suddenly looked guilty as Judas. He looked around, leaned over closer, and said, "Ben, you got to promise you won't tell your brother. I felt sorry for that woman, and I let her stay in the Cathedral last night."

"I'll bet you went and got her food, too."

"I did. She was nigh starved. How'd you know?"

"Because I've done the same thing for her myself. Don't tell Jake."

"I won't. But I'm glad to know it. She has a way of making you feel worried for her, don't she?"

"Indeed she does. But you talked like you knew something about those papers she carries."

Roscoe looked even guiltier. He dipped his head low. "Ben, I sneaked a look at them. I was just trying to find out her name, that's all. She wouldn't tell it to me, and I felt like I ought to at least know who she was, considering I was breaking the rules of the house for her. So I waited until she was sleeping, and I looked."

"Probably shouldn't have done that."

"I know."

"Well, what did you see?"

"Nothing. That's the strange thing. Them papers in that pouch, the ones you say are supposed to get this brother of hers in trouble, they was blank. Nothing written on them at all. Not a blessed word on a single one I looked at."

CHAPTER 13

The next day, Ben took his first real walk since the beating. He was glad to know that his attackers were gone; he could roam Ferguson, as far as his sore body would let him, at least, without fear of turning a corner and coming face-to-face with them.

It was a beautiful day, the sky clear and blue, with that indescribable crystalline quality seen in the highest altitudes. Ben felt grateful to be alive, and even somewhat at home. An odd feeling, that one. He hadn't felt at home in years, no matter where he was, and he wasn't quite sure why he should feel at home now, in a town where he was still depending on his brother for security, and where he'd twice been pounded upon by strangers.

He was thinking of such things when he encountered her. Deborah Bray, still dressed in masculine fashion, was suddenly before him, and in his reverie he had failed to notice where she came from. The sudden appearance gave her a rather ghostlike quality, and he stared at her oddly.

"He's after me," she whispered. "Still chasing me, still planning to hurt me. I've seen him this very morning!"

"Your brother?"

"Yes! Yes! Who else?" She looked at Ben differently all at once, just then noticing his bruises and hobbling manner. "Merciful heaven! Has he gotten to you? Did my brother do this to you?"

"No. No. I just got into a row with some scoundrels. Deborah, listen to me. Are you sure that your brother is in town?"

"Of course!"

"And are you sure he's dangerous to you?"

"Why are you asking me this?"

Ben glanced down at the inevitable leather packet in her hands. "Is it those papers he's after?"

"Yes." She instinctively drew the packet close to her.

"Then why don't you find someone you can trust to turn the papers over to?"

"Because there *is* no one I can trust. I trust only you, Ben. And the nice man who has been at the Cathedral. He's kind, like you are. He let me stay, like you did."

"That's Roscoe. He is nice. He's also got a few doubts about your story. And I have to admit, so do I."

She looked betrayed, an expression so intense and pure it made Ben feel quite guilty. "Doubts? Why?"

Ben wasn't about to reveal that Roscoe had looked at her papers while she slept. He was beginning to develop a theory about this woman, and if it was accurate, he didn't want to give her reason to be angry at Roscoe. He wouldn't mention the blank papers.

"Because there's something odd in all this. Why do you keep roaming the same town, dressed the same way, supposedly running from the same man who nobody but you ever sees? It just doesn't seem right."

"So you...you're one of them, too?"

"I'm not one of anybody. I'm just me, trying to figure out this wild story you keep telling, and the crazy way you behave. Listen to me, Deborah. If you need a place to stay, food and shelter, I believe I could help you. My brother is a prominent man here. He's also a kindhearted man, and he can probably find you a place to be. Maybe even a way to support yourself until you get all...all your problems worked out."

"Would he hide me? From my brother?"

"I don't know...maybe. He'd help you. I think...you'll have to let me ask him. Tell him about you. Can I do that?"

She thought about it, holding the packet tight against herself. "I'll tell you later."

"When's later?"

"Tomorrow. I'll tell you tomorrow."

"Where will I see you?"

"I'm going back to the Cathedral tonight. The nice man, Roscoe, he told me I could come back again. It's the only safe place for me. But I'm not sure it really is safe. I think maybe Daniel knows I've been staying there."

Ben wondered if there really was a Daniel. He had strong doubts.

"I'm sure that Roscoe can keep you safe."

"I hope so. He's such a kind, gentle man. So different from Daniel. There's nothing kind about my brother. Nothing gentle."

She turned and was gone, vanishing into the crowd so fast that, again, she seemed ghostlike.

Ben shook his head, wondering if it was always this way in the thin atmosphere of a high mountain town. Was there something in the very air that brought out the bizarre in people and situations?

Turning slowly, he hobbled back toward Jake's house, fancying that he was moving a little more freely and easily than he had even an hour earlier. He hoped so; this being laid up and hobbling about like some old ancient got a man tired very quickly.

He was nearly to Jake's when he saw Marshal Fraley come stomping down the street, a shotgun in hand and a very upset Roanie Piatt before him. The shotgun was poked right into the small of Roanie's back, and he was waving and gesturing and talking loudly and distraughtly, declaring that he "knowed" he'd "made a mistake," that he was "sorry, and it ain't going to happen no more," he swore.

Ben frowned and wondered what was going on, then realized there was a third member of this little parade, a man trailing along behind the marshal. Ben turned his eyes to him.

He tensed so suddenly that every sore muscle in his body sent a throb of cramping pain through him.

The man was Henry Champion.

Henry Champion, sure as the world. Older, grayer, broader, but *him*.

Ben felt light-headed all at once. The world suddenly lost all its patterns and threw aside all its laws. Henry Champion was alive! It was impossible, yet there walked the evidence before him, on two thick legs. And if Champion could be alive, then the law of gravity could be suspended at any moment, two plus two might sometimes equal five, and a circle could be a square while still remaining a circle.

Then the object of Ben's astonished gaze turned his head and showed his face more clearly, and the world became sane again.

It wasn't Henry Champion at all. The resemblance was remarkable, but only at first glance. Now he saw that "Champion" was much bigger in the nose than the authentic item had been. And Henry Champion had never possessed ears that were out-thrusted and long-lobed. Further, Champion hadn't been nearly as barrel-chested as this fellow. Despite a healthy weight of muscle and bulk

Champion had carried around on his frame, the frame itself had been entirely average in size. This man, however, had a rib cage that could accommodate a hogshead inside it.

Ben closed his eyes, took a deep breath, and trembled all over. Then he chuckled, and the day became brighter than ever.

All wondering was over now. Any subtle wondering about the possibility that maybe, somehow, Champion really was alive, now vanished.

It was all very clear. Roanie Piatt had indeed seen a man he thought was Champion. The same fellow who now followed him and the marshal down the boardwalk. But it never had been Champion at all, just someone who resembled him.

Ben wondered what the story was behind the three-man parade that had just passed. Maybe Jake would know. As a merchant in an excellent position to hear every tale of the day, he seemed to know most everything that went on in the overgrown mining camp of Ferguson, Colorado.

———

Just as Ben hoped, Jake did know.

"Yes, I heard about that," he said over his well-laden plate at another late supper. "Really peculiar thing, but it makes sense of what you and I were talking about, Ben. It seems that Roanie Piatt, once freed by the marshal after his first questioning, headed out determined to find Henry Champion for the murder of poor Billy Piatt."

"Henry Champion!" Sally exclaimed. "But that's the name of the man who was hanged right after the war!"

"Yes, dear. I'll explain it all to you later. It's all a big misunderstanding on the part of one of our local Negroes, that's all. Anyway, Ben, Roanie went out, located this man who apparently does look a lot like an older version of Champion—"

"Yes, he does," Ben interrupted. "I saw him myself today, and almost fainted dead away. But when you take a closer look, you see he's quite a different fellow."

"Right. Apparently Roanie came to realize that, too, but only after he'd jumped the man and was about to beat him to death."

"Amazing. It's a good thing he realized his mistake in time."

"It is. It would have been a shame for a traveling preacher to have been beaten to death, mistaken for a long-dead bush-whacker."

"Preacher?"

"That's right. This fellow was a preacher. Just arrived in Ferguson ten minutes before Roanie Piatt jumped him. Some kind of welcome, eh?"

"Yes." Ben grinned and returned to his supper. Old Roanie, getting everybody stirred up over nothing! Claiming that Henry Champion was around, when really it was nothing more than some old traveling Methodist, come to spread the gospel among the highland heathens.

"This old Christian, as I hear it, has decided to put his faith into his works and forgive poor old Roanie. He's not going to press an assault charge. But the marshal apparently is going to leave Roanie locked up overnight anyway, kind of a warning not to go jumping anybody else."

"Poor Roanie. He'll probably be laughed at from now on because of this."

"Yes. But sadder than that, this will probably make the marshal even less likely to really pursue whoever killed Billy Piatt. The whole affair will seem like some sort of bother or foolishness to him, he'll forget the whole thing, and likely as not, Billy Piatt's killer will never see any justice done to him."

"Is Roanie Piatt that colored wagon driver?" young Judy asked.

"Yes, honey."

"Life isn't fair to colored people, is it?"

"No, honey. It's not."

Ben felt almost healed by the time he turned in that night. He was getting over the beating faster than he had hoped. As hard as the mine work was, he was almost eager to get back to it. Maybe he'd be able to tomorrow...No, maybe not that soon. Maybe the next day.

Ben was almost asleep when he opened his eyes suddenly and frowned into the darkness. Earlier today, he'd mentally folded, boxed, and filed the case of Roanie Piatt and Henry Champion, but new thoughts arose that suddenly threatened to make it come undone.

Like a cross-examining attorney, Ben's mind began asking him questions.

If Roanie's belief that Henry Champion was alive was to be explained by his having seen this preacher a time or two, and mistaking his identity, how was it that the preacher arrived only today, while Roanie has been claiming to have seen Champion well before that?

Also, what about Roanie's claim that Henry Champion himself tried to assault him in the hills? The preacher wasn't in Ferguson then, and even if he was, would a preacher attack a man, or have cohorts do it?

It proved harder to get to sleep than Ben had anticipated.

CHAPTER 14

The alarm sounded at three in the morning, a clanging, disruptive bell that pierced into the sleep of every resting denizen of Ferguson and told them that the most dreaded demon that could come to a mining town, just had.

Fire.

Ben sat up, blinking, trying to make sense of it. The bell clanged on. Jake, clad in a nightshirt, appeared at Ben's door, Andy just behind him, similarly dressed. Ben made out the shadowy figure of Sally, pulling a cloak around herself and the gown-clad, rounded form of young Judy.

Jake spoke. "There's a fire, Ben."

"Where?"

"I don't know."

Ben went to his bedroom window and looked out. "Jake...I can see the light of the fire. It's coming from the direction of the Cathedral."

"The Cathedral..."

Ben was hardly aware of his aches and pains as he dressed hurriedly and joined the general throng racing, like moths drawn to a giant candle, through dark streets and alleys toward the leaping, orange light that licked at the sky. Jake,

Andy, and the rest of the family were already at the scene by the time Ben made it.

It was indeed the Cathedral. Flames shot through the high roof just as Ben arrived. The heat was intense, and the local fire brigade, working frantically, was concerning itself only with saving nearby buildings. The Cathedral itself was beyond hope.

One of Jake's fellow local merchants, clad, like most there, in trousers and nightshirt, came to Jake and touched his elbow. "I'm sorry, Jake. A big loss. And it's tragic, too, about that poor fellow."

"Oh, no...someone was still in there?"

"Only one, Jake. Only one. The rest got out. The only one trapped inside was the man you had overseeing it for you. So I'm told by those who've gotten out."

"Roscoe ..." Ben whispered. He stared, disbelieving, at the hellish flame and felt sick. "Roscoe. No!" Part of him said to lunge forward, find Roscoe, and somehow pull him out of the burning building. Another part told him how foolish and hopeless that would be. He couldn't even draw close to such an inferno, much less enter it. And Roscoe by now would be beyond all help. Gone.

So Ben did nothing but stand like a statue, staring at the flames until they seared their light into his eyes and were still visible even when he closed his eyes and at last turned away.

She was there, beside him. Again she had appeared in phantomlike fashion. She was in the same clothes as always, but much more dirty, covered with ash and soot and smelling of smoke.

"You're alive," Ben said softly. "You were inside?"

"Yes. It was Daniel. Daniel set this blaze."

"How do you know?"

"Because I saw him."

Ben frowned. "You saw him? He was inside the place?"

"No. Outside. He set the fire in the alley, against the building. I saw him there."

"Deborah, I'm trying not to doubt you"—though he did indeed doubt her strongly—"but I'm not understanding something. There was no window in the overseer's sleeping chamber. So how could you see into the alley from inside?"

"Through the knotholes. There were two knotholes through the wall, on the side looking out onto the alley. I heard a noise in the alley, smelled smoke, and looked out and saw him through the knotholes."

Ben tried to remember whether there had in fact been knotholes in that wall. He couldn't, try as he would. But if there had been knotholes, it would have been possible to look out through them directly into the alley. The pine walls of the Cathedral of Rest had been only one board thick.

Another soot-covered figure, apparently a survivor of the blaze, approached Ben and Deborah. He put out his hand to her. "I wanted to thank you, sir, for giving the alarm. If you hadn't, we'd all have died."

This man obviously took Deborah's male garb at face value, believing her a male. He was far too distracted at the moment to look closely enough to see his error. Deborah smiled at him, made a guttural grunting noise of affirmation, and quickly shook his hand.

If he noticed that the hand was unusually slender, it didn't show in his reaction. "I owe you my life, mister," he said, and turned away.

Ben said, "You fooled him, at least. So it was you who gave the first alarm?"

"Yes. I yelled. With my voice as low as I could make it sound. Roscoe was the first to wake up. He stirred the others and got them out. All out... all but Roscoe himself."

Ben lowered his head and felt tears rise. Embarrassed to cry before her, he quickly brought himself under control, dabbed his cheek very fast, and looked up at her again. She was not crying. He could not read her face at all.

"I suppose it gives credence to what you said, that man saying you were the first to give the alarm."

"Did you doubt what I said?"

"I don't remember seeing any knotholes in that wall, that's all."

"Did you ever look?"

"No."

"Then you don't know that there weren't any. And I'm telling you that there were." She sounded perturbed. He didn't blame her.

The fire brigade began pushing the crowd back. Ben grasped her elbow and moved her along with him, not wanting to lose her before he had a chance for some further conversation. It was time for some answers. He moved all the way across the street and into the shadows, getting out of the light of the fire and away from the likely earshot of anyone else.

"I want you to answer a question for me. That packet you carry, the papers you said would implicate your brother in the murder of your father—why were those papers blank?"

"Blank?" She frowned. "What do you mean?"

"The papers. There was nothing written on them."

"You *looked* at my papers? My private papers?"

"No. But Roscoe did. Maybe he shouldn't have, but he did. And he told me there was nothing written on them."

"He was wrong. There were letters in that packet. Documents."

"Why would Roscoe lie to me?"

"He didn't."

"Mercy, woman—talking to you is like talking to a walking riddle! Either those papers were blank, and you've been lying about them, or they had something written on them. Which was it?"

"Both. The documents were hidden in the lining. Most of the rest of the paper was blank. Stationery."

Ben thought about it. Again, it made sense...maybe. Like the knothole story, he couldn't say it was true, but neither could he say it was false. Roscoe had looked through the packet in pressured circumstances. And the man, noble as he had been, hadn't been the smartest of fellows. Maybe he'd just not looked closely or deeply enough to find the written material.

"Where is the packet now?" Ben asked.

She glanced toward the burning warehouse, now thoroughly engulfed in flames. Most of the roof fell in even as she watched, sparks and flame shooting to an incredible height as it happened and making every onlooker cringe and pull away.

"Deborah, I'm going to ask you something, and I want an honest answer from you. Is the story you've told me, about your murdered father, and your half-brother, and the documents and the danger you're in—is that story true?"

She looked him squarely in the eye. "It is true."

"Every word?"

"Every word."

"Swear to God above?"

She lifted her hand. "I swear before God." She lowered her hand. "Do you believe me?"

He took in a deep breath and let it out slowly. Finally he nodded. "I believe you."

One of the walls of the Cathedral fell in, sending out another explosion of flame, sparks, and heat, causing the crowd to gasp as one and pull back even farther. The heat was baking, the light dazzling. Ben squinted into the brilliance, entranced by it, horrified as well, thinking how dreadful it must have been for poor Roscoe to die in such a place. The tears rose again, drying on his face even as they fell, evaporated away by the intense, attacking heat.

He watched the fire a while longer, then turned to speak to Deborah.

She was gone.

———

They buried Roscoe Hammel, or what bits of charred bone remained of him, in the graveyard outside of town. Far more people stood at his graveside than would have been there had he died like most who filled this cemetery, of accident or illness. Roscoe Hammel had died a grander death, a heroic death, died while making sure the men under his charge safely escaped. And so the people came to see him laid away.

But when the grave was filled, they dispersed, and Ben stood beside Andy, Jake, and the other Woolards, and knew that before long Roscoe would be forgotten. The blackened rubble of the Cathedral would be cleared away, and Jake would put up some other business, or sell the lot to somebody else who would. Before long the fire would be forgotten and the man who died in it would become a distant memory.

It seemed to Ben a sort of analogy of life itself. Men were born, live, thought themselves and their tasks important, but suddenly it ended, one way or another, and the men and their lives were forgotten. No longer mattered. The world progressed without them, filled with new people operating under the same delusions of significance as the others before them, now forgotten, now moldering away in their graves.

Or so it all seemed to Ben Woolard just now, and so it was that when evening came, he was seated not at Jake and Sally's supper table, as usual, but in one of the local saloons, staring at a brown bottle of cheap whiskey purchased an hour before. Purchased but so far not imbibed from.

Ben longed to open that bottle and take a drink. Then another, and another, and forget about the fire, about life and loss and suffering. The death of Roscoe had done something to him, opened wounds left by the death of his own family, wounds that had only recently begun to heal over enough to let him get on with living.

Now he wasn't sure living was worth it. Maybe he'd been right to turn to liquor after he lost his wife and children. Maybe it made more sense to numb one's self to life rather than subject one's self, unprotected, to its tortures.

He reached for the bottle.

"Ben, I hope you don't do what I think you might be about to do."

Ben looked up at the man who had approached him from the side. He smiled without mirth and chuckled without pleasure. "Sit down, Andy. Care to join me for a drink?"

Andy looked at the bottle. "Maybe I will at that." He scooted out the chair opposite Ben and settled into it. He looked closely at the bottle, then at Ben, beyond it.

"You and me have both about drowned in that stuff, Ben."

"Yep."

"Right now drowning don't seem such a bad thing."

"Nope."

"How long you been sitting here?"

"I don't know. An hour."

"So why ain't you took a drink?"

"I don't know as I can answer that."

"Maybe because down deep you don't really want to."

"Maybe. What about you? You want to?"

"I do. And I don't. Because, you know, even if I take it, and get good and drunk so that it doesn't hurt to think about Roscoe, when I come out of it on the other side, the hurting's going to still be there, and Roscoe's going to still be gone."

"Good point."

"So if we ain't going to drink, what are we going to do?"

"What do you mean?"

"What are we going to do? For Roscoe?"

Ben crossed his arms before him on the table and lowered his chin onto them in the fashion of a bored schoolboy, and stared into the amber bottle, looking at the distorted image of Andy on the other side of it.

"Well, the only thing I could think of to do for Roscoe would be to find the person who set that blaze, and see him punished for what he did."

"I been thinking along the same lines. But we don't know how it started. Might have caught on fire by accident."

"Seemed to me I smelled a bit of coal oil in the air during that blaze."

"So did I."

"Besides, I talked to a woman who said she saw a man setting it. She was inside the place, and said she looked out through knotholes in the wall of the overseer's sleeping chamber, and saw the man doing it."

"A woman? In the overseer's chamber? Wait a minute... you're saying Roscoe had a woman with him? *Roscoe?*"

"No. He was sleeping out in the main section, and let her stay in his bed. Alone. He did it because he felt sorry for her. It was against house rules, of course, but he did it, and the truth is, I'd done the very same myself a time or two before. Same woman. I'd just as soon you not tell your father. Not that it really matters now. By the way, do you remember there being any knotholes in the wall at the overseer's chamber?"

"There were two or three, as I recall."

"So she was telling the truth about that. I guess she was probably telling the truth about the rest, too."

"What was the rest?"

"That the man who set the blaze did it because he knew she was somewhere inside, and wanted to kill her. Her name's Bray. Deborah Bray. The man who set the fire, according to her, is named Daniel Bray. Her half-brother."

"You telling me straight? Her half-brother?"

"That's right. And he's supposedly killed before. Their own father."

"Sounds like quite a fearsome devil, this Daniel Bray."

"He murdered Roscoe. That's what matters most to me. And he may murder Deborah, if he finds her. I wish I could find her first. Take her somewhere safe and protect her. But she has a way of appearing and disappearing, and right now I have no notion about where she might be."

Andy frowned into the amber, thoughtful. "Ben, I got an idea. Why don't we leave this whiskey sitting right where it is, and get out of here. And then why don't we lay aside mining for a while, and spend a bit of time looking for this Daniel Bray. See if we can't catch him and make him pay— by the law or outside it, I don't care which—for killing poor old Roscoe? What do you say?"

"I say it sounds good to me."

"You up to it? Healed up enough from that beating?"

"I'm up to it. And I'm going to do it even if I ain't up to it."

"Let's go find that son of a bitch."

"Let's do. And let's find Deborah, too. It's important to me to find her."

"Pretty woman?"

"Very much so, as best as I can tell. I ain't seen her a time except that she's been dressed in a man's clothes."

"What? Why?"

"To disguise herself from her brother."

"Sounds like sort of a strange kind of woman."

"She is. I've wondered a time or two if she's sane. But as

it appears right now, she's been telling me the truth all along. I believe she's who she says, and what she says, and I believe she's in true danger from her own brother."

"Let's go do something about it."

"Let's do."

"Should we go have a word with the marshal?"

"I don't like the marshal. I don't trust the marshal."

"Neither do I."

They stood and walked out. In a crowded mining town saloon, a full bottle left unguarded at an empty table wouldn't remain where it was long, and theirs did not. It was picked up almost immediately by a broadly built, gray-haired man who had been watching that table, unnoticed, from the shadowed corner since long before Andy joined Ben. The bottle in his hand, he sauntered slowly to the door of the saloon and looked out into the falling evening, watching the pair walk off together, and merge into the ever-present milling crowds of Ferguson.

Chapter 15

J ake Woolard loosened his collar, tugged and adjusted his armbands, and slipped off to the back room of his store, gently closing the door behind him, and even more gently settling a locking bar into place.

Once alone, he grimaced, yawned, stretched, and listened to his joints pop. Lord, what a day! Busy from the moment he opened. His back ached from having unloaded a new shipment of mining supplies earlier in the morning, and with a lunch freshly settled in his stomach and store traffic momentarily diminished, he was ready to do something he did more often than he would want anyone to know: Leave the store momentarily in the hands of his two clerks outside, and stretch out for a few moments of rest on a cot nicely hidden behind stacked crates here in the storeroom.

The clerks knew what he did, and he knew that they knew, but the accepted approach was for them to pretend they didn't, while he pretended, in turn, that he didn't know they were pretending. Easier all around that way. He suspected that the clerks were just as glad to have the boss out of their hair for half an hour each afternoon as he was to escape the labor of merchantry for those same blissful minutes.

He stretched out on the bunk and wondered if this daily need for a nap had anything to do with getting older. No. Surely not.

Jake drifted soon into a pleasant but odd dream, something involving drifting along on a cloud high above the mountains, enjoying the risky feeling of flight while also knowing that, no matter what, he couldn't really fall, when a bumping sound on the other side of the wall jolted him awake.

He opened his eyes and glared at the ceiling. Somebody was out in the alley, just behind the storeroom. Oh, well. Folks in Ferguson walked everywhere, through yards and alleys as much as down the street and boardwalks. He closed his eyes again. Another bump.

This time he sat up, realizing that the bump came from an area of the alley that he had enclosed with a wooden fence built up against his building, a place he could set out trash and so on without fear that dogs or wildlife would get into it. Something, apparently, had gotten inside the fence.

Blasted clerks! How many times had he told them to make sure they closed the gate securely after putting out refuse?

A small, high window looked out into the fenced area. He got up from the bunk and stepped onto a crate, bringing his face up to the window. He looked out in anticipation of seeing a dog knocking about in the garbage.

He had barely gotten his face up to the glass when another face appeared on the other side of it. A man's face, inches from his own, separated from his only by the thin glass.

Jake yelled and fell back off the crate, landing on his rump on the storeroom floor. He looked up wildly at the window. The man was gone.

Both clerks rattled the barred storeroom door. "Mr. Woolard? What was that noise? Are you all right?"

The door burst open on them and Jake Woolard came out on a run, heading through the store, around the front, into the alley....

The gate on the high fence was open, creaking and swinging in the wind. The man who had been in there was gone, having fled very quickly, maybe as startled to have seen Jake's face as Jake had been startled to see his.

Jake stopped and gazed at the open gate. He panted like a dog. Having gone so quickly from rest to violent motion, with a good scare thrown in besides, had left him winded.

The clerks pounded around the corner and up to him. "Mr. Woolard? What in the world is going on?"

Jake continued to stare at the open gate. He said nothing.

"Mr. Woolard?"

"You fellows need to be careful to keep that gate closed," he said. "I've told you time and again."

He turned and walked back up the alley, leaving them frowning and puzzled. They looked at each other; one of them shrugged. The other walked to the gate and closed it, checking it to make sure it was securely closed.

"I suppose the boss man's nap is through for today," he said as he rejoined the other.

"I suppose so. I wonder what that was all about."

"We'll likely never know."

———

Jake was unusually silent at supper that night, but none of the others particularly noticed. All were in a pensive mood, except perhaps for Judy, who as the youngest was the least understanding and least affected by the terrible death of

Roscoe Hammel, to her a virtual stranger despite his frequent visits to this very table.

With the Cathedral gone there were no Woolard beds to be had except those in the house itself. Ben volunteered to make a pallet on the floor for himself, but Andy quickly overrode that idea, pointing out that Ben was still bruised up from his beating. And besides, he noted, he'd gotten awfully used to sleeping on floors during his drinking days.

Ben and Andy said nothing to Jake about their plans to seek out Daniel Bray. They were unsure what he would think about their putting aside their mining in a project that he had grubstaked with his own dollars and equipment. They were even more unsure how he would take to the idea of their effectively taking the law in their hands and searching for a criminal on their own, rather than through the official channels.

Their silence, though, was unnecessary. Jake was in no mental state to even think about the mine or his grubstake, or even who had set fire to the Cathedral. He had another thing to occupy him, something he wasn't sure he would share even with his own wife. It seemed too absurd.

But that night he did share it. Rolling over and facing her in the darkness, he stirred her from the edge of sleep with a question. "Sally, why do you think a man would sneak into an alley and peek into the back window of a general mercantile's storeroom?"

She lifted her head slightly from her pillow. "That happened?"

"Yes. Today. I heard something bumping around in the alley, back where the fence is, and looked out that little window to see what it was. I figured I'd see a dog, but it wasn't. It was a man, and he stuck his face up to the window at the same time I did. Almost scared me to death!"

Her face was invisible to him in the darkness, but he

could tell that he had just worried her. "That's strange, Jake," she said.

"I know. And it's been on my mind ever since. Why do you think somebody would do a thing like that?"

She paused, then said, "I'd as soon not think it, but the first thing that comes to mind is that they might be thinking of robbing the place. Maybe he was looking for a way to get inside after dark."

"I've thought just the same. But I've also wondered if maybe he was looking inside not so much to see into the store itself, but to see if he could see *somebody* who was in the store."

"Well, I suppose. But it seems an unlikely explanation, to tell you the truth. Robbery seems a more likely one." She hesitated. "Oh, Jake...what if somebody's down there now, robbing the place?"

"I had a word with the marshal today about it. Asked him to have a deputy keep an eye on the store after dark for two or three days. He said he'd do that."

"Good." She settled back down again, but sleep wouldn't come for a while now. She had unsettling things to mull. After a few moments, she asked, "Jake, why did you say that about somebody trying to see a person inside the store? I mean, what made something like that come to mind?"

There was an answer to that question, but he didn't want to tell it to her. It seemed too foolish and impossible, too close to notions he'd already derided to his own brother not long before. "Oh, it was just a silly thought, that's all. You know how things like that can get your mind to thinking crazy things." He leaned across and kissed her. "Good night, sweetheart."

"Good night. I love you."

Ben, having declared himself fit to work, left with Andy the next morning as if they were going together to the mine. They diverted course once out of sight of the house, and realized they weren't quite sure how to proceed from there.

"We won't keep this hidden from Pa for long, you know," Andy said. "The town is his domain, and we'll not spend much time poking around for this Bray fellow without it getting back to him."

"I know," Ben replied. "That's why I hope it doesn't take us long to find him. But it isn't just Daniel Bray we'll be looking for. We've got to find Deborah Bray, too."

"Where do you think she's gone?"

"I don't know. She tends to appear and disappear at will."

"Or against her will."

Ben thought about it. "Andy, you thinking that maybe he's got her?"

"You'll never know without looking. So let's look."

And as the day rolled past, look they did. Ben had no idea where Deborah spent her time. Did she roam the streets? Settle into the background in the saloons and cafes? Hide in the alleys and rows?

The question was no nearer an answer when, in late afternoon, a weary Ben Woolard began to suspect he'd not find Deborah Bray that day at all. He'd spent exhausting, dull hours roaming and looking, staring at strangers, trying to examine the inhabitants of the shadowy rears of cafes and drinking houses. So far he'd seen no sight of Deborah.

But as he began to wind his way back toward Jake's house, his still-healing body now very sore from the day's exertion, he did see Roanie Piatt, crossing the street ahead of him.

"Roanie!" he called. "Roanie! Hold up!"

The black man turned a solemn face toward him, eyes

narrowing. No smile, no glimmer of gold. For a moment Ben thought that Roanie was angry, but as he drew closer he saw that his expression was more one of sorrow. And frustration.

"Roanie, good to see you free."

"Thank you, sir. No reason I shouldn't be free. I ain't done a wrong thing. None but one, anyhow."

"The one being that you attacked a preacher that you thought was Henry Champion. Right?"

"That's right, sir. He looked a right smart like him, so much you'd think it was the same man just to glance at him."

"I know. I happened to see the same fellow while he was following you and the marshal down the street."

"Yeah. Humiliating, that was, sir. But I believe the marshal likes to humiliate me. I don't find he thinks very high of a colored man."

"Roanie, I need to know something. Your talk about Henry Champion...was all of that just a mistake, like the mistake about the preacher? Maybe somebody who just looked like Champion?"

Roanie shook his head firmly. "No, sir. No, sir. Not at all. The business with the preacher was a mistake, and I admit it. But Henry Champion is here, sir. He *is*. Impossible as it seems. I swear it."

Ben had hoped that Roanie wouldn't say that.

"And it ain't only Champion who's alive, sir. There's some of his old gang with him. After all these years, still with him!"

"Who?"

"One name of Rellon, sir. Arthur Rellon. And another called Masker. I don't know his first name."

"Jim," Ben said, his heart sinking inside him. "His name is Jim Masker. And I think I've seen him."

Roanie actually brightened. "Then you believe me, sir, about Henry Champion?"

"Roanie...I don't know what to believe. It's one thing to

see Jim Masker or Arthur Rellon alive. Nobody ever hanged them, after all. But Champion is a different matter. We both saw him die. You and me. And my brother saw it, too. He can't be alive."

"Can't be... but he is. And he murdered Billy, and pulled out all his teeth."

"Do you have any evidence besides your own claims?"

"Yes, sir," Roanie replied. "It so happens that I do. There's an old fellow out in the mountains, a prospector who's struck a bit of silver here and there, and lives now up under Goatbeard." The reference was to a certain peak in the vicinity with an undercrop that many fancied bore a resemblance to the beard of a goat. "This man, I'm told, knows for a fact that Champion and some of his old gang are here. And he knows where he's staying."

"You talked to this man yourself?"

"No."

"You aim to?"

"I do. You want to come with me, sir?"

Ben found himself actually considering it, but after a few moments of thought he shook his head. "No, Roanie. I don't believe I will. To tell you the truth, the notion of Champion being alive is one I ain't too keen to explore too much. It bothers me just to think of it. Besides, it ain't possible. Whatever you think we saw in that prison yard, I *know* what I saw. I saw a man hanged until he was dead,"

Roanie looked at him in a way that, oddly, made him feel he had just said the most hurtful and irresponsible words possible. So he went further, explaining. "But the real reason, Roanie, is that I've got something else that has to be done now, something more pressing to me than searching for bushwhacker ghosts. I'm trying to find somebody who may be in bad trouble. Maybe in danger of her life."

"A woman, huh?"

"That's right."

"Your woman, sir?"

"No. Not really. Just a...friend."

Roanie nodded. "Friends is important, sir. I hope you find her."

Roanie turned and walked away, shoulders slumped.

Chapter 16

"Wonder where Andy is," Jake said for the third time since the meal had begun.

Ben glanced at Sally and saw the worried puzzlement in her eyes as she watched her husband. Indeed Jake wasn't himself. He was distracted and seemed quite worried. About Andy? Probably, but Ben figured there was more to it than that. Andy had been late for supper many a time, had missed suppers entirely during his time of drinking, with Jake not getting nearly as distracted as he was now.

"I expect Andy'll show up anytime now," Ben said, the same answer he'd given the first two times Jake had asked.

"I hope he ain't drunk again," Judy said, filling her mouth with potatoes.

"Judy, don't talk that way. Andy has given up his drinking."

"Sometimes people go back to drinking, though. Ain't that right, Uncle Ben?"

Ben said, "Well, I guess so."

"Like you. I bet you'd like to go back to drinking sometimes when you think about your dead family, wouldn't you?"

"Judy!" Sally erupted. "Good lands, child, have you no notion of other people's feelings?"

Judy looked more unhappy at being scolded than sorrowful. She delved back into her food and shut out the world around her.

Sally grimaced at Ben. "I'm sorry."

"Never mind. The fact is, Judy's right. A man does think about drinking sometimes, once he's got himself used to it. The fact is, I was sore tempted because of what happened to poor Roscoe. But I didn't touch a drop, and I'm glad of it."

Jake, who normally would have been deeply involved in such a conversation, sat silent, lost in his own thoughts, his brows knitted.

They ate a while longer. Jake said, "I wonder where Andy is."

Sally and Ben glanced at each other again. Judy kept eating.

Sally found Jake alone in the backyard after supper. He paced and smoked, staring at the sky, the mountains, the ugly lumber-colored backsides of the nearest buildings.

"Jake, you've got to talk to me. Something's wrong."

He looked at her as if she were a stranger, still frowning.

"For heaven's sake, Jake! What is it?"

"It's Andy. I'm worried about why he isn't home yet."

"It is not Andy. He's a grown man, and you never worried this much even when he was at his worst. There's more to it than that, and I want you to tell me."

He considered it, drawing slowly on his cigar, then tossing it to the ground. He stared at the red coal as it flickered and sizzled in the evening damp. "Nothing. Really, honey, it's nothing. I'm just tired. Maybe coming down with a spell of sickness."

"I don't believe it. I think this has to do with that man who looked into the storeroom window. Am I right?"

"No. It's just that I'm feeling sort of sickly. Nothing bad. That's all."

She looked at him closely. "Are you sure, dear?"

He smiled. "Of course. Don't worry. I'm sorry I've acted this way. And I do wish Andy would come home."

Her manner warmed and she came to him, wrapping her arm around him. "Andy'll be in later. And if you're feeling sick, you ought to get inside and go to bed early. Get some extra sleep. I'll tell you when Andy gets home."

"All right." He hugged her. "I love you, dear. I wouldn't know what to do if I lost you."

"Then don't lose me."

———

Ben's confidence that Andy would soon return faded as the evening dragged on. Tired as he was, he didn't go to bed when he wanted, but instead went to the porch and planted himself there, looking out into town and waiting to see Andy appear.

Jake joined him about ten o'clock. "Thought you were in bed, Ben."

"No. Kind of wanting to see Andy get home, you know."

"Me, too." Jake sat down in a rocker and stared over the porch rail. "Ben, let me make mention of something. Did I tell you about what happened at the store yesterday— me catching a fellow looking in through the storeroom window off the alley?"

"No."

Jake related the story succinctly. Ben voiced the obvious concern that the man might have been looking the place over in anticipation of a robbery.

"I don't think that's it, Ben. I truly don't. There's something about that man that I haven't mentioned to Sally. Or to anyone else, either." He hesitated. "I knew the fellow. It was Bill Helm."

Ben sucked in his breath, a little more loudly than he wished. "Bill Helm...*the* Bill Helm?"

"The one who rode with Henry Champion, yes. The one who sat through every minute of that trial, and had to be carried off by soldiers to keep him from barging in on the hanging, yes."

Ben felt cold all at once. "That makes three, Jake. Three men who either happen to look just like some of Champion's gang, or three who really *were* some of Champion's gang. And all here in the same town, the same one where a colored teamster swears that Henry Champion himself is alive, too."

"You're talking about Roanie Piatt?"

"Yes. I spoke to him again just this very day. Jake, he swears that Champion is alive and here. He says the preacher he mistook for Champion isn't the same man he's seen before. It was coincidence, he says, just a mistake. And that has to be true. I got to thinking about this here lately. Roanie's been claiming to have seen Champion since well before the preacher he mistook for him even got to town."

"But what can it mean, Ben? And how can it be? Even if some of Champion's old bushwhackers are here, that can't explain how a dead man can be walking again."

"I know. Which is what I always come back around to. No matter how odd it seems, it can't be Champion, because Champion is dead and buried."

Conversation lagged. Both men rocked fast, tensely, staring into the darkness and looking for Andy.

"Ben, why would Bill Helm be looking into my store-room window?"

"Maybe thinking to rob it, like I said."

"Or maybe he was looking in hopes of seeing me. Seeing if the Woolard who runs the mercantile in Ferguson is either of the Woolards who helped put Henry Champion on the gallows."

"Maybe."

"Which means there could be danger. It might be more than mere curiosity. Helm might have notions of avenging his old partner. He was devoted to Champion, you know."

"Yes." Ben played through his mind an almost-forgotten image—Bill Helm being dragged away from the Nashville prison yard, his arms and legs flailing, screaming curses and all but weeping as he demanded to be allowed to witness the execution of the murderous bushwhacker whom he had called friend. Ben had never known what became of Bill Helm after that.

Maybe now he did.

Ben rocked and thought. The night seemed more ominous than before. At length he said, "Blast it, Jake, I'm not going to let myself get eaten up over all this. Champion's dead. So is the past, and I'm not going to spend my time looking over my shoulder for it to jump up like some spook or booger and yell 'Boo!' I'll not do it!"

Jake listened to the impassioned talk, flipped his brows up to show he was impressed, then smiled slightly. "All right, then. I reckon that's settled. So, how's mining?"

"Well, to tell you the truth, Andy and I didn't do any mining today."

"Why not?"

"We spent the day looking for somebody. A woman I met."

"A woman!"

"Why do you sound so surprised? I might begin to feel insulted."

"I just... I don't know. I didn't think you were to the

point of looking at other women yet. After what you went through."

"The truth is, I'm not looking, not in *that* way. This isn't what it sounded like. The reason I'm looking for her is that she might be in danger. She claims to be, anyway."

"What kind of danger?"

"She's hiding from a brother she claims killed their father. A half-brother, actually. She says she's seen him in Ferguson, and all at once I can't find her."

"How'd you meet up with her in the first place?"

"Just a chance meeting, that's all." He saw nothing to be gained in telling the full tale of how she slept unauthorized in the Cathedral.

"When you find her, what are you going to do?"

Ben realized he didn't have an answer. He'd thought no farther than simply finding her and making sure she was all right. "I don't know," he admitted.

"Well, if I can help her in any way, let me know," Jake said.

Ben smiled his appreciation and wondered if Jake would be so magnanimous if he knew that it might have been to kill her that his Cathedral of Rest was torched.

"What's her name?" Jake asked.

"Deborah Bray."

"What's she look like?"

"A man."

"Huh?"

Ben chuckled. "She looks like a man because she's been dressing as one to throw her brother off her trail. His name is Daniel Bray, incidentally. If you should happen to run across him or hear of him somewhere, let me know."

"You really believe he's a danger to her?"

Ben paused, then nodded. "There's been times I've wondered about her, how stable and truthful she is...but yes.

I do believe her. My gut says she's truly in danger. Andy is helping me look for her, by the way."

Jake nodded. "That makes me wonder all the more where he might be. You think this Daniel Bray might have done something to him?"

"The thought has crossed my mind, and it ain't a welcome one. I'd feel awful, pit-of-hell awful, if anything bad happened to that young man because of me."

And just then, as fate would have it, they saw him. Andy trotted into the yard and up to the porch. Breathless, he nodded a quick greeting to his father and said to Ben, "I need a private word."

"Have you found her?"

Andy looked surprised and cut his eyes quickly toward his father.

"It's all right," Ben said. "I told him about her. Did you find her?"

"No, but I found a man who claims he knows where she is. Or, at least, someone who fits her description. He's in town right now, half drunk, and waiting for us. We need to talk to him tonight, Ben, or else we may lose our chance. He seems a shiftless kind."

Jake asked, "Is she in danger, Andy?"

Andy, no doubt wondering if Ben had told his father *everything,* including Deborah Bray's possible connection to the Cathedral fire, said, "She might be."

"How?"

"This man, he's told me little so far, demanding that I give him more money—and I've already cleaned out my pockets for him. But he's hinted around some, and I believe what he's going to tell us is that Daniel Bray has found her, and maybe taken her away."

Ben whispered a curse and came to his feet.

"Ben...take this," Jake said, handing him something. Ben took it. A small pistol, compact enough to lie fully on a big man's hand. "I wanted to give it to you anyway...just in case the other business we talked about has something to it."

Ben took the pistol. "Thank you. I will take it. But not because of Champion. That's a figment, nothing more. The man I'm concerned about is flesh and blood, and I hope to God we're not too late. I hope to God he hasn't done anything to Deborah."

CHAPTER 17

A "figment," Ben had called Champion. Now it seemed that the knowledgeable man Andy had claimed to find was a figment as well.

"He was here, I swear," Andy said, looking around the crowded saloon, thick with out-of-tune piano music and blue-tinted, reeking clouds of smoke. "He said he'd stay right there, in that chair, until I got back."

"Well, he didn't, obviously. How much money did you give him?"

"All I had on me. Ten dollars."

"He's gone off to some other saloon, I'll bet you. Off buying himself more liquor."

They began a saloon-to-saloon search that ate up more than an hour, but the man could not be found. Discouraged, they headed back to Jake's house, weary and swearing to try again the next morning. Jake was still up, still on the porch.

"Any luck?"

"He was gone."

Jake didn't seem surprised.

Ben slept very little that night. It seemed absurd to be lying in bed, trying to rest, when there was no telling what

Daniel Bray might be doing to Deborah. Even now he might be lifting a pistol to her forehead in some lonely mountain spot. Or maybe throwing a noose over a limb, or laying out a wrist for slitting. Maybe the act was already done, and he was disposing of the body.

Finally Ben did sleep, somehow, and awakened early the next morning ready to begin again. Andy, who had slept well, was rested and vigorous, and apologetic for having let his informant disappear.

"It was a foolish mistake, and I won't make another one like it again."

"What was this fellow's name?"

"He wouldn't say. But I'll know his face."

Four hours later, the town of Ferguson had been pretty thoroughly scoured, and that face hadn't shown itself. "I'm thinking we may have hit a wall," Ben said. "This man probably has moved on. And I'm betting he didn't really know anything. He just strung you along for the money."

Andy said nothing, and Ben figured he'd just inadvertently insulted his nephew. But he hoped he was right, and that the man really didn't know of any harm coming to Deborah. He'd rather know nothing of her whereabouts than to know that anything bad had come her way.

———

They found the man as soon as they stopped looking for him.

Ben was the first to spot him, and though he hadn't laid eyes on the man before, something about him caused him to look twice, and point him out to Andy.

"That's him!" Andy declared. "You! Hey, there! Stop right there!"

Andy raced forward with such fervor that Ben expected the man to pee his pants and take off on a run. But instead the fellow stayed where he was, looking dumbly at Andy from beneath heavy gray brows. Ben followed Andy along the boardwalk, hobbling a little and not quite as fast.

By the time Ben got there, Andy was already quizzing the man intensely, and scolding him at the same time for his failure to be where he said he would be the night before. The man, a small and frail-looking fellow, age hard to determine because of the effects of drinking, seemed to be having trouble remembering a thing about the prior night.

But as Ben stood by and listened to Andy pummel the fellow with questions, comprehension began to dawn in the thin face. At last the man put on a look of great concern, and said, "Many pardons, friends, many pardons.... The fact is I wasn't feeling well last night, took a bit of medicine to help me sleep, and woke up just as confused and forgetful as I could be. I'd purely forgotten what we'd talked about, young man, but now it's coming back... slowly, slowly. Maybe I'd remember better if I had a bottle of stimulant."

"Forget the 'stimulant.' I want you sober this time."

"Ah, yes. Sobriety. A virtue, sobriety. Virtues are to be lauded, unlike evils...evils such as, oh, poverty ..."

"You cussed devil," Ben said, surprising the fellow. Ben dug in his pocket and handed the man a coin. What little money he had was merely the remains of his meager pay as Cathedral overseer, and he had little to spare for drunks who might know nothing at all. "That's all the money you'll get from us, and if you have no information to provide, I'll beat you until you beg to give even that back. You savvy, friend?"

The man cocked his brows aristocratically. "Sir, you are a barbarian."

Andy said, "Talk, friend. What do you know about Deborah Bray?"

"Well, quite truthfully, I don't know that I know anything about this Bray woman, sir, in that I don't know the name of the woman I saw. Might you describe this Miss Bray?"

"I described her last night."

"Yes...but perhaps a reminder ..."

Ben impatiently described Deborah Bray and her masculine disguise, the lively brows of his listener wiggling above brown eyes. "Oh, indeed, that is the very woman I saw!" he said. "But I can't be sure that the man I saw with her is the one you are after. Might you describe him, too?"

"I can't," Ben said. "I've never seen him. But he would be roughly her age, not many years' difference."

"Brown hair?"

"I don't know."

"Well, sir, the man I saw had brown hair, a youngish appearance, well dressed and groomed."

"And what was he doing?"

"He was with the young lady, speaking to her harshly. He seemed angry that she was dressed as she was. He grasped her arm...."

"Did you hear any threats?"

"Threats? Why, yes. He was quite threatening. I couldn't understand his words, but he seemed to be threatening to carry her off somewhere."

"Where?"

"I couldn't hear. But his manner disturbed me sufficiently to make me follow him and the lady some distance."

"Wait... you *saw* him take her away?"

"I did."

"And where did he take her?"

"To a cabin. Above the place where the pressure cannon work."

"One of the old gold miner cabins?"

"Yes. One quite close to the rim of that sheer bluff left by the blasting of the water cannon. The one visible from the mountain road."

"I know the place. And all this happened yesterday?"

"Indeed."

"Andy, we have to get up there."

"I know. If there's any point. He might have already ..."

"Might have, but maybe not."

The little man, looking from face to face, apparently realized that they were finished with him. He backed away, cautiously, then tipped his round little hat and scurried off.

"We've got to arm ourselves," Ben said.

"There's two rifles at the house. We'll get a couple. But I don't want my mother to see us do it. She'd not be happy to know what we're doing."

"I hope Deborah's alive. I hope she's all right."

They hurried back toward Jake's house, the little man watching them from an alley. When they went out of sight, he bit the coin Ben had given him, nodded his satisfaction, cocked his hat to one side, and scurried toward the nearest barroom.

———

They knelt behind a jumble of boulders, eyeing the little cabin.

"Don't look like there's been anybody there for a long time," Andy whispered.

"I know. But we'll have to get closer to be sure."

"Ben, do you think that little varmint was telling us the truth?"

"I don't know. It seemed believable while he was saying it."

"Ben, I ain't ever done anything like this. Have you?"

Through Ben's mind flashed images of himself, in the company of bushwhackers whom he hated but pretended to admire, creeping through wartime forests toward the unsuspecting homes of men soon destined to feel the sting of

Henry Champion and his band. "Yes, I have. But it's been a long time."

"Maybe you should lead the way. You being experienced, and all."

"Maybe so."

But as Ben led the slow creep toward the cabin, he didn't feel experienced, or like a leader. He felt old and battered and ill-suited for such a grim task.

The cabin was small, but seemed to grow as they approached. Ben's mouth was dry, his hands trembling, causing him to grip his rifle tightly to hide it. He felt more like a foolish old man with every yard he advanced, and Andy seemed more a boy. And the mysterious, unseen Daniel Bray seemed more demonic, a fearsome being Ben dreaded even to meet.

"Ben, you think they're in there?"

"I don't know...Listen, Andy. This isn't your matter. There's no reason you should go any farther. What would I tell your father if something happened to you?"

"I'm coming with you," Andy said, trying but failing to sound brave.

Ben nodded. "All right. If you feel like you—"

He cut off quickly and dropped to his face as Andy did the same. A terrible, explosive roar had erupted, making the very ground rumble and shake. A stinging white mist blasted up from somewhere just beyond the old cabin, raining back down upon them.

The water cannon had erupted into operation, grinding down the mountain a little farther as the last of the high country's gold miners manhandled the land with an effectiveness their dish-swishing predecessors could only have envied.

"Scared me nigh to death," Andy said, though Ben could no longer hear him. The cannon roar was far too loud and endless. Ben motioned for Andy to continue.

At least any sound they made in approaching would be masked.

Nearer they came, slowly creeping, eyes stinging in the fine spray bursting up from below the edge of the bluff, rifles growing wet in their grasps.

They reached the rear of the cabin. Ben sucked in a deep, moist breath and edged to the window....

He gazed in for several seconds, rifle at the ready, eyes exploring the dark interior.

"What is it, Ben?" Andy asked. He went unheard.

Ben lifted a leg and put it through the empty window, then pulled the rest of himself through, vanishing from Andy's sight.

———

A minute later, both men stood inside the cabin, protected momentarily from the blasting mist. The roar of the water cannon was sufficiently muffled by the log walls to allow them to speak to one another. If the sound had suddenly shut down they would have discovered they were shouting at each other. As it was, they had to strain to hear what each other said.

"I should have known, Andy," Ben said. "I should have seen that shrimp was lying to us. He never saw a thing."

"But he said he saw her, even described what she was wearing."

"No, he didn't. *We* described it. We fed him everything he needed to know in the way we questioned him, and he just threw it right back to us. For the money."

Andy pondered and nodded. "We've been fools. Me the biggest of all. I'm the one who led us to that lying drunk."

"Well, in one way maybe it's all for the best. If he'd been telling the truth, most likely we'd have found her dead up here."

The cabin quaked and rumbled, the blasting sound growing louder as the cannon fired their jets at a point just below the top of the bluff.

"What now, Ben?"

"We get out of here and back to town. Then we keep looking, at least for a while. If you're willing, at least."

"And if we don't find her?"

"Then we go back to the mine, and start doing what miners are supposed to do."

"There's something I ain't mentioned to you about the mine, Ben. Something that happened the day of the night that Roscoe got burned up."

"What?"

"We hit a horse down in the shaft."

"You hit a *what!*"

"A horse...you know what I mean. A big block of iron. Seems to be right monstrous."

"So all that digging..."

"Has been for nothing."

The roaring was growing louder, the cabin beginning to shake and shiver, making strange, twisting, straining noises... but Ben was preoccupied with what he'd just been told, and hardly noticed.

"But ain't there some way we can—"

He saw the look on Andy's face, the fear that rose suddenly in his eyes, the opening of the mouth to scream, but the scream was never heard. Something struck the cabin that felt like the very fist of God, slamming the base of it, ripping it asunder and pushing it up and back, the course suddenly reversing as the cabin, cut loose by a stray blast from one of the water cannon, now spilled out and down, pitching over the edge of the bluff and tumbling, turning, crashing down the slope into the white hell of water and stone below, carrying its two screaming human occupants with it.

CHAPTER 18

B en felt nothing. He was numb all over... no, not completely numb. There was cold. A chill that embraced him from head to foot. Wetness. And a shaking, ear-attacking, grumbling roar, like the growl of Satan angered.

Ben opened his eyes and saw a gray-white blur. All a jumble, nothing making sense, everything askew, twisted, bent at incredible angles. His focus came back, partially, and he saw Andy amidst it all, lying on his back. One leg was stretched out before him. The other was bent impossibly, as if he'd gained a new joint in the middle of his thigh. Andy didn't move. His eyes were closed.

Ben closed his eyes, too, and wondered if he had gone to hell. If so, all the usual tales were wrong. Hell was supposed to be hot, not cold and wet.

————

The roaring was gone, replaced by a steady, dull buzzing that seemed to come from inside his own head. No more cold, either. He was warm now, and lying on something soft. He opened his eyes again, and looked into a face, and blandly thought, *I was right. I have gone to hell.*

The man looking back at him was Henry Champion.

Odd that it should be Champion who came to welcome him to the infernal regions. Or maybe not. Maybe it was part of the torment of damnation that your most hated enemies became your eternal companions.

"Mr. Woolard, I'm so glad to see you awake," Henry Champion said in a voice that wasn't Henry Champion's. "We were quite worried about you."

Ben stared at the face. A gentle and smiling face. His mind cleared a bit, and now he knew. This wasn't Henry Champion at all. He'd made the same mistake that Roanie had. This was that newcomer preacher, the one who merely happened to resemble Champion.

"Am I alive?"

"Yes."

"So I've not gone to hell?"

The preacher gave him an odd look. "No. Oh, no. You're in your brother's house. You were found yesterday afternoon, almost dead, soaked and covered with dirt and rubble and gravel. You were at the place where the huge water cannons blast away the mountain. Do you remember?"

Ben felt his heart begin to race. "I remember."

"You wouldn't have survived much longer. It's astonishing that you survived as long as you did. Had you fallen facedown instead of on your back, you'd have drowned."

Another memory..."Andy. What about Andy?"

"Alive. A badly broken leg. But he seems well otherwise. And you, sir, are remarkably blessed. Not a single bone of your body broken."

"I hurt anyway."

"Well you should. It appears that you and the younger Mr. Woolard fell inside a cabin from the top of the bluff all the way to the base of the pit."

"That's exactly what happened."

"Why were you there?"

"First you tell me why you're here."

"They were afraid you'd die. They knew I was a minister of the gospel. Thus I was called in."

"Tell them I don't plan to die."

"Gladly. Now, why were you in such a dangerous place?"

"Looking for somebody. A man named Daniel Bray."

Silence for a moment. "How odd."

"Why odd?"

"Because, Mr. Woolard. you've found the man you were looking for. My name is Bray. The Reverend Daniel Bray, and I'm quite pleased to have the pleasure of your acquaintance."

———

Ben gazed at the preacher for a long time, wondering if he'd really heard what he thought he'd heard. His head buzzed; he realized he'd probably been administered some sort painkiller before he fully regained consciousness.

"Did you say your name is Daniel Bray?"

"Yes."

"You don't look as young as I thought you'd be."

"Tell me, sir, how you had heard my name, and why you were looking for me."

The buzzing in Ben's head grew louder. He didn't know what he should or shouldn't say to this man, but his tongue seemed loosened by whatever he'd been administered, and he spoke freely. "I heard of you from Deborah Bray. Says she's your half-sister. Says you murdered her father, your own father."

He slowly shook his head. "Oh, dear girl. My dear girl... so beautiful. So ill. So...destroyed."

Ben wasn't in much shape or mood for talking, but this intrigued him. "What do you mean, 'destroyed'?"

"Deborah isn't well, Mr. Woolard. She's ill. Not physically. Her mind."

"Are you saying she's insane?"

Bray was slow to answer. He suddenly seemed older. ' T suppose that's what I am saying. But they're not easy words. Not for a father to say about his daughter."

If Ben had felt like it, he would have sat up. "Daughter? Deborah is your daughter?"

"Indeed she is. You see, Mr. Woolard, there is no half-brother named Daniel Bray. That's what she told you, I suppose—that she is fleeing from a wicked half-brother named Daniel, that he committed some dread crime, that she has information that can lead to his downfall, and that he's after her, intent on killing her."

"That's what she told me. She said that Daniel killed her father... killed *you*.'"

"Mr. Woolard, I am the only Daniel Bray still alive. Daniel Bray my son—the twin brother of poor Deborah—died when he was eight years old. A terrible accident. Deborah saw it, the only one who did. I gave up years ago trying to determine the exact circumstances of his death. Deborah would never say...at least, she would never say the same thing twice. It involved fire, that much I can tell you. The poor boy, my son, burned to death in an abandoned house that he and Deborah had been playing in together."

"I'm sorry."

"Yes. In any case, when he died, he and I were at odds. Nothing important, just a case of his misbehavior and my punishment, and him holding resentment over it. I gather that he'd made comments about having bad intent toward me. Perhaps he said he'd kill me; childish metaphor, if he did. No true intent. But Deborah seemed to believe he was serious. She believed he really wanted me hurt or dead."

"Reverend Bray, are you trying to hint that..."

"I'm trying to hint that it's possible that Deborah killed her own twin brother at the age of eight. Not certain. Possible. It took me years to be able to admit even the possibility. But suffice it to say that after Daniel's death, Deborah began a slow and continual slide into very dark places. Her sanity failed her. Her mother and I did all we could for her, sought her the best care and wisest men. She improved. She became very much a normal young woman, her perspective in the right place. Only when the matter of Daniel came up did she seem...abnormal. Unable to cope. And when her mother died, she lost everything she had gained, and more. She began talking as if Daniel had killed her. She claimed to have papers —just blank sheets of paper, nothing more—that proved he intended to kill me. And she would sometimes dress in a man's clothing, and claim that she was him."

"Wait...she was in man's clothing when I met her. But she didn't claim to be Daniel. She claimed to be hiding from him, dressing that way to disguise herself."

Bray shook his head. "No. Perhaps she was clever enough to use that story because it was more acceptable to others. But the fact is, she dresses in male clothing not to escape Daniel, but to *be* him. She and Daniel are one and the same, Mr. Woolard. One and the same."

Ben was so caught up, so fascinated and appalled by all this, that he was hardly aware of his own injuries. "Mr. Bray, I need to tell you something. When I met Deborah, it was while I was operating a sort of hotel for my brother. Not really a hotel, just a big warehouse full of bunks where men, only men, could pay for a bed for a night. Deborah came in, dressed as a man, and to make a long story short, I realized she wasn't what she appeared." He quickly related his other condescensions to Deborah, and how Roscoe Hammel had treated her with equal protectiveness and liberality. Then he paused, and went on: "This sleeping house, sir, was destroyed very recently by fire. On a night Deborah was sleeping there. And afterward she told me that she saw Daniel do it."

The old reverend went pale, and sat weakly down in a chair beside Ben's bed. So far none of Ben and Andy's kin had come into the closed room, and for this Ben was glad, because only in privacy could such a delicate and informative conversation as this one proceed.

"Oh, Mr. Woolard, it pains me to hear that. She set it, then. Deborah set that fire." He squeezed his eyes tightly closed a few seconds, pursing his lips. Then he looked at Ben again. "Did anyone die?"

"One man."

"God help us. God help us."

"I'm sorry to have told you that."

"Mr. Woolard, don't be sorry. It's providential that we met, you and I. I mean that literally. Our meeting was intended, because through you I've found my daughter's track at last, and learned things, however painful, that I needed to know."

"And so have I, sir. I believed Deborah's story. She's quite persuasive."

"Of course. After all, she believes it herself."

"Is there any hope for her? Can she ever be sane?"

"I don't know. Perhaps. There are those years of lucidity that she enjoyed. Those give me hope. Maybe she can return to them, and this time not lose touch again." He paused. "But this death, this fire...that makes it all different. If she's responsible for a man's death ..."

"Sir, if you would, say nothing to anyone about that. The fact is that we don't know that she set the fire. Maybe someone else did set it, and she saw them, and in her state of mind interpreted that person as her half-brother."

Bray, obviously eager for any hope he could find, seized on that idea eagerly. "Yes! Yes! Perhaps so. I'll assume the best for now, for Deborah's sake."

"You must know, sir, that I haven't seen Deborah since the night of that fire. That's why Andy and I were looking for Daniel Bray—the imagined one, not you. We thought he'd found her and taken her off. In fact, we met a man, a town drunk, who swore to us that he'd seen a woman who sounded like Deborah being carried off by a young man."

"Mercy! Might he really have seen something, somebody taking her away?"

"No. I'm convinced he didn't. Andy and I went about questioning this fellow in entirely the wrong way. We fed him his answers in the very questions we asked, and he gave us back what we seemed to be looking for so that we'd pay him. He lied to us for money, told us we'd find the people he saw up in that cabin above the rock pit. But when we got inside, it was obvious that no one had been in that place for years."

"So Deborah is still missing."

"Yes. Perhaps she's gone on elsewhere, sir."

"Perhaps. She travels far. I've been trying to find her for a year now. A full year, following rumors, tracing down clues about her whereabouts.... It's hard. Terribly hard."

"Maybe she's still in town. Maybe we can find her. There's new people streaming into Ferguson every day, Reverend. Huge crowds of folks. A person can lose themselves in such a town with ease."

Reverend Bray bowed his head, and Ben wondered if he was praying. But when he lifted his face again, his eyes were red and wet. The weary, worried man had been crying. Weeping for a missing, insane daughter who might have once more slipped out of his reach.

If Ben had any doubts about the veracity of Bray's tale, he let them go at that point. At times all that could be trusted were instincts. He believed Bray. Everything about him had the aura of authenticity.

"I'll help you search for her, Reverend. I'd consider it a privilege."

"I don't think you're in much shape to help just now, my friend."

"You'll be surprised. I've come through two beatings already, and I'm not out yet. If I can do that, and then slide down a mountain and come out without a single broken bone, then I believe I can do most anything. I'll be up and about in no time, and you and me will find your daughter, sir."

Bray smiled and nodded. "God bless you, Mr. Woolard. You are a saint."

"No. I just sense your concern for her. You care about her. And so do I."

Bray stood. "Mr. Woolard, I've done you a disservice. Here I've been brought in to sit with you and pray over you until you awakened, and now that you have, all I've done is chatter on about my own situation. Your brother doesn't even know that you've come back to the living!"

"Then maybe you can go tell them."

Bray nodded, smiling more firmly. "That I shall. And thank you, sir. Thank you for your pledge to help me."

"Not at all."

Ben settled back into the pillow as Bray left the room, and waited for the others to come to him.

CHAPTER 19

Andy was quite jealous. With his painful broken leg, splinted and bound and propped up before him, he would be abed for heaven only knew how long. And yet Ben, merely a week after that tumble over the bluff and not that much farther past the second of two beatings, was already up and about and doing quite well.

Not bad for a man working through his fifth decade of life. Andy could only lie as still as possible, and envy him.

He had other things to think about, too. Like his father's odd manner. For the last three days, Jake Woolard had seemed very distracted, not himself at all. Something was on the man's mind, heavily so, but he denied it each time Andy asked him about it.

At the moment, Andy was fairly comfortable, but it wouldn't last. The doctor was scheduled to stop by later in the day, and, as usual, he'd poke and prod about at that broken leg until it was so sore Andy wanted to weep. Then he'd tell Andy to remain still, leave the leg alone, and wait for him to come back in a day or two and torture him some more.

Andy closed his eyes and decided to nap. If he could.

Laid up in bed, about all a man could do was nap, and after so much sleep, more of the same wasn't much appealing.

Andy drew in a deep breath, moved a little to resettle himself—wincing at the pain this caused to shoot through his leg—and vowed never again to join Ben Woolard on any quest for any woman or any mysterious stranger.

Once he was out of this bed, Andy Woolard would return to mining and be glad to have no further adventures.

———

Ben rocked slowly on the porch, looking out into the evening, when the door opened behind him and Jake emerged.

"Well, howdy, Ben. I didn't realize you were out here."

"I don't have to be, if you were looking for some privacy. I can go back inside."

"Oh, no, sit still." He pulled up the other rocker. "What makes you think I'd want you to go away?"

"Maybe the fact that you've had a kind of distant manner about you this week."

"Have I?"

"Yes. Andy and me were talking about it only today. And Sally has mentioned it more than once. I think she's worried about you." Ben paused. "I am, too. It isn't like you to act like this. Is something wrong at the store?"

"No. Everything's fine at the store."

"But something's wrong somewhere. Right?"

A moment of silence, then Jake looked over at his brother. "Ben, I saw Henry Champion."

"What?"

"I saw him. The day after you and Andy went over the cliff in the cabin. I saw him standing in the doorway of a saloon, looking across the street at me. He was in the shadows, and I don't think he realized I could see him...but it was him. Not the preacher Bray, either. There was no mistake this time."

Ben felt tense all over. "Jake, could it really be that somehow the man really is alive?"

"It has to be. I know because I saw him."

"We saw him hang, too."

"But maybe we didn't see him die."

"Surviving a military hanging? No. Can't be. You heard the sound when that rope jerked tight. You could feel the force of that snap when he hit the end of that rope. A jerk like that would break any man's neck. He couldn't have made it through alive. And if he had, wouldn't it have been known right away?"

"I can't explain. All I know is what I saw. And that I'm scared by it. He was looking at me, Ben. Right at me! Staring with those same cold eyes that I felt on me when I was testifying in his trial."

"I don't know what to say."

"Neither do I. Just be sure to keep that pistol I gave you with you all the time."

"I will. You stay armed, too. Just in case." He thought about it some more and shook his head. "Jake, he *can't* be alive! It isn't possible."

"I saw him, Ben. I saw him just like that colored man said he saw him."

"Roanie... And you know something, Jake? Roanie hasn't been around lately. I haven't seen him, anyway."

"Maybe Champion got him."

"I'd just as soon you not say that kind of thing. Makes me nervous."

"Ben, there's more to it than me just seeing Champion, as if that wasn't enough. I did some investigation. I found out that there's a mining claim in the Goatbeard area held by a man named Marcus Fellers."

"Fellers...good Lord, Jake. Ain't that the name that Jim Masker used for himself from time to time?"

"It is. Maybe it's coincidence, but a mighty odd one if it is. And from what I was able to find out by asking around among the miners I know from around Goatbeard, this Fellers man matches the looks of Jim Masker, and there's men with him, some of whom sound like they might be Champion and Art Rellon. And a couple of younger men, too, apparently grown-up sons of the others."

"Jake, this scares me to death."

"Don't it, though."

Ben rocked a few moments more. "I think I might go inside now, Jake. All at once I don't feel too safe sitting out here."

"I'll join you."

They rose and entered the house, seeking the shelter of protective walls in a night that suddenly seemed more than a little ominous.

Ben spent the next day with Reverend Bray, searching the town for Deborah. Bray was intense and focused on his quest, talking only of what they were doing at the moment, unable to know that when his still-limping companion cut his eyes here and there to examine the throngs of Ferguson, it was not only for Deborah Bray that he looked.

The aging preacher began the day full of hope that he would find his daughter, and it was sad to watch his spirits declining as the day waned. "We'll find her tomorrow," Ben said as brightly as possible.

"Can we not continue to look a bit longer?" Reverend Bray pleaded. "Just a bit more? The night brings out more people in a town like this one."

Ben was tired, increasingly suspicious that Deborah had

already left Ferguson entirely, probably fleeing because somewhere in her troubled mind she knew that it wasn't any phantom half-brother, but she herself, who had burned down the Cathedral. And there was something else nagging at Ben, too, a feeling that he needed to return to Jake's house, that it was very important that he be there very soon.

But the old preacher's sad, pleading face was hard to deny. "A while longer," Ben said. "Just a half hour or so. Maybe we'll find her after all."

"I'm sure of it!" Bray said, suddenly bright and full of life. "Thank you, sir! You are indeed a godsend to me."

And so they searched on, but no Deborah was found. And the unsettled feeling that had plagued Ben, calling him vainly back to Jake's house, only grew. At last he could continue no more, and told the preacher that he'd now be heading back but would be ready to continue the search the next day.

Ben set out toward Jake's house on a trot, and was almost there when a small boy intercepted him. "Mr. Woolard, sir? Mr. Ben Woolard?"

"Yes."

"I got something for you. A message."

"Who from?"

"I don't know. Just a man who gave me two dollars to watch for you and make sure you got it." He handed Ben a folded piece of paper, sealed with wax, then waited expectantly. Ben sighed and reached into his pocket and handed the boy a coin. He was completely out of money now, relying on handouts from Jake to get him by, and he didn't like parting with even a small amount of cash. The boy grinned and trotted away with his money.

Ben unfolded the paper and read. Wadding it, he crammed it into a pocket, turned, and ran back up Center Street as hard as his bruised and tired body would allow.

———

He found the store locked and dark except for a single light burning back in the storeroom, where Jake kept a desk upon which he worked through the store's books and ledgers each evening.

"Jake!" Ben yelled, pounding the door with his fist. "Jake! Are you in there?"

Jake appeared in the storeroom door, frowning and gazing across the dark store interior toward whatever maniac was pounding down his front door. "Ben? Is that you?"

"Let me in, Jake!"

Jake hurried across the store and admitted Ben. "What the devil is wrong?"

"Nothing, it appears. But I got a note on the street—a boy handed it to me—and it said you were in here, hurt and bleeding, and that you'd be dead by the time I found you."

"What? Ben, I'm fine, as you can see. Nothing's happened to me."

"I know. I can see that. Either this is some kind of a joke...or a warning ..."

Jake looked solemn. "Or maybe an attempt to keep you from going where you were going at the time. Where were you heading when you met this boy?"

"To the house. Your house."

A pause. "Ben, let's go. Let's go now."

They left the store together, not even pausing to shut the door behind them, and ran hard up the street, through the milling and half-drunken crowd, toward Jake's house.

———

Andy had tried to fight them, impossible though it was. He'd somehow dragged himself out of his bed and gone for one of his father's rifles in the rifle case, but someone had gotten to him long before it was within reach, and pounded him senseless with the butt of a shotgun. He lay now with his bleeding head cradled in the lap of his weeping mother. She was bleeding too, shot through the shoulder, and her nose was broken and dripping scarlet liquid that washed over her lips and fell onto her son's pale face.

Jake all but fell before her, groping out, weeping, asking her what had happened, and who...

"They got Judy," she said. "They got Judy, they took her. They took her, Jake!"

"Who was it, Sally?" Ben asked urgently.

"I don't know...men.... They left a letter with your name on it, Jake."

"Where?"

Ben had already spotted it, lying on the supper table. "Here it is." He grabbed it, handed it to his brother.

Jake shook his head. "My hands are trembling too much. Open it, Ben. Read it."

Ben's hands were almost as tremulous, but he managed to get the envelope open and the paper spread. He read it silently, then read it again.

"Champion?" Jake asked.

Ben nodded and let the paper fall from his fingers.

"He wants us?"

"Yes. If we want to see Judy alive again, he says, we have to come to him, to his claim at Goatbeard. For a 'reckoning.' That's what it says. A 'reckoning.' And we have to come alone, and unarmed. Any weapons, any law in sight, and he'll kill her."

Sally sobbed, out of control. Andy groaned and moved, an encouraging sign, but hardly noticed under the circumstances.

"We've got to do it, Ben."

"I know."

Sally screamed, "No, Jake! They'll kill you! I saw them, I know what kind of men they are.... They'll kill you!"

"I have to do it, honey. For Judy."

Sally leaned across her unconscious son and wept like a child.

CHAPTER 20

F unny, Ben thought, how there seemed nothing to say. Two brothers, walking alone in the night along a trail that would lead to their deaths at the hands of a man long believed dead—and there was nothing to say. He and Jake strode side by side, looking straight ahead, walking unarmed and unfollowed into the night, and neither had a word to say to the other.

Though the night was quite dark, the trail was relatively easy to keep to once their eyes fully adjusted. Many a miner traveled the route between Ferguson and Goatbeard day after day, and footfalls and hoof beats and wagon wheels had made a road of what had once been untrampled mountain soil.

They strode on, ever silent.

They saw the fire, just as promised, a bonfire flickering below the overhang of Goatbeard. They made for it. A beacon to guide them, put there by Champion and his cohorts. A beacon to lure two men to their deaths...and yet they had no option but to follow, because of Judy.

Jake stopped, turned, and looked behind them. "Did you hear that?"

"No," Ben said. "What was it?"

"It sounded like someone following."

"I didn't hear."

"I hope no one followed. My God, what will they do to Judy if someone followed, and they detect it?"

Ben listened hard. "Jake, there's no one back there. I think you imagined it."

Jake shook his head. "I heard something."

"A critter, probably. Now let's move on. If we're late, Judy might pay the price."

They trudged up the mountain, toward the flickering light.

———

Art Rellon was the first person they saw. They were close enough to the bonfire now to make out the figures of men around it, and Art Rellon was suddenly before them, stepping out onto the trail with a shotgun in hand.

"Ben Woolard!" he said in an oddly warm voice. "So that really was you I met on the street a while back! Who'd have thought we'd wind up in the same town!"

"Where is she, Rellon?"

"The girl? Why, she's fine. Henry's got her."

Jake spoke. "If he lays a hand on her to harm her or to shame her in any way, I'll slice him into pieces, a little at a time."

Rellon laughed. "My Lord, ain't you two the somber ones? What's wrong? You afraid somebody's going to betray you? Put you into a situation that endangers your life? Is that it?" He paused. "I guess you're pretty much an expert when it comes to betraying folks, eh, Ben?"

"Where's Judy? When will you let her go?"

"Ain't up to me. It's up to Henry." Rellon laughed. "I'll

bet that strikes you odd, hearing talk about Henry, when you've thought him dead for so damn long!"

"Henry Champion can have me, as long as he lets Judy go," Ben said. "And there's no reason he should want to harm my brother. It was me who put him on the gallows."

"Your brother played his part, too. I do believe it was him you reported back to, betraying Henry, betraying all of us, all that time you were pretending to be one of us." He waved the shotgun. "Now come on. Let's let you go say hello to an old friend."

———

Ben was sure that at any moment he would open his eyes and find himself staring at Jake's ceiling. Maybe even the ceiling of the Cathedral, with all that had occurred in the last few days proving to be no more than a bizarre dream.

But every time he closed and reopened his eyes, the same vision was before him: Henry Champion, alive and in the flesh, standing beside the bonfire with a rope in his hand, the other end of which was tied around Judy Woolard's plump neck.

The murderous old bushwhacker had her leashed like some dog! Ben felt his blood surge hot. He wondered if there was some symbolic significance to the rope being around her neck—a subtle reminder that he was Henry Champion, the gallowsman who had somehow managed to survive his own hanging. Was he hinting that the Woolard brothers were going to be forced to watch a mere child hanged as punishment for their long-past offense?

Henry Champion looked Jake up and down, then turned a far more lingering gaze upon Ben. He evaluated him silently, eyes trailing his entire form, expression never changing. In fact, Champion seemed to have no expression at all, just a chilling, unrelenting gaze.

"Hello, Ben," he said at last. "Last time I seen you, I was about to have a hanging mask pulled down over my face."

"How'd you live through it, Champion?" Ben asked. "I saw you drop. I saw the rope jerk tight around your neck."

Champion smiled for the first time. His smile had always made Ben shudder back in the old days. It was no different now. "What you think you see and what really happens ain't always the same thing. I did drop. I did jerk that rope tight. But it wasn't my neck that took the impact of it. There was a harness around me, under my arms, with a sort of hook on it. That rope was linked to that harness, so that when it pulled tight, I took the force of it around the chest, not the neck. God, that hurt, but damned better it was than the alternative. All I had to do was hang there limp and play dead."

"Wait a minute...are you telling me that your hanging was a hoax?"

"I'm standing alive before you, ain't I?"

"But that would require the complicity of the Federals... Somebody defied the order of the court."

"My, my, ain't you just as smart as you ever was! You got it just right, Ben. There was complicity. Several layers of it, matter of fact. You see, even the Yankees had some among them who knew that it wasn't just for a man like me to hang when others who'd done as much or more than I had had been pardoned. There was several in that courtroom who knew, even while I was being sentenced to hang, that it would never happen. There was a plan to fake the thing almost from the time the sentence was read. When I mounted that gallows, I knew I'd be coming off it alive again."

Ben had nothing to say. He'd never have believed such a thing as Champion was describing could have happened... but the evidence stood alive before him. His own government, his own side, illegitimately sparing the life of the man he'd risked his life to bring down. Suddenly Ben understood what it must have felt like to Henry Champion to see someone he'd trusted testifying against him in trial. The very Federal justice structure that Ben had aided and trusted without question had betrayed him.

"So you've been alive all these years."

"That's right. Alive and kicking. Oh, I laid plenty low for many a year, and traveled many a mile. Came west eventually, using this name and that. I was a sodbuster for a time, and a rancher. I've been a merchant and a horse trader. Now I'm a miner. But all the while I've done what I could for the old cause. I've wore the white sheet and the white hood with pride. I've done my share to let Mister Nigger know that, free or not, he's still Mister Nigger, and I'm still his better."

"It was you who killed Billy Piatt."

"Who's Billy Piatt?"

"A Negro. Murdered and his teeth pulled out."

"That gold-mouth negro! Oh, yes, that was my doing." Champion laughed, but quickly turned his look very hard and sour. "Damned negro, going around flashing them gold teeth, thinking himself fine because of it! Damn, but it made my blood boil inside me! I reckon old gold-teeth had a different attitude by the time I finished with him! That was one negro I particular enjoyed killing."

"You've killed a lot of men, Champion. Men who didn't deserve it. Even boys."

"I have. And I ain't through killing yet."

Ben glanced at Judy, who was biting her lip, crying, but doing her best to be brave. "You ain't going to stoop to hurting a little girl, are you?"

"I don't quite know what I'm going to do with this girl," he said, giving the rope a small jerk. "I believe I'll keep her close by for now, just to make sure you Woolards have good reason to cooperate."

Jake spoke. "We'll do whatever you say...but please, please, let my girl go. Don't hurt her. I beg you."

"You beg me, do you? You beg me. If I'd begged for my life on them gallows, would you have felt bad for me? Would you have listened? Hell, no."

"Let's get on with it, Henry," Masker said.

"Let's do," Champion said. "Here. Come take this little gal's rope. Take her and tie her to a tree over yonder."

Masker led Judy off her head turning as she walked so she could maintain eye contact with her father. Masker tied his end of the rope tightly around a tree, then aimed a finger at Judy's face. "You try to get loose, and you'll regret it, girl!"

Champion walked slowly to Ben and looked him in the eye. For a long time he said nothing, then slowly he shook his head.

"Ben Woolard. Good Ben Woolard, who rode with me, told me time and again he supported what I believed in, what I did, what I was. You know, Ben, I trusted you. I took you at your word. You were like a son to me. I swear it's true. Like a son."

"You were a murderer, Champion. A murderer then, and a murderer now."

"I was a faithful, true son of the South. A man who knew the rightful scheme of the world and wasn't willing to let a bunch of negroes and negro-loving bluebellies mess it all up. And I was a man who paid an eye for an eye. That's all I was."

Ben said, "I'm not sorry for what I did. I've been proud of it all these years. I was proud that evidence I gathered was what convicted you, and proud that it was me who brought you to the noose."

Champion actually looked sad. "Them words hurt, son. They do. I wish you'd been true to me. I wish you'd been what I thought you was."

"Let me go, Champion. You'll gain nothing by doing harm to me now. And whatever you do, please, I beg you to let Judy there, and my brother here, come to no harm. Please."

Champion made no promises. It was as if he didn't even hear. "It hurt me bad, seeing you Judas me like you did, son. Every word you said in that court, every word burned me like a brand.

"But I didn't carry my grudge against you close to my heart. No, sir. I could have sought you out in secret when it was all over, or could have had any one of these faithful men of mine do it, but I didn't. I let it be. Let you be. But then, when it begun to come clear that fate had brung us together once more, then I knew that justice had to be done.

"I didn't believe it at first. Here comes Rellon saying he'd seen you in town, face-to-face. I didn't believe it. Then Masker tells me he seen you, too, and that the Woolard who runs the mercantile was none other than your brother. Still I didn't quite believe, not until the day I seen you with my own eyes in a saloon in town, staring at a bottle you never touched."

"You were there?"

"I was. I watched you and the young fellow with you.

When you were gone, I even took your bottle. And I drunk it, and thought, and drunk it some more, and thought some more, until I knew what had to be done. The old score had to be settled. And settled it'll be. Right here. Tonight."

Champion waved back across his claim. A typical kind of operation, not much different in looks than the one Ben, Andy, and Roscoe had worked. A pen with a couple of mules, a rough log storage shed for tools, heaps of dirt and stone, and a shaft with a wooden pulley frame—a "gallows," ironically—built atop it. And Champion's men, faces from Ben's past, and two younger men he knew were sons, though of which men he couldn't know. Ben took it all in with a sweep of his eyes, and felt sad to know that this would be the last scene he would ever see.

"Time for reckoning, son," he said. "I'm sorry it's come down to it." With that he wheeled quickly toward Jake, drew a heavy, ancient pistol, and swung it hard, smashing it into Jake's jaw, breaking open the flesh, knocking Jake cold in a bleeding, collapsing heap.

Judy screamed and began to sob. Rellon turned and cursed at her, told her to shut up, and she somehow managed to stifle the sounds of her weeping, though the weeping went on.

Champion reholstered the pistol. "We'll deal with him later," he said. "You're the one who matters most, Ben. You're the one who dies first."

CHAPTER 21

The horse was big and black. Champion's own and quite a prized beast, Ben was told. Ben sat astride it now. No saddle, just the horse between his legs, his hands tied behind his back, and a noose around his neck.

Champion stood to his side, looking up at him with that same sad expression, like a father sorrowful to see a wayward son bearing the cost of his own ill decisions.

"I'm awful sorry, Ben," he said. "What makes it even harder for me is knowing how you'll suffer. Not enough height to give any drop to the rope, so I guess you'll just have to choke it out. God have mercy on you, son."

"I wonder what God thinks, hearing the voice of a man like you calling his name," Ben replied. He was determined to meet his end with all the dignity and defiance he could muster.

"Why don't you ask him when you see him, which won't be long now," Champion replied.

Ben could no longer look at the man. He lifted his eyes and took a final look at his brother, still crumpled unconscious on the ground, then up to where Judy was tied...

...and he began to smile.

Champion saw it, and his eyes narrowed. "What are you smiling at, son? This ain't no time for smiling. You ought to be praying."

The smile lingered. It wasn't forced. What Ben had seen caused it to well up from inside, and he couldn't stop it if he tried.

Masker, off behind Champion, glared at Ben's grinning face, then turned to see what he was looking at.

"Henry...look."

"What?"

"She's gone, Henry. The girl is gone."

"What the hell..."

Champion looked. Masker was right. The rope that had held Judy Woolard bound was still tied to the tree, but Judy was gone. Champion swore and turned to Ben again.

"Where'd she go? How'd she get away?"

Ben smiled down at Champion. "Maybe a ghost got her loose. Maybe the phantoms of all the men and boys you murdered gathered and swooped down out of the sky and set her free."

"Damn you, answer me straight! What happened to her!"

"Looks to me like somebody cut her loose. Now, don't that give you cause to ponder! Somebody out there... somebody to witness what you're doing here, somebody to testify about it in court."

Champion tried to hide it, but fear came over him then. His eyes shot fire at Ben, and he turned to his men.

Masker spoke. "Henry, even if there ain't nobody else, and she just wiggled loose, she could still tell what happened."

"Get out there," he said. "Find that girl, and if there's anybody else about, find them too. Now!"

Every man scurried to respond. Henry Champion was still an unquestioned leader after all these years.

"Wait, Jim," Champion said to Masker. "You stay here with me. I want two of us guarding in case that one on the ground begins to wake up."

Masker seemed glad to oblige. Ben, who just kept on grinning, could understand the feeling. There was something quite ominous about that dark forest, a sense of a presence there that was almost diabolical, like the great Goatbeard peak itself had come to life and moved monstrously and vengefully in the blackness.

"Maybe the night is going to swallow them alive," Ben said to Champion. "Maybe all the wickedness you've done has come to life. Maybe it's hungry for the flesh of bad men."

"Shut up!" Champion bellowed.

"Let's hang him now," Masker said. "Just slap the horse out from under him and shut him up for good!"

"Not until I have that girl back. Not until I know there's no witnesses out there."

They heard a sound in the forest, an odd, gurgling noise. A human sound, it seemed. And then a soft, muffled thud.

"That's one," Ben said. "One gone. I wonder which. Rellon? I'll bet it was Rellon."

Champion aimed his finger up at Ben. "Damn you, Ben, if you keep that up, I *will* go ahead and move this horse. You understand me?"

Ben kept up the smile. Champion glared at him, and Masker's look was one of dark and pure hatred.

Another noise—a faint, masculine grunt, perhaps a muffled cry. Another soft thudding sound, like a heavy bag of grain being dropped as quietly as possible on the ground.

"That's two," Ben whispered, and Champion cursed at him again and made as if to slap the horse from beneath him. But he didn't. And Ben knew he wouldn't, not until he knew for sure that he could commit this murder without being witnessed by hostile eyes. Champion, for all his talk, all his power over others of his ilk, all his attempts to justify himself for his crimes, was at heart a coward. Surrounded by protection, he would act. Alone, he would falter.

Time passed. The horse fidgeted but did not move out from beneath Ben.

He kept on grinning. By heaven, he'd still be grinning when they pulled the horse from beneath him, if it came to that. He'd not give Champion the satisfaction of seeing him whimper or cringe from death.

More sounds from the forest, more silences. Then more noises, men falling in a silent battle. One of the sounds this time was a very distinct cry of pain. One of the younger men, Ben thought.

"I believe that's all of them, Champion," Ben said.

"You brought someone with you," Champion said. "After what I ordered, you had somebody follow!"

"No. We didn't. We followed your orders, told no one. But I believe maybe somebody has followed us anyway. Somebody has followed us all on their own."

"I'll kill you!"

"No you won't. Not until you know you can do it without being seen. You only kill in the dark, Champion. Men who you'd never face in the light, and never face alone. You're a coward. You've always been a coward."

"We'll see how brave *you* are, Ben, when you feel that horse move out from under you." Champion turned to Masker. "Jim, maybe you'd best get out there and see what's going on."

"What?"

"You heard me."

"You think I'm going out there? There's something out there, Henry. Somebody."

By the light of the bonfire, Ben saw Henry Champion's face go crimson. Champion opened his mouth to reply to Masker, but before he could speak, another voice did from the darkness.

"Henry Champion!"

Ben, still smiling, watched the ruddy face of a moment before suddenly go white.

"Somebody's calling you, Henry," he whispered.

"God..." Masker said, backing away. "God, Henry, that voice don't even sound human!"

Champion's lips moved, but his ability to speak seemed to have escaped him.

"Henry Champion!" the phantom voice called again. "Time for you to pay the price!"

Ben watched pure panic envelop two men. Champion's mouth moved silently, like a fish's. Masker wasn't trying to speak, but he backed away, looking wildly around, clearly unsure what to do, where to run....

A shot erupted out in the darkness. Masker yelled. Blood spurted from a hole that suddenly appeared in his belly. He doubled forward, gripping his middle, making high noises in his throat.

The horse moved a little beneath Ben. His smile faded.

The second shot caught Masker in the top of the head and drove him back. He hit the ground dead, just as the horse spooked and ran forward, pulling out from beneath Ben. As the rope squeezed incredibly tight around his neck, Ben saw Champion run out of the clearing and into the forest, away from where the shots had come.

And then the pain became too great, the choking too intense, and Ben felt his consciousness begin to fade, his feet kicking wildly, his hands struggling with bonds that would not give, and his neck burning, stretching, constricting, unable to pull in air, unable to do anything but hurt like nothing had ever hurt him before.

The bonfire flickered brightly, shooting sparks to the sky. Then, in Ben's eyes, it began to grow faint, the flame losing its brilliance, dying away with his consciousness, fading toward nonentity like the spark of life inside him.

Jake Woolard opened his eyes and found himself gazing into the fire. His face hurt, and felt wet and warm. He tried to move and found it difficult, but a second effort succeeded and he sat up slowly. He touched his face, grimaced, and pulled in a sharp breath.

His face was laid open and bloody; he fancied that he had just touched his bare jawbone, exposed in the midst of the wound.

He looked at the fire, trying to think, and his eyes drifted to a rope tied to a tree.

He remembered, and came to his feet. Miraculously, he did not fall. "Judy," he said. "Judy."

But Judy was not there. He looked around the clearing.

No one was there. Not Champion, not any of his men.... And where was Ben?

There, on the ground. Lying flat on his face, unmoving, with a rope around his neck. Jake stared. "Ben?" His eyes drifted up and saw the other portion of the rope still hanging from the limb above Ben. It appeared that Ben had been hanged, and the rope cut while he was still swinging.

Jake stumbled toward his brother and fell to his knees beside him. "Ben, are you alive?"

He touched him. The flesh felt warm. He pressed Ben's shoulder.

A groan. Ben was alive.

"I'm going to roll you over, Ben. Going to roll you over so you can breathe...."

It took almost all his strength to do it. Ben was limp and unhelpful in the effort, a deadweight sack of flesh and bone that almost struggled against him. Even so, in a few moments Jake had him on his back.

After that he just stared at Ben's face, watching him suck

in air, watching him gradually come to life again, like some sunken swimmer slowly rising to the surface of the water.

Ben opened his eyes.

"Ben, it's me. It's Jake. They hanged you, Ben. But somebody must have cut you down."

Ben groaned again.

"It wasn't me who did it. I was out cold...you were already on the ground when I came to. Ben, where's Judy? Where did they take her? Where's my daughter?"

Ben seemed to be trying to speak, but his throat was damaged. He had no voice.

"Can you stand, Ben? Do you have the strength?"

Ben managed to nod.

"I'll help you...we'll go back to town, get help. Come back and find Judy. Got to find Judy."

Rising was difficult for Ben, and when at last he was on his feet he wasn't sure he could remain there. But with his bleeding, gash-faced brother serving as a human crutch at his side, Ben managed to take one step, then another. On and on, over and over, until they were in the dark forest, heading along the trail toward town.

"Who did it, Ben? Who cut you down?"

Ben tried to answer, but still that crushed throat was unable to produce sound.

They walked on, hurting and weak, but growing stronger in the effort. They would make it. Reach Ferguson, and find help.

And somehow, they would find Judy. Somehow.

———

They did find her, without even trying.

Moving along the street, two battered brothers, they attracted much attention from Ferguson's nocturnal populace. Crowds of gaping men parted like water before a ship's prow as the pair moved along, holding each other up, heading for Jake's house. Jake talked to those around him, urging them to help him find his girl, babbling on about old Civil War bushwhackers and lynchings and men who were supposed to be dead but weren't, and no one paid heed because they couldn't make sense of it.

They continued down the street together, and when they neared the place where the Cathedral had stood, Ben saw something that stunned him so that his voice, or a part of it, stirred to life again.

"Jake... it's Judy." A coarse, soft whisper, but Jake heard it and understood.

"Where, Ben?"

"There," he whispered, and pointed.

And indeed she was there, weeping and terrified, seated in the lap of a woman who held her close and caressed her gently. An angel, she appeared in the eyes of the two men. A kind angel, comforting a girl who had been through an ordeal no girl should have ever had to face.

Judy saw her father, and the tears abruptly stopped. She stared at him, saw the wound, and for a moment her expression was impossible to read. Then she wailed out again, left the lap of the comforting woman, and ran to her father, throwing her arms around him and sobbing against his chest.

"There, girl, there now," Jake said. "It's all right, dear heart. It's all right."

Ben, leaving Jake with his daughter, walked slowly toward the woman, who stood to meet him. She was a pretty woman, hair unkempt but beautiful nonetheless, dress tattered and a little large, yet flattering and feminine. Her gaze was unblinking and firm.

It took Ben several moments to comprehend that he was looking into the face of Deborah Bray.

CHAPTER 22

It was after midnight. Judy sat alone by the stove, on her stool, a plate of food in her lap. Untouched. Not a bite had been eaten, and her stare had hardly broken from the opposite wall in the last fifteen minutes. She'd asked to be left alone, and her wish had been granted, though they had to nearly tear her mother away from her. Sally Woolard slept now, having taken an opiate to calm her ragged and ruined nerves. Jake, his face now stitched back together, slept beside her, similarly drugged. Andy was no longer in the house. He'd been taken off by the doctor to be placed in a bed at the doctor's private little ward, where he could be watched. But prospects looked good for him. He was expected to recover.

Ben walked in slowly and looked at Judy. Her eyes drifted over and met his. He advanced and sat down slowly in a chair near her.

"I know you want to be alone, but you and me need to talk," he said. His voice was still a whisper and would remain so for a long time, until the rope bruise healed. "About what happened out there. And the person who helped you."

"Did you see him, Uncle Ben?" Her voice was a whisper, too, but he did not know if this was because she was unconsciously mimicking him or because she sensed the need for confidentiality.

"No. Just a shadow of movement, that's all. But I think I know who it was. I heard his voice later, when he called out to Henry Champion. Did you hear that?"

"No. I was running then. That's what he told me to do. He cut me free, carried me off on his shoulder, away from that place, and set me down on the trail. He pointed his finger and told me the way to go. And he told me to run. It was hard to see him well in the dark, because his skin was—"

"No, Judy, don't tell me that. It's best I don't really know. That way, if there are questions, I don't have to lie. I don't want you to tell me any more about how he looked, what kind of man he was, anything like that. Do you understand why I don't want to know?"

"No."

"Because this man, if he's who I think he is, is a good man, but he could be in trouble if it was found out what he did."

"Because he let me go?"

"No. Because of what he did after that."

"What did he do, Uncle Ben?"

Ben hesitated; this did not seem the kind of thing to be telling a child. "He...destroyed them. He killed them."

"All of them?"

"I don't know. I only saw one of them actually die. A man who was shot in the clearing, from out of the darkness."

"I heard the shots. While I was running."

"But I think he killed others, too. Champion, the leader, sent his men out into the dark to find him, but he found them instead. I believe that when morning comes, the law will explore that claim and the area around it, and I believe they'll find the bodies."

"Did the man in the dark kill the leader?"

"I don't know. Champion ran away, out of the clearing,

away from where the others had gone, and from where the shots had come. I don't know what happened to him after that."

"Are you going to tell the law people about the dead men, Uncle Ben?"

"I've been thinking about that, Judy, and I don't think I will. I don't want to get this man into trouble. He saved my life. Henry Champion planned to hang me. And the horse did go out from under me, but somebody cut me down before I could die. It had to be the man...the man in the dark, like you said. It couldn't have been your father, because he was unconscious. And something came to me a few minutes ago, Judy. When I came back to consciousness again, the body of the man who had been shot in the clearing was gone. Somebody had taken him away. It must have been the man in the dark."

"Why would he take away a dead man?"

"To hide him, I suppose. To protect himself."

"Maybe he took the others away, too. Maybe they won't find them when they look."

Ben knitted his brows. "You know, Judy, you may be right. I hope you are. I don't want this man to get into trouble. What he did was a good thing. Those men deserved to die."

"I know."

"So you and me, we'll say nothing about that man, all right? I mean, it was dark. And you can't see people clearly in the dark, right? Maybe you just found an old knife blade on the ground, and cut yourself loose."

"Right."

"And I never saw any of those men who went into the woods actually get killed. And the one I did see get killed... maybe it was my imagination. I was on the back of a horse, about to be hanged. A man might imagine any number of things at a time like that. Right?"

"Right."

"So I'm thinking, maybe I won't say anything at all about seeing anybody get shot. I might be wrong about it, you see, and I'd hate to be wrong about a thing like that."

"You're right, Uncle Ben."

"Maybe we'll both just kind of not say too much about anything at all, huh?"

She smiled, very slightly. "Maybe we won't."

He hugged her. "I'm glad you're not hurt, Judy."

To his surprise, she kissed him on the cheek. "I'm glad you're not hurt, too. And the man in the dark. I hope he's not hurt."

"I have a feeling he's just fine."

"I think I want to eat my food now."

"You go right ahead, honey."

———

The Reverend Bray was at the door come morning. Haggard and weary, having not slept at all since his daughter was brought to him, he was nevertheless a happy man. His daughter had been found. He knocked on the door, and Ben answered.

"Hello, Reverend," he whispered raspily. "Come in. Is Deborah with you?"

"She's right here." Deborah stepped out from behind him. Ben gazed at her a few moments, still unused to seeing her in feminine dress. He wondered where she'd found the dress. Someone's castoff, perhaps. It was ragged and stained, but she made it look good anyway. "Deborah wanted to speak to you. She and I have been up all night, talking. Good talk."

"Please, come in." Ben stepped back and let them enter. "I'm sorry for looking like I do. I been sleeping on that sofa yonder. The others are all still in bed. The doctor gave Jake and Sally something that pretty much knocked them out."

"How's your neck?" Bray asked.

Ben gingerly touched the red, tender place where the rope had bruised him. "Sore. And my voice ain't the same. But the doctor tells me no real harm was done."

They sat down. Ben could hardly keep his eyes off Deborah, and yet found it hard to keep them on her at the same time. She was the same, but not the same. A stranger now, even more so than before.

"Deborah has something she wants to tell you," Reverend Bray said.

Ben looked her in the face and waited.

"Ben...I told you false things before. Stories about my brother, and my father being dead. They weren't true."

"I know. Your father already explained things.'.'

"But I want to tell you myself. I didn't really lie to you, because what I told you, I thought it all was true. My mind, you see...things aren't right. With my mind."

Ben smiled because he didn't know what else to do. "You seem fine right now."

"Yes... for now. It's been that way with me. There are times when everything is clear. The clear times last for a long time, sometimes. Then the clouds come. From somewhere. And I start to believe in things again that aren't true."

Ben knew nothing about mental illness. What could he say to her? "Maybe this time the clouds won't come back at all."

"We may only hope and pray," the reverend murmured.

She lowered her head. "Sometimes, when the clear times come, I don't remember all of what happened when the clouds were there. But this time I remember one thing. The fire."

Ben was sure she was about to admit to him that she set the blaze. He didn't want to hear it. He didn't want to associate this lovely woman with the death of Roscoe Hammel. "Deborah, please...if you're going to say what I'm afraid you are, I'd rather not know."

"Do you think I'm going to tell you that I set the fire? I'm not. Because I don't know. I remember the fire, but I don't know how it began. It's not clear... the clouds are there. But I'm afraid...afraid it was me. Because I've done it before, in my worst times. There have been other fires."

"Listen to me. You don't know how that fire began. I don't know. Nobody does. You can't assume you caused it."

"But neither can I be sure I didn't."

"So what are you thinking of doing?"

Reverend Bray cleared his throat and answered in her place. "We don't know what to do. Who can we turn to? Am I to take my own daughter to the law and tell them that maybe she was the cause of a fire that killed a man? It would be wrong to do that without being sure. Yet do we not owe it to that poor man who died to open up every possibility to examination?"

"To what end? Roscoe can't be brought back."

"Yes, but—"

"There is nothing for you to do now, Reverend, but to take care of your daughter, speak only what you know really is, as opposed to what merely might be, and to, well...pray. You ought to be familiar with that process. Pray. Ask that the truth come out, so that you can quit wondering."

"You honestly believe we are under no obligation to voice our suspicion to the authorities?"

"I honestly do." Ben pondered how strange it was to have a preacher, of all things, come to him for moral advice.

"Then we'll take your advice. We'll keep quiet for now, and pray for the truth to be told. Whatever it may be. And when it is...then we'll deal with it."

Ben smiled. "I think that's the wisest course."

"Yes. Thank you for your counsel. And for all your help

lately, and...before. When Deborah was still, as she says, clouded."

"No thanks needed. But, Reverend...there's something you can do for me."

"You merely have to name it, sir."

"When you're doing that praying, also pray for a fellow I know, I don't want to say his name, who might need some protection. Pray for this fellow, if you would. That he'll not find trouble for a thing that he did."

"A bad thing?"

"No. A good thing."

Bray nodded. "We'll remember your friend, Mr. Woolard. Just as you ask."

———

The marshal arrived an hour later, throwing around questions in an irritable and almost accusatory fashion. Who did the kidnapping? Where are they now? What did they mean, Henry Champion the bushwhacker really was alive? That was the same talk that crazy gold-toothed black boy had talked. Did they not know that a man of the law had no time to waste on foolishness?

When the marshal was gone, Jake shook his head. "So much for all those notions of this fellow being the peace officer Ferguson needs. I believe maybe the way he handles his cases is just to complain about having them, accuse all the witnesses, then ignore it."

"Let him ignore it," Ben said.

"What? You don't want to get to the bottom of this? You don't want to see justice administered to those men?"

Ben stood. "I believe it likely that it already has."

———

The first of Reverend Bray's prayers was answered the next day. He held a copy of the latest newspaper edition in his hand and wept as he read the story: A local drunk had confessed to starting the fire that destroyed the Cathedral of Rest and took the life of one Roscoe Hammel. The motive as yet remained unclear, but evidence backing up the confession had been found and the man was in custody, awaiting indictment.

Ben saw off Bray and Deborah later the same day. They did not wish to linger in Ferguson any longer than they had to now that the only matter holding them was eliminated.

"What will you do for her?" Ben quietly asked the preacher, out of Deborah's earshot.

"All that I can," he replied. "There are new things being learned about the human mind, I'm told. People who can perhaps help her to keep those clouds of hers away. But I'm under no illusions. She's done this before, moving from insanity to lucidity, all in the snap of a finger. But it has never lasted. Always she goes back. Always there are more clouds."

Ben looked at her, perched on a wagon the preacher had hired to convey himself and his daughter out of the mountains. She was a lovely lady, appealing despite the storm that he knew brewed inside her. He thought briefly of what might have been had circumstances, both his and hers, been different. Then he put out his hand and shook that of Reverend Bray.

"God go with you, sir, and keep the clouds away forevermore."

"Amen, my friend. Amen."

Ben watched the wagon rumble away, then turned back toward the house, feeling for the moment quite sad, and quite lost in clouds of his own.

CHAPTER 23

Ben heard the tapping on his window and sat up. A storm had swept in, lightning flashing, wind rattling shutters and making the roof creak, but the sound he had heard was not the result of the weather.

As he squinted toward the window, a lightning flash revealed something there, an object that moved and fluttered.

He rose and opened the window, momentarily letting in rain and wind. Retrieving what he had seen, he closed the window again, cranked up the lamp that burned low beside the sofa upon which he slept, and read the soggy note he had just snared. It had been pinned in place on the windowsill beneath a fist-size stone.

Ben did not lie down again for the duration of the night. When the note had dried, he lit it in the lamp and let it burn to ash on the hearth.

When Sally rose to cook breakfast, the storm was past and Ben's sofa was empty. He had dressed and left with the first light of dawn.

Walking on this particular terrain gave Ben a very troubling feeling. He looked about, seeing the place by daylight for the first time. There was the mule pen, empty now. Apparently the marshal and his deputies had removed all livestock since there was no one seemingly about to see to its care. There was the tree, with the rope that had hanged him still swinging from the limb. It looked quite innocent now, nothing to gain anyone's attention. After all, many folks in these mountains hung their foodstuffs in sacks from ropes just like that, to keep them out of reach of animals.

The place where Masker had died revealed no bloodstains. Someone had stirred the dirt considerably and managed to mask them all. As for any bodies being found close by, there had been none that Ben had heard of. Someone had removed them. The same someone, Ben was sure, who had made Masker's corpse vanish, and who had left the note on the windowsill a few hours before.

Ben stood in the middle of Henry Champion's claim and wondered what had become of the old bushwhacker. He'd fled in pure fright into the night, then vanished as if the earth had swallowed him.

"Ben."

The voice startled him, though he had been expecting it. He turned. "Howdy, Roanie."

"You doing all right, sir?"

"I'm fine, thank you."

Roanie Piatt looked closely at him. "What happened to your neck?"

Ben narrowed his eyes. "I kind of figured you knew what had happened to my neck. How somebody strung me up from that tree yonder the other night, and then somebody else cut me down in time to save my life. Yes, sir, I figured you'd already know all about that."

"How would I know that, sir, unless I'd been close by to see it?"

So now they understood each other, and how this conversation was to progress from here on out. Nothing said directly, words carefully chosen, some things mutually known but mutually unspoken. Ben agreed with that approach. Better that way, in case the marshal ever should decide to do his job after all, and launch a true investigation.

"Good point, Roanie. I suppose you don't know a thing about what happened here at that."

"Only what I've heard, sir, from this man I talked to."

"What'd that man have to say?"

"He said there was a bunch of men killed hereabouts the other night. Said there'd been some poor little girl took prisoner to lure some others up here after her so they could be killed. But this man, he'd been watching this here claim close for some reason. Spying out them who worked it. When he seen them two men coming up unarmed, he fell in behind. Followed. This man, he seen what was going on, and decided he might ought to help out. He got the little girl free, this man did, and that drew a whole gang of bad men into the dark, after him."

"And what happened after that?" Ben asked.

"This man I talked to... he hinted around to me that maybe he killed them bad men, one at a time. Out in the dark. Didn't say it to me direct. Just hinted. And then, later on, maybe this man gathered up all the dead ones and hid them where they'll never be found."

"I see."

"Yes, sir. And I'm thinking that maybe it was this man who cut the rope you was hanging from."

"If that's the case, then I owe this man my thanks," Ben said. "You'll tell him for me, won't you, if you see him again?"

"I surely will, sir. But this man, I won't be seeing him. He's long gone now, sir. Long gone. Miles and miles away."

Ben nodded. "And what about you, Roanie? You planning to maybe leave, too, like this man did?"

"Maybe, sir. Maybe that'd be a good thing. You know, there's always folks who want to stir up trouble. Like marshals and such. Poking around, stirring up things, accusing folks of this and that that they don't know nothing about."

Ben said, "You know, that man you were talking about might have been worried that somebody would stir up trouble for him. Accuse him of something. Maybe that's why he left."

"Maybe so, sir."

"Too bad he didn't know that the marshal and his deputies came up here and poked around and didn't find a blessed thing. No dead men at all. He hid them well. And from what I hear, the marshal doesn't have much heart to go poking any further. I hear he's not sure that anything happened up here at all, and don't much care even if anything did."

"I suspect, sir, that this man would still have left even if he knowed that. He ain't the kind to take chances. And besides, maybe he just don't want to be around these parts no more. For personal reasons, you could say."

"Makes sense to me."

"Well, sir, I'm glad you and me run into each other. Funny how that just happened. Especially since this man told me there's something he'd like you in particular to know. Said you didn't need to worry about Henry Champion no more. He said he could promise you firm that Henry Champion won't never bother you nor nobody else ever again."

"That's good news. I wonder how it is that this man could know something like that?"

"Sir, I wouldn't know. Sure as the world, I wouldn't.

Maybe this man tracked down Henry Champion in the dark after he run off, and took care of him."

"Maybe he did."

Roanie tipped his hat. "Well, sir, I believe I'll be going my way now. Don't expect we'll see each other again."

"I'm glad I got to know you, Roanie. Mighty glad."

"Me, too, sir. Good-bye." Roanie turned and began walking away, up toward the Goatbeard.

"Roanie...wait. If you were to see this man again, the one who cut my hanging rope, and if you were to ask him for me how Ben Woolard could know for absolute certain that Henry Champion was gone, what do you think this man would say?"

"I believe, sir, that he might say there was an old abandoned mine claim up two miles beyond that there Goatbeard peak. I believe he'd tell Ben Woolard to maybe go pay a visit there sometime."

"Maybe Ben Woolard will do just that. Good-bye, Roanie. And thank you."

"Ain't no reason to be thanking me, sir. I ain't done a thing. Not one thing."

He turned again and walked away. Ben watched him until he was out of sight.

————

This was one of those claims that obviously had not come to much, for it had been abandoned early. Ben, winded from the long trek, looked the place over, puffing hard, hurting in every joint and every bruise ,and of these he had plenty.

A shed stood nearby and he looked inside, holding his breath. Nothing. It was empty. An examination of every hole and crevice and nook failed to reveal anything of Henry Champion at all. Ben stood frowning, wondering if he'd come to the wrong place, or if Roanie had deliberately misdirected him.

He sat down and rested for almost an hour. He still hadn't adjusted fully to this thin, anemic high-mountain air. Pulling in big lungfuls of air, he tried to satisfy his body's craving for oxygen.

And in the process he caught a foul whiff of something. The breeze had shifted. He stood, wrinkling his nose and frowning. Quite a stench. Looking into the wind, he saw that it was blowing toward him over the mouth of the mineshaft.

A miner's "gallows" stood over the shaft. And from it, a rope descended into the dark hole. A rope not hanging loosely, as would be expected at an abandoned claim, but pulled tight.

Ben advanced to the shaft. The stench grew stronger. Something dead and decaying. Or someone.

He looked into the shaft and saw only black shadows. Testing the rope, he found that indeed there was something quite heavy at the unseen end of it, stretching it tight.

Ben put his hand to the pulley crank and began to work. The rope inched up slowly, heavily weighted. He had to stop and rest three times before at last the job was done.

Henry Champion's back was toward Ben when his body finally emerged from the shadows. Ben fixed the pulley in place and backed away, hand over his mouth and nose. The smell was terrible, making him want to retch.

Ben stared at Champion's back for a few moments, then circled the shaft to see the face. An ugly, blackened face, eyes half open and sunken, lips swollen and drawn back, revealing the interior of the mouth.

Ben looked close, and winced. Every tooth had been pulled out of Henry Champion's head.

Ben shook his head. "Roanie, I wonder why that man you met went and did a thing like that. I surely do wonder."

Ben pulled out his folding knife. Placing one hand over his mouth and nose again, he advanced toward the hanging body of the late Henry Champion, reached out, and sawed the rope in two. Champion's blackened corpse dropped into the shaft below him.

Ben Woolard folded and pocketed his knife, and turned his steps toward Ferguson and home.

Henry Kidd,
Outlaw

Chapter 1

Lightning seared through the sky, silhouetting the abandoned water tank on its teetering tower, illuminating the barren, water-swept main street of what once had been a town. The young mountaineer, far from his home and his element, saw by the lightning's flaring light the broad flatlands, the chaparral blown flat by the wind, the wind-whipped river, the horizon far more distant than any the cloistering mountains of his childhood years had ever allowed him to glimpse.

He saw it all but scarcely noticed it. His attention was on the dark, lean rifleman who darted across the muddy street, headed for the cover of a narrow alleyway between empty buildings.

Oblivious to the rain that buffeted him on this dark Texas afternoon, Marsh Perkins left his own refuge behind a rotting pile of ancient firewood and mounted the boardwalk in front of the vacant saloon. He ran down the creaking porch, heading for an alleyway of his own when the rifleman fired off a shot that smacked into the wall just beside him. By reflex, he lunged to the right through the gaping and glassless front window of the abandoned saloon.

He hit the floor hard and felt its rotting wood yield beneath him. Marsh plunged through splinters and grit to the cool, dank ground below.

The wind knocked out of him; he lay there unmoving for a few moments, stunned at first, then realizing that fate had—perhaps—just done him a favor. He crabbed forward, looking out through a gap in the crumbling foundation. More lightning. The rifleman was there, not fully visible, peering every few moments around the edge of one of the buildings siding the alleyway.

Marsh checked his rifle—an unusual weapon with a revolving cylinder like that of a pistol—and quickly reloaded the three cylinders he had already emptied in this gun battle. Working his way closer to the opening in the foundation, he looked out again, positioned himself as comfortably as possible, and nestled the familiar butt of the rifle against his shoulder.

He took aim at the place where the outlaw Henry Kidd had last thrust out his head. "Go ahead, Kidd," Marsh whispered through gritted teeth. "Get curious. Wonder where I am. Stick that head out one more time and take a look."

The moment he did, Marsh Perkins would be ready. He would fire the shot that would end Henry Kidd's life and bring to an end, at last, the long quest that had led him to this remote part of Texas all the way from the mountains of western North Carolina. It would be over, thank God, and he would be able to go home and report that he had done what he'd been sent to do.

There it was, the quick look, the head popping out from around the edge of the building just like the turkey heads that Marsh used to shoot off back in Carolina at turkey-shoot competitions down near the trading post. Turkey behind a log, corn scattered at its feet, head bobbing up and down, up and down... Turkey shooting was a matter of

timing. Of being ready, of sensing when and where that head would next appear...

Henry Kidd bobbed his head out, then quickly withdrew it again. Marsh had missed his chance. He gnawed at his lower lip, disappointed. A trickle of mixed sweat and rainwater dripped from one eyebrow, stinging his eyes. He kept ready, kept his aim steady, waiting for that next glance around the corner. Henry Kidd's last look at the world.

It came. Marsh was ready. The finger squeezed, the pistol-style cylinder in the rifle revolved, the hammer fell...

A dead click.

For the first time in Marsh Perkins's experience, the rifl given to him by his grandfather, a rifle the old man prie from the clutching fingers of a dead reb bushwhacker, faile him. He couldn't believe it. He pushed the rifle away, glarin at it in disbelief.

Quickly, though, he turned his attention again to tl alleyway in which his nemesis hid. The next cylinder wou not misfire. He settled the rifle against his shoulder agai squinting down the barrel, aiming at the precise spot frc which Kidd had been looking out.

Lightning, more wind, a harder surge of rain... but Henry Kidd. Had he moved?

There he was, darting out and across the street. T move was unanticipated; Marsh wasn't ready for it. He ag missed his chance to get off a shot.

Thunder rumbled across the flatlands. Magnificent, d thunder... but when it had rolled off into the distance, M; detected another kind of rumble, coming from the e; itself. What the devil? Then he knew. Horses, many of th coming in a hard rush.

The rumble grew louder. They passed. Marsh saw blur of their mud-slinging hooves as they passed the fror the old saloon that hid him. He heard voices, shouts, the hammering percussion of rifles blasting.

"Got him!" someone yelled. "We've killed Henry Kidd!"

Marsh went weak. Kidd was dead?

Who were these men who had just done his work for him?

He felt a draining mix of relief that, at last, the quest was over, but disappointment that it had been others who brought it to an end. He had traveled many miles and endured many hardships to bring down Henry Kidd, and it seemed unjust that any but him should end Kidd's life. In fact, he'd always believed, based on something told him by his grandmother, that it was actually his personal destiny to be Kidd's destroyer.

He crabbed forward again, working his way out of the gap in the foundation. He tried to make little noise because he didn't want to startle this band of armed strangers.

Just in case, he lifted his rifle high above his head as he walked toward the riders. He counted ten of them, several now dismounted and gathered around the body of the man Marsh had tracked for so long.

When they detected Marsh's approach, a couple of men reacted quickly by leveling weapons at him. Marsh just kept on approaching, though, his rifle held aloft to show he was not going to use it.

"Who are you?" one of the riflemen yelled in a threatening tone.

"Marsh Perkins, out of North Carolina!" he called back. "I heard someone say Henry Kidd is dead. Is it true?"

"He's deader than stone," someone said.

"Look at him... just a rawboned kid," another said, and Marsh couldn't tell if he was talking about him or Kidd. The description would fit in either case. Both he and Kidd had the boyish kind of look that made them seem ten years younger than they were.

"What are you doing here, boy?" the first man

demanded. All this gang of strangers was looking at him now.

"I was shooting it out with Henry Kidd before you rode in," Marsh said. "I've been tracking him for months now. I come plumb out of North Carolina to get him."

"Carolina!"

"That's right."

"How do we know you ain't a partner of Kidd?" another man challenged.

"You don't," Marsh replied. "That's why I'm handing you this rifle." He turned his rifle over to the man, who inspected it.

"I ain't seen one of these in years!" he said.

"My grandpap gave it to me and told me to kill Henry Kidd with it," Marsh said.

"You've missed your chance, boy," a man said, and the others chuckled.

Marsh went to the dead man's body, which lay prone on the ground. He rolled it over with his foot. The face was muddied, but the rain washed it away in moments.

"No, I ain't," he replied. "I don't know who this is, but it sure as the devil ain't Henry Kidd."

CHAPTER 2

A hulking fellow in a big coat eased out of his saddle and walked heavily over to Marsh's side. He had a gray, wide mustache and small eyes. He'd not said a word so far.

He spoke now. "You sure about that, boy?"

"I'm sure," Marsh replied. "I can see how anyone might think this was Kidd from a distance.

Same build and general look. But it ain't Henry Kidd."

"Then we've been mightily fooled."

"No more than me. I thought it was Kidd, too. If I'd been closer, I'd have been able to see it wasn't."

"My name's Campbell. Andrew Campbell. I'm the sheriff here," the big man said. "You say your name is Perkins?"

"That's right, sir. Marshall Perkins. Most call me Marsh for short."

"And you've been trailing Henry Kidd all the way out of North Carolina?"

"I can't say I really started trailing him until I got to Texas. But I came to Texas to find him and kill him, so in that sense, yes, I've been tracking him all the way from Carolina."

"Why?"

"He murdered three men and a woman back in Carolina, where I live. Killed them and mangled them up just for meanness. One was my father."

"When was this?"

"Back during the war."

"What? You been tracking Kidd for a decade?"

"No, sir. Just the last six months or so since I've been able to pick up his track."

The sheriff evaluated Marsh for a few moments. One of the other men nudged at the dead man with his foot and said, "Maybe this ain't Henry Kidd, but it sure as hell is the man who killed Rogers."

The sheriff said to Marsh, "Sounds like you've got a story to tell. I want to hear it. I'm requesting that you come back with me to my office and tell it once we deal with this dead man here." Then he turned to the man who had just spoken. "Yes, this is the man who killed Rogers. We were just wrong about it being Henry Kidd."

"There's been a murder, then?" Marsh asked.

"Yes. An old man used to be a dentist until his fingers got all stiff and sore in the joints, and he couldn't work no more. He was robbed and murdered by this fellow on the ground here. We got a posse together, sniffed out his track, and trailed him here to the ghost town. Looks like you were ahead of us."

"I thought it was Kidd," Marsh said. "He's around here, somewhere. I know it for a fact because I've tracked him for eighty miles. I reckon I've lost the track now, though. This dead man here led me astray."

"You're right. Kidd is in the area. I got a wire out of Hooper County saying he was believed to be coming this way. That's why we believed it was Kidd who killed Rogers. You're certain this ain't Henry Kidd?"

"I'm certain."

"I'll need you to fill out an affidavit to that effect and sign it. You read and write?"

Marsh Perkins stood up a little straighter. He was literate, one of the few who were in his remote mountain home in an obscure part of western North Carolina. "I can, sir."

"Good. Well, gents, let's gather up this dead man and get him back into town. Maybe somebody will be able to figure out who he is."

"Even if it ain't Kidd, it's a good thing we got him," one of the others said.

"It is," the sheriff said.

"But it means Henry Kidd is still out there," Marsh said. "And that's real bad."

"I can't argue with that," Andrew Campbell said. "Henry Kidd alive means other people dead. And it's meant that for way too long."

"It'll end once I finally get hold of him," Marsh said.

"You speak with confidence."

"It's from being a Perkins. A Perkins is always confident, especially when it comes to hunting."

"Manhunting included, eh?"

"Especially manhunting."

The lawman nodded. "Let's you and me go talk some."

"Let's do," Marsh replied.

CHAPTER 3

The dead man was on the slab at the local undertaker's office, coffee bubbled on the stove in the sheriff's office, rain pattered on the roof, and Marsh Perkins sat on a chair with Campbell as his enthralled audience.

He had just signed the affidavit vowing that he knew the face and general appearance of Henry Kidd and that the man killed by the sheriff's posse was not said, Henry Kidd. Now the affidavit was laid aside, and Campbell leaned across his desk, lower lip sagging as he listened and occasionally responded to Marsh's tale.

"Let me understand this," he said. "Kidd actually cut the dead man's face after he killed him?"

"Into a kind of smile, that's right," Marsh said. "Cut away the flesh of his jaws so that the hole angled up like this." He ran a finger along the side of his face. "Then he dumped the corpse in the midst of the road so that we would find it. He wrote his name on him in blood. 'Henry Kidd,' just like he usually does."

"Why'd he kill him?"

"Because my father had refused to give him an old saddle. Kidd demanded it. No right to it, no grounds for claiming it, but he demanded it. It wasn't my father's, though, just on loan to him, so he couldn't give it away even if he wanted. We later figured that he made the demand just so he would get turned down and have a reason to kill him. Not that Kidd needs a reason."

"He does it for pleasure, from all I hear," the sheriff said. "I've heard of people like that, but never until now have I brushed up this close to a real live one."

"My father was a good man. A churchgoer who'd do no wrong to nobody. He'd even tried to stay clear of the war because he had folks on both sides and couldn't bear to go against none of them. But Henry Kidd wouldn't bear a man like that to live. Had to kill him."

"How'd Kidd come to be in North Carolina? Born there?"

"Ain't nobody knows. If he was born there, it wasn't in the same parts as me. He just showed up in the mountain country one day, him and some other bushwhacking types. No more than bandits and killers, really. The war meant nothing to them except as an excuse to kill."

"The others he murdered... he mangled them, too?"

"He always mangles them he kills. At least when he has the chance. He's a man with a demon in him, my grand-mammy always said. A man with a demon in him. I believe it. I've never run across so wicked a human being."

"You couldn't have been more than a boy when all this happened. You look to be little more than a boy right now, to be honest."

"I look young. Always have. Baby-faced, they call it. Baby-faced Marsh. I used to fight boys who called me that."

"So, how old are you?"

"Twenty-four years old."

"I'd put you at seventeen, not a day more."

"I'm twenty-four. I'll vow it on a Bible."

"About Kidd's age?"

"I'm about four, five years younger than Kidd, I figure it. I was fourteen, maybe fifteen when Kidd did his murders in Carolina."

"I don't understand this. Henry Kidd shows up, murders folks in your neighborhood, and then, a full ten years later, you get sent after him by... by who?"

"By my grandmother, most directly. By the community as a whole, really. They picked me to do the job that needs doing."

"Why you?"

"Because I'm the best tracker and hunter that ever come out of the Stone Creek valley. And because back during the war, me and my uncle, Harve Jonely, tracked down a horse thief who'd beat a farmer nigh to death. I was the one who found his trail, and when he shot Uncle Harve out of hiding and left him wounded, it was me who tracked him up a steep ridge with the sun already setting... and brought him back."

"Dead or alive?"

"Dead."

"You were a tough and hard young man."

"I was what I had to be. I was what the mountain made me and what the war made me. I still am."

"So this quest for Henry Kidd... how exactly did it come about, and why did you wait a full decade to do it?"

"From the day Henry Kidd vanished from the mountains, my granny had it in mind that someday one of her men would find him and avenge them he'd murdered. She had a vision of it... things like that happen with her. But she always thought it would be my pap who did it. Not me."

"Why not your uncle?"

"He died. His heart. He wasn't an old man, but it failed him like it says in the Bible. Young men's hearts failing them. You probably know that verse."

"I don't go to church as much as I should, to tell the truth."

"Well, Pap died, and it fell to me to be the one to go after Henry Kidd...but there was no sign of him. No way to know if he was even still among the living. Until that newspaper, I showed you arrived."

The sheriff reached to his desk and picked up a crumpled, yellow newspaper page that Marsh had shown him earlier. It was a Texas paper, a small-towner, mostly news reprinted from the bigger papers from San Antonio and Dallas. But there was one item, the story of a murder in which the victim had been left mangled. The murderer was gone, but it was thought, according to the paper, that it was a drifter named Henry Kidd."

"How'd this newspaper get back to North Carolina?"

"It was mailed there. A man who'd grown up on Stone Creek and lived there through the war sent it to my granny. He'd come to Texas after the war, wanting to be a cattleman. He saw the story, remembered. He mailed the newspaper back because he knew we'd need to know."

"And so now you're here."

"Yes."

"How'd you have the traveling money?"

Marsh hesitated at this point. To answer that question fully was something he naturally balked at doing because it involved a secret that was kept among the mountain folks. But here, miles away in Texas, it probably didn't matter. He cleared his throat and, for the first time in his long journey, revealed to another person the source of his quest's backing.

"Old Sam Bird. He's a Cherokee who's lived up in the mountains above Stone Creek for as long as the mountains have been there... or so it seems, anyway. Everybody knows that old Sam has a mine. The purest silver, Cherokee silver. See the sight on this rifle? That's some of it. He mounted that sight for me told me it would bring me good luck. But the main thing he did for me was to give me coin."

"Counterfeit?"

"I guess so, in one way of looking at it. But purer silver than anything the government ever pressed out. That's how he's got by with it. His money is worth more than its face value, so nobody who has it gets hurt."

"You got a coin of it on you?"

Marsh reached into his vest pocket and pulled out a rough-edged silver disk, and plopped it down before the sheriff.

"There's one. I don't carry many of them. Most of them are in a bank. Anytime I need to, I just send a telegram, and they'll do something or other to get money to me. I don't know just how it works because I ain't had to do it."

"So you're a wealthy man."

"No. Just fixed well enough to keep going for as long as it takes to find Henry Kidd."

"But you ain't found him yet."

"I've come close."

"When you came to Texas, where did you go?

"Looking for the man who'd sent the newspaper. And I found him. I said a prayer for him by his grave."

"Kidd?"

"That's right. They said he'd gone after Kidd himself. Found his track and decided to take care of the job himself. Henry Kidd left him hanging upside down by one foot with his throat cut. The name 'Henry Kidd' carved into his forehead. So they told me."

"And Kidd himself was gone."

"Like always. He kills and vanishes. Nobody can catch him, not lawmen, not possess. The army went after him one time. But he just disappears. Like a ghost."

"Or a devil."

"He's worse than the devil."

"You know, son, it's probably not right for me to sit here and tell you that you're doing the right thing. The law ain't something a man should take into his own hands."

"I'm not taking the law into my own hands. Henry Kidd's a wanted man."

"There's a reward, that's true."

"The only reward I want is to take his right hand back to my granny. There's a scar on it, they say, that marks him like a brand. She wants to see it and know he's dead."

"I've heard about that scar. A circle with a kind of slash through it."

"I need to tell you something. Marsh. A man who kills like Kidd kills draws attention. There's plenty of others after him now. Sooner or later, one will get him, especially since there's a reward. It may not be you."

"It'll be me."

"How can you be sure?"

"My granny. She saw it in a vision."

The sheriff toyed with the silver coin again, watching it glint in the light of the lamp, then handed it back to Marsh. "I like you, son, though you frighten me a bit. I'm always frightened by men who are obsessed with something, even something so righteous as bringing down Henry Kidd."

"Make me one promise: When you do what you have to do, stay on the right side of the law. Watch out that going after a devil don't turn you into a devil yourself."

Marsh dropped the coin into his pocket. "I'll remember that, Sheriff. I will."

CHAPTER 4

It would not be hard to remember. From what he knew about Henry Kidd, Marsh had nothing but loathing for the man Kidd was. Robbery Marsh could understand if the robber was desperate and in true need. Even killing could be abided if a man did it in self-defense. But the kind of crimes Kidd committed often had no secondary motives and seemed to be done for their own sake. They were foul, wicked. Cruel. More than anything else, cruel.

The hotel in this Texas backwater was nothing to grow excited over. Most of it was on one floor, a long, low structure reminiscent of many Mexican dwellings, but over part, there was a second story. The man behind the counter was a mix of Anglo and Mexican.

"Room for you?" he asked Marsh in heavily accented English.

"Yes, *si*."

"You are in luck...business is slow," the man said, grinning with a flash of gleaming yellow.

"Sorry to hear it."

"It was a joke. Business is always slow," the man explained.

"Oh." Marsh could have figured as much.

"Except for when cowboys come through, looking for women of sport. You like women of sport, *si?*"

"I always steer clear of them," he said.

"Maria, you'd not steer clear of, Maria is a beauty. I'll send her by, no?"

"No."

"You should see her before you say that."

"Is every hotel in Texas a whore parlor?" Marsh had experienced something almost exactly like this in two other locations.

"Not everyone. Just the best ones."

"Don't send anybody by my room. Not Maria, not anybody. I want to be left alone."

The man looked disappointed and shook his head subtly. Marsh wondered how much of Maria's earnings he took for his referral services.

Supper was taken in a small cafe down the street. Steak, eggs, and biscuits, the latter soaked in good gravy thickened with flour and served well-peppered. It was late for coffee, but Marsh had three cups anyway because he craved it. And he needed its mind-sharpening effects to help him plan his next move.

How could he track Kidd now? The trail had been broken. He could have cursed himself for letting himself get off onto the trail of the wrong killer. What were the odds that two young murderers of similar physical appearance would be in the same area at roughly the same time? But it had happened, and now Kidd was out there somewhere, and Marsh had no way to track him down.

He ate a piece of rhubarb pie for dessert, making it all the better by having sugared cream poured over it, and finished off his coffee. He paid with coins—not the silver coins he'd brought from home, but with currency, he'd traded them for at a bank three or four towns back. He realized how fortunate he was, having resources to travel without having to odd-job his way along.

But self-sufficiency had a price. As it was, depending on no one, he was always alone. Following the bloody trail of a moving murderer, he had little cause to stay long in one place. With no work to do, his contact with other good people was minimal and short-lived. He was left to live with thoughts of little but where Kidd was, where Kidd was going, what Kidd would do next...and where the next mangled body would be found.

It was depressing. He longed for it to be over so he could return home, his promise fulfilled, and have a bit of peace again, and think of something besides the devilish young murderer who obsessed him.

In an odd, twisted way, Marsh had developed a sort of admiration for Kidd. Not for what he did—he loathed that —but for his ability to do it without ever being caught. It was downright astonishing that a man could commit the kinds of crimes Kidd did and get away every time. Posse after posse had pursued him, lawman, after lawman had sworn to get him. None had.

A few had wound up dead for their efforts. There was a terrible story out of Arkansas about a county marshal who left town to find and kill Henry Kidd—and came back in dragging on the ground behind his own horse, his foot tied to the stirrup and most of his face cut away. They said the man's own mother was the first to see him making his last homecoming.

Marsh wasn't sure he believed the story. Kidd's crimes were so horrific that it was inevitable that legend would grow up around him. Some said he'd killed twenty people over the last two years; Marsh had it figured at more like ten, maybe twelve.

But you never could be sure. An active killer like Kidd might have victims no one even knew about, drifters who could die and be missed by no one. And Kidd required no reason to kill. He did it for its own sake whenever the mood struck him. Who could say who might have died by his hand in places where the crime would never be detected?

Marsh in some ways knew Henry Kidd better than any other man, though he'd never truly met him, not in the face-to-face, words-sharing kind of way. He'd seen him twice from a distance, for certain, and one other time closer at hand... not so certain. It might have been another case of mistaken identity, like today.

He wondered sometimes if Henry Kidd had seen him in turn and would remember his face whenever the day came that Marsh put a bullet through his heart.

If Kidd knew, somehow, that Marsh was following him, Marsh figured Kidd was more flattered than worried. Henry Kidd was proud of his sinful work. Only a proud man would do what Kidd did to his dead victims, only a man struttingly pleased with his own wickedness.

With his belly full, almost to discomfort, Marsh walked the dark streets of the town. He wasn't tired enough to go to bed or willing to endure the boredom of sitting still.

His horse was in the livery, his weapons locked in his hotel room, except for the one small pistol he wore beneath his coat, a hideout gun that he carried in violation of the laws of most towns, probably this one included. He didn't worry about it. Most men carried guns somewhere on their person, and it wasn't an issue unless a show was made of it. Marsh couldn't afford to be unarmed when his quarry was one such as Kidd. There was always that chance of rounding a corner and encountering Kidd. Should that ever happen, Marsh did not intend to be unarmed.

———

He detected the man behind him as he turned a corner. Big fellow, broad, yellowish hat that was much battered and greased, clothing that was dusty from the trail so that the color was hard to make out. Though he moved in shadows, it appeared that his hair was sandy, nearly blond. He wore a mackinaw and boots; no more details than that could Marsh make out.

Marsh made no show of having seen the man but walked nonchalantly along the boardwalk onto which he'd just turned and ducked into the first alley after the next turn. When the man passed, looking here and there in an uncertain way, Marsh stepped out and gripped his shoulder, pulling him around to face him.

CHAPTER 5

The man almost jumped out of his boots. "What the—"

"You looking for me?"

The man, who had a ruddy face and eyebrows that were so light they blended right in with his skin, was speechless a few moments, then burst out laughing. This surprised Marsh, to say the least, and he actually took a step back and began to slowly reach for his pistol.

"Something funny?" he said.

"Nothing but myself... What a fool I am to let myself be outsmarted by a boy!"

The accent was nothing American but subtle and hard to place.

"I'm no boy. Haven't been for years."

"Well, you look it. You look like you've still got mama's milk on your lip there. Or might that be the start of a wispy mustache?"

Marsh could tell he didn't like this fellow. Anyone that would trail a stranger in a strange town, then mock him to his face, was unusual if nothing else.

"I do believe it's a mustache," said a voice from behind.

Marsh turned and saw another man, similar in size, coloration, and accent to the first. He'd approached while Marsh was preoccupied with the first fellow. "No lap child, this one, though he may look it."

"Who are you men, and why were you following me?" Marsh demanded.

The first man laughed again and stuck out a big hand. Marsh wasn't inclined to take it and didn't, for fear the man would yank and restrain him while the other pilfered his pockets.

"Very well, then," the man said, lowering his hand and remaining as jovial as ever. "I suppose a man is right to be wary of strangers. So I'll make us strangers no longer. My name is Knutsen. Rolph Knutsen. This is my brother, York."

"Pleased to meet you, young manhunter," York said.

Manhunter? What was this all about?

"I'd say I was pleased, too, except I don't know why you were following me."

"Simply wanted to meet you, that's all. We have something in common, you and us," Rolph said.

"We're on the track of Henry Kidd," York said.

Marsh eyed them cautiously. "Bounty hunters?"

"Indeed. There are sizable rewards being posted for bringing in Henry Kidd, both private and public. We intend to claim them all," said Rolph.

"Too bad for you, I'm afraid," York said condescendingly. "We heard it told of you that you've trailed him all the way from the East."

"Who's been talking about me?"

"There's a deputy sheriff here who loves to drink, and when he drinks, he tells what he's overheard young manhunters saying to the local sheriff."

From the smell of York's breath, Marsh surmised he enjoyed drinking, too.

"That's right," Rolph threw in. "He tells us all about this

eager boy manhunter from the East who says he's trailing
Henry Kidd, and about how this boy manhunter nigh got
himself killed today trying to do what should be left to
grownup men... and it ends up the man he thinks is Henry
Kidd isn't Henry Kidd at all! So York and I look at one
another and decide we need to meet this boy manhunter and
tell him to go back east and leave the tracking to men who
know what they are doing."

"Yeah," said York, though it sounded more like "Ya."

Marsh looked at the brothers. "Well, gentlemen, I have to
disappoint you because I can't back off from what I'm
doing. I've gone too many miles to quit now. And I made a
promise that I'd bring back Henry Kidd's scarred hand to
show that those he'd murdered back home have been
avenged."

The brothers glanced at each other and laughed. "You're
going to cut off his hand?"

"That's right. I'll cut it off, pack it in salt, and take it
back to North Carolina."

They laughed again. "You should be in dime novels,"
Rolph said.

"Ya," York chimed in. "They could call it 'The Boy
Manhunter Who Went After Henry Kidd's Hand and Got
Killed.'" They roared. This apparently was high humor in
their book. Marsh stared at them, not even blinking.

The laughter died, and Rolph suddenly was serious. He
thumped a forefinger on Marsh's chest. "Listen to me, boy
manhunter. That reward is ours. You nor anyone else will
get it."

"Ya," York said.

"I'm not after reward," Marsh replied. "I just want
Henry Kidd."

The brothers laughed again. Rolph had a touch of
alcohol on his breath, too, Marsh detected. He wasn't sure
what was funny about what he'd just said.

"You let it go, boy. Get back home to your mother," Rolph said.

"Ya," said York. "We're the ones who have the track now. Not you. Go home, or we'll shoot at you."

Track? These men had a lead on Kidd? Marsh wasn't sure how much credence to give that claim, but if it was true...

These men had just gained themselves a follower, like it or not.

"If you want to go after Henry Kidd, go after him," Marsh said. "I can't stop you. But you won't stop me, either."

"You stay away from Kidd and from us," Rolph said firmly. "You don't, we'll make you regret it."

Marsh said no more. Simply stared at them.

"You understand us, ya?" York said.

Marsh just kept on staring.

The brothers looked at each other, laughed, and went on their way down the street, talking in a language Marsh could not understand.

He waited until they were nearly out of sight and fell in behind them.

Chapter 6

I f they had a lead on Kidd, they didn't follow it right
away. They wound their way to a saloon, drank for an
hour, and came out staggering drunk. Marsh followed them
again and smiled to himself as they entered the same hotel in
which he had a room.

As drunk as they were. Marsh was sure they would not
rise earlier than he, and he was right. By the time the sun had
cleared the horizon, he was already up, out of his room,
making breakfast out of a cold biscuit he had filched from
the cafe the day before. His horse was saddled, and he
watched the hotel with infinite patience, nibbling his biscuit
slowly.

They emerged about nine o'clock, a little earlier, actually,
than Marsh would have guessed. Even from a distance, their
hangovers showed in the way they squinted, the way they
moved, the grim looks on their faces. They went to the livery
and emerged with their horses, took them back to the hotel,
vanished inside, then came out again with saddlebags packed
with a few goods they threw over their mounts.

Booted Winchesters rode beside them on both saddles,
and they wore large Colt revolvers in open defiance of the

town's gun-carrying prohibition. But it didn't matter; this pair was obviously leaving town anyway.

They rode out, and Marsh followed, keeping at a distance and, he hoped, out of their sight for as long as possible. He had only a meager hope that they actually had some kind of lead on Henry Kidd's whereabouts, but a meager hope was better than none, which was all he had otherwise.

Marsh found it amusing that it took the supposedly crack manhunters more than two hours to realize they were being followed. Rolph, who had seemed the less dim of the pair, was the first to see him, and he twisted around in the saddle and pointed in agitated fashion. When York saw Marsh, he pointed as well. Two fools, Marsh thought. He could imagine their invisible eyebrows knitting together as they tried to figure out what to do.

At first, they did nothing. They simply rode on ahead, a little faster than before, as if they could outrun him that way. It was futile. Marsh stayed with them, actually a little closer than before because now there was no reason to hide. Eventually, they did what he anticipated. Rolph took out his rifle, aimed it high, and fired it a good thirty feet over Marsh's head.

He didn't think they'd ever actually try to shoot him— they seemed like fools more than murderers—but he took the message and fell back. He let them get ahead, almost out of view, then fell in behind again, riding off the trail so that the meager brush hid him, at least part of the time.

He didn't know if they really knew where Henry Kidd was, but they did ride like men with a clear destination in mind. With nothing better to do, Marsh Perkins would continue to follow.

Port McGee had run the little blacksmith shop near his house for fifteen years, and he did good, steady business despite a crotchety attitude about life. All the citizens of the Black Fork community knew him and joked about him and his eternal sourness, made up for by his very sweet and friendly wife. Port knew his reputation and was smart enough to play along with it, acting sometimes more sour than he really was because, oddly, it was expected and good for business.

He had just immersed a horseshoe in a bucket of cold water when the young stranger came in, slipping off his hat and nodding in a friendly manner. Port nodded back, eyeing the remarkably ugly newcomer, who was clad in somewhat oversized clothing that had not been washed in weeks and whose hair stuck out like stiff straw from his somewhat misshapen head.

The newcomer sniffed loudly and said, "Howdy, sir. I see you're making a horseshoe there."

"That's right."

"I need you to make one for me."

Port looked down at the young man's feet. "Don't make 'em in that shape."

This comment seemed to throw the young man. He frowned, mumbled something, then chuckled. The chuckle grew to a full laugh, but it wasn't pleasant to hear, as most laughs are, but a sporadic coughing sound, interspersed with loud sniffs. The newcomer swiped his sleeve under his nose, and Port noted with un-revealed disgust how crusted the sleeve was.

"You were joking me," the young man said. "Took me a minute to get it."

"Aw, I just don't smile enough when I tell my jokes," Port said. "Folks tell me that all the time. What happened? Your horse throw a shoe?"

"Yep."

"I'll take a look."

Port followed the young man outside. A pale mare stood there, looking underfed and ill-used. One shoe was gone. On its back, though, was a fine saddle, quite expensive and out of keeping with the ragged and impoverished look of both owner and horse.

Port took measurements, grunted, and rose. "I'll get your shoe made right now if you don't care to wait."

"I'll wait," the man said. "Glad to have company. These are dangerous times hereabouts."

They went back into the smithy. "You're talking of Henry Kidd, I reckon."

"Yeah. Scares me to death to have such a killer roaming about. Makes me afraid to ride alone."

"I don't blame you. I keep an eye out myself."

"Hell, I'm as afraid of the posses and the lawmen as I am of the killer hisself," the visitor went on. "A man my age and size, out riding, why, they might think I was Kidd."

Port was hard at work on the shoe. "Could happen. I hear tell that over at Palmerville, they shot a killer and didn't know until after that it wasn't Henry Kidd. They thought they'd killed the murdering son of a bitch." He glanced up at his visitor as he said this. "Too bad they didn't, huh?"

The fellow gave a flickering smile. "Yeah."

Silence held a few moments while Port hammered and shaped and worked the bellows and tongs. The visitor wandered over to the window that looked toward Port's house.

"What's that smell?"

"Dried apple pie," Port replied. "My wife makes it at least once a week. Best in Texas."

"I believe it. Smells real good."

There was a loud sizzle and hiss of steam as the horseshoe descended into the bucket. Port pulled it out again and laid it aside to cool.

The stranger turned and found Port standing there with a small revolver aimed at him.

"Hello, Mr. Henry Kidd," Port said. "I knowed it was you when you rode up."

"What the hell?"

"You heard me. Now get that gun belt off, slow, and toss it over toward the corner. One hint of a slick move, and I'll shoot this pistol and not quit until all six bullets are in you. You understand me, you murdering bastard?"

CHAPTER 7

The visitor's face lost all color, and his eyes went wide. He drew back his lips in a ghastly way, revealing his dirty and uneven teeth. And to Port's surprise, a great circle of dampness suddenly spread down his canvas trousers. The fellow had actually peed himself!

The first flicker of doubt came into Port's mind. Maybe this wasn't Henry Kidd after all. Would a cold-nerved killer who laughed at posses and vanished like a ghost time and time again pee his own pants just because somebody drew a pistol on him?

The newcomer fell to his knees. "Oh, God, oh, Lordy... don't kill me! I ain't no Henry Kidd! I swear it!"

"The gun belt!"

Weeping now, face twisted and streaming with tears, the terrified man fumbled at his buckle, loosened the gun belt, and tossed it to the corner as he'd been instructed. Then he thrust his hands high in the air as if trying to touch the ceiling from his kneeling position. "Please," he said again and again. "Please don't kill me, don't kill me, don't kill me..."

"Shut up and stand," Port ordered, trying to sound authoritative and like a man with a definite plan, though in fact, he was making this up as he went along. "Turn around and clasp your hands behind your back. Don't let go."

The young man nodded and complied. Port glanced about, looking for something to tie him with and also realizing he had a logistical problem: How could he tie up this man without laying down his pistol?

His wife was up in the house; they could go up there, and he could have her hold the pistol while he tied up Kidd... if it really was Kidd. He certainly hoped it was. If not, he might have bought himself a whole wagonload of trouble he didn't need.

It all was very uncertain, though. Emily probably couldn't shoot anyone if she had to. But he wasn't willing to let her be the one to tie him, either. He didn't want her getting that close to him in case he grabbed at her.

He remembered something, all at once. Over in the shed was a pair of irons he'd made for a past sheriff. They'd gotten damaged along the way, had been brought in and repaired, then the sheriff lost the election, and his replacement never came to collect the irons. They'd work perfectly to hold this man. Port would make him put them on himself.

"Out of here," he ordered. "Walk toward that shed."

"Oh, no, no... You're taking me out to shoot me!" The crying intensified.

"I ain't going to shoot you. I'm going to put you in irons and take you to the sheriff. He can sort this out. If you ain't Kidd, you can prove it to him, not me. I ain't taking no chances."

The fellow went a shade paler. "I think I'm going to get sick."

"Don't do that. You've already got piss all over my floor. I don't want no vomit on it too."

"I'm feeling mighty weak."

Good Lord, the young man was actually about to faint! It was more doubtful by the moment that this was the infamous Kidd. Henry Kidd was cold and hard and shaken by nothing, or so folks said. This behavior didn't fit.

"Don't you pass out! Get up like a man."

"I'll try... I'll try..." He started to rise, then his eyes went out of focus, almost crossed. He moaned and flopped over onto his belly, right into the puddle of his own urine.

Port muttered a curse and went over to him, grabbing him by the back of the collar and yanking up. "Get up from there, you sorry, son of—"

The young man rose swiftly, a lightning-flash move, and something bright in his hand flashed as well. Port grunted and staggered back, suddenly weak, and looked down to see profuse bleeding from his stomach.

The other was on his feet, and at him, in scarcely the time it took for Port to realize he'd been stabbed. The knife flashed again, again. Port dropped to the floor, limp as a rag, no longer able to hold the pistol. Yet he somehow managed to teeter on his knees and not fall over completely, not yet. His foe reached down and swept up the fallen pistol.

"I'd have left you alone if you'd left me alone," he said, a grin on his ugly face. "Hey, how'd you like the peeing? That throws them off every time. Ain't nobody believes that Henry Kidd would do that. But let me show you the kind of thing Henry Kidd does do!"

He glanced over and saw the hammer on the anvil. He picked it up, hefted it in his hand, and raised it. Meanwhile, he cocked the pistol and aimed it point-blank at Port.

He brought down the hammer hard on the anvil and pulled the trigger in tandem with the ringing blow, which masked the sound of the shot. Port fell over. The shooter laughed, proud of his timing, and tried it again. Once more, perfectly simultaneousness. The third time was just as well-timed.

"Did that well, didn't I!" he said to the dead man on the floor.

Then it struck him: The blacksmith was dead, and the shoe was not on his horse. He'd have to do it himself as best he could.

Swearing violently, he fired another bullet into his victim, along with another hammer ring, just for dying on him at an inconvenient time. Then, because it was his way to do such things, he kneeled and mutilated the face. Not as much as he sometimes did, for he felt potentially exposed here, with the wife in the house. Still, he made the blacksmith look horrific. At last, he gathered up tools, nails, the horseshoe and went outside. He moved his horse up a little so that it was hidden from view from the house and did a clumsy job of putting on the horseshoe. He wasn't sure it would hold and again cursed the blacksmith for having gotten himself killed a little too soon.

Briefly, the murderer returned to the smithy and poked around. To his delight, he found an excellent Winchester rifle locked in a cabinet with boxes of ammunition. He loaded up his new treasure, found a rifle boot that would fit his saddle in addition to the one he already had there, and returned to his horse outside.

He mounted and glanced toward the house. The scent of that pie reached him again. He'd surely love a piece of it. But maybe there was somebody else in the house beside the wife. Instinct told him to forget the pie and go on. The wife was lucky; she'd live this time. Other times he might have just sent her soul over Jordan to join her husband's.

He rode back the way he'd come for a little over a quarter-mile, then turned into a grove alongside a small stream.

"I got the shoe replaced," he said to the person awaiting him there.

"Good, Starky," the other replied. His way of speaking was that of a simpleminded man.

"We need to go on now. Get your horse. We need to ride.

I got that feeling again. Somebody's after us, and we need to move fast."

"There's blood on you, Starky. You smell like pee. You wet your pants, Starky."

"Never mind all that. Let's move."

"Did you hurt somebody again, Starky? Did you kill somebody?"

"Shut up! I'll not say it again: Let's move!"

CHAPTER 8

Marsh had to hand it to the two Knutsen brothers. Dullards though they seemed, they'd managed to lose him, and that was no easy task when it came to Marsh Perkins, who folks back in Carolina claimed could track a will-o'-the-wisp through a windstorm. He was glad those same folks couldn't see him just now, outsmarted by two hard-drinking idiots with no visible eyebrows.

He stopped, made a fire by the roadside, and cooked some bacon. At the moment, he was at a loss. No track of Henry Kidd, nor of the two men who claimed they had a notion of where Kidd was. Right now, there was nothing to do but wait and keep his ears open for news of another Kidd murder.

It was a horrible way to track a man. Sometimes it made Marsh feel a little ill when he thought about it. Ill, and astonished, too. How could such a violent man have gone so long, so far, without being caught?

There was another mystery about Kidd: What had he done during the years between his wartime crimes back in Carolina, Tennessee, and—some claimed—Georgia, and the present, when he'd turned up murdering again in Texas?

Had he lived peaceably during all that time, only to bloody his hands again all these years later?

Marsh nibbled his bacon and pondered it all. He doubted Kidd had gone a decade without killing. Murder seemed too much part and parcel with the man to imagine that he had ever gone long without it. No, Kidd must have been in some other part of the country, or maybe out of the country altogether. Mexico or someplace.

Marsh looked across the Texas landscape and felt very lonely. It was like that at these times when the trail was cold. When he was on the chase, preoccupied with Kidd's next move, he thought little about home and all the miles he'd come. When the trail was cold, he had time to reflect and to miss his kin and his beloved, familiar mountains. He couldn't wait to get back again. When he did, he'd never talk about this time of his life. He'd never bobble grandchildren on his knee and talk about the time he traveled all the way to the great West to find the murderer who had ravaged the home community. He knew others would tell the tale, and he couldn't do anything about that, but he'd not take part himself. He wanted only to finish this, then forget it.

With the meal done, he led his horse to a nearby stream and let it graze nearby while he leaned back against a tree, tilted down his hat, and took a brief, shallow nap.

He never lost full awareness of what was going on around him, but he did lose track of time. When he stirred back to awareness again, the sun had traveled far across the sky. The afternoon was well underway.

Marsh's horse was a trusty one and never wandered far. He mounted and rode, following nothing but instinct now. Kidd was to the west. He couldn't prove it, didn't really have any particular intuition about it, in fact. He just had to go somewhere. And the Knutsen brothers had headed west, so maybe that was the way to go. Couldn't hurt.

He wasn't sure what made him look behind him, but

when he did, he saw a rider. Distant, hard to make out. For a moment, he wondered if it could be Kidd, but when he squinted and looked hard, he could see that the build wasn't right. This man was bigger than the wiry Kidd. He wore a long-tailed coat of some sort, perhaps a mackinaw or duster. Marsh watched him awhile, trying to ascertain if the man might be following him. He couldn't tell but decided not to linger and let the man reach him. You never knew these days where you might find danger.

He'd gone a mile when a delicious scent reached his nose. Cooking beef...maybe venison. The aroma of boiling vegetables and fresh biscuits mixed in, borne on wood smoke. He saw smoke clouds rising over the low hillside to the south. Lots of smoke... There was some sort of sizable gathering underway on the far side of that hill.

A glance ahead revealed a sign beside the road. He rode up close enough so that he could see it if he squinted, WOODHAWK, TEXAS, 2 MILES, the sign said.

He left the road and headed south, going up the rise to the top of the hill. There he stopped and looked down on a remarkable scene.

Wagons and tents were spread across a big expanse of land. Fires burned everywhere, and people milled about, cooking, eating, talking. Quite a few were reading, and though he was still too far away to see clearly what they read, he knew right away it was the Bible. There was a big brush-covered platform standing in the midst of the gathering, with a pulpit in the middle and a big wooden cross standing at the rear, with a few chairs scattered along the rear of the stage.

A camp meeting!

Marsh hadn't encountered one of these extended religious gatherings since he'd run across one in Tennessee while on his way west. He smiled, feeling a certain nostalgic warmth for a familiar institution that reminded him of home.

In the absence of new leads on Henry Kidd, he knew what he'd be doing the next couple of days. He'd visit this camp meeting, get to know some people, share some good food, and listen to a few stirring sermons. Who knew? Maybe he'd learn something here to help him find Henry Kidd.

He rode down toward the camp and was first noticed by a man who was dumping the dregs out of a coffee kettle. The man eyed him closely, with some suspicion, and Marsh knew just what he was thinking. Any lone young man in these parts these days could easily be suspected of being Henry Kidd. Especially a baby-faced one like Marsh. He was reminded anew of how careful he should be.

The man evidently decided that Marsh didn't look like a killer, for he smiled and nodded a greeting.

"Hello, brother, and good day to you," he said to Marsh.

"Howdy, sir." Marsh looked around. "Mighty big camp meeting."

"Yes indeed. Have you traveled here to join with us?"

"To tell you the truth, I wasn't even aware of it. I just sort of stumbled across it."

"It's a good one, now in its third day, and going strong." The man walked up to Marsh and put out his hand. "Bailey Jones. I live over at Woodhawk."

"Marsh Perkins, out of North Carolina."

"North Carolina! Well, I had some people from there. Your speech is like theirs. What part of the state?"

"Western. The mountains."

"Beautiful place. But mighty remote and rugged. A lot different than Texas, huh?" Yes, sir.

The man had not, and would not, ask what had brought Marsh all the way from North Carolina. There was a code on the western plains that said a man's business was his own. Inquisitive people were not looked on in a kindly way. Even now, Marsh wasn't sure whether Jones was being truly friendly or simply trying to get close enough to him to keep an eye on him in case he really wasn't who he said he was.

"I'd like to invite you to join the meeting," Jones said. "There's been much moving of the Lord's power here. People are turning to God in a time of distress."

"What distress would that be?" Marsh already knew, but he didn't want to be the one to bring up the matter of Henry Kidd.

"There's a terrible, pestilent murderer in these parts just now. People are afraid and with cause. Have you ever heard the name, Henry Kidd?"

"I have."

"Then perhaps you know what I'm speaking of."

"I was in Palmerville and heard the subject being discussed. There was a killing there, and people thought Henry Kidd had done it. But when the posse killed the murderer, it turned out to be someone else."

"I heard the same story myself, only this morning, from another family that rode in to join us. Kind of an ironic thing, I guess... Henry Kidd being so wicked is causing people to want to be more good. This camp meeting seems the place to be... for practical reasons as well as religious ones. There's safety in numbers. People feel safer in the midst of a crowd, safer than if they are isolated off in their own homes."

"Makes sense."

"Come join us. We've got food."

"I just had some bacon a while ago. Don't need anything right off."

"Join us anyway."

"I will."

"Maybe eat some supper with us later."

"I'll do that, too."

CHAPTER 9

Jones was one of those sincerely friendly people who have little pretense about them. If at first, he checked Marsh over pretty thoroughly, at last, he seemed to relax about him and take him at his word regarding who he said he was. Still no questions about purposes in being in the region and so on. And Marsh had not given up that information voluntarily.

If Bailey and his wife, a rotund woman named Virginia, were not prone to ask Marsh his business, their young daughter was not so reticent. She was about eleven years old, freckled and sandy-haired, and very forthright. The western code of silence wasn't a concept Martha Jones had yet fully grasped.

"What's your mother's name?" she asked Marsh at supper that night. The sky was darkening, and singing was underway over near the pulpit area. Three preachers were warming up to deliver at top volume as soon as the music had everybody softened up for the message.

"Martha, don't ask questions like that," her mother said.

"It's all right," Marsh said. "I don't mind it. Her name is

Emma June, Martha. Emma June Marsh. She was a Shelton before she married."

"I like the name Emma June. If I ever get a real doll, I might name her that."

"Honey, the dolls your papa makes you are real dolls," Virginia said.

"I mean a store-bought doll," she said. "With a china face."

She was a charming little thing. Marsh had a young cousin she reminded him of a lot. If he was near a store, and if the parents didn't mind it, he'd buy this girl a store-bought doll right now, with his own money. Of course, there was no store within miles except whatever typical kind of general store would be in Woodhawk, two miles down the way, and Marsh suspected it didn't sell dolls with china faces.

"What kind of work do you do?" Martha asked.

This time both parents chided her in unison. She looked puzzled and a little hurt.

But Marsh noticed both parents, then looked expectantly at him, unable to disguise their own interest in how he would answer.

"Well... right now, I'm not really working, in the usual sense," he said, measuring every word. "I have some support from family and friends back home while I search for somebody."

"Oh," Martha said, not really understanding. "Is it your brother?"

"No."

"Your father or uncle?"

"Martha, that's enough," Virginia said.

"It's not a relative. Just somebody who was in our community one time," he said.

It was clear, he hoped, that he would say no more. He wasn't about to reveal the details of his mission, not in front of this child and not in the setting of a camp meeting. He wasn't at all sure what kind of reaction he would receive.

"Martha, it ain't polite to ask people too much about their business," Bailey said. "Folks take offense to that."

"Ah, she's just asking questions like children do," Marsh said. He gave her a friendly wink. "No problem, I can see."

Conversation moved to other subjects, but Marsh heard little of it. He'd just spotted someone a few campsites over who, for the moment, had his full attention.

Her hair was auburn, her skin somewhat pale and completely unblemished. Her gingham clothing was modest, as one would expect of a decent girl from a decent, camp-meeting-attending family, but it did not fully hide a beautiful, very feminine frame.

But it was her eyes that made his heart race a little faster. Big, perfect, heavily lashed eyes that for a few moments caught his and held just long enough to make Marsh lose his breath.

He almost rose, almost went to her. But Marsh was shy; women at times actually scared him, though he had never dared admit it to anyone. Something in her eyes simply made him freeze, and when she turned and disappeared into the crowd, he was unable to pick her out again.

"Who was that?" he asked the Jones family in general.

"Who?"

"The young lady who was over there."

Bailey smiled. "Some young beauty has caught your eye; I take it."

Marsh was oddly embarrassed by the question. "Uh...no. No, she just looked like somebody I met before, and I wondered if it might be her."

Marsh had just lied in the midst of a camp meeting. He wondered how serious a sin it was.

"I don't see who you are talking about."

"She's gone now. Never mind. It wasn't important."

The preaching began, and Marsh learned just how deeply the presence of Henry Kidd had affected this part of Texas. The danger of the present moment was the subtle, or sometimes not-so-subtle, undertext of almost everything said or shouted from behind the pulpit. Marsh found himself caught up in the sermons, inspired by them, but not in the way most would be. His unique relationship to the subject at hand made the sermons quite personal to him, and when one of the preachers began openly talking about the "demon roaming these plains" and the "pale horse of death" that had the region in fear, Marsh trembled with awareness of the importance of his mission.

The third preacher, less fiery than the first two, preached a sermon not as obviously inspired by the depredations of Henry Kidd. Using the text "Here am I, send me," he sought to inspire evangelistic fervor among the flock.

But the preacher halted the sermon abruptly, saying he felt led to do something unplanned. He had the big outdoor congregation bow heads in prayer. "O Lord," he prayed, "send us a protector, an avenger. Send us hope in our time of fear. Send us one who will destroy the wicked man, Henry Kidd, who defies your law and murders the innocent, young and old. Send us one who will face him without fear and persevere until the demon is slain. Send us one who will destroy the great evil, O Lord. Send us one who will go in the name of righteousness and avenge the innocent. Call his name, Lord, and let him answer."

Alone at the fringe of the crowd, Marsh Perkins bowed his head and quietly whispered, "Here am I, Lord. Send me."

CHAPTER 10

Dawn, the next day. People across the campground were beginning to stir; fires glowed, food sizzled on skillets. Marsh, always an early riser, had been up an hour already, as had the Jones family. Bailey Jones was talkative, but Marsh had an on-edge feeling he couldn't account for. There was something stirring in the air, a feeling not unlike that of a coming storm. But the sky was clear.

He saw her. An unexpected sighting, like the first one. She was walking across the camp, carrying a bucket of water dipped from the little spring that watered the campground.

In the dim light of morning, she looked even more beautiful than she had the day before. She had not noticed Marsh just now, as best he could tell, so he stared rather openly at her, thinking how perfect a creation she was and how much he wished he had the courage to speak to her. A murderous, maiming devil-like Henry Kidd, he could trail with little fear, but a pretty girl made him tremble and lose his words.

He watched her until she reached her campsite, where a man, presumably her father, took the bucket from her. She immediately went to tend the breakfast that was frying in a big iron skillet over the fire. Her mother, herself an attractive woman, though somewhat plumped by the years, joined her daughter at the fireside. A boy of about ten, probably a little brother, was receiving instruction from his father about some task or another needing to be done and not looking happy about it.

The sound of a horseman riding in fast finally drew Marsh's attention away from the lovely girl at the campfire. He turned to see a man coming at full speed, hardly slowing even as he entered the camp. He rode among the campsites at reckless speed and headed toward the arbor-covered pulpit, nearby which the preachers and leaders of this religious meeting had their tents.

That sense of foreboding that had affected Marsh increased. Something was afoot here, and the horseman's wild and desperate manner indicated it was not good.

Marsh quickly moved up through the camp in the hope of getting near enough to hear what was being said. But by the time he did, the words had already passed.

The Rev. Jonah Cacey, a bearded, somber, barrel-chested man with a long gray beard and the manner of an Old Testament prophet, was mounting the stage. It was not time for preaching, but clearly, he was about to say something.

"Attention!" he boomed from behind the pulpit. "All attention to me! Heed me, saints... I have news to give!" Cacey's voice was as loud as a cannon blast emanating from that big, resonating chest of his. No wonder he had such success as a preacher. It was Cacey who had given the prayer for a divine protector the night before.

"Gather near, saints," he said. "Come close so that you can clearly hear what I tell you."

People moved in from their campsites, faces somber because it was evident from Cacey's look and tone that his news would not be good.

As focused on Cacey as he was, Marsh still managed to sneak a glance across the crowd until he spotted the lovely young lady. When he saw her looking back at him, he quickly looked back to the stage. She did the same. Marsh's heart, already thumping fast, thumped a little faster yet.

Cacey's stentorian voice boomed. "There has been the work of Satan among the people of this region, yet again," he said sadly. "I must inform you of the murder and mutilation of Mr. Port McGee, the blacksmith, many of you, know well."

A gasp and murmur passed through the crowd, followed quickly by the sound of a few women beginning to cry and children tugging on their parents' coattails, asking in loud whispers for an explanation of what the preacher had just said.

"The evidence is that the work is that of the devil Henry Kidd, a man whose soul belongs to Beelzebub himself and who is the enemy of God and his people wherever he goes."

"God curse his soul!" a man shouted emotionally.

"My brother, the curse is already upon his soul, placed there not by God but by Henry Kidd himself, who has chosen the dark way over the light. And we bring a curse upon ourselves if we allow him to continue unmolested! The law has tried to find and destroy Henry Kidd; the law has failed. Hunters for bounty have gone after this human devil; they, too, have failed. Fathers now tremble in fear for their families, and children cry in their beds, comforted by mothers as fearful as they are. Can we allow this abomination to stand?"

"No!" many voices shouted in ragged unison.

"Then I call upon you, men of faith and courage, to go to your wagons. Fetch out your arms, put on the sword of faith, gird up your loins, and join me in pursuit of this demon from hell! We will form a mighty army of God, sweep this countryside, and sweep out this sinful creature! Let us ride out together and find this outlaw, Henry Kidd!"

The roar that went up in response to this was deafening.

Marsh was caught up in the same excitement that prompted it, but with it in his case was a strong sense of doubt. Though the preacher could call it an "Army of God" if he chose, in fact, what he was proposing was just one more posse, and Henry Kidd had evaded posses time and again. It was one of his dark talents.

Still, a man never knew what might happen. Maybe this time, it would be different. So Marsh, along with the rest, readied himself to ride, loaded up the revolver rifle, and sent up a prayer to heaven that today, at last, would be the day that Henry Kidd was brought down.

He was riding out with the big conglomeration of armed and determined men when he glanced to his left and noticed the object of his adoration watching him. Or was she looking at the group in general? No... she had her eye on him. He felt a thrill of excitement and hoped that he looked sufficiently dashing to impress her.

The Army of God thundered away from the camp meeting grounds, Cacey leading the band with his long beard blowing in the wind.

CHAPTER 11

Marsh was quite uncertain about this huge, informal, unofficial posse. No question that these men were motivated, and many of them were probably capable. The very size of the group, though, made it unwieldy and hard to hide. Henry Kidd would see this bunch coming from miles away. Marsh had his doubts that they would actually bring him in.

Nevertheless, there was something stirring about riding with such a purposeful and impressive group. Marsh felt like part of something big and fearful and righteous... and it did not take him long to realize that the immediate situation presented him a handy if somewhat self-serving opportunity.

Riding to Marsh's left and somewhat behind him was the father of the pretty young lady.

Here was a chance to introduce himself to the family, which might lead to meeting the girl a little later on.

Marsh drifted back, letting his horse fall in beside the man's. He looked for something to say, but before he could speak, the man spoke first.

"Quite a task we have before us, eh, young man?" he said to Marsh.

"Yes, sir." Marsh leaned over, hand thrust out. "Marshall Perkins, from North Carolina. Folks call me Marsh."

"Jim Serandon. You're a long way from home."

"Yes, sir. You live hereabouts?"

"Yep. Over the other side of Woodhawk. Got a little ranch."

"Family?"

"Wife and daughter. God knows it's a hard time to have a family, with a murderer roaming the countryside."

"I suppose your family is back at the campground."

"Yes. I'm grateful the meeting is going on. There's more safety with the crowd there. If not for that, I'd not be leaving them."

"You look like a young man; your daughter is small, I guess."

Serandon grinned widely. "Mr. Perkins, Marsh, you may as well come honest with me. I saw you taking notice of my daughter back at the campground. I figured she was the reason you drifted your horse over near me. Am I right?"

Marsh was stunned and to taken aback to speak. There was no real shame in what he'd done, but it was still embarrassing to have the plain facts so openly laid out by none other than the father of the girl he admired.

"Well...I...the truth is... I'm sorry, sir. You're right. She's mighty beautiful, and I couldn't help but think she looked like a fine young woman. I beg your pardon, Mr. Serandon."

Marsh began to drift his horse back over, away from Serandon.

"Hold up, Marsh," Serandon said. "No need for that. I know she's a beautiful girl. She looks just like her mother did at her age when first I laid eyes on her, and I was just as struck by her mother as you are. No need to go red-faced on me."

Marsh managed a grin but couldn't think of a word to

say. He rode along in silence, staring straight ahead, then started whistling softly in a forced nonchalance.

Serandon couldn't help but smile. "Marsh, maybe when this is done, you can join the family and me for supper."

"Maybe so. Kind of you, sir."

"I'll introduce you to Corinne."

Marsh nodded, no words. This was going well, in a way. Serandon was certainly open to him and not averse to his interest in his daughter. He'd actually received an invitation to meet her. But it was all a little strange and embarrassing.

It all faded into the background, though, when there was a flurry of loud voices and pointing fingers near the front of the band of riders.

Marsh at first could not ascertain what the commotion was about, but after moving a few paces spotted what those at the front had already seen: a lone man, mounted, out on the plains.

"It's Kidd!" someone declared. "We've found him, sure as the world!"

"Sweep down on him!" someone else hollered. "Don't let him outrun us!"

But the lone man on the horse didn't look interested in running. He sat slumped in the saddle, looking back at the Army of God, no doubt wondering what kind of strange conglomeration of armed humanity this was.

Marsh quickly rode forward, working his way through the band of riders until he reached the preacher Cacey. "Sir," he said. "My name is Marsh Perkins. I need to tell you that that man out there ain't Henry Kidd."

The preacher's gray eyes pierced him. "How do you know that, young man?"

"Because I've trailed Henry Kidd for months. I came from North Carolina, where he killed innocent folk back during the war, just to track him. I've not been real close to him, sir, but I've seen him from a distance and can tell you that ain't him. That man out there is far too big a fellow." Marsh looked at the distant figure and the distinctive long coat he wore. "I saw that man before, riding behind me, about the same distance he is from us now. I recognize his form and his coat. But I don't know who he is. But he ain't Kidd."

Others, who were not able to hear what Marsh said, just then whooped in unison and started to ride toward the man on the plains. Marsh looked at them in shock, afraid that some overeager avenger might actually gun the man down before asking any questions.

"Sir, you've got to stop them," he said.

Cacey, who had seemed uncertain the last few moments, suddenly became resolute. "Halt!" he called. "Desist, men! That isn't our man out there!"

The riders stopped, turning and looking bewildered. "That could be him!" one said.

"No," Marsh said. "I've seen Henry Kidd. That ain't him."

"Then who is he?"

"I don't know."

"I suggest we go find out," the preacher said. "But slowly and without threat. If he isn't Kidd himself, perhaps he will have seen something of him. Don't frighten him, men. Keep your guns ready but not leveled." Marsh swung out and joined the small band of riders, led by the preacher, who slowly traveled toward the lone man.

CHAPTER 12

I f the stranger was concerned by the approach of armed
strangers, he didn't show it. His posture in the saddle
was utterly relaxed; he exuded a confidence and fearlessness
that Marsh could detect from far away and had to admire.

It was obvious before long that this man was a Mexican,
though perhaps not fully. His eyes and nose had a distinctly
Anglo quality about them.

He was a fine-looking fellow, dark haired and somewhat
swarthy. His clothing was dirty from the trail yet fit his
broad-shouldered, narrow-waisted form quite finely. He
smiled at the riders who approached him.

The preacher spoke first. "Hello, sir. My name is the
Reverend Jonah Cacey, servant of the Lord. These men here
with me are saints and citizens of these parts, and we ride
together in search of one Henry Kidd, an outlaw, and
murderer."

The man lifted one dark brow. "You say much in a few
words, Reverend. I am impressed." His English, though
lightly accented with the intonations of Mexico, was
elegantly spoken. He put out a strong hand toward the

preacher. "I am Juan Carlos and am honored to make your acquaintance, sir."

The preacher shook Carlos's hand. "We held suspicion about you, sir, when we saw you from a distance, that you were, in fact, Henry Kidd."

"Any lone traveler in these parts is subject to that suspicion...which is a danger, eh, sir? Fear and caution can cause danger to the innocent...yet Kidd seems to roam free with impunity."

"You are aware of his depredations, I take it."

"Very aware, sir."

"Do you know anything of his possible immediate whereabouts? Seen or heard anything?"

"I know nothing. Only that Henry Kidd is a man pursued by determined avengers." As he said this, he looked directly at Marsh, which surprised Marsh, who wondered if the look was coincidental or meaningful. Coincidental, surely. How could this man know anything of who he was or his quest?

"There has been another murder," the preacher told Carlos. "A local blacksmith has been killed, and his body left damaged, as is Kidd's wicked way."

"You are a posse, then? I ask your pardon for this question, sir, but why would a posse be led by a priest?"

"Not a priest," Cacey said, somewhat snappily. "I am no Papist, sir. I am a preacher of the word of God. The men you see here are good men of this region who were already gathered for worship at an extended camp meeting a short distance from here. When we learned of the latest murder, we felt it our obligation to respond as a divine army, sweeping to find and stop Henry Kidd once and for all."

"My best wishes for your success," Carlos said. And he glanced at Marsh again.

There was something beneath the surface here. Marsh could tell it. Juan Carlos, whoever he was, seemed to know him, or at least know what he was doing. Marsh wondered who Carlos was and why he was here, riding alone at a place and time in which riding alone could get a man killed by an overly nervous populace.

"You are welcome to join us," Cacey told Carlos. "All help is welcome, and you are safer with a large band such as ours."

"Thank you, sir. But I have business that requires me to remain as I am."

As the smaller delegation of riders rejoined the larger body awaiting them, Marsh looked back. Juan Carlos was riding slowly away, circling toward the southwest, moving slowly. Marsh frowned, overwhelmed with curiosity about the man, wondering if he would encounter him again.

Cacey led his "army" onward, a band of Christian soldiers sweeping the plains with a sense of pride and cockiness that faded somewhat when finally they rode into view of the blacksmith shop where Port McGee had died.

The county sheriff was talking gently to the weeping widow when the Army of God came up like a band of angry angels. The corpse had just been removed by the local undertaker and was on its way to town in the back of an enclosed black wagon. The sheriff, who had been seated beside the widow on a rickety bench outside the smithy, came to his feet as the big band of riders rumbled in.

His face went red, and his eyes wide. The Reverend Cacey rode right up to the sheriff and dismounted with great dignity, and the sheriff all but grabbed his collar.

"Preacher, pardon my French, but what the hell do you think you're doing?"

Cacey puffed up and seemed to gain about a foot of stature. "We, sir, have come to learn the grim facts of this case and to chase down and destroy the outlaw, Henry Kidd." He paused and looked at the widow. "My condolences, ma'am, in this horrible time of loss. God will sustain you if you let him."

Another man, wearing the badge of a deputy, emerged from the smithy. He gaped to see the Army of God. "The tracks!" he bellowed. "Sheriff, they just trampled over all the tracks!"

"So they did," the sheriff replied. To Cacey, he said, "Do you see that, Preacher? We had a good, clear set of tracks left by the murderer, and now they're gone. All your horses here have trampled them away."

Cacey looked bewildered, but only for a moment. He wasn't one to let himself look disadvantaged in front of his audience.

"Well...regrettable, then. But it doesn't matter. With a band this large, we can sweep this countryside and find this devil, with or without tracks."

"Preacher, that devil has evaded posse after posse. You might catch him; you might not. Suffice it to say that without tracks, the likelihood is strongly lessened."

"Regrettable," the preacher said again. "Regrettable." He cleared his throat and looked vainly for something else to say.

"Regrettable, you say. Yes, indeed. If we fail to catch this bastard, Preacher, because of you trampling up his trail, I'll hold you personally responsible."

The preacher looked a little pale but soon collected himself. "Perhaps you should quit your profane complaining about our arrival and make use of us, Sheriff. I have an army of men here willing to look for the devil Henry Kidd until he is found. If we've trampled a few tracks, what of it? You saw which way they went, did you not? Let this army of righteous men sweep the entire countryside. We'll uncover him. Well, sweep the evil being straight into perdition."

"You may not have noticed just how big this entire countryside is, Preacher," the sheriff responded. "Your group is big, but the countryside is a hell of a... pardon me, a way whole lot bigger. Henry Kidd will see you coming long before you see him, and he'll vanish like he always does."

"I have every confidence God will deliver him into our hands."

"Beg pardon, Preacher, but I'd have been glad for the Lord to deliver him into my hands at any time, and so far, he ain't seen fit to do it."

The preacher and the sheriff argued, growing more vigorous by the moment. The widow wept; the deputy stood around looking angry...and Marsh moved toward the rear perimeter of the group of horsemen, staring off toward hills limned against the sky.

He'd just seen something.

CHAPTER 13

The glint of light on glass is what had drawn Marsh's attention. To the west was a line of low but rough-and-rocky hills, well covered with brush. From a gap between two rocks, he'd caught that quick flash of reflected sunlight, and a closer look revealed two familiar forms, kneeling in the brush and watching the commotion around the smithy.

He wondered if the Knutsen brothers had noticed him in particular and if they'd had any luck in finding Kidd. Probably not. If they had Kidd, they'd be trumpeting it proudly, hauling in his corpse over the back of a horse and heading for the nearest saloon for some liquid celebration.

Marsh kept watch on the poorly hidden brothers while also listening to the argument between the sheriff and the preacher. It seemed the preacher was on the losing end, the sheriff telling him that he had no use for posses formed outside the bounds of the law. Cacey's answer was that he served a higher law, but that did little to persuade the sheriff. It seemed likely to Marsh that the Army of God had gone as far as it would go.

Good enough for him. He didn't believe they would catch Kidd anyway. Time to discharge himself from the army and begin following the brothers again. Maybe they had a lead to Kidd or would stumble across one.

Quietly, Marsh rode away from the group, trying to draw no attention. It wasn't easy, and he was also aware that there was no way to do this without the Knutsen brothers seeing him. Probably they'd vanish well before he got near them, but at least he might be able to track them.

"Marsh!"

The voice came from the perimeter of the crowd. Marsh turned in the saddle. It was Serandon, riding out after him.

"Where you going?"

Marsh was irritated. He'd hoped he could just disappear. He saw no alternative but, to tell the truth.

"There are a couple of brothers I met who are looking for Henry Kidd like we are. They told me they had a lead on his whereabouts. Well, they're watching us right now, through field glasses, over in those hills."

Serandon looked in the direction Marsh subtly indicated. "I don't see... wait. Yes, I do. I see them!"

"I'm going to try to work around where I can follow them."

"You think they really know where Kidd is?"

"No. If they did, I doubt they'd be lying in brush watching us. But they've got a better chance of finding him than this big group does."

Serandon looked intrigued. He glanced back at the arguing sheriff and preacher. The fire was certainly being diminished in the Army of God. He turned back to Marsh.

"I'll go with you."

"Sir, there's no need for it. I've tracked Henry Kidd alone all this time, and I don't know I'd work well with somebody else."

"You've tracked Kidd? What do you mean?"

"I've been tracking Henry Kidd for months now. I came here from North Carolina to do it."

"Why?"

"He killed my father and some other good people back where I come from, a long time ago. I was sent to find him and avenge the dead."

Serandon rode out close to Marsh. "You telling me the truth?"

"Yes, sir."

"I'll be! Now I really do want to go with you. That's impressive, son! You're on a righteous quest...it's downright biblical!"

"I need to go, sir. I hope to see you again and maybe take you up on your offer of hospitality with your family."

"I'm coming with you."

"Sir, I—"

"No arguing. It's safer with two. I'm coming with you."

Marsh sighed. Clearly, there was no point in arguing. And probably it didn't matter. The Knutsen brothers probably had no more idea than did Cacey or the sheriff where Henry Kidd really was. He and Serandon would poke around a bit, follow the Knutsens if it was feasible, then head back to the campsite. "Very well, sir. But let's be as quiet as we can about it."

"Wait just a minute." Serandon went to another man and spoke to him. Marsh could make out enough of what was said to determine that Serandon was sending a message back to his family, not to worry about him if he did not return as soon as the entire band.

Serandon joined Marsh, his manner eager. Marsh had the odd sense that he, by far the younger of the pair, had a much more mature perspective on what was going on here. Serandon seemed to view it as something of a lark.

They rode out together, slipping southward until the swell of the land hid them, then circling back toward the hills where the Knutsens hid.

They reached the hills and found tracks there, but the two manhunter brothers were not in sight.

"We'll follow as far as we can," Marsh said. "If we find them, maybe we'll find Kidd, too. They claimed to have a lead on him, but I've got my doubts."

"Why would they say it, then?"

"Reward. They want it for themselves. I think they were trying to put me off to lessen the competition. They were afraid I'd get him before they did. And they're right. I will be the one who gets him. My granny dreamed it, and her dreams always happen."

"I'll be. She's never wrong?"

"Not so far."

They rode out, following the trail, but as all Marsh's trails had lately, it grew cold. Hours passed, the day rolled by. Marsh had food in his saddlebags, not much of it, and when shared with Serandon, it went twice as fast. He wished the man would just go away.

He had a bad feeling about him being here. It was something that just wasn't supposed to be.

———

While the sun declined toward the western horizon, the newspaper had literally blown into the hidden little camp that hid the two Kidd brothers. It had so startled Starky Kidd, the venomous young man known to the world as Henry, that he had whipped around and drawn a pistol when it came blowing into the brush, hanging up and flapping there. He quickly collected the newspaper, most of which was gone, and looked at the date. It was only a week old, part of a weekly printed in the next county. Starky Kidd, who could read a little, with effort, sat down and spread the paper before him, grinning as he took in the headline he'd hoped he'd find.

"Listen at this!" he said. "It says, 'Henry Kidd, Murderer of Six or More Men, Has Region'..." He paused, squinting and mouthing out letter sounds. "'Has Region Quaking in Terror.'"

Starky's brother looked puzzled. "What does that mean?"

"It means we got everybody around here scared bad, Henry. It means folks are looking for Henry Kidd because he kills people."

"I don't kill people."

"Why, it says right here that you do! Right here in the newspaper! Says you killed at least six men! Now, why did you go and do such a thing, Henry?"

"I didn't! I ain't killed nobody! It's you, Starky! You're the one who hurts people and does bad things! I don't like the things you do!"

"I do what I got to do, Henry. Can't help myself. Never could!"

"So why does the paper say it's me?"

There was an easy answer to that question, but Starky Kidd, murderer, wouldn't give it. Simpleminded though his brother was, it might just be possible that he would understand the answer, and that was something Starky did not want ever to happen.

"Why, it must be a mistake! Now everybody thinks it's you, Henry! Everybody who reads this paper believes it's Henry Kidd who done all them bad things. Know what they'll do if they catch you, Henry?"

"No."

"They'll hang you! They'll say, 'There's Henry Kidd, the murderer...let's hang him!' And they will."

Henry's eyes were wide and full of fear. "Starky, you got to tell them it ain't me! You got to tell them I never killed nobody!"

"It's too late, Henry. Nobody would believe it. So I

reckon you're stuck in the mud hole, huh? Now all you can do is to mind your brother. You do what I say, always and every time, and I can keep you safe. If you don't...well, there's a lot of ropes out there and a lot of tree limbs."

Henry Kidd was pale and breathing hard. "Don't let them hang me, Starky. Promise me you won't let them hang me!"

Starky Kidd smiled darkly. "Why, I wouldn't let them do that, Henry. I'm your brother! I've took care of you since we was both boys! Have I ever let anybody hurt you?"

"No."

"Then you don't worry. You just always do what I say, and you'll be all right."

"I will, Starky. Don't let them hang me."

"I won't...if you'll always mind me."

CHAPTER 14

Henry sat back against a tree, his knees pulled up close to his chin in the posture he always took whenever he was scared. Starky read the newspaper laboriously; he enjoyed learning of the terror he was spreading across this part of Texas. At last, he laid the newspaper aside and looked over at Henry, who had fallen asleep.

He pondered his younger, simpleminded brother, feeling the combination of love and loathing he always felt toward him. The love came from the fact that they were brothers, had endured together the horrors of life under the beating rod of a drunken father, and had fled together on the stormy night that he had used the ax from the woodpile to finally end their father's existence. An eventful night, that one had been. Starky's first killing. And later, as he and his brother fled through a stormy Kentucky forest, a lightning bolt had stolen young Henry's intelligence in one swift stroke, leaving him alive but forever a child.

Starky had cared for his brother ever since that night, and it amazed him when he thought enough about it that they were still alive and together after all these years. Together they had left Kentucky, settled in Tennessee. There Starky had committed his second murder, a woman killed in a rage when she refused to give him the intimate favors he desired because he was "just a slip of a boy." His stabbing knife had by accident mutilated her face as she collapsed, and he'd found that intriguing. From then on, mutilation had been part of the ritual of almost all the murders he committed.

It was in North Carolina that he'd struck upon the strategy of taking on his brother's name when he killed. Just a little safety measure, that's all it was. Henry Kidd was a burden to him, after all, so why not get some use out of him? Let his name be the one associated with the murders... and maybe, if ever things went truly bad, it would be Henry's neck, and not Starky's, that would feel the pinch of the noose. Starky didn't want that to happen... but if ever it did, better his brother than himself. Brotherly love went only so far, after all. And at times, when Henry was his most whining and fearful and cloying, Starky didn't feel he loved his brother at all. Three times in the last six months, he had stared at him while he slept and thought about trouncing him unconscious, stringing him up from a limb, and leaving a note from "Henry Kidd," announcing his suicide. Starky would be free then. Everyone would think the great murderer was dead, and he could go his way free of worry.

He might just do it yet.

Thunder rumbled suddenly, far away. Starky looked with concern toward the darkening western horizon, then at the sleeping Henry. He hoped the storm would pass. Lightning terrified Henry beyond anything else. If a big storm rose, Henry would become overwhelmed with fear, hard to console, hard to control. Starky didn't want that right now.

He watched the clouds, hoping the storm would blow on by.

The storm did not blow by. As darkness descended, the winds rose higher, buffeting the landscape and all those who ranged upon it. Night was coming, and it would be a wet and windy one, with plenty of lightning.

Marsh held his hat on with his left hand and stared out across the wide plains from the vantage point of the hills.

The Army of God was long gone. Marsh and Serandon had watched its departure less than an hour after they'd slipped away from the group that morning. Obviously the sheriff had managed to overwhelm Cacey's authority, or passion, or both...In any case, the riders had moved in a great mass back toward the site of the camp meeting.

"Maybe you should go back to the campsite," Marsh had suggested to Serandon. "This storm could cause a real mess if it turns out as bad as it appears."

Serandon shook his head. "There's plenty of people there, and they'll help each other. I'm a lot more concerned about getting rid of this murderer than I am the storm. I'll stay with you."

"Well, I appreciate that, but—"

"Look!" Serandon said suddenly, pointing south. "He's still out there."

Marsh saw him: Juan Carlos, still alone, riding in his perpetually relaxed manner across the plains, the dramatic and darkening sky spreading above him, the massive landscape around him. He was heading in Marsh's and Serandon's direction.

"I wonder who that man really is?" Marsh said. "There's something about him that just makes questions start coming to mind."

"There are some caves in these hills," Serandon said, looking at the sky. "Some of them big enough to hold men and horses, too. Unless we want to get wet, I suggest we find one of them. If you'll follow me, I think I know where one is."

Just then, a huge lightning flash seared through the sky

and struck a tree about a mile away. The flash and electric tingle in the air made Marsh's hair stand on end.

"Lead on," he said to Serandon as he tried to calm his spooked horse.

The pair rode back farther into the hills, Serandon leading the way.

CHAPTER 15

I t was times like these when Starky Kidd hated his brother.

Henry was terrified, inconsolable, screaming with every flash of lightning. His fear of lightning was primal, unerasable, branded into him years before by the hot stab of heat and electricity that had damaged his brain. Even in minor storms, his suffering was great; in large ones such as this, he was like a tortured soul on the brink of hell.

He was also a danger to his brother at these times. Starky Kidd lived a life in the shadows, a life of hiding, and a man couldn't hide very well with a screaming babbler at his side. Starky's rage was rising, and he played with the thought of taking out his pistol and ending Henry's screaming forever. He could dump the corpse out on the plains where it could be found, and folks would believe the killer plaguing the region had been shot by some helpful soul, for Starky and Henry bore a strong resemblance to each other. Starky would be able to relax a little... at least until he murdered again.

But even in the dark soul of Starky Kidd, there was a flicker of primitive morality, at least where his brother was concerned. His brother was the only other living human being who had endured with him the sufferings of their childhood. No one else had been at his side all these years. As substandard a piece of human company as Henry was, he was at least a companion, someone who kept Starky from being utterly alone in the world. And so Henry let him live on, as he would let him live on tonight—unless he grew so out of control that Starky had no choice but to quieten him the only way possible.

The storm had driven the Kidds from their original hidden campsite. The same factors that had made it hidden also made it prone to flash flooding, and that had come shortly after the first torrents began to fall. The Kidd brothers had scrambled out of their little hollow, drenched to the skin. Starky saddled their horses in the rain, and off they went, looking for new shelter in the darkness, fearing the lightning—Henry screaming like a scared child all the while—and Starky hoping there were no hidden eyes in the low, brushy hills to see the region's most wanted outlaw scrambling across the plains by the light of the storm.

A lightning bolt flashed, moving horizontally across the sky. Henry screamed, bending forward on his horse, covering the back of his head with his hands. "Don't let it hit me!" he screamed. "Starky! Don't let it hit me!"

"Shut up, you damned fool!" Starky called. "Keep riding. Look yonder—I seen a cave over there when the lightning flashed. We'll go there."

But just then, he saw something else in the darkness, a dim, flickering square of light farther ahead.

"I'll be damned... there's a ranch house yonder," he said. "Maybe some food for us out in a shed or smoke-house or something. I'll take you to the cave, Henry, and then I'll go to the house and see what I can find." The talk of looking in sheds and smokehouses was for Henry's benefit. Starky had no qualms about looking in the house itself and simply killing any occupant who got in the way of it.

"Don't leave me alone!" Henry wailed.

"Shut up and head for that cave."

"I don't see it!"

"Follow me. I'll get you there."

The cave was easily reached and surprisingly dry, thanks to the angle of the cave floor. With effort, they were able to get their horses beneath a rocky overhang and at least mostly out of the bad weather.

Henry, though, was not much better off than before. From inside, the cavern entrance formed a wonderful frame for the wild activity of the storm outside. Henry stared wide-eyed and blubbering at the lightning and rain, tears mixed with the rainwater on his face, his lower lip bulging out like that of a cowardly boy. Starky looked at him in disgust and barely restrained himself from hitting him.

"I'm going to that spread now, and I'll bring us back some food," he said.

"Don't go, Starky!"

"I'm going. You sit down yonder and close your eyes. Don't watch the storm. You'll be fine, and the storm will pass."

Starky headed out of the cavern and into the rain.

Henry sank to the cave floor and buried his face in his hands.

A quarter mile away, Marsh Perkins and Serandon huddled in a cave quite similar to that occupied by Henry Kidd but more spacious. Their horses were safely back deeper in the cavern, and except for a rivulet of water that ran back in from the mouth of the cave, the temporary partners were dry and relatively cozy.

But Marsh was very frustrated. He was convinced that he could have successfully gotten back on the trail of the Knutsen brothers if only he'd been alone. Serandon, though a well-intentioned and good-hearted man, was not a manhunter. He was loud and visible and clumsy and in the way. Now Marsh was stuck in a cave, waiting out a storm, with no idea of what he'd do or where he'd go when the storm ended. Another cold trail... not to mention wet. Come morning; he had no notion as to how he'd continue his quest. One thing was sure: He'd find a way to dump off Serandon.

"Wonder how it's going back at the camp meeting," Serandon said.

"Most likely, they're getting a little wet. But I'm sure they're fine."

"The lightning worries me. It's dangerous to be out there on the flats when there's lightning."

"Yes, sir. But I feel sure they'll come through fine."

"I'll head back come morning... I'd like to keep on helping you hunt, but I need to check on my family. You'll come too, maybe? Meet the family, eat a meal or two with us?"

Marsh thought about it. Why not? The storm was washing away much hope of successful manhunting. Back at the camp, there would be food and companionship and that promised chance to meet Corinne Serandon. "I'll come too. Thank you."

"Things haven't quite gone the way the preacher thought, have they? The 'army' didn't ever make it to battle."

"It's likely to be one man, or two, who bring down Henry Kidd," Marsh said. "He's too sly to be caught by a big, loud, visible group."

The rain continued, even intensified. The lightning was strong and closer, the air very damp and cold. Marsh huddled under his coat, waiting for the storm to end and wondering where the mysterious Juan Carlos was. He smiled slightly to himself, picturing him riding with that same utterly relaxed posture through the midst of a driving storm. Every time he'd seen Carlos, that's the way he'd been.

He wondered who Carlos really was. He had a feeling about that man and recalled how Carlos had looked meaningfully at him. Maybe their paths would cross again, and if so, Marsh might have a few questions for the mysterious Anglo-Mexican.

CHAPTER 16

Starky Kidd was halfway to the ranch house when the lightning flared with particular brightness and revealed the unexpected sight of two men standing beside two horses, pressed up against the side of a small bluff in a vain attempt to escape the brunt of the rain.

The lightning flared for several seconds, giving him a good look at the pair, and them, in turn, a good look at him.

It might have amounted to nothing, this chance meeting with two strangers, but in the world of Starky Kidd, chance meetings seldom amounted to nothing. And such was the case now, for as soon as the pair spotted him, one of them shouted out spontaneously, "It's Kidd!" And he knew then that they were among the many who looked for him.

The man's shout had a funny sound to it, some kind of foreign-sounding inflection.

He reacted quickly, veering to the side and running through the darkness toward the nearest rocky hill. He ran blind, based on his memory of the terrain as revealed by that last lightning flash, and avoided running straight into a stone mass only when another lightning bolt fired down its light just in time to let him see the stone before him. He cut to the side and worked his way up and around the stone, seeking a hiding place. A glance back, another flash of lightning, and he saw that they were coming after him, on foot, with rifles in hand and horses abandoned back at the base of that bluff.

If the scenario were only slightly different, he might be able to circle around unseen and reach those horses, steal one and send the other running away. He couldn't do it, though —not easily, anyway—because the two pursuers were between him and the horses.

The best bet was to find a hiding place and let the storm and darkness serve as his protectors. If he got the chance, he'd kill one or both of these men, but under the circumstances, he doubted it was wise to shoot unless he had a truly good opportunity. Shooting would reveal his location, and the odds of drawing a bead on and then shooting his targets in the brief span of a lightning flash didn't strike him as good.

He was clambering blindly around a boulder, seeking a hiding place, when the first shot was fired. One of the two men fired in tandem with a lightning flash and very nearly hit him. He heard the bullet ricochet off stone not a foot from his head and felt the sting of splintered rock against his face.

Starky swore, flipped the leather hold-down strap off his pistol, pulled it out, and fired randomly in the direction from which the shot had come. It was an act of anger, not planning, and as soon as he did it, two more shots fired back at him, aims guided by the flash of his own pistol. One of the shots struck even closer than the first one.

He dove behind a rock, abrading himself, pinching his foot in a space between two boulders, and slamming his shoulder hard against a rock. It was hard to maneuver in the darkness— but he reminded himself that the same things that disadvantaged him also disadvantaged the two manhunters after him. He'd been in tighter spots—and at least Henry wasn't here to be in the way.

Starky's heart pumped, energy coursing through him. He was frightened, fully aware of the danger he was in, but he was also full of a strange, cold energy that usually overtook him at such times. It sometimes literally felt like a cold hand gripping the back of his neck, filling him with icy courage and aggression that actually made him enjoy the danger. At such times he would grow bold and reckless, but in that very transformation, become a more fearsome warrior. That energy carried him through, filled him with a dark joy and satisfaction that found its apex in the acts of murder and mutilation.

Two against one. That was the worst of this situation. One could engage him in a firefight, making him expose his position, while the other slipped around and gunned him down.

He had to change those odds. He had to play this his way, not the way they wanted him to. They were counting on him to panic, to shoot at them wildly as he already had, and thus to reveal his position very precisely. That, then, was the very thing he would not do.

Another shot fired, singing overhead. Starky Kidd grinned to himself there in the darkness. Let them shoot. He would be patient.

The odds would shift in his favor very soon.

At the sound of the first shot, Marsh came to his feet. "That ain't no thunderclap," he said.

"No, sir. That's a shot."

The follow-up shots confirmed what Marsh had already suspected. "No hunter is out in the midst of a rainstorm. And that pattern of shooting...

"A gunfight," Serandon said.

"That's right."

"Kidd."

"Very likely."

"So, what do we do?"

Marsh did not have time to answer. He was already heading out of the cavern into the rain, his hand wrapped around the cylinder of his unusual rifle to keep it as dry as he could.

Serandon stood there uncertain and suddenly—if he dared admit it to himself—very afraid. A gun battle! And this time, there was no massive "Army of God" surrounding him. Just him, Marsh Perkins, the darkness...and whoever was shooting.

He trembled so badly he could hardly move, and his breath came hard. He knew what he should do, but he couldn't find the courage to move. He stared out into the darkness, praying for strength to do his duty... but still not moving.

Huddled in his own cavern, cringing from the storm and lightning, Henry Kidd also heard the shots. He sucked in his breath and said in a sharp whisper, "Starky! Starky!"

Despite the storm, he came to his feet and edged toward the mouth of the cave. Starky was out there, and there was shooting... He had to help his brother.

How, though? What could he do? And the lightning was so terrifying....

But Henry Kidd was nothing if not loyal to the brother who took care of him. Despite the storm, he would have to move. He had to find a way to help Starky.

Though he had never been taught to pray, Henry Kidd did pray as best he could, an unconscious pleading for safety and for his brother. Armed by it, he bit his lip, whimpered softly, and plunged out into the violent, rain-driven night.

CHAPTER 17

Starky Kidd was not moving, scarcely breathing. His heart, though, hammered like a drum played too fast. The position in which he lay had him mostly on his back, looking upward, rain hammering into his face and eyes, making him blink to keep his vision as clear as possible. But he didn't need to see much to do what he had planned.

He gnawed his lip, hand gripping the pistol tightly, the other cupped over the end of the barrel to keep the rain out of it. There he waited, ready, and listened to the slow approach of a man who would soon be dead.

———

Rolph Knutsen crept slowly through the rocks at the base of the hill, heart in his throat and his pulse racing like a scared Texas jackrabbit. He was more scared than he would ever admit... but excited as well. They'd done it! In the most unlikely way, they had actually stumbled across the murderer they had chased for months. He was trapped, and they were closing in. Rolph was already spending the reward money in his mind and talking big, braggadocious talk to the pretty saloon girls who would be so impressed by the man who killed Henry Kidd.

He could not see York now, not even when the lightning flashed. The terrain was too rocky and rough and blocked his view. But he knew where Kidd was, and in a moment, he would be in position to make his move. A quick lunge, a fusillade into Kidd's cramped hiding place, and it would be done. The morning sun would find him and York bearing the corpse of the west's most vile killer in for the reward.

He reached the spot. Lightning flashed, so close it startled him. He swallowed hard, said a fast and fervent prayer...

Time to move.

With a great heave, he lunged forward.

———

Marsh heard the shots, three of them in quick succession. He caught a glimpse of the flash of the shots as well.

A lightning flare made him aware of someone behind him. He turned quickly, in time to see the outlined figure of Serandon, clambering down through the rocks toward him.

He almost swore, his grandmother's firm teaching on that subject notwithstanding. He'd wanted Serandon to stay put. This was not his kind of affair, and he would only be in the way. But he didn't want to shout at him and betray his presence to the others.

Maybe the shots would drive Serandon back into his hiding place. Marsh wondered who had fired them and at whom.

"Rolph!" he heard a voice shout. It was York Knutsen. "Rolph, did you get him?"

There was no reply.

"Rolph?" York called again, and Marsh thought him a stupid man, for every shout revealed his general location. If Kidd had killed Rolph—and who else could it be but Kidd?

— York was all but waving a target above his own heart and daring him to put a slug through it.

Marsh moved forward, forgetting about Serandon, hoping to get himself into a strategic position without being detected.

———

Henry Kidd, the real one, wanted to scream but could not. He was too scared, his throat too tightly constricted. He did not know if his brother was alive or dead, or if whoever was here, he had a feeling of men being all around him—would want to hang him like Starky had said they would.

Then came lightning, the biggest and closest blast of it so far. It struck a tree atop a nearby knoll and exploded it in a flash of fire. In the brilliant, blinding light, Henry made out the spectacular but horrifying sight of the knoll itself splitting apart under the impact of the bolt.

It was just like the bolt that had struck him when he was young, and it sent a primal terror through him that took away any rationality or self-control he possessed.

He began to run, blindly and without thought, heading by instinct toward the dim, yellow light of the ranch house to which Starky had said he would go. He ran as hard as he could, saying not a word nor giving any outcry. He ran long and hard, leaving the hills behind and making the yellow square of windowpane light before him grow ever larger.

Something huge and dark loomed up beside him. He had reached a barn. Another lightning flash sent him scurrying inside it. He scrambled into an empty stall and cast himself down in the straw, burying his face in it and wailing almost like an infant.

———

Her name was Marian Stevenson, and she had lived in the ranch house with her husband, Ned, for a decade. In the beginning, Ned had done most of the ranching, leaving her to the domestic chores, but time had brought illness to her husband, and now he lay perpetually in his bed, on his back, looking at the ceiling and not speaking, usually not even looking around.

He was a sad man now, bitter at his ill health and sometimes taking it out on his wife. But Marian was strong, not one to yield or even weep—not often, anyway. Nor would she give up this ranch that she and Ned had built, even though now that meant running the ranch almost entirely by herself.

Protecting the ranch, too, which was why she was so interested when she saw a figure dart into her barn moments earlier. A man, running right in the midst of the storm...

Very odd. Why would anyone do that? This had not been someone merely dodging out of the storm—he had run like a man terrified. Why was anyone out on foot in the night, anyway? And mixed in with the thunder—had that been shots she'd heard from somewhere far out in the darkness?

Marian's life was quite isolated; she had only meager contact with neighbors, all of whom lived miles away. She knew nothing of the camp meeting going on over near Woodhawk. She had not heard of the death of the blacksmith, nor indeed of any of the depredations of Henry Kidd, outlaw. She had not even heard the name. The talk of the land did not often reach her. She was an odd and off-putting woman to many, and most left her alone and did not seek her out for gossip and the sharing of news.

She went to Ned's bedside and spoke to him, though she knew he would give her no indication as to whether he heard her. "I'm going to go check on something in the barn," she said. "I'll be back shortly."

He stared without blinking at the ceiling above him as if it was her fault he was sick, and he was mad at her for it. It made her angry sometimes when he did this, but lately, she'd begun to suspect that he truly did not always hear her. Part of his illness, she had concluded. He was drifting away from her by the day, cut off from her most of the time.

She went to the closet and quietly took out the shotgun she kept there, always loaded. She checked it just to make sure it was, then slipped on her coat and hat and headed out the front door and around to the barn.

CHAPTER 18

One thing Starky Kidd had not counted on: Rolph Knutsen's corpse falling upon him after he shot him. As he struggled to free himself from the limp, heavy body, he cursed himself for not having anticipated this. Positioned as he was, firing upward just as his attacker lunged forward to shoot down on him, it was inevitable that the body would plunge down right atop him.

He struggled beneath the dead man's weight, shoving at his bleeding body with everything he had and having quite a lot of trouble getting him off. And the worst was, the falling body had knocked his pistol out of his hand, and it lay somewhere down in the black rock crevice into which he was wedged.

And even now, the second manhunter—the one who kept saying, Rolph! Rolph!—was approaching. Coming up on almost the same spot as had this first one... the one named Rolph, Starky presumed.

He swore again because it was fast becoming evident he wasn't going to be able to wiggle out from under this dead man in time. The other would be above and upon him, and there would be nothing Starky could do to defend himself.

But wait... His hand brushed something. The butt of a pistol strapped into the holster worn by the dead man who was all but crushing the breath out of him. He was so wedged as to be barely able to reach it...

"Rolph? Rolph, answer me! Are you all right?"

Starky strained, managed to get his hand around the butt of the pistol. He pulled, but it held in place. A leather strap, across the thumb grip of the hammer. Starky tugged at it, but it held tight. He tried again, again... His thumb was unable to angle itself correctly to slip the leather strip.

"Rolph?"

The man was just above him now. Starky gave a hard, wrenching pull and the leather strip snapped. The pistol came free.

And somehow, in the same action, Starky managed to finally shift the dead Rolph into a position that let him wriggle out from beneath him. His breath coming hard, Starky wormed and writhed...

———

York knew something was wrong. Rolph wasn't answering him, yet neither was there any noise from Kidd, other than some movement down among the rocks.

At least one of them was alive... God above, let it be Rolph!

York edged toward the crevice. The lightning was less now, farther away, but still sizzling and bright. A flash in the distance cast a clear electric brilliance across the stony hillside, just in time to let York see the figure that burst up out of the crevice, pistol leveling...

———

The pistol was unfamiliar and kicked harder than what Starky was accustomed to, but it did the job nicely. He had emptied three bullets into the new intruder even before the man could squeeze his own trigger.

The man teetered on his feet there at the edge, his form barely discernible to Starky, outlined vaguely against the sky. A lightning bolt revealed him clearly for a moment, though, and in anticipation of this possibility, Starky had put a wicked grin on his face.

"Don't you go falling on me, too," he said to the man even as he died on his feet.

York Knutsen accommodated Starky's request. He fell backward, sliding down the rocks and coming to rest unseen somewhere in a rainwater-filled natural basin at the bottom of the hill.

Starky Kidd climbed the rest of the way out of the crevice and clambered across the rocks, a happy man now, for he had again overcome the odds. Two men looking for him, two dead. Served them right!

"Rolph?" he muttered to himself, imitating York's accent. "Where are you, Rolph?" Then he laughed.

Lightning flashed across the sky, illuminating the entire landscape.

Starky Kidd sucked in his breath. There was another man, a third one! He was coming up the slope toward him—and froze when he saw Starky.

The two stood there a moment, paralyzed by surprise. A lightning flash gave them each a good look at each other.

For Starky, this was a revealing moment. As soon as he clearly saw the face of the third man, he knew he'd seen that face before. Twice, in fact, not close up... but he'd seen him. And that odd rifle, too, the one in his hands right now.

This man was pursuing him over many miles and many months. And now here they were, within yards of each other.

Starky raised his pistol and aimed it at the place the man had been. He thumbed back the hammer, but a new flash showed him...nothing. The man was gone! It was so swift and thorough a disappearance that Starky was for a moment uncertain that he'd actually seen a man there at all. Maybe it had been a trick of the light or his own mind.

Then came a gunshot, and Starky Kidd fell with a yelp, hand groping toward the side of his head. He felt a wound, blood gushing...

Dear God, he'd been shot! The boyish-looking fellow had dropped, rolled, and pinched off a shot with that revolver-style rifle.

Starky screeched in a high-pitched voice and staggered back. He stumbled, fell, and in so doing avoided losing his life, for a second slug sang just above him after he went down.

Terrified, head going numb around the wound, blood dripping down the side of his head and through his fingers, Starky scrambled up and ran deeper into the rocks.

———

Though he'd reacted quickly and well to finding himself face-to-face with Kidd, Marsh had been just as taken aback as Kidd had been. All this time, all those miles, and finally, it had happened. The pair had looked into each other's eyes and known each other. Marsh could tell, even in that brief lightning-light illumination. Kidd had recognized him. If he didn't know his name, he'd known his face and why he was there.

The two prior times that Marsh had gotten within view of Kidd he'd wondered if Kidd had seen him in turn. That look of recognition on Kidd's face gave him his answer.

It ends tonight, he thought. *He's in my grasp now, and I'll not see morning before I see him go down.*

He ran up the hill, following directly after the fleeing Kidd.

CHAPTER 19

Marian Stevenson entered the barn slowly, shotgun ready and senses on alert. Since the time she'd left the house, she'd heard other shots out in the darkness, some distance away but too close to be casual about. And the pattern of fire indicated a fight of some sort.

She moved into the dark barn and immediately backed into a corner. Holding her breath, she listened closely. Her eyes narrowed, and she felt puzzled.

Gathering her courage, she advanced slowly, trying to make little noise but, of course, failing to do so. She headed toward a nearby stall.

"Who's in there?" she demanded. "I know you're in there—and I've got a shotgun I'll use!"

"I need some help—he's hurt!" The voice was plaintive and childish, in a way, though it was obviously the voice of a man.

"I'm opening this door...you don't move a muscle!" she ordered.

A battered lantern hung on a nail driven into a beam. Nervously, she dug a block of matches from her pocket and lit the lantern, feeling vulnerable because, during that lighting, she wasn't in real control of the shotgun. But the man in the stable did not emerge or do anything threatening. But she did hear, to her surprise, a canine whimper.

The lantern flooded light through the barn. She opened the door of the stall and thrust the lantern forward.

"Dear Lord," she said. "What in the world is happening here?"

———

Starky Kidd was ready when his pursuer came around the stone. He fired off a quick shot that almost struck him in the head, but the fellow ducked back just in time. The bullet sang off into the storm, which was now beginning to wane a little.

"Who are you!" Kidd bellowed. "I've seen your ugly face before!"

"My name's Marsh Perkins, Kidd! I've tracked you for many a mile, and tonight I'll end your trail for good!"

"You're messing with the wrong man! I'll leave your corpse cut up for the crows to eat!"

Marsh took a shot at him, missed. Kidd yelled in fury and returned fire. His shot sang high.

Marsh scrambled for cover, difficult to do in the darkness and on rain-slickened rocks. Kidd took another shot and missed again.

"You remember the war, Kidd? Remember them you killed and cut on back in North Carolina? Their people ain't forgot! I've been sent to kill you, and I will!"

"Damn you!" He took another shot, this time aiming so wide that Marsh could tell he really didn't know where he was.

"I'm taking your scarred hand back to show the others," Marsh said. "That way, they'll know that you're dead!"

Kidd roared in fury. Marsh realized that the man probably was not at all used to being taunted. Normally he was in the position of power, probably mocking those he murdered. To have someone throw defiance in his face infuriated him.

Good. A man out of control is a man more easily tripped up. Marsh promised himself to bring this quest to an end tonight.

Kidd yelled, "I'm bleeding here, you bastard! You've done shot me, and I don't let nobody do that!"

"Come get me!" Marsh yelled back.

He heard Kidd moving. He was looking for him. But Marsh would give him no further clues. He was through throwing words back and forth. From now on, silence let Kidd grow puzzled and nervous. And, with luck, careless.

"Where are you, fool! What did you say your name was? Perkins? Come out like a man if you want to fight me!"

Marsh held quiet. Let Kidd come to him.

"Where are you, coward? You afraid of me all at once?"

Marsh hardly breathed. Kidd was coming closer.

"What the hell's wrong with you? Come out and fight!"

Closer yet. Marsh got ready. In only a moment, he should be able to confront Kidd at point-blank range.

"Damn you, show yourself!"

From out in the darkness somewhere, another voice sounded. "Marsh! Is that you?"

Marsh could have dropped where he stood. Serandon! Of all times for him to appear!

"Who the hell—" Kidd wheeled.

"Mr. Serandon—get away from here!" Marsh yelled though he despised revealing his location so close to Kidd. "Kidd is here! Get away!"

"I'll not leave you here alone!" Serandon hollered. "I'll be up to help you!"

Marsh came out from his hiding place, ready now to take on Kidd, whether from an advantageous position or otherwise. Serandon would either run Kidd off or get himself killed.

But Kidd was gone. He'd simply disappeared. Marsh was left puzzled. He heard movement below, Serandon climbing up.

What if Kidd had gone down after him?

"Mr. Serandon!" Marsh yelled, oblivious now to his own danger. "Get away, fast!"

"Well, Perkins, looks like old Starky won this one," a voice said.

Marsh turned. Kidd was just behind him, pistol up, finger squeezing down...

Marsh did the only thing he could and flung himself back, off the rocks on which he stood. He did not know whether he would strike an embankment or plunge off a bluff. The move, though, saved him from Kidd's bullet. It sang above him even as he fell.

Half a moment later, he struck hard, rough stone and fell, rolling. Blackness engulfed him. He twisted, a half-turn, then struck the water that immersed him in cold darkness. He lost all perception of direction and location. His rifle, in his hand earlier, now was gone.

Marsh splashed and flailed, and a few moments later, his head broke the surface of inky water, and he gulped in air. He was in deep blackness, only a circle of relatively brighter blackness above him to give him any point of perception. Rain peppered onto his face as he looked up.

He'd plunged into a pit, or sinkhole, or oddly angled cavern. It was full of water—moving water, he noticed. An underground stream, perhaps existing only after hard storms like the current one.

The water was rising. Panic threatened; if it rose too high and he couldn't make his way out, he could drown. But if he made his way out now, Kidd would be up there, waiting for him...

A dark figure loomed above, partially obscuring the hole. Marsh reacted just in time, sucking in air and pulling himself beneath the water's surface, clambering down by pulling himself down the rough, submerged wall. He heard the shots from above through the muffling water roaring in his ears and was aware of the slugs zipping through the water beside him. But he had pulled himself back beneath a submerged overhang, and as long as he was here, Kidd could not find an angle to shoot him.

He wondered how long he could hold his breath. To get his next breath, he would have to break water at the same exposed place as before. Kidd would be waiting and shooting him as soon as he appeared.

He held his breath as long as he could, mentally voiced the prayer of a man about to die, and kicked his way back out and up.

When his head came through the surface of the water, no shots sounded. But there was commotion above, voices, shouts, the sound of a struggle.

Something large and dark plunged into the hole and down toward Marsh. He barely had time to suck in a breath before he was driven deep beneath the water, pinned there by the heavy thing that had struck him. He struggled to free himself but could not. His lungs began to ache for air, his vision to fill with bursting stars. He was trapped beneath cold water and passing out...

The blackness claimed him just as his lungs lost their ability to hold air. In moments, he would breathe, filling his chest with water.

It would be over soon. He ceased struggling, and with his last flickering consciousness, he readied himself to die.

CHAPTER 20

"Ah! You are still with us, I see. Very good!"

Marsh blinked, opening his eyes. He squeezed them closed again, though, as light assaulted them. He groaned, winced violently, then very slowly opened them again.

He managed to hold them open this time. He saw a cloudy, gray sky, dim with either evening or morning light. Then, moving into his field of vision from one side, a face appeared, smiling down on him.

"I feared you would never wake up," Juan Carlos said. "God was with you, my friend. In a hundred different ways, you could have died between the time you went into that pit and the time I found you. Yet you live."

Marsh groaned, then asked, "How did you find me?"

"I heard the sounds of the fight in the night, from some distance. I came, but no one remained. No sign of anything beyond a few spent cartridges I found among the rocks. Then, when the sun rose, I found the pit, and in it, you. And the other man, too, may God rest his soul."

Marsh began to remember. His last consciousness was of being pushed beneath the water by something heavy, something he could get out from under. He remembered his final prayer and his expectation of drowning.

"How did I survive?"

"I can't know," Carlos replied. "It appears you floated to the surface of the water and managed to drag yourself into a place that held your body in place after you passed out. Your face was barely above the surface."

"How did you get me out?"

"A rope. And muscle. It was not easy, my amigo."

"Thank you for saving me."

"I accept your thanks. I only regret I could not save the other man."

"Other man..."

"Yes. In the pit with you, a corpse, floating. I was able to fish it out. It lies yonder. God rest his soul."

Kidd? Could it be? Marsh remembered the sound of struggle above the mouth of the pit. Maybe Serandon had been gotten the advantage of Kidd while he was distracted. Maybe the dark and heavy thing that had plunged into the pit and pinned him down had been the corpse of Henry Kidd.

Marsh managed to sit up. Carlos said, "Perhaps you should—"

Marsh waved him off. "I want to see that dead man."

Carlos reached down, lent him a hand as he rose. Marsh shook his head slowly, blinking, and managed to find his balance. He coughed a few times.

"The unfortunate man is over here," Carlos said.

Marsh walked over and looked down at the body. Carlos had laid it out in dignified fashion, on its back, hands crossed over the chest. Two of the fingers were broken, Marsh noticed, probably during the fall into the pit.

He hadn't known Serandon well; in fact, he had been somewhat annoyed by him, but he'd known him to be a good man. It would be difficult to tell his wife and daughter that he was gone.

Marsh looked into the face of his dead former companion and vowed again that the one responsible for this would pay.

"I had hoped it would be Henry Kidd," Marsh said sadly.

"*Si*," said Carlos. "The day Henry Kidd dies will be a blessed day for this world."

Marsh looked at Carlos's handsome face. "You know about Henry Kidd, do you?"

"I know much about him. I have been tracking him since he left Mexico."

"Kidd was in Mexico?"

"For several years. At the cost of several lives."

"I've been tracking him, too."

"I know. I know all about you, Marsh Perkins."

Marsh stared at Carlos, astonished. "But how?"

"When a man follows a trail that another also follows, it does not take long for him to find that other person. I began to detect you quite some time back. And from those few along the way who learned of your quest, I was able to learn much about you. As much, anyway, as can be gleaned in such a fashion."

"Tell me what you know."

"I know you are Marshall Perkins, a young man from North Carolina who has come to Texas on the trail of Henry Kidd, who killed several in your home area many years ago. Is my information correct?"

"It is. But you have the advantage. I know nothing about you."

"We shall have to change that, no? Especially if we are to work together."

"Work together?"

"It makes sense, does it not? You and I together can do

more than we can apart. If we are to ride the same trail, we should do so together."

"I don't know you. I don't know if I can trust you."

"I saved your life. Does that count for nothing?"

"It counts for much. But I can't do anything that would endanger my quest."

"I understand fully. I would not ask you to do that."

"Who are you, then?"

"To most, I meet, I am a traveling writer, in Texas to follow the outlaw Henry Kidd and tell about his depredations. There is much interest in him in Mexico. He entered Mexico after your great war and killed several innocent people. Afterward, he vanished for a year, then appeared again, some miles away. Still killing. Still the diablo. Among those he killed was my brother. He cut his throat, then damaged his body in ways that are shameful even to describe."

"It's always his way to do that."

"I vowed that one day I would find this Henry Kidd and see justice done to him. So you see, our quests are much the same, and as different as we are, we are much alike."

"Yes. But there's one difference: It will be me, and not you, who kills Henry Kidd."

"How do you know this?"

"My grandmother had a vision about it."

Marsh waited for Carlos to laugh, but he did not. "I knew a woman once with the same gift," he said. "She was old and wise, and I missed her when she died. She was the mother of my wife."

"You left a wife behind to chase Henry Kidd?"

"No. My wife is gone. I buried her a year ago."

"I'm sorry." A dreadful possibility came to mind. "Mr. Carlos...the death of your wife...it wasn't..."

"No. It was not Kidd. She died naturally. But it was only

after she died that I was free to begin pursuing him, as I had vowed to do."

"Are you, in fact, a writer?"

"Yes, and the day will come when I will tell the story of this quest and its fulfillment."

Marsh looked down at the corpse of Serandon, a man who had died trying to save him. It was difficult to keep his emotions in check. "When you write that story, this will be one of the sad parts. This man was named Serandon. He has a wife and daughter. They are at the camp meeting some distance from here. And I'll have to ride to it and tell them the news that will destroy them."

"It is the legacy of Starky Kidd, no?"

Marsh looked quickly at Carlos. "Starky?" Something triggered in his mind. Among the last things Kidd had said to him...he had used the name "Starky" in reference to himself.

"Why did you call him Starky just now?"

Carlos looked seriously at Marsh. "I had come to believe that you did not know the full truth about who you are tracking. It took much time and thought for me to surmise it myself."

"Are you telling me that Henry Kidd is not Henry Kidd?"

"As you perceive Henry Kidd, that is exactly what I am telling you."

Marsh sat down, hands on the side of his head, and slumped forward. This was all too much to deal with. A man who had tried to assist him had gotten killed for his efforts. Kidd had escaped once more. And now it appeared that the very premise upon which Marsh had based his quest was not correct.

"Talk to me," he said to Carlos. "I want to know all you can tell me."

CHAPTER 21

Starky Kidd touched the aching wound on his head left by the grazing shot fired by Marsh Perkins. He cursed the fellow, whoever he was—or had been—and hoped his death down in that pit had been slow and hard.

He was rather proud of the idea of having tossed the other man's body into the pit—an idea inspired by his own experience in that rocky crevice when the body had fallen atop him.

He even had a prize from the night before: the interesting revolver-style rifle carried by that baby-faced North Carolina manhunter, Perkins. He'd lost it when he fell into the hole, and Starky had retrieved it. He'd enjoy toying around with it later when there was time, and he was at some safer place.

Starky's happiness at his own survival and diabolical cleverness was muted, though, by his worries about Henry. His brother was gone. Starky had returned to the cave in which he'd left him, but Henry had vanished. The horses remained, along with their meager personal possessions, but no Henry.

So now Starky Kidd was a man with a problem. He desperately needed to flee these parts, especially now that he'd added even more murders to his history, but he couldn't leave without his brother. Family loyalty had a degree of hold even in his black soul, but more than that, he feared what Henry might reveal. In his half-witted innocence, he might give away the locations of the places in which they roamed and hid or present some crucial clue that would assure the gallows for Starky.

He had to find Henry. But how? The storm had washed away all tracks.

"Think, Starky!" he muttered to himself. "Try to think like Henry—why would you have run out in a storm that way? 'Especially with the lightning going so hard. Because of the shooting?"

It was the only possibility he could think of. The sound of the gun battle might have drawn him out. Either that or something in the cave had frightened him out. But Starky was relatively sure the cave had been free of animal occupants when they entered it. Maybe something wandered in during the storm, seeking refuge.

But once out of the cave, where would Henry have gone? He hadn't returned. Maybe something had happened to him. Maybe there were other pits like the one Marsh Perkins had fallen into.

Starky rode down a swollen creek, leading Henry's riderless horse behind his, hiding their tracks in the water, going nowhere in particular, just moving because it was his compulsion. Yet he wouldn't leave, not yet. Not until he'd found Henry again.

Where would Henry have gone? And why? He racked his brain...and then a possibility arose.

Starky thought it over and nodded. It was the only likely possibility he could think of. There was really no other place in the vicinity that Henry would have gone. He should have thought of it right away.

He guided the horses out of the creek and turned toward the northeast.

———

Back among the rocks that had been stage to all the violence of the prior night, Marsh Perkins sat listening to Juan Carlos as the mystery of Henry Kidd slowly clarified a little in his mind. Links were clicking together, murky experiences becoming clear.

"It's amazing," Marsh said, having heard Carlos's information. "I feel a right fool for having never figured it out myself. I've been trailing two men, not one—all this time, two men. It takes away any pride I had in my tracking skills."

"Don't be critical of yourself," Carlos said. "It took me a long while to figure it out myself. Starky Kidd is an adept man in his own wicked way. Simpleminded yet fiendishly clever in terms of his ability to hide his tracks and activities. He has hidden away the real Henry Kidd for years, keeping him as it were in his pocket, close by but out of sight of all others."

"'Fiendishly clever,'" Marsh repeated. "That's the truth. Living as one man but committing his crimes using the name of his brother. Shifting the blame so that if ever the trap springs, maybe it would spring on Henry instead of him. I'd have never figured such a thing out if you hadn't come along. I thank you."

"You would have come to the same conclusion over time," Carlos said. "If you think back, I suspect there are times along the way that you've encountered situations that will make more sense when you reconsider them with the knowledge that you have been trailing two men rather than one."

Marsh nodded. "There were such times," he said. "They

seemed hard to account for...until now. Once, when I was very close on the trail, I noticed the tracks of two horses rather than one. But I dismissed it as Henry Kidd riding one horse and leading a packhorse. I guess it wasn't a packhorse after all. And twice I encountered people who told me of meeting a man named Henry Kidd, and they described him as kind, gentle... simple. I just dismissed those people as having made some sort of mistake. The Henry Kidd I was following wouldn't have helped an old woman fix the broken wheel of her wagon. He wouldn't have carried a little boy with a broken ankle back to his home, carrying him for nearly a mile on a hot day so that his family could get him to the nearest doctor. I heard these tales of a kindly Henry Kidd from time to time, but I couldn't make them fit the man as I knew him. So I just put them down for mistakes or misidentifications. There have always been some people eager to paint a good face on outlaws and scoundrels, anyway. Makes for good legends." He paused. "Are you absolutely certain that what you say is true, Mr. Carlos? There are, without any question, two Kidd brothers?"

"It is true. I know it to be so because I once met the real Henry Kidd."

"Face-to-face?"

"Indeed. And at the time, I had no idea to whom I was speaking. I found him alone in a hidden camp, a simple, homely, friendly fellow who seemed to welcome my company. I noted he seemed to resemble the man I was track-ing, the one who in my mind at that time was Henry Kidd—this was not the same man. He was friendly but nervous, waiting for the return of his brother, whom he called Starky. He did not say his own name; I believe now that he'd been instructed not to reveal it. I talked briefly with him, gave him some smoked meat I carried with me, then went on my way. Later, I learned there had been a murder and mutilation on a farm about two miles from that location, about the same time I was talking to the simple fellow in the camp. It bore all the usual marks of a Kidd murder. Then there came a report from a boy who saw two men riding away from the area, one of them with a description exactly matching that of the man to whom I had given the smoked meat."

"But how do you know he is the real Henry Kidd?"

"I learned it from a drunkard in a small town near the border. He is one of the few who have encountered Starky Kidd and come away from the experience alive. Others dismissed his story, but I believe it. He claims he drank with Starky Kidd one night in a little cantina and that Starky revealed the entire affair to him—his true name, his use of his brother's name in association with his crimes, his scheme to have his innocent brother pay the penalty for him if ever they are caught. Have you not thought it odd that this killer has always taken pains to make sure the name 'Henry Kidd' has been left behind at the scenes of his crimes? How many murderers leave behind their names, sometimes written in the blood of their victims?"

"Or even carved into their flesh a time or two."

"Yes. I have heard that, too."

"But why would Starky have revealed so much to this drunk?"

"He was drunk himself at the time. And I believe his intention was to kill the fellow afterward. But he drank too much and passed out. The other one simply slipped away."

Marsh thought it over. "If there are two Kidd brothers, where was the real Henry last night?"

"Somewhere nearby, I am sure. By now, his brother has undoubtedly retrieved him, and they have moved on. I anticipate that Starky will leave this region now. There has been too much activity for him to feel sufficiently safe to remain here."

"It's the usual pattern. A few killings within fifty or sixty square miles of territory, then he moves on. Yes, I think you're right. He'll be leaving the territory now."

"Which means we must find the trail soon."

"Yes."

"What next, then?"

Marsh paused. "There is one thing I must do right away. Mr. Serandon's body must be returned to his family. I dread it deeply."

"I'll go with you," Carlos said. "I'll help you out. From now on, until our common quest is done, I propose that it be that way: I help you, you help me. Agreed?" He thrust out his hand.

Marsh, for all the time he'd been on the trail, had never envisioned taking on a partner. It was in his nature to work alone, and his quest was so unique and private that he'd never anticipated encountering anyone else following almost the identical path. But he liked Juan Carlos, and trusted him instinctively. Thanks to what he'd learned, he understood much better just who he was pursuing. So with no hesitation, he shook Carlos's hand. "Agreed," he said.

CHAPTER 22

Marian Stevenson walked to her husband's bedside, looking at him in the light of morning streaming through the window. He was asleep now, or so she felt reasonably sure; it was often hard to tell, given the effects of the strange, debilitating disease that controlled both his body and mind. She looked by lamplight down into his face and spoke to him even though she doubted he heard, understood, or cared.

"There is another man here tonight, dear," she said softly. "I found him in the barn, in a stall, hugging a dog that had been hurt in the lightning and had run to hide in the barn. Just like he had himself, he seems such a tender soul... but he isn't right in his mind. He's very slow, not smart. But so kind! He was so tender with that poor dog. Just like you were back when we were young, always tender toward hurt animals."

She stroked her husband's brow and gave him an unseen smile. "I miss you, Ned. When you are aware, you are sad and angry and won't speak to me. When you are not aware, just lost in your world, wherever that is, you are out of reach to me. It's as if you are gone already sometimes." She reached up and wiped away a tear. "I'm glad that the young man has come. It's good to have someone here who is kind and tender. But I think he's ill. He's coughed a lot, and he doesn't look well. And I don't know why a man so simple-minded would be alone. He talks about a brother who takes care of him, but he doesn't know where he is. Maybe he will come to find him. I don't know. Henry's sleeping now. It was hard for him to go to sleep, though. He was very upset. The poor dog didn't survive."

She looked at her unresponsive husband a minute more in silence. It crossed her mind that it was not only her new visitor who seemed sickly. Ned himself had an odd pallor, and his breathing was slower than usual. He was sleeping very, very deeply.

"Oh, Ned," she whispered because she sensed a time might be fast approaching that she had long dreaded. "Oh, Ned, please grow stronger. Don't go away and leave me here even more alone than I am now!"

She leaned over and kissed him, then pulled up a cane-bottomed chair near the bed, sat down on it, and pulled a comforter across her lap. Then she simply sat, staring at her husband and wishing things were different than they were.

———

For Marsh, the ride to the camp meeting site was slow and silent. Carlos talked about the Kidd brothers, seemingly unmoved by the fact that they were carrying a dead man's body on a dragging litter attached to the back of Marsh's horse. Marsh wondered if the man was hardhearted but reminded himself that Carlos had not known Serandon at all. He had not seen his wife and lovely daughter and did not have to dread, as Marsh did, what it would be like to share with them the terrible news.

As they neared the campsite and heard the swell of a

hymn being sung, though, Carlos apparently sensed Marsh's feelings. He went silent for a time and grew somber.

"This will be a difficult moment for you, eh, amigo?" he asked.

"Yes. He had a wife and beautiful daughter, both of whom believe he is still alive and well and helping me search for a murderer. They believe right now that their husband and father is a hero."

"And so he is."

"Yes. But a dead one. And dead heroes cannot hug their daughters and kiss their wives."

"Come, my friend. Let's go on and get this done. It is hard to share bad news, but I'll be beside you."

Marsh nodded. At the moment, he was glad to have a partner, any partner, at his side.

———

Noon. On a typical day, Marian Stevenson would be preparing a simple meal for her silent husband and herself. Today she had not even thought of food. She was growing more alarmed by the moment.

Someone came to the door of the room, making her turn with a gasp. She had become so preoccupied with her husband's fast-declining health that she had actually forgotten Henry Kidd was in the house.

"Henry...you scared me."

"I'm sorry. I didn't mean to." He looked at Ned. "Is he your father?"

"No. He's my husband."

"He looks too old for that."

"He is older than I am. But he is also very sick."

Henry stared at him and coughed deeply. Marian said, "Henry, I think you're sick, too. A different kind. How long have you coughed that way?"

"I cough a lot. This whole year I've coughed a whole lot. My brother, he says, 'Quit that coughing!' But I cough anyway because I can't help it."

"Do you have any idea where your brother is?

"No. He's just out there. Somewhere."

"Will he come to get you?"

"I don't know where he is. I guess he don't know where I am."

"Is he good to you, Henry?" She had her doubts that he was good. Henry had been so filled with fear when she first found him, unwilling even to reveal his name without an hour of prodding, that she knew he had suffered in his day.

"He gives me food. He gets me clothes and such when I need new ones. He lets me stay with him."

"He's a good man, then?"

Henry's face darkened. He would not look at her. "I don't think he is. I think he may be a bad man."

"Henry, will he come here, do you think?"

"I don't think he will." He looked worried. "How can I get with him again? I don't know where to look for him!" Then he coughed some more, deeper than before.

"It was bad for you to be wet in the storm last night. It's made you ill. You should go to bed and stay warm. I'm going to go fetch someone who will help you. And Ned. I think both of you need a doctor."

"I've never seen no doctor. Not ever."

"The man I'm thinking of isn't a real doctor, either. But he's as good as one, most times. He has a talent for helping the sick." But she looked at her weakly breathing husband and doubted that any doctor, even a highly trained, authentic one, could do much for him now.

She did not allow herself even to mentally voice the words, but she knew Ned was dying. It made her sad but also furious. It was wrong that a man could die of so strange a malady, an illness that ate away both body and mind and sent folks to their graves without even a name for their loved ones to attach to the ailment that killed them.

"Don't leave," Henry pleaded. "When Starky left, I couldn't find him anymore."

She thought a few moments, eyes narrowing. "I heard shooting out in the darkness last night, off some in the distance. Could any of it have been your brother shooting?"

"I don't know. I thought maybe it was. I heard the shooting, too, and went out to see. But I got scared of the lightning—lightning is real bad to me—and I just ran. I ran and ran and ran until I found your barn. And there was the poor dog inside, all hurt and crying." Henry's eyes began to moisten and grow red. He coughed hard and made a face that showed it hurt.

"You go to bed, Henry. I'm going to fetch Joe Parker. He's the man who helps sick people. I think you're ill, Henry...and I'm afraid my husband might be dying."

Chapter 23

Bounty hunters. Starky Kidd had learned to spot them long ago. You could always tell. Sometimes he could all but smell it on them.

This was a big band. Four of them encamped together. He actually recognized one of them, a big fellow who had tracked him and Henry for two days before Starky could figure out a way to give him the slip. There was a second one, too, who looked vaguely familiar. Maybe he'd tracked him too, at one time or another.

He was hiding in the rocks, not far from that pit into which the baby-faced tracker out of North Carolina had fallen and into which Starky had thrown the body of the other man he'd killed. It was odd indeed to be stuck at such a place, and it had not been his intention to get into such a situation. It's just that the sorry bounty hunters had camped themselves in such a place that he now could not come out without being seen. The unwitting idiots had trapped him and didn't even know it.

Starky always followed a rule when it came to bounty hunters: When they start showing up in bunches, it's time to strike off for new territory.

He was ready to do that. He'd not leave Texas, not right away, but he'd go to another part of it. That was the good thing about Texas: It was big. A man could lose himself in it.

Right now, though, he'd do nothing but sit tight, hiding in these rocks and waiting for the bounty hunters to move on. He could be here for hours, maybe even into the night, depending on what they did. He cursed and thought himself a most unfortunate man. It was important to get away from here, but he couldn't do it without Henry, and he couldn't get to the place he thought Henry would be as long as these bounty hunters hung around.

He settled himself as comfortably as possible, hoped his horse would not make too much noise, and tried to be patient because that's all he could do.

———

The storm had done much damage at the camp meeting site, tearing down the arbor above the speaking platform, whipping down makeshift tents, turning wagon ruts into small rivers and low-lying areas into ponds. Yet the people had not scattered. They'd stuck it out, and still, the preaching and singing had gone on.

It was not going on now. The grim word had spread through the camp: Mr. Serandon had been murdered! It had brought to a halt all music, all preaching. The praying went on, though, grieving prayers, wails of sorrow and bitter anger sent up to the heavens from a people who had seen one killing too many.

Bailey Jones happened to be the first who had spotted Marsh and Carlos bringing in the dead body. This was unfortunate. He raced up, saw the corpse on the litter, and rushed back to the camp shouting the terrible news well before Marsh and Carlos could provide any explanation.

Thus, from the outset, the news ran out of control,

unguided by facts and bolstered by speculative answers to the inevitable questions. Serandon is dead! How did he die? Henry Kidd...it was Henry Kidd!

Carlos had explained the true facts to the Reverend Cacey, telling him about Starky Kidd, but Cacey barely seemed to grasp it. Since the sheriff had sent him and his "army" sneaking back to the camp meeting with tails neatly tucked between legs, Cacey was deflated and dejected. He listened to the truth about Henry Kidd and the revelation of the existence of Starky Kidd, but didn't seem much interested. He did not mount the pulpit to share the truth with the others—and now it was too late. No one was listening to anything but rumors at this point.

So, like a fire in dry brush, the fury spread through the camp meeting, uncontrolled and growing, becoming more exaggerated and inaccurate by the minute.

Marsh knew it was happening but was too preoccupied to ponder it. He focused on only one thing: Corinne Serandon and her mother huddled together, weeping, friends trying vainly to console them. It hurt to see it. He felt partly responsible for their bereavement.

What hurts most of all was that Corinne, the admired girl he had never met and now probably never would, apparently held him responsible as well. She had turned a few moments before and glared at him with obvious hatred. He had been the one whom her father had followed out to look for Kidd. It was he whom Serandon had died trying to save. He was the reason her father was dead!

Marsh wanted to vanish. Just close his eyes and go off into some oblivion. He didn't care about Starky Kidd, Henry Kidd, or his quest. The cost was just too high. It was too much for him.

Carlos came to him and grasped his shoulder rather hard. Marsh looked up at him.

"What is this?" Carlos said sternly. "Do I see you trying

to hold back tears? Listen, amigo, there is no time for pitying yourself. Do you know what is happening here?"

"What do you mean?"

"What is happening here is wrong. The rumor is sweeping through this entire camp that Henry Kidd is responsible for the death of Serandon. We were fools, you and I, to bring the body in as we did. We should have gone first to the preacher and told him the story and told him that it is Starky Kidd, and not Henry, who is the murderer. He could have told it all to this group in a way that made them understand, and then we could have broken the news about Serandon to them gently, without stirring them as they are now. Now it is too late. Look!"

Marsh looked where Carlos pointed. A group of seven men, well-armed, were riding out of the camp. Nearby, another band was saddling up.

"What are they doing?" Marsh asked numbly. His brain seemed to be functioning slowly right now.

"What do you think? They are going to find and kill Henry Kidd."

"But Henry Kidd didn't kill Serandon. It was Starky."

"*Dios!* Of course, we know that! But *they* don't know it! They believe like Starky Kidd has wanted them to believe, that it is Henry who is the killer! They don't even know of the existence of Starky Kidd! We were fools, amigo, fools. We did not do this task as we should."

Marsh watched the second band ride out. The "Army of God" whose ignoble career had been cut short by a sharp-tongued sheriff and a leader with short-lived determination was now energizing again, but with a difference. This time they were divided into small bands. This time they were truly, deeply, bitterly angry.

Marsh's nerves were raw, his body and mind tired. Temper flared. He glared at Carlos. "I don't much care whether we did it right or not," he said. "I don't even care much about Henry Kidd or Starky Kidd just now. I'm just too tired and sick, to my stomach because of what happened."

"You don't *care?* What has happened to you? You've traveled your road all the way from Carolina, and now you don't care that armed men are going after an innocent man?"

"I can't help it that Henry Kidd was unfortunate enough to be born with an evil brother who is willing to betray him to save his own skin. That's not my fault, Juan Carlos. It's not your fault. None of this is our fault!"

"I am speaking less of fault than of justice, amigo. Justice. If Henry Kidd, the true and innocent Henry Kidd, is found, he will be shot down or hanged, and the true murderer might well go free. That would be a mockery. It would be Starky Kidd spitting on the graves of every person he has murdered."

"Juan, even if we could make every person here understand the truth—which we can't— what difference would it make? These people aren't the only ones searching for Henry Kidd. There are bounty hunters, lawmen, common folks guarding their families—they've all heard of Henry Kidd and know nothing of Starky."

"But *we* know. We must seek to stop the injustice if we can."

Marsh looked over at the weeping Serandon women and felt another pang of remorse and guilt, even though he knew in the rational part of his mind that he bore no fault for Serandon's death. That thought gave rise to another, though: If he found it painful and unfair that Corinne Serandon held him in wrongful blame for her father's death, was it any different for Henry Kidd, blamed falsely for the crimes of another?

"All right, then," Marsh said. "Very well. We must try to set things right. But what do you suggest we do?"

"It is not possible for us to make half a nation suddenly

understand the truth and start blaming Starky Kidd rather than Henry. We must be the ones to find the Kidd brothers. We must destroy Starky Kidd, but protect Henry. No one else but us will do that."

"That's a tall order."

"We are almost certain to fail. But we must try for the sake of justice. Remember, few people are alive who know the face of Starky Kidd or Henry. If the pair is caught, Starky will probably be able to persuade them that his brother is the man they seek. He is clever enough for that."

"How can we hope to find them?"

"We have as good a chance as any of these armed bands—see? There goes another! Come with me, Marsh. Let's go back to where you fought Starky Kidd, and see if the Almighty might bless us with clues and a successful hunt."

"I have no rifle," Marsh said. "It was lost in the fight."

"Then we will find you one to replace it. There are plenty of them in this camp. Now let's go. I have the strongest sense that if we look now, we may be successful. God will ride with us, my friend. He will deliver Starky Kidd into our hands."

To Marsh, that sounded like the things the Reverend Cacey had said the day before as the Army of God amassed. And look how wrong he had been! But he didn't say this to Carlos. Like everything else at this moment, it just didn't seem to matter much.

CHAPTER 24

S tarky Kidd, still hidden in the rocks, swore bitterly but not loudly. The band of bounty hunters was still encamped and showed no signs of being about to move, and now a whiskey bottle had been brought out and was being passed among the members of the increasingly merry group.

These men were going nowhere anytime soon. And from his higher vantage point among the rocks, Starky could see a second group of riders, three men, heading in his direction.

He couldn't remain. It was growing far too dangerous. Nothing to do but creep away and forget for now about finding Henry.

Starky took one last look toward the place he'd been trying to reach: the ranch house whose light he'd seen in the darkness the night before, just before that wild fight for his life. He didn't know Henry was there, but it was a reasonably strong possibility. Henry had known that's where he was going. He might have gone there himself, looking for his brother.

Disappointed, dejected, and more scared than he would admit, Henry Kidd withdrew into the rocks, worked his way back to the little draw where the horses were hidden, mounted up, and rode away, leaving the rocky hills between himself and the bounty hunters.

Could he circle around toward the house from some other, safer direction? Perhaps, but it would take time and force him to ride in the open for a long distance. He hardly dared do that. Perhaps after darkness fell—if he could stay hidden that long.

Hiding held a lot of appeal. Too many people were looking for him. He had to find a place to roost where he would not be found. And it looked like he would have to do it, for the moment, anyway, without Henry.

———

Marian Stevenson's horse was familiar with the road to the community of Parmeter and apparently liked it because it always traveled at a fast and efficient clip when she went there. There was not much to Parmeter, but there was a trading post from which she bought the items she could not make or find on her own. And there was Ben Rumley; the old Civil War wound dresser who now served as the closest thing this region had to a practicing physician.

Ben was a wagon maker by trade and was hard at work on a buckboard when Marian rode up and told him about her husband's condition. Preoccupied with Ned, she did not mention Henry.

He greeted her description of Ned's decline with a grim expression. "I'll look at him, but this isn't a broken arm we're talking about here, Marian. Ned is very sick. I don't even understand the nature of his illness. I think he needs a real doctor."

"It's too late for a real doctor, Ben. I know that. And I know there is probably nothing you can do, either. But still, I owe it to Ned to do all I can. Maybe you can help me make him comfortable, if nothing else. Maybe you'll think of something unexpected that can make him better. All I ask is that you look at him."

Ben looked down at the unfinished buckboard. Going back to the Stevenson spread would throw him behind on finishing it, and the commissioner of this project was already growing impatient. But duty was duty.

"Come on," he said. "We'll take a look. Give me a moment to pull my things together."

———

Marian's degree of worry became clear to Ben when they were within a mile of her ranch. A band of armed riders went by on a trot, a quarter of a mile away, and she didn't seem to notice. She was pushing hard to reach the house, as if fearful that too long a delay might have a cost she did not want to pay.

Ben watched the riders disappear over a swell in the land. He was vaguely comforted to have seen them. Because of the outlaw Henry Kidd, there were many such groups ranging through this region. They were tense, trigger-happy, dangerous bands, but with such a murderer as Kidd around, Ben felt safer for their presence.

He felt a little guilty, too, when he considered that he had given no thought to the situation of Marian and her bedridden husband. Living out like they did, alone and with little contact with others, they were in a particularly precarious situation with Henry Kidd roaming around. Nobody knew how Kidd survived, so the presumption was he stole to survive. An outlying ranch whose only male occupant was disabled was a strong potential target. Ben decided he'd been amiss in not checking on the Stevensons. But the truth was that he hadn't even thought of them until Marian showed up today.

They came within view of the house. Marian seemed both relieved and anxious to be home again.

"You look worried, Marian," Ben said as he stepped onto the yard. "Are you concerned that Ned has been here alone?"

"Oh, he's not been alone," she said. "There's another man here. He's slow in his mind but very gentle."

"I didn't know you'd hired help."

"I haven't. He just showed up. I found him in my barn, and I guess just took him in."

"Who is he?"

"He says his name is Henry. Henry Kidd."

Ben jolted to a stop and froze for several moments. "My God!" he declared. Drawing his pistol, he rushed to the door, paused there...

"Ben, what in the world—"

He didn't wait for her to finish. He pushed the door open and burst inside, pistol drawn. No one there. He looked back toward the bedroom and saw motion.

"Ben, for God's sake, put away that pistol!" Marian said, coming in the door behind Ben.

Ben did not heed her at all. He rushed into the bedroom and again froze, astonished and appalled by the scene that met his eyes.

CHAPTER 25

"There they are," Marsh said, eyeing the rocky hills where he had endured his own violent encounter with Starky Kidd. "I'll never forget what happened among those rocks. That pit almost killed me... but maybe saved my life, too. If I hadn't fallen in when I did, Starky Kidd would have killed me."

"Why don't we take a look among those hills," Carlos suggested. "This is largely flat country, and Starky needs to hide. He might be drawn to these hills."

"Even after all that happened here? He may have gotten away, but he was close to disaster himself."

"One never knows. A man seeking to hide can only go to where hiding places are. Perhaps in one of those caves, we will find him, or at least some clue."

Marsh nodded. They had been searching for a good while but with no luck. They'd seen other riders, but they weren't the Kidd brothers, but others like themselves, out in search of Starky—though all but Marsh and Carlos, of course, did not know of Starky and were in their own minds looking only for one Kidd, Henry. A good number of them had only hours before been among the number of Cacey's failed Army of God.

Marsh didn't say it, but he considered this nearly hopeless. This was the classic kind of situation in which Kidd was able to vanish. Marsh had seen it before, twice. Kidd killed, evoked panic, drew swarms of manhunters... then vanished. It happened every time. If Marsh was more superstitious, he might be tempted to attribute some sort of supernatural capabilities to Kidd.

He did not believe it likely that he and Carlos, or any of the other manhunters, would find whom they sought.

He and Carlos rode into the hills, looking around, hoping to find some track or clue. There were some fresh tracks and other indicators of the presence of someone in the hills very recently, but who could say who it was?

Though it sent a chill down his spine to be in the area of the pit that had swallowed him, Marsh looked around on the slim hope he would find his rifle. He didn't, of course, and knew that Kidd had probably taken it. It might have fallen down into the pit with him and now be forever lost deep in that dark subterranean water.

As Marsh had anticipated, their searching led nowhere. He was discouraged by this entire process and not fully in accord with Carlos, who seemed righteously determined to make sure that the innocent Henry Kidd did not wrongly take the punishment due to his brother. Marsh cared... but he was tired. He'd traveled very far, over a long time, to reach this place. He was so sick of manhunting; he could almost consider casting it aside and heading back to North Carolina.

A time or two, he'd been tempted to actually do it. The odds were he could go back home, claim that Kidd had been killed and that he knew about it, but had been hampered from bringing back the evidence of Kidd's scarred hand. In the remote North Carolina mountains, no one would probably ever learn he'd lied.

He'd toyed with the idea, but never seriously. He would know the truth if no one else did. He'd spend the rest of his days waiting for that next stray newspaper clipping or rumor from the West revealing that Kidd had murdered yet again. Then everyone would know he had lied.

There was nothing for Marsh to do but stay on the task until it was done.

They had dismounted and were walking among the rocks, Marsh halfheartedly looking for his rifle but not expecting to find it. From atop a boulder, he looked across the flatlands below the hills and noted a ranch house alone in the distance.

"Juan," he said. "There's a ranch yonder. I wonder if the Kidds might have gone there. For food, to steal something or whatever reason."

Carlos joined him atop the boulder. "Perhaps so. There is no harm in going to see, no? But let's look through these hills a while longer. I believe that Starky Kidd may yet be hiding here. So be careful, amigo."

———

"Get off him!" Ben yelled as he raised his pistol.

Henry Kidd, leaning across the bed with his hands upon the mouth and throat of the stricken Ned Stevenson, looked back across his shoulder at the unexpected intruder. His eyes were wide and wild, glaring, and at that moment, he looked fearsome and murderous.

"Stop choking him, or I'll kill you!" Ben shouted again, his finger already beginning to tighten on the trigger.

Henry Kidd reflexively ducked, his hands slipping away from Ned. Henry collapsed back onto the floor on his rump beside the bed and threw his hands across his face. "No!" he screamed in a high pitch. "No!"

Marian burst into the room. "What in the world—" She looked at Ned, went to his side.

"He's going to kill me!" Henry wailed.

"I ought to kill you, you murdering son of a bitch!" Ben said. "But I believe I'll just haul you in and let the law do it."

"Ben put down the pistol," Marian ordered firmly.

"Marian, do you know who this is? Do you know all he's done and what he was doing when I came in here?"

"This is Henry Kidd, a kind young man, and I demand that you put that pistol away, Ben! What has gotten into you?"

"Henry Kidd is a murderer, Marian. Maybe you don't know about him, cut off like you are out here. He's a murderer who has killed more people than anybody even knows. He killed poor old Port McGee in his blacksmith shop. This whole countryside has been crawling with manhunters looking for him!"

Marian took that in but couldn't quite grasp it. It was impossible to make it fit with the gentle Henry Kidd she knew.

"He was leaned over Ned, choking him, when I came in," Ben went on.

"I wasn't!" Henry declared through tears. "I wasn't! He was choking all by himself, and I was trying to stop it! I was trying to save him! To save him!" Then Henry broke off into a burst of violent coughing and was able to say no more.

Marian nodded. "I believe him, Ben. That happens sometimes—you know that. Ned's throat will close down, and at times he has literally nearly choked on his own tongue. When that happens, you have to pull his tongue clear to let him breathe. I told Henry to watch for that happening and how to deal with it when it did."

"Why are you taking this murderer's side, Marian? There's so much you don't know. This whole part of Texas is living in fear of this bastard right now, and he's managed to convince you he's some innocent half-wit!"

"You can't be right, Ben," she said. "This young man is no murderer—I can tell you that very firmly!" In her tone, though, the vaguest flicker of doubt was beginning to form. She recalled hearing those gunshots shortly before Henry showed up at her barn.

"Marian, I have to take him in. I have no choice. If this is the same Henry Kidd that has this county in an uproar, he has to be taken to the sheriff."

"I just can't believe that..." She faltered away. "Henry?" she asked. "Is it true?"

"No!" he declared. "No, no, no! It's Starky who does bad things! Starky, not me!"

"Who is Starky?" Ben asked.

"My brother!"

"I've never heard of anyone named Starky Kidd. I've only heard of Henry Kidd. Marian, you take my pistol and hold it on him while I look at Ned. Then I'll take him on to the sheriff."

"There's no need to look at Ned," she said softly. Her husband's still form and half-open eyes had just caught her attention. "He's gone, Ben."

She lowered her head and wept.

Chapter 26

Two manhunters, both young, neither particularly adept at it, both of them drunk from whiskey they'd bought earlier in Woodhawk. Camped now near a little stream, they were passing the bottle back and forth, talking big talk about what they would do with their share of the reward money once they brought in the feared Kidd.

"I'm going to buy me a bunch of busted rifles and take them to my uncle and get him to fix them, then I'll turn around and sell them," one was saying. "I know a man who did that in Arkansas, and he makes all kinds of money now selling guns. Once I get enough, I'll open me up a full gun shop. Then I'll marry Annie Prince and have me a houseful of children in no time."

"Yeah, you would. The way she looks, you'd not be able to keep off her. You'd have a lot of children, all right."

"Don't talk about Annie that way. She's special. You can talk about other girls that way, but not Annie."

"Well...Mickey's in love! I always knowed you were fond toward her, but I sure didn't know you were all lovey-dovey." The speaker's voice was slurred badly, the whiskey taking its toll.

"Don't you mock, Perry. I'm serious about this."

"I won't mock. Hey, you know what I'm going to do with my share of the reward?"

"What?"

"Buy into that new saloon. Same one we got this whiskey at."

"What makes you think they'll let you?"

"I already talked to them. They said if I could get the money, I was in."

"You'll drink up all the stock."

"Reckon I might." He laughed and turned up the bottle, closing his eyes as the hot liquor drained into his mouth and down his throat.

When he opened his eyes again and lowered the bottle, he was surprised to see Mickey sitting there with blood all over the front of his shirt and a stunned look on his face. He tried to talk but couldn't. Slowly he tipped to one side.

Perry stared up in horror at the grinning man standing behind Mickey. He had a bloodied knife in his hand. "You ever cut a throat?" he asked Perry. "It's mighty easy. Good way to dispatch a man." Starky was proud to use the word "dispatch." He considered it a ten-dollar word, like an educated man would use, and enjoyed throwing it out from time to time. He lost his smile suddenly, however. "Hey! You're spilling that whiskey! I want that!"

Perry was trying to get to his feet, but he was drunk and terrified, and Kidd had the drop on him, anyway. Starky raised Marsh Perkins's revolving rifle and fired off three rounds that sent Perry staggering back, to collapse with his face to the sky. He stared at the moon as he died.

Starky had already rescued the whiskey, not much of which was lost. He lifted the bottle to his lips and took a swallow, then swiped the back of his hand across his mouth.

"You fellers got any food?" he asked the dead men. "I'm about starved."

He dug around in their supplies and found some cold biscuits, rather dry, along with equally dried-up fried sausage, some parched corn, and a hunk of cheese gone orange instead of yellow. Not the best fare, but good enough. Starky sat by the fire of his victims and dined, talking to them as if they were still living company.

"Well, got to go, boys," he said when he'd finished the food. "I'll take the whiskey with me. Oh, and I guess I better have brother Henry leave a note."

He used the blood from the first one he'd killed to scrawl the words "Hello from Henry Kidd" on a white shirt he'd found crammed in among their supplies. He stretched it out across the ground near the fire. With his knife, he did some of his usual insulting work on the bodies.

Satisfied and feeling he'd made quite a telling commentary on the bands of amateur manhunters trying to find him, Starky smiled down at his victims. "So long, boys. Got to go a ranch house yonder way and see if my brother is there. I believe he might be. If he ain't, well, I guess he and me has finally parted. Kind of sad, huh? Oh, well."

Starky Kidd selected the better of the two horses that grazed nearby and transferred the saddle from his own exhausted mount. Mounting, he rode off in the direction of the ranch house of Marian Stevenson.

Two hours later, in the deep of night, Carlos stood outside the ranch house door with a look of concern on his face.

"I vow to you, Marsh, that there was a light inside. I saw its flicker, small and dim, like a candle. But there was a light. Someone is here!"

"I saw no light, Juan. I think this house is empty. It feels empty to me, you know what I mean?"

"He may be in there."

"Yes, or there may be some terrified rancher in there with a rifle aimed at the door, waiting for us to come in. He probably figures Henry Kidd is paying a call."

"I'm going inside, Marsh."

Marsh sighed. "I know. I guess we have to."

"You need not if you don't want. I can go in alone. It's my instinct and not yours that I am following."

"We're together in this. Try the door. If it's open, we'll both go in."

The door was indeed open, but the latch had an odd, unworking feel to it as if the door had been forced and the latch damaged in the process.

Marsh and Carlos looked at each other. Carlos hefted up his rifle a little, and Marsh drew out his pistol, the only weapon he had left since he'd lost his rifle. Only the leather tie-down strap had kept him from losing the pistol when he plunged into the pit during his fight with Starky.

"All right, amigo...one, two...*three!*"

They lunged inside, weapons waving about. All they found was a dark and empty room.

"I guess nobody's here," Marsh said softly.

"I don't know...I have a feeling..."

"Let's look in the back."

"Wait."

Carlos found a lamp and lit it. With his rifle gripped in one hand and the lamp aloft, he advanced to the back, with Marsh just behind him.

"Look," Marsh said, pointing at the bed.

Very clearly, there was a body lying there, with the cover pulled across the face. The partners glanced at each other.

"Kidd?" Marsh whispered.

"Starky Kidd doesn't put covers tidily across his victims. He displays their bodies in terrible ways." Carlos reached over and gently lowered the cover, revealing the dead face of Ned Stevenson.

"No marks on the body," Marsh said.

"Yes. This was a natural death. But for some reason, whoever else lives in this house is now gone."

There was, however, one more door, one more room beyond it. Marsh gestured toward it.

Carlos moved that way and sat the lamp on the floor far enough back so that it would not be tilted when the door opened. He grasped the knob and opened the door.

Light spilled in on the man standing just on the other side, with Marsh's revolving rifle upraised. Starky fired before Carlos could react. The bullet passed through Carlos's extended forearm, making him drop the rifle from suddenly limp fingers.

Marsh moved, raising his pistol, but Starky was faster. He was on Carlos in a moment, grabbing him, turning him, jamming the muzzle of the rifle up under his chin.

"No, sir, mister manhunter. You drop that pistol right now, or I blow off his head. Lay it down and kick it to the corner there."

Marsh knew Kidd. He knew that he would probably blow off Carlos's head anyway. But he had no option but to comply. He slowly lowered the pistol to the floor and left it there. He kicked it away as Starky had ordered.

In the glint of the lamplight, though, he noticed the shotgun that hung above a small fireplace to his left. Loaded? No way to know.

Starky grinned at him. "Good boy. How the hell did you get out of that pit? Never mind... you're dead for sure this time. Time for a little pleasure... time to watch your friend die, with you to follow!"

Carlos moved quickly, with no warning, pulling his head down and jamming the elbow of his good arm into Starky's gut at the same time. Starky grunted; the rifle fired, but the muzzle had been deflected, and the bullet went out through the ceiling and roof.

Carlos pulled free and reached for his pistol. Marsh, meanwhile, went for the shotgun on the wall. His own pistol was out of sight, and there was no time to grope for it in that dark corner.

Starky fired just a little more quickly than Carlos. The slug passed through Carlos's belly and snipped his spine. He fell like a sack of oats, dropping his pistol.

Marsh yanked the shotgun down, pulled back the hammers, turned toward Kidd.

Starky had the rifle aimed right at him. He pulled the trigger.

A dead click. For only the second time in Marsh's experience, the rifle had misfired.

Indeed the shotgun was loaded. Its roar was like a cannon in the enclosed room. The shot blasted out, caught Starky's right arm just below the wrist, and blew his hand off. The rifle, though, was in his left hand at that moment, and he did not lose it.

Starky let out a horrible wail, glared at his bleeding stump, then turned and plunged out through a window, shattering the glass. Marsh heard him come to his feet and run off into the night.

He would not pursue. There was Carlos to deal with.

He knelt beside the wounded man. "Juan...I'll find you help, Juan. I promise."

Carlos looked up at him. He smiled faintly. "I was not at my best tonight. In a better time, I would have had him."

"No doubt."

"I must go now... This is your quest alone from here out."

"No, Carlos. We'll get you help. You'll live."

"I'm afraid...it is too late...to harbor that hope...pray for me...pray for my soul...and when you do kill Starky Kidd, do it in my name...along with all the others...he has...murdered..."

Carlos went limp, his brown eyes no longer seeing, his lungs no longer drawing in air.

CHAPTER 27

In a room in the only hotel in Woodhawk, Marian Stevenson looked out the window and watched the crowds gathering outside the sheriff's office fronting the jail. She shook her head.

Despite all that Ben had told her, she still could not reconcile the gentle Henry Kidd she had met with the brutal killer Ben described. Yet all the rest of the world seemed certain that Henry was a murderer and mangier. How could it be?

Like so much tonight, it all seemed unreal and impossible to understand. She pulled up a chair at the window and sat down, still watching the crowd and wondering how long it would be before demands began being made for the sheriff to turn Henry over to them for immediate justice.

One sheriff, two deputies...and a crowd of at least sixty angry men, armed, ready to have a hanging before the sun came up. How long would the sheriff resist? And if he did resist, how could he possibly prevail?

She prayed for Henry. He simply could not be what they claimed. She imagined him huddling, terrified, back inside that dark jail, locked in a cell. It was for his sake that she had come here, leaving Ned's poor corpse there alone in the house. But what did it matter? Ned was gone, his body only an empty dwelling in which he used to live. But Henry was still alive.

Not for long, though, if what was happening outside progressed.

Marian stood. She was going down there. She would stand on that porch and face the crowd of lynch men and tell them that they had the wrong man. If there was a Henry Kidd who committed murder, it was not the same man now in the cell.

They would not believe her. She would not be able to stop them any more than the sheriff could. But it was her duty to make a stand no matter what the outcome.

She walked out of the hotel and toward the crowd, pushing her way in and through, making a path to the porch where the sheriff stood alone, shotgun in hand and a look of defiance thrown across his face like a mask that tried, vainly, to cover the face of fear beneath it.

———

An hour later, Marsh rode slowly into the edge of Woodhawk. Carlos's body was draped across his horse and tied in place. It seemed an ignoble way to carry the body of a friend and partner, but he had not been willing to leave him there in his blood on the spot that such rubbish as Starky Kidd had killed him.

He hoped Starky was out there on the plains, bleeding to death from that stumped forearm. He hoped he died slowly and hard and that wolves and vermin mangled his body like he mangled so many he had killed.

Marsh stopped when he saw the crowd at the jail. He studied it, identified it as looking for all the world like a lynch mob, then rode forward. He thought better of it, though, and paused long enough to lead the horse bearing Carlos's body back into an alley. Riding up with a dead man just now might generate more confusion than it was worth, and he wanted to have a clear idea of what was going on here.

It surely had to do with Kidd. Right now, in these parts, everything had to do with Kidd.

He dismounted and walked to the edge of the crowd. An eager boy of about thirteen was bobbing up and down, trying to see a little better what was going on.

"What's this all about?" Marsh asked him.

"They got him! They got Henry Kidd the murderer in that jail! And all these men here are ready to take him out and hang him!"

From the porch came a woman's voice, drawing Marsh's attention.

"I tell you, this is not the right man!" she said. "This is a gentle man, weak of mind but kindly and sweet... He cried like a child over an injured dog as it died. In fact, a child is what he is in his mind! He's no killer!"

Marsh knew right away that they had Henry Kidd in there, not the murdering, falsely identified Henry Kidd who was really Starky, but the true Henry Kidd, the innocent.

"Move out of the way, Mrs. Stevenson!" someone demanded. "There's no call for you to involve yourself in this. Go back home and care for your husband!"

"My husband died tonight... and Henry Kidd tried to save him. He is no killer! Please, go home and don't do this lawless thing you're doing!"

"She's right," the sheriff said. "This is a clear violation of the law, and if you harm or kill the man in my custody, I know every one of you and will see you prosecuted for it!"

"Will you prosecute the whole county, Sheriff? Because the whole county is behind us! Hell, half the men in the county are here!"

That was quite an exaggeration, but the basic point was strong. The sheriff was bluffing, and everyone knew it.

The crowd surged then, moving in and up, closing in on the porch. The sheriff raised his weapon, and the surge stopped, but clearly, the next time, it would go on through.

Marsh knew what he had to do. He began pushing through the densely packed crowd toward the front. He sensed another surge, the final one, about to take place, so when he was only halfway through the crowd, he shouted, "Wait! Wait! I have something you need to see!"

Men glared at him, an upstart intruder interfering with their business, but he persisted and, at last, made it through to the porch. He stood there; a leather pouch he'd found in the ranch house slung across his shoulder. Marian looked at it, recognized it.

"That's my Ned's hunting pouch," she said softly, confused.

"Do you live in a ranch house with a man lying dead on the bed in the back?"

"Yes."

"Then I guess it is your Ned's pouch. I'll explain it all later." Then he turned to the crowd. "Tell me something: Does anyone here know about the scar on the hand of the murderer Kidd?"

"I've heard of it!" a man called back. Others echoed.

"Well, the story is true," Marsh said. "There is a scar on his right hand. And the man inside the jail, I'm willing to bet, has no scar. Right, Sheriff?"

"There is no scar," the sheriff confirmed.

"Are you saying that the man in the jail isn't Henry Kidd?" someone called.

"I'm saying that the man in the cell is not guilty of any murders. His name indeed is Henry Kidd, but he has a brother named Starky, who has committed all the crimes. Starky Kidd is an evil man, and he leaves the name of his half-wit brother at the scenes of the crimes so that he will take the blame instead of Starky himself! It's his scheme, and it must be a good one because you men are just about to fall for it! If you lynch Henry Kidd, you've lynched an innocent man. The real killer, Starky Kidd, is still out there —and in much worse shape than he was earlier tonight because I shot off his hand."

That brought a stunned reaction from the crowd.

"You're a liar!" someone shouted.

Marsh reached inside the leather pouch and brought out the shot-off hand of Starky Kidd.

"Bring that torch up here," he directed a torch-bearing man at the front edge of the crowd.

The torchlight revealed it clearly: On the back of the bloody, ugly hand was a jagged, very visible scar.

CHAPTER 28

Corinne Serandon sat beside the creek, in the place she went when she was sad, staring into the water and wondering why she could not cry. Her father was dead! Murdered! Her sadness was deep, but she was unable to vent it. It festered in her, painful somewhere deep in her chest, and she wished she could turn back the clock and tell her father not to ride out with that absurd "army" that the preacher had pulled together. If only he'd stayed at the camp! He would be with her now. Her mother would not be alone in her room, her face buried in her pillow and the space beside her on the bed vacant.

Her mother could cry, and Corinne had at the beginning. Then sorrow had been overwhelmed by anger, and the tears had stopped. The anger was at her father for having ridden out with the preacher's foolish army, for having not come back when the rest of them did, and for getting himself killed when his family needed him so badly. She was angry at the young man whom her father had died trying to save. She was angry at the Reverend Cacey for having drummed up the idea of a citizen army, anyway. She was even angry at God.

Most of all, she was angry at the murderer Kidd. A man who killed for no reason other than his own wicked mind. A man who stole away life, the best possession of all, and left girls without fathers.

It was a deep night. The house, visible through the brush from where she was, was full of relatives and friends, sleeping on couches, spare beds, cots, blankets on the floor. It was that way when people died; all their loved ones piled in to make the grief easier to bear.

For Corinne, however, it had all seemed stifling. She had waited impatiently until the others slept, then she'd crept out here in the darkness to her secret place.

She had come to cry. So far, there had been no tears. Just anger, interspersed with periods of astonishing numbness.

It was hard to imagine how she and her mother would go on.

Then, from somewhere inside, a wall broke, and her eyes filled. Seated on the ground, her knees up and her arms folded around them, she bowed her head and wept into her sleeves.

The pain was intense, the bitterness deep, but the tears softened them both. She cried for a long time—then raised her head sharply and suddenly.

She had just heard something behind her.

Corinne stood and turned. She saw no one, but her conviction that she was not alone was strong. "Hello?" she said.

No reply.

"Hello?" she said again. She began to suspect it was her uncle Martin. He was the kind to sneak about in silence—he made her uncomfortable very frequently.

The form emerged from the darkness, silhouetted dimly against the house. It was indeed her uncle.

"Uncle Martin? What are you doing out here?"

The figure moved, and Corinne drew in her breath

sharply. It wasn't Uncle Martin! This man had only one hand. She could see only a stump where the other hand should be. There was a cloth of some sort tied over it, bound tightly with a strip of cloth.

"Who are you?" Corinne asked. She stepped back toward the creek.

"Hello, miss," the man said. He spoke softly and with no sound of threat. He sounded rather weak. "Miss, I am in need of help. I've had a terrible accident."

"Your...your hand?"

"Yes."

"You need a doctor, then."

"Maybe I do. But I can't go to one." He paused. "There's folks after me."

She hesitated, and a dreadful possibility arose in her mind. She backed away another step.

"I need somebody with me...so they'll leave me alone."

God help her, it was Kidd! It had to be—and what he was talking about was hostage-taking.

She backed away to the very edge of the creek and was about to scream, but with his good arm, he raised a rifle. "No, miss. No. You just keep it quiet. You scream you're dead. You understand me?"

Corinne looked longingly at the house that earlier she had so wanted to escape. Now she wished she'd never left it.

"Please..." she begged. "Please don't do this!"

"I got to do it, miss. Every son of a bitch in the country is after me. I'll never live unless I got somebody who they're afraid I'll hurt."

"If you take me, they'll try even harder to find you."

"They're going to try hard anyway. Now, come on. Keep your mouth shut and move."

She could tell from his voice that he was in pain. Her mind raced, looking for a ploy. "There's whiskey in the house," she said. "I can get it for you to make you not hurt."

"Hell, no. I know what you're up to. I'll get whiskey later, somewhere else but here."

He was scared. She took note of it. This man was terrified, and that made him all the more dangerous. But it might also make him careless and give her an advantage.

This is the man who killed my father. The thought was overwhelming, hard to wrap her head around. *This is the murderer who killed my father and threw him into a pit.*

Despite her terror, despite the fact that her knees quaked so much she feared she would fall, and her hands trembled like aspen leaves, she vowed right then that he would not kill her too. No matter what, she would not let that happen.

No, she would kill him instead.

"Move!" he ordered again, in a sharp whisper.

She toyed once more with the idea of screaming. There was a houseful of people within earshot. They would be outside in a moment, and Kidd would have no chance.

But she knew that they would find her dead. So she did not scream.

He approached her and nudged the gun into her back.

"Let's go, girl," he said. "Don't make me kill you because I will. Believe me, I will."

CHAPTER 29

Marsh was growing hopeless. Part of it was pure exhaustion, and part of it was the fact that, once again, Starky Kidd had managed to evade capture. The night was his friend, not that of those who sought him. Marsh was beginning to wonder if he would make it away yet again—minus one hand, but still alive.

That lost hand, though, was the biggest source of hope for Marsh. If the bleeding was bad enough, Starky might already be dead out there somewhere in the darkness. If he had managed to stop the bleeding with a tourniquet, he might still feel compelled to seek medical help. That could expose him.

Part of Marsh hoped that Starky wasn't dead yet. If Starky was lying in some draw or in some hidden recess or cavern, his corpse might never be found. Marsh would be left with no way of knowing whether his quest was finished or not.

Marsh's quest aside, though, it would be best for the world if Starky Kidd had already left the mortal veil. Hell could have him, and innocent people could rest more easily in their beds.

They had reached the Stevenson spread and continued from there, searching in a widening swath all around in the hope of finding Kidd either dead or dying from loss of blood. No luck. Reassembling, they had tried again, this time with different searchers going in different directions. Again there was no luck, but one man, by torchlight, did find a strip of bloodied cloth on the ground, about a hundred yards from the ranch house.

Kidd had made himself a bandage or tourniquet, it appeared. That indicated a certain state of ability and presence of mind despite the loss of his hand. The hope of finding him dead right away dwindled.

Discussion had followed. There was general agreement that Kidd was probably trying to cover a lot of ground under the veil of darkness. In his physical condition, though, he probably would be attracted to settled areas, outlying ranches like the Stevenson's was where he could find better bandaging, maybe something to purify his wound.

"Or a hostage," Marsh suggested.

The words laid a cold pall over the entire body of manhunters. It made sense. Kidd was alone now, fleeing, and if found, would have no way to protect himself unless he had another person he could threaten.

"I have a suggestion," the sheriff said. "I refuse to sit here and wait until daylight. Let's continue on to the Serandon spread. It's the closest one to this one. If there were lights visible, as well, there might be given the bereavement there and the houseful of people that brings about, Kidd might have been attracted. It can't hurt to look. We may chance even to stumble upon his body between here and there."

It seemed as good a plan as anyone could come up with. Marsh pulled together his last fragments of strength and rode out with the determined band.

They were within sight of the Serandon ranch when the sheriff raised a hand and brought the band to a halt.

He did not have to tell what he had seen because they all saw him now: a man riding pell-mell in their direction, frantic and fast.

"Kidd?" someone asked as rifles began to go up.

"I don't know—hold your fire until we are sure," the sheriff replied.

"That ain't Kidd," Marsh said. "I can see his hands, and he's got both of them."

"It's Michael Buckwood," said Port Bailey, who was among the manhunters.

"Ain't he Serandon's brother-in-law?" the sheriff asked.

"He is."

"What's he doing out like this at this hour?"

Buckwood thundered up and reined to a halt. "Sheriff, thank God you heard! How did you know?"

"Know what?"

"She's been took!"

"Who?"

"Corinne! My niece! She's gone, and we believe she's been took!"

The sheriff looked at Marsh. "Kidd," he said.

Marsh merely nodded and felt he might become ill right where he was.

———

Marsh could not bear to look at the weeping widow Serandon. A husband lost, and now a daughter mysteriously vanished. It was clear from the tracks around the nearby creek side that she had been there and that a man had been there as well. The torchlight had revealed some blood, too, indicating that the man was wounded. Not much blood, but not much would be expected if Kidd had applied a tourniquet.

"Where would Kidd go from here?" the sheriff mused

aloud. "He knows that he is pursued— the fact he has taken a hostage shows that he is afraid and anticipates being caught."

"How well does Kidd know the country here?" Marsh asked.

"Fairly well, I believe," the sheriff replied. "I've heard it said that he came up into Texas some during the years he was in Mexico and that he even killed a couple of people during that time. He would have had the opportunity to get to know the terrain."

"Where would you go if you were on the run?" Marsh asked.

The sheriff paused, then said, "To the old McCade ranch. It's empty since McCade died... since he was murdered, I should note. He is one of those they say Kidd might have killed."

"Then let's go there."

"Let's do."

CHAPTER 30

The fear was still there, but the anger was stronger. Her hatred of the man who had taken her—the man who had murdered her father—now coursed through her like the blood in her veins.

She tried but failed to not cry out when he slammed her onto the floor of the loft of the empty barn. Her hands were tied behind her, but not too tightly, because a man with one hand had no advantage when it came to tying knots. She had clenched her hands tightly when he tied her, and the ropes would be slippable...she hoped.

Her breath was knocked from her when she struck the loft floor; her eyes filled with grit and the dust of straw. She grimaced and lay still, for she had learned that any sort of unanticipated movement was always interpreted by Kidd as resistance, making him curse her and hit her.

"You just lay there, pretty thing," he said. He'd been calling her "pretty thing" for the last hour, which worried her. But when she'd realized how hurt he was, how much in pain and exhaustion, she ceased to worry that he might misuse her. He simply wouldn't have the strength.

"Sit up, you," he said. "Why you lying there?"

She sat up and looked around.

"You know this place?" he asked her.

"Yes," she said.

"I know it, too. I come here quite a few years ago. Had to deal with a fellow who give me some trouble. Deal with him, I did. They found him lying about a hundred feet in that direction...and that direction...and that direction..." Kidd laughed.

"You cut him in pieces," Corinne said.

"Yep."

"Why?"

"It's just what I do."

"Why do you kill?"

"Because...well, I don't know a man needs a reason to do what's in his nature. I kill because I hate the damned old world and because it hates me. I kill because...because I *like* it."

"You killed my father."

He looked at her in surprise. "I did?"

"You killed him and threw him into a pit in the hills. The ones who brought him back told about it."

"Hah! That was your father? I'll be damned!"

She was so full of hate at this moment that words failed her. She quietly and unnoticeably began working at the poorly tied bonds around her wrists. The moon was out now, spilling into the barn, and she was able to watch him with ease and quit her wriggling when he might notice them.

"I'll say one thing for your father: He fought hard. Surely did. He come out of the dark and fought me like a mad dog, that old fool did. But it was his mistake. I snapped his throat." He leaned over suddenly and raised his arms, making a claw shape with his one hand. "Ka-snap!" he said and laughed.

But as he looked down at his stump, the laughter died. He shook his head and gnawed on his bottom lip a minute.

"Damn him!" he said. "Damn him for shooting off my hand!"

She gave a little tug; one of the bonds came loose. She looked around, and in the moonlight, noted that unusual rifle was lying on its side across the loft. She didn't know if it was loaded, or if so, in how many chambers, but there was a use she could make of it, loaded or not.

"They'll find you, you know," she said. "They're determined to find you and stop you."

He laughed. "Hell with them! You know how many folks have tried to get me? Hundreds of them! Know how many have caught me? Not a one! Not a damn one!"

"This time, they will. My kin won't let you take me."

He lunged toward her, kneeling, and shoving his ugly face close to hers. "Take you, you say? Girl, if it wasn't for the pain I'm in, if it wasn't for having to keep my eye and ear out in case them bastards come looking here." He paused, and his face grew more menacing. "If they do come... you let out one peep, and I'll put a knife through your throat, slow and rough, so it hurts like nothing you ever nightmared of... and you'll die slow, girl, and in pain."

She almost spat on him, but instinct warned her off.

Her hands were free. Her opportunity would come.

He backed away, then sat back against a post of the barn, about ten feet from her. He studied his stump in the moonlight.

"God, it hurts," he said. "Hurts so bad."

She said nothing. He stared at the stump, and for a long time, said nothing, and in fact, did not move. She began to suspect he was asleep, but his eyes remained open, blinking from time to time, staring at the stump. He remained that way for almost an hour, in that odd, waking sleep—but every time she began to move, his eyes shot up and glared at her in the moonlight.

She looked away at the rifle on the floor. Her hands, free

now, were gripped together behind her. She could move, lunge for that rifle... She tried to calculate how long it would take to reach it, how quickly he would react.

He moved. Broke out of that strange stupor and came to his knees, staring out the open door of the loft to the dark but moonlit land beyond.

Riders. She heard them too now.

And she moved. She came to her feet and moved toward that rifle, getting her hands on it before Starky Kidd could even turn. He pivoted, glared at her in shock, and saw the rifle butt coming like a battering ram toward his face.

He threw up his hand to block it—but habit made him throw up the right arm rather than the left. There was no hand there, only a crusted, painful stump, and the rifle butt hit it hard, knocking loose the cloth tourniquet and making him scream in agony. He staggered back, tripped, and almost fell out of the window, his upper body actually passing out backward through the opening. There were a couple of old ropes hanging there, however, and his left hand managed to grab one of them and hang on. He tried to pull himself back inside.

She lifted the rifle, pulled the trigger. Either the gun was empty, or it misfired because nothing happened. He was almost back in again, and the riders were now actually visible out there on the plains, coming in like phantoms in the moonlight.

She pulled the trigger again, and again nothing happened.

He made it back in. She panicked, but only for a second. Turning the butt of the gun toward him again, she pushed forward with it and caught him in the forehead, hard. He fell back again, teetering on the edge of the window. He grabbed at the rope again, but this time missed it. She hit him again, and he fell out of the window completely, hanging on by his one hand to the window's lower edge, his body swinging and dangling.

A dark inspiration struck her. She leaned out over him, grabbing the rope he had tried to save himself with. She looped it around his neck as he swatted at her with his handless stump. She looped it hard and tight and tied it.

The riders were coming in close. She called to them. "I'm here! I'm here!"

Kidd cursed and roared at her, his hand beginning to slip....

She had dropped the rifle at her feet, but now she picked it up again. She pounded his fingers with the butt of it, again and again, until at last he lost his grip and swung out, hanging by the neck above the barn door, choking, kicking...

The riders saw him and watched in silence as he swung and flailed.

"Let's show a bit of mercy," the sheriff said. He pulled his rifle from its boot and raised it. Others saw and did the same.

"Out of the loft, Corinne!" a man yelled. "Come down now!"

She vanished from the window, and a couple of moments later was running out beneath Starky Kidd's kicking feet, racing toward the riders and safety.

"Ready...aim..."

The volley was deafening, and almost every shot struck the swinging target. Starky Kidd was hammered by scores of bullets; his body destroyed in less than a second, his miserable life shot out of him. One of the bullets missed him, though, and struck the rope, clipping it almost completely. Kidd swung dead a few seconds, then the rope snapped, and his corpse fell with a thud at the barn door.

No one spoke for almost half a minute. The sheriff rebooted his rifle.

"Well, folks, I guess that's that," he said.

EPILOGUE

"I t really didn't come out like I thought it would," Marsh Perkins said to the widow Serandon. He'd talked with her and with Corinne and told them of his sorrow that their loss had come, indirectly at least, because of him. And they had forgiven him. That was easier now that Starky Kidd was gone. Forgiveness, peace of mind, hope—they all came easier now that the demon was dead. "It really wasn't what I thought it would be at all," he went on. "My grandmother had a vision that showed me killing Kidd."

"In a way, you did," she said. Having heard his story, she was impressed by the dedication with which he had searched for the killer. "If not for your pursuit and persistence, Kidd might not have been finally stopped."

"I'm just glad it's over. But sorry, it came at the cost of lives. Good people. Juan Carlos. Mr. Serandon. All the ones murdered."

"What will become of Henry Kidd?" Corinne asked.

"The widow Stevenson, a fine woman, is taking him in. He'll work for her, live in her home. For the first time in his life, he'll have a good situation. It's good. He's an innocent soul, as innocent as his brother was wicked. I hope no one will hold against him the sins of his brother."

"And what will become of you now, Marsh?" Mrs. Serandon asked.

"I'm going home," Marsh said. "I've seen done what I was sent to do. I even have the hand of Henry Kidd to bring back, as I was told to do. I'm eager to get there. It will be good to be home again."

"You will come back someday?"

He couldn't help but cast a glance at Corinne.

"I'll come back someday," he said. "You can be sure of it."

A Look at: Cherokee Joe and Jerusalem Camp
Two Full Length Western Novels

Writing with power, authority, and respect for America's frontier traditions, Cameron Judd captures the spirit of adventure and promise of the wild frontier in these two full-length novels in one volume.

The lawmen call him *Cherokee Joe*, but his given name is Joe Wolfkiller. He's a rebellious half-breed wanderer wanted for numerous crimes in the Indian Territory. Despite the danger, Joe ventures back into the Cherokee Nation when he learns his father is at Death's door.

Deceived by the white man and deeper in trouble, he befriends an eccentric old Indian who carries an ulunsuti, an ancient crystal credited with awesome, but fickle, powers. Joe agrees to help the old man in his final quest: to find his long-lost daughter and bequeath to her the mighty legacy of their people... a journey that will bring bitter vengeance and mortal danger.

In *Jerusalem Camp*, when a mysterious, on the lam drifter named Tellico rides into the isolated Sierra Mountains town of Jerusalem Camp, he soon finds himself snowed in by a fierce winter storm in a town where an unknown killer has begun stalking the populace for reasons no one can seems to fathom. Killing with a long knife and further mutilating his victims by severing one thumb, the unseen murderer soon begins leaving hints that his actions may not be as random as they appear...

As he is drawn into the effort to find and stop the "Gray Man" who terrorizes the town, Tellico joins with the local blacksmith-turned-reluctant-town-marshal in trying to determine why death has descended upon Jerusalem Camp, and just what, and whose, long-buried sin it is that the Gray Man is determined to avenge.

"Brilliant characterizations . . . The classically suspenseful,

neatly ironic ending is flawless." – Publishers Weekly (for Jerusalem Camp)

AVAILABLE NOW

About the Author

Cameron Judd is the author of more than fifty published novels of the American frontier, two of his works having been national finalists in the Spur Awards competition of the Western Writers of America. He has written under his own names and pen names including Judson Grey, Tobias Cole and Will Cade. A native and lifelong Tennessean, he has three adult children. He and his wife, Rhonda, share their Northeast Tennessee home with a cornbread-loving dog named Lola. He is a former award-winning newspaper journalist and editor.